LAURA WILSON

THE RIOT

Quercus

First published in Great Britain in 2013 by Quercus
The paperback edition published in 2014 by

Quercus Editions Ltd
55 Baker Street
7th Floor, South Block
London W1U 8EW

A CIP catalogue record for this book is available
from the British Library

PB ISBN 978 1 78206 308 7
EBOOK ISBN 978 1 78206 307 0

10 9 8 7 6 5 4 3 2 1

Printed and bound in Great Britain by Clays Ltd, St Ives plc

Typeset by Ellipsis Books Limited, Glasgow

Laura Wilson's acclaimed and award-winning novels have won her many fans. The first novel in the series, *Stratton's War*, won the CWA Ellis Peters Award. Two of her novels have been short-listed for the CWA Gold Dagger. Laura is the *Guardian*'s crime reviewer. She lives in Islington, London.

Praise for *The Riot*

'As well as being a crime narrative of great authority, the texture of the piece is immensely evocative'
Financial Times

'An academic historian's accuracy and a born writer's imagination . . . a most impressive piece of work'
Literary Review

'The tang of Wilson's period detail pops off the page . . . a richly imagined, compassionate story'
Metro Herald

'Offers startling insights into an unfamiliar world. A party goes disastrously wrong, ending in a riot, and the novel is a sombre reminder of just how poor and divided London remained in the 1950s'
Sunday Times

Also by Laura Wilson

A Little Death
Dying Voices
My Best Friend
Hello Bunny Alice
The Lover
A Thousand Lies

DI Stratton series:

Stratton's War
An Empty Death
A Capital Crime
A Willing Victim

To George and Florence

Well, believe me, I am speaking broadmindedly
I am glad to know my mother country
I've been travelling to countries years ago
But this' the place I wanted to know
London, that's the place for me.

To live in London you really comfortable
Because the English people are very much sociable
They take you here and they take you there
And they make you feel like a millionaire
So London, that's the place for me.

From 'London is the Place For Me'.
Calypso by Lord Kitchener (Aldwyn Roberts,
1922–2000)

Author's Note

In the 1950s, a legal loophole existed whereby anyone could set him or herself up as the chairman of a building society and – provided that he or she could persuade the public to invest by offering a slightly higher rate than normal – make use of the money to fund their own property empire. Comparatively little capital was needed (enough to open an office and pay for some advertising), but the potential rewards were great and it is surprising that more entrepreneurs did not take advantage of the situation to make themselves a fortune.

CHAPTER ONE

August 1958, Notting Hill Gate: *Puncture wound to chest, entered right-hand side in 4th intercostal space, 4 in deep, penetrated to the heart . . .*

DI Stratton shifted irritably in his office chair – it was half-past midday and sweltering, and his shirt seemed to be plastered on to his back – and pushed the pathologist's report aside. In the black and white photographs Herbert Hampton looked more annoyed than dead, and the stains on his clothing might easily have been the result of carelessness with ketchup or HP Sauce. Seated on the floor in his underwear, with a bald head and a petulant expression, he made Stratton think of a giant baby who'd been pushed over by an older sibling and was preparing to start howling about it. At least, Hampton's top half made him think this. His lower half – a map of varicose veins and a partially visible scrotum so low and loose that it looked like pebbles at the bottom of a pigskin bag – just made Stratton think of the sad indignities of getting old and being murdered in your vest and underpants.

He'd been found by a girl: Shirley Maples, aged seventeen,

typist, on her way home from the ABC Royalty, Ladbroke Grove, where she'd attended the six o'clock performance of a film with her friend Sandra Mills. Glancing at the map of his new manor, he saw that Shirley Maples lived in Colville Terrace and Sandra Mills – also a typist – lived in Talbot Road, which was just around the corner. Stratton thought he could picture the streets: rusted railings, crumbling front walls, and rows of tatty five-storey Victorian houses, each one occupied by a dozen – or perhaps even two dozen – people.

Both girls lived with their parents. They had watched *Raintree County*, which apparently, with the rest of the programme, lasted three whole hours, and Shirley arrived back home at half past nine. When she'd climbed the stairs to the family's top floor flat, her father had sent her back down again and across the road to give the week's rent to Mr Hampton and, while she was at it, to fetch him a bottle of Mackeson from the pub down the road. He never got his beer. Stratton imagined her pushing open the door of Hampton's flat and standing hypnotised, before she began to scream. He shuffled the papers until he found her statement. Scanning to the end, he read: *My dad says it's the coloureds that do these things.*

The office door swung open and a large man he recognised as PC Jellicoe – two days into his new post, he hadn't got all the names down yet – appeared with a cup of tea and a rock bun on a plate. "Ot, ain't it? 'Ere you go.'

The voice was an exaggerated Cockney – the London equivalent of the country dweller's exaggerated yokel act, put on for strangers – and there was a sort of menacing joviality about it, as if daring him to pull rank. Stratton wondered if he'd been put up to it. As the first appointment of a Superintendent who'd only been there a year himself, he was bound to be an object of suspicion, especially as his first task was to investigate a crime that the natives had failed to solve.

PC Jellicoe, who'd put the tea and bun on the table, nodded encouragingly. 'Thought you might like a cuppa after your lunch.'

'Thanks,' said Stratton. He took a sip of the tea, and picked up the rock bun.

'Just like Muvver useta make.'

Stratton took an experimental bite and encountered a concrete-like substance. 'Yes, if Muvver was a bricklayer. Still, it's the thought that counts.'

No snorts of laughter from outside, so it obviously wasn't a set-up, just Jellicoe having a sniff round the newcomer and, presumably, reporting back. Jellicoe studied him in a manner that made him think of a man trying to decide whether a piano would fit through a doorway. After a moment, his face broke into a grin. 'They are a bit of a facer.' Pointing at Stratton's map, he added, 'That's where that bloke Hampton was done a couple of Saturdays ago, isn't it?'

Stratton, well aware that Jellicoe knew exactly what he was looking into, took this to be an olive branch of sorts and said, 'That's right – Colville Terrace.'

'What that little lot –' Jellicoe nodded at the papers on

the desk – 'won't tell you is that all round there, Colville Terrace, Colville Road, Powis Terrace, Powis Square . . . most of them houses belong to Danny Perlmann. He's got quite a lot in St Stephen's Gardens too,' indicating the street with a stubby finger, 'and Chepstow Road, Westbourne Gardens, Pembridge Square. Got a bloody great mansion in Hampstead, I heard, and he drives about in a Roller full of blondes. Hampton was one of the rent collectors. But . . .' Jellicoe heaved a big, puffy sigh. 'It's a disgrace, really. Not saying it hasn't always been a problem round there – gyppos and all sorts, more your criminal class than your working class, if you see what I mean – but now with the darkies everywhere, it's got to be the worst slum in London. Some of them club together and buy a house and then they want the tenants out so they can bring in their own sort. We had a Nigerian bloke a couple of weeks ago trying to evict a bunch of Irish – brawling in the street, they were, furniture thrown about all over the place, and what with that business in Nottingham over the weekend, coloured stabbing whites and all sorts . . .'

'The Chief Constable said that wasn't a racial riot,' said Stratton, who'd spent quite a lot of the previous Sunday morning reading about the 'milling mob' of fifteen hundred people who'd rampaged through the streets of St Ann's.

Jellicoe sniffed. 'Not a racial riot my arse – wouldn't have happened if the darkies hadn't been there. Anyway, bit different from your old patch in the West End, isn't it?' In other words, thought Stratton: let's see what you can do in a really tough manor, glamour-boy.

Jellicoe did have a point, though. Stratton's old division, C – St James's, Soho and the surrounding area – certainly had its problems, and a fair amount of poverty as well, but there wasn't anything that approached the unrestrained squalor he'd seen on his brief tour of the Colville and Powis area.

'Perlmann's got a club up West too,' said Jellicoe, 'but you'd know about that.'

'I don't, actually.'

Jellicoe looked surprised. 'It's called Maxine's.'

Stratton had only once glimpsed Maxine's plush interior, but he knew it, and its smart clientele, by repute. 'I know Maxine's. It's in Wardour Street. I didn't know it was his, though.'

Jellicoe nodded. 'Him and another bloke. He's got another club in Earl's Court. Rumours of unlicensed gambling, though he's never been had up for it.'

'Sounds as if he's doing all right for himself.'

'Not short of a bob or two, that's for sure.'

At least, Stratton thought when Jellicoe had taken himself off, I've got one potential ally. There was no record of money being found in the man's room, which made robbery a likely motive and the money stolen would, presumably, have belonged to Perlmann, from whom he could find no statement. Putting the map and Shirley Maples's statement to one side, he turned back to the photographs. There were five or six, and the police photographer had done a better-than-average job: different angles and everything in sharp focus. The accompanying plan of the third floor flat showed a living room – where Hampton had met his death – with a tiny kitchen partitioned off on one side.

In the first photograph, Stratton could see, next to Hampton's body, a television set encased in a wooden cabinet with doors that hinged out on either side like an altarpiece. From what he'd seen of Colville Terrace so far he doubted if many of the residents could have afforded such a luxury, but perhaps Hampton, as the rent collector, had been in an unusually privileged position. On top of the cabinet was a lace-edged runner, on which stood a china donkey and a framed photograph of a young woman. Stratton wondered if this was Mrs Hampton, who, according to the notes, had died the previous year. The television, according to Shirley, had still been on when she'd entered the room.

The second photograph showed a collection of empty and unwashed milk bottles, together with a clutter of opened tins, two overflowing ashtrays and several plates of congealing leftovers, one of which was furred with mould. Clearly, Hampton hadn't kept up with the housework after his wife's death. The lino, Stratton could see from all the pictures, was haphazardly strewn with newspaper. As Hampton was sitting on some of it, he felt it was unlikely to have been put there by the man's assailant – more likely it was a feeble attempt to keep the floor clean. The pages weren't crumpled or dirty: Stratton could clearly see advertisements for Radio Rentals, Double Diamond and, by Hampton's left foot, Kellogg's Cornflakes – the sunshine breakfast with the wide-awake taste. Turning the photograph through ninety degrees, he made out another advert – Chilprufe vests, a must for the school outfit – and a headline: 'Little Rock says shut schools to bar Negroes'. The paper was the *Daily Express*. Obviously recent, but he couldn't make out the date underneath the masthead – he supposed it would be somewhere in the notes.

Stratton read through the statements from the neighbours, who struck him as an exceptionally cagey lot. There seemed to be fourteen different people living in the same building as Hampton – not counting any children – and none of them had noticed anything unusual. What was interesting was that all of them, whether white or black, appeared to have liked Hampton: words like 'kind', 'helpful' and 'nice' kept recurring. Several of Hampton's immediate neighbours, plus quite a few from surrounding houses, agreed with Shirley Maples's dad's assertion that 'it was coloureds', but without elaborating further. None of the coloured neighbours had an opinion as to what might have happened – or anyway not one they were willing to voice – and, thinking about it, Stratton couldn't blame them.

He lit a cigarette and had another look at the pathologist's report: *Caused by a single-edged knife . . . Wound edges protruding, probably owing to rapid withdrawal of instrument . . . No other marks of violence about the deceased . . . No evidence of rigor . . .*

Hampton's last meal – consumed, according to the report, at least three hours prior to his death – consisted of minced lamb, peas and potatoes. This, Stratton knew from the statements, had been taken in a nearby cafe, along with a cup of tea, between 5.30 and 6 p.m. The pathologist estimated that Hampton had been dead for between two and four hours before he was discovered by Shirley Maples at approximately 9.45 p.m. That would mean that he'd been killed sometime between, say, 6.05 and 7.45 p.m. At that time, thought Stratton, the older children would be coming in for their tea and the adults either home from work or off out for the evening, it being Saturday. Anyone in the house who had a television would have been watching it, as Hampton had been: the *Six-Five Special* for the kids and later, *The Black and White Minstrel Show* for the whole family.

Perhaps, though, the neighbours weren't being as cagey as all that. With fourteen adults and Christ knows how many children clumping up and down the stairs, the place wouldn't have been exactly quiet. Any stranger would have been assumed to be an acquaintance of another of the inhabitants, one of whom, Stratton could see from a hand-written note helpfully pinned to her statement, was thought to be on the game.

At the bottom of the pathologist's report was another handwritten note: *It is possible that this wound was caused by the deceased rushing at his assailant while he (the assailant) was holding the knife in his hand. In the absence of other evidence to the contrary, I am unable to suggest any satisfactory theory by which the wound could have been self-inflicted.*

Stratton was just about to go through the paperwork again to check he'd not missed anything significant when the door opened, revealing the immaculately suited and ramrod-straight form of his new boss, Detective Superintendent Matheson. Stratton started to rise from his chair, suddenly very conscious of the sweaty and crumpled appearance he must present.

'No, no. Stay where you are, man. How's it going? I see they've given you all the gen.'

'I'm catching up as fast as I can, sir. Just about to go to Colville Terrace.'

'I told the station sergeant to make sure there's a car at your disposal.'

'I thought I'd walk this time, sir. Get the lie of the land, so to speak.' As he said this, Stratton was aware that, as in their previous exchanges, he didn't sound like himself but like something out of a war film: decent, doughty, doing his damnedest in a gruff, self-effacing sort of way. It was the effect the man had on him: the clipped, upper-class tones, distinguished countenance and military bearing, not to mention the background and reputation, plus the fact that, at forty-two, Matheson was a whole eleven years younger than him. He had, as anybody who read the papers knew, joined the Met in the thirties, under Commissioner Trenchard's ill-fated scheme for recruiting an officer class. At the time Stratton had, like most serving policemen, viewed the Hendon 'boy wonders' as a bunch of ineffective public-school washouts, which a lot of them were, but not Matheson. His successes had been celebrated, the newspapers had fawned on him, and five years ago he'd become the youngest officer ever to be appointed Detective Superintendent by Scotland Yard. And – as if this weren't enough

– he'd had a good war too. He'd been a captain in the Desert Rats and taken part in the Normandy invasion.

'Jolly good,' said Matheson. 'I'll leave you to it. Take whatever time you need to talk to people – learn a bit about them. Come to my office whenever you've finished. I've a fair bit to do myself, so I shall be here until at least eight o'clock this evening. You can give me your ideas over a drink.'

'Yes, sir. Thank you.'

Blimey, thought Stratton, there's a turn-up for the books. In all the years working under Lamb at West End Central he could only remember being offered a drink once, and that was because the man was retiring. Dragging his jacket over his uncomfortably clammy shirt, he headed for the lobby to inform the desk sergeant of his whereabouts for the next few hours.

CHAPTER TWO

The desk sergeant had his hands full dealing with a man so drunk that his speech was as slurred and slow as a gramophone record played at the wrong speed. Stratton was content to wait. For one thing, the desk sergeant had managed to lay hands on an elderly fan – its incessant clacking being more than compensated for by the movement of air, even if it was warm – and for another, it gave him a chance to take stock of the place. Not that there was anything new to him: an elderly woman with violently dyed ginger hair was telling one of the young coppers that she'd lost her dog, and a couple of teenage Teddy boys were waiting to be booked in by another, who looked barely older than they were. Stratton eyed the pair. He'd seen it all before – the sharp clothes, the jittery insolence, the way they jingled the change in their pockets as if they couldn't wait to unleash the next sixpenny-worth of strident music from an imaginary jukebox. Whether it was their frank air of villainy or simply their youth and appearance Stratton didn't know, but he felt uneasiness creep over him like an infestation of lice and suddenly found he couldn't wait to get out of the place. It's because I'm getting old, he told himself. The world's moving on, away from me, and things don't make sense like they used to.

The sensation of discomfort was intensified when Stratton walked down Colville Terrace. There were about two dozen people there, either sitting on the steps of the houses or just standing about chatting, but every single one of them, apart from a couple of housewives carrying shopping, was black. It wasn't, Stratton told himself, as if he'd never seen a coloured person before. He must have seen hundreds over the years in the West End – and there were several coloured clubs – but just not all at once, and not milling about in the street like this. They seemed friendly enough, cheerful and animated, and anyway, they were only people, the same – when you came down to it – as any others. Nevertheless the scene was still disconcertingly alien, especially against the background noise of bawling Cockney stallholders from Portobello market, which could be glimpsed at the end of the road.

What was I expecting? he asked himself. It wasn't as if he hadn't been warned at the station – there'd been plenty of comments: dirty habits, can't be trusted around women, lazy and work-shy, playing music at all hours, touchy ... Stratton decided he'd prefer to make up his own mind, although he wondered about the 'work-shy' bit as it didn't look as if any of these blokes had jobs – unless, of course, they'd come home for lunch. Colville Terrace was, as he'd expected, a street of large crumbling and unpainted terraced houses, whose front porticoes were blocked by overflowing dustbins and empty milk bottles. Music was blaring out from at least three different locations, and the gutters were filled with dry rivers of old newspapers, rags, broken-up wooden fruit boxes, used French letters and the like. Already he knew what they'd be like inside: rigged meters, vermin and no hot water.

Then again, Notting Hill Gate had never, as far as he knew, been an area that anyone would live in if they could have lived anywhere else. He looked at the groups of people again, but surreptitiously, to avoid giving the appearance of staring. He'd seen coloured people arriving in Britain on the television news. It had been back in January, and they'd been filmed bewildered and apprehensive in their thin, unsuitable clothes – straw hats, even – amid piles of luggage at Waterloo station. They must have seen newsreels, too, in their cinemas in Kingston or Port of Spain or wherever they came from, showing the best of Britain. Now it occurred to Stratton to wonder what the hell they must have been thinking as, standing on the station platform, they'd turned to the camera with those wide, brave smiles.

There weren't any people sitting on the front steps of number 19, where Hampton had lived, but the front door was ajar. Stratton skirted the evil-smelling dustbin and entered. The hall was dingy: cracked lino ingrained with dirt and peeling wallpaper. The place smelt of a combination of paraffin, dirt and cooking, and there were a number of unclaimed letters, circulars and pools coupons – many

of which, judging by the footprints on the envelopes, had
been there for some time – lying on the mangy doormat.
On the first landing was a blackened saucepan on a solitary
gas ring and on the second, a filthy lavatory with no bolt
or handle on the door. From above, he could hear music
punctuated by crackles of static. Rounding the bend of the
stairs, he was able to identify it as 'All I Have to Do is Dream'.
Looking up, he saw a pair of shapely legs rising from sling-
backs and topped by a tight, shiny skirt, a low-cut blouse
and a come-hither smile.

'Looking for someone, darling?'

'Yes,' said Stratton. 'I'm investigating the death of Herbert Hampton. Do you live here?'

The girl – Stratton supposed she couldn't be more than
twenty, although the air of professional carnality made her
seem much older – looked disappointed. 'Is that all? I live
upstairs, as it happens, but I've already told the coppers I
don't know nothing about it.'

'What's your name?'

'Vicky.'

'Vicky what?'

'Allardice.'

Stratton pulled his notebook out of his jacket and looked
through the list of names he'd compiled from the witness
statements. Vicky Allardice seemed to be the only woman
in the place who lived alone – assuming that she actually
did live there and didn't just use the room for business purposes. 'How much rent do you pay, Vicky?'

'What's that got to do with you?'

'Mr Hampton collected the rent, didn't he? It's possible that he was killed during a robbery.'

'I suppose.' Vicky shrugged. 'But the rent weren't due till the next day, so he wouldn't have had it, would he?'

At least, thought Stratton, that explained the lack of money in Hampton's room. 'How much?' he persisted.

'Two pound a week.'

'Really?' This wasn't the West End, where a working girl might pay as much as £15 or even £20 for a flat, but Stratton was surprised by the disparity. He'd be willing to bet that she was paying a fair bit more than she'd said – but of course to admit that was tantamount to confessing how she earned a living. Deciding not to press the matter, he settled for raising a single eyebrow in a clear show of disbelief.

Vicky folded her arms. 'I don't know why you're asking me about any of it,' she said defensively. 'I wasn't even here.'

'But you do *live* here?'

'Mm-hm. Ask anyone.'

'So where were you?'

'Out.'

'Out where?'

'I went shopping.'

'By the time Hampton was killed the shops would have been closed.'

'We stopped out for tea.'

'We?'

'Me and my friend.'

'Her name?'

'Marion.'

'Marion who?'

'Marion Lockwood.'

Stratton glanced at the notes he'd made summarising her statement – so far, everything tallied. 'Where did you have your tea?'

'The Larchwood Cafe on Queensway.'

'That's off the Bayswater Road, isn't it?' Stratton had seen the scores of tarts who lined the railings – one every few yards – right down Bayswater Road and along Park Lane.

Vicky stared at him as if he'd just dropped out of a spaceship. 'Last time I looked.'

'What time did you finish eating?'

'Dunno – half past six.'

'What did you do after that?'

'Went for a walk.' Her eyes were defiant.

'Along the Bayswater Road?'

'No law against it, is there?'

'Depends on the purpose of the walk – as I'm sure you know. What time did you get home?'

'About half past eight.'

'Slow night, was it? Still, it was early, so presumably you went out again afterwards.'

Vicky sighed. 'Yes. About ten to nine.'

'And you came back again when?'

'I suppose . . . Quarter past nine, something like that.'

'Kerb-crawler, was he? Gave you a lift back afterwards?'

'I did get a lift, yes.' This time the admission came sullenly, and she didn't look him in the eye.

'I'm not here to give you any trouble,' said Stratton. 'I

just want some information. All right, you brought a punter back here – and you went out again when?'

'Half past nine, twenty to ten, something like that.'

'Did you see Shirley Maples when you went out?'

'Who?'

'The girl who found Mr Hampton.'

Vicky shook her head. 'The only person I saw was one of the coloured blokes who live downstairs. At least, I think it was him – the bulb's gone on the landing, so I couldn't really see. He was coming out of the lav.'

Stratton consulted his notebook. 'You identified him as Horace Conroy when you made your statement.'

'It *could* have been. I mean, he lives here and he's tall, and so was this bloke. Frankie – that's the other one who lives here – is small and skinny, so it couldn't have been him, but I never saw the face, so I can't be certain.'

'Fair enough.' Stratton made a note to this effect and said, 'Frankie would be Francis Crockett, would he?'

'I suppose so – I don't know. Frankie and Horace share a room. They've got another bloke living with them now. I think he's called Jackson or something like it but he won't be no use to you because he only come here last week.'

'What about one of the others . . .' Stratton consulted his notebook, 'Ernest MacDonald or Jeffrey Royce?'

'They live on the ground floor so they use the lav in the basement.'

'You mean they share it with the . . .' Stratton had another look at his notebook, 'the Tyndall family?' He could see from the notes that not only did the Tyndalls have four children, there were two other adults and a baby living on the ground floor, as well as MacDonald and Royce.

'Well, they've got to go somewhere, haven't they? And up here we've got one lav for ten people – and that's not including Winnie and Eddie's kid.'

'Winnie and Eddie?'

'They're the new people in Mr Hampton's rooms. Coloured couple – moved in a few days ago. Not very nice when the poor old boy'd been murdered like that, but beggars can't be choosers, can they?'

'Might MacDonald or Royce have been coming up to use the bathroom?'

'What bathroom?'

'Haven't you got one?'

'Nope.' Vicky shook her head, her mouth a thin, emphatic line. 'Some of the rooms got basins, though,' she added. 'Wish mine did.'

'Get on with your neighbours all right, do you?'

Vicky shrugged. 'Don't see that much of them, really.'

'What about Mr Hampton?'

'What about him?'

'Did you get on with him?'

'He was all right.' Vicky uncrossed her arms. 'Can I go?'

'In a hurry, are you?'

'Not particularly.'

'Good. Did your client see the man on the landing?'

'Dunno. He never said. And he was coming down the stairs behind me – and, like I said, the bulb's gone – so I doubt it.'

'What was his name?'

'His name?' Vicky gave him a scornful look. 'Well, he said it was John, but it wasn't his real name so it doesn't matter, does it?'

'What did he look like?'

Vicky shrugged. 'Like a punter. Bit fat, horn-rimmed glasses . . . Oh, yeah – he was a kink. Wanted me to give him the cane. That should narrow it down for you,' she added sarcastically.

'Not one of your regulars, then?'

'Never seen him before in my life.'

'Who lives upstairs with you?'

'Nobody lives *with* me, but there's a couple of students next door. They're English. Posh, arty types.' Vicky rolled her eyes. 'Bruce and Jimmy.'

A glance at his notebook told Stratton that Bruce Massingberd and James Hartree were visiting their families in, respectively, Sunningdale and Bexhill-on-Sea – presumably to give themselves a break from playing at starving artistically in a garret – at the time of Hampton's death.

'What about this floor?'

'Winnie and Eddie and the baby in there.' Vicky jerked her head towards the door behind her. 'And –' she indicated the door adjacent to it – 'Bill has that room.'

Stratton looked at his notebook again. William Harkness was a fifty-year-old railway worker who hadn't – according to him, his mates and the barman – returned from the Walmer Castle on Ledbury Road until gone eleven. 'OK. And underneath them, on the first floor, there's Horace Conroy and Francis Crockett, and who else?'

'Two old girls who run a sweet stall down the market. They're twins. Should be about because they usually come back for lunch. Lived here for donkey's years – probably since the place was built.'

'Margery and Mary Lewis?'

'That's right. And on the ground floor you've got Ernie and Jeffrey, and Mr Russell – he's an old bloke, lives by himself. Then there's Jean – she's the Tyndalls' eldest – and her baby. He's halfcaste – father's Jamaican. He comes to see her sometimes, but he doesn't live here. The Tyndalls are down in the basement, with their other four kids, and that's your lot. *Now* can I go?'

When she'd clattered off upstairs Stratton addressed himself to his notebook once more and discovered that, at the time Hampton was killed, Horace and Frankie were at home and so were the Lewis sisters and old Mr Russell. Ernest MacDonald and Jeffrey Royce had gone straight from work for a meal in a cafe, then for a drink in a pub, and then on to a basement club called the Calypso – this was confirmed by three separate sources – and Jean Tyndall had been downstairs with her mum. Her dad had been at the pub – the same one as Harkness, which wasn't the one patronised by MacDonald and Royce – and had returned home at around half past ten. Jean, Stratton could see from the notes he'd made, was seventeen, and the other Tyndall kids were fifteen, thirteen, ten and five. They'd all been home all evening except for the fifteen-year-old, Tom, who'd been out until around 9 p.m.

The two rooms occupied by the Lewis twins were, by contrast with the rest of the house, immaculately kept with fresh wallpaper, spotless linoleum and a gleaming collection of china cats. Elderly and identically prune-faced, sitting poker-straight on either side of the gas fire in matching cardigans and slippers, the two women confirmed that they'd been in all evening and had heard Horace and Frank's record player through the wall. They'd heard people coming and going too, on the stairs, but as Margery – or possibly Mary – pointed out, 'It's always noisy, so you don't pay any attention.'

'And you didn't speak to anyone else or leave your room at any time?' asked Stratton.

'Only to make our supper. We prefer our own company. In any case, there's some here that no decent person would mix with. The Tyndall girl's got a baby by a coloured man and there's no sign of him marrying her, and the girl upstairs brings men back every night.' Margery-or-Mary's mouth pursed in disapproval.

'I've just been talking to her.'

'Then you'll know exactly what she is.'

The two rooms shared by Horace Conroy and Frank Crockett were, in reality, one large one divided by a plywood partition, and they weren't half as well maintained as those of the Lewis sisters. A huge chunk of plaster was missing from one corner of the ceiling, and there was a map of cracks spreading across one wall. It certainly didn't look big enough for three. A glimpse through the door into the bedroom told Stratton that it contained only two beds with barely a gap in between them. Where did the new arrival – Jackson or whatever his name was – manage to sleep, Stratton wondered. Perhaps the three of them occupied the beds in shifts.

The few bits of furniture in the main room were shabby: a scarred wooden table and two chairs and an armchair pitted with cigarette burns. Next to this, an orange box with some fabric tacked round it served as a coffee table.

Conroy himself was tall – about the same as his own six foot three – and slim. He was, Stratton guessed, in his late twenties and had a strong West Indian accent. When Stratton introduced himself he was instantly apprehensive, as if he feared he might be accused of something.

'I just need to ask a few questions, that's all. Is Mr Crockett here? I don't need to bother your other friend.'

Conroy shook his head. 'Crockett working. I get the day off and Jackson not here anyway. This about Mr Hampton?'

'That's right. The girl who lives upstairs, Vicky Allardice. You know who I mean?'

Panic flashed in Conroy's eyes. 'I know she, but I ain't do anything against the law.'

'It's OK,' said Stratton, 'no one's suggesting that you have. As I said, I'd just like you to help me out with a bit of information. You see,' he added, 'I'm new here myself.'

Conroy looked baffled. 'I mean,' Stratton continued, 'this is a new patch for me – a new part of London – so I'm just finding my way round the place.'

Seeing from the confusion on Conroy's face that his attempt at finding some common ground had failed entirely, Stratton continued, 'Vicky said she saw you upstairs that evening. About twenty to ten.'

Conroy looked alarmed. 'I never saw she.'

'But you were here? She said you were coming out of the lavatory.'

'I'm here all the time, and Frankie, in this room. We go out to the shops, come back, stay home. Save money – my wife makin' child and I send she money so she come here when the baby born. We ain't see anybody. Maybe I go upstairs sometime – for *that* – but I don't remember.' Clearly fearful that he wasn't being believed, Conroy said, 'That Mr Hampton a good man – make us welcome right from the start. When we arrive—'

'When was that?' asked Stratton.

'April. Me and Frankie. We meet this fellow, he from Africa, face all scratch up,' Conroy drew several lines on his cheeks with his fingers, 'he say, "Go see Perlmann, man." So we come here and Mr Perlmann rent us this place. Mr Hampton, he collecting money from the tenants every week. He tell us maybe it have a cheaper rent if we speak to the council, the tribunal . . . I don't know. He going to come and talk to us about this thing, but we thought if Mr Perlmann willing to rent to coloured people, well . . .'

'You thought it best not to complain,' finished Stratton.

'That's right. Mr Hampton tell this to the Jamaican boys too, downstairs.'

'You're not from Jamaica?'

An almost imperceptible flicker of irritation crossed Conroy's face. 'Trinidad, man.'

'How much rent do you pay here?'

'Eight pound. Me and Frankie pay half, every week – it have less each now Jackson staying with us.'

Stratton blinked. High rents to prostitutes were one thing, but Conroy was, according to his notes, a labourer. 'Eight pounds? For *this*?'

Conroy nodded.

'How much do you get paid?'

'Seven pound ten a week. So does Frankie. I can't get a better work here. I'm a carpenter – cabinet maker. Trained. Frankie's a trolley bus driver but he can't get a work like that – he get a factory work.'

Stratton thought that Conroy was probably telling the truth – a coloured man might well get less than his British workmates. He looked round the room once more, feeling uneasy, adrift. Conroy, he felt instinctively, was honest. It was just the strangeness of him – of all of them, and of this unfamiliar place – that was causing this feeling of not quite having a grip on things.

A shout from the road outside – 'Nigger-lover!' – like a whipcrack across the torpid air, made both men jump. Stratton went over to the window. A group of Teddy boys were hanging about on the corner of the street. Or rather, six of them were dressed in the Teddy boy style – the other five, who appeared older, were more conventionally clad. Coloured people were hurrying past them, in groups of two or three, heads down, eyes averted. As far as Stratton could tell the insult must have been aimed at the two English girls he could just see disappearing round the corner. There didn't seem to be any weapons on view but, despite the fact that half of them were lounging, leaning against the wall, there was an unmistakable air of aggression about the group, a dangerous alertness, like dogs sniffing for signs of threat. He could see people retreating from their doorsteps and curtains twitching, so that the very houses seemed to exude an air of tension, as though the street were holding its breath. Something's going to happen here, thought Stratton. Maybe not today or tomorrow, but soon.

As he watched, another coloured man came into view, walking by himself. The heads of the group swivelled, as one, to stare at him. Stratton was too far away to make out their individual expressions, but there was a menacing rigidity to every jawline and pair of shoulders that told him all he needed to know. As the coloured man drew level with the group, one of the Teddy boys took a step forward and spat, catching him squarely on the side of his face. The man didn't break stride but carried on walking, taking a handkerchief out of his jacket pocket and wiping off the spittle. Stratton looked round to see if Conroy, who was standing just behind him, had witnessed this. Conroy's face was completely devoid of expression, the dark eyes opaque, but – in apparently unconscious mimicry of the man in the street – his hand was lifted up to his cheek.

CHAPTER THREE

By the time Stratton had got downstairs to the front door, the group of men had disappeared. He walked to the end of Colville Terrace but could see no sign of them. Now they'd moved off he could see, chalked in big letters on the brick wall they'd been lounging against, the letters KBW. He stared for a moment, wondering what they meant.

As he doubled back, he noted that people had begun to reappear on their front steps. They were chatting as before, but now the talk seemed more fragmented, broken off for glances up and down the street. As he climbed the steps to Hampton's house again, he was aware of half a dozen pairs of watchful eyes upon him and suspicious mutterings in his wake.

Alfred Russell sat so stiffly that Stratton might have thought, if it were not for the fact he'd heard him croak 'Come!' in answer to his knock, that rigor mortis was already upon him. His single room smelt sourly of mortality, with a sharp overlay of piss. The heavy curtains were drawn and when a knife of light from the hall sliced across the room as Stratton gingerly opened the door, his first impression was that Russell had recently been burgled. The furniture was good quality, solid stuff – the best he'd seen in the house – but there were drawers pulled out and the floor was strewn with items of clothing garnished with dog-ends from an overturned ashtray. He spotted a row of three brimful basins lined up against the wall – the source of at least one of the odours – and, tottering beside them, a pile of unwashed crockery.

When Stratton explained who he was Russell said, in surprisingly cultured tones, 'Please draw back the curtains. I'm afraid I tend to forget.' He added, as Stratton did so and opened the window for good measure, 'Don't have much use for the sun these days, you see.' Turning, Stratton saw, as the dusty light flooded into the room, not only that Russell was even older than he'd at first thought, but also that he was wearing a pair of dark glasses and had a white stick at his side. 'Do sit down – if you can find a space to park yourself, that is.'

Stratton cleared a tray with the remains of some sandwiches off the only available chair and sat down. 'I hope the place isn't in too much of a mess,' said Russell, 'although I fear it probably is. I pay the girl next door a few shillings to clear up from time to time and visit the launderette and so forth, but she hasn't come in recently.'

Stratton, taking in the man's unshaven appearance and the stained and dishevelled condition of his linen suit and grease-spotted club tie, said, 'If there's no one else who can help – no family – I can always speak to the welfare officer if you need—'

'I do not need,' said Russell firmly. 'While I am – naturally – grateful for your concern, the last thing I want is to be treated like a mentally deficient toddler by a bunch of do-gooding women. The coloured boys who live on the other side of that wall –' he gestured behind him – 'are kind enough to do any shopping I might require. Between them and the girl, I can manage. She's a good enough sort in her way,' he added, 'but ignorant, like a lot of people nowadays. Asked me the other day if Barbados was part of Jamaica! I was in the West Indies, of course. Colonial Service . . . You've not been here before, have you? With the other chaps who were asking questions, I mean.'

'No,' said Stratton. 'This is a new patch for me.'

'Then,' Russell leant forward, clearly pleased to have a new audience, 'I'm sure you're wondering how I've ended up in a hole like this.'

This, thought Stratton, definitely came under the heading of 'learning a bit about people', as Matheson had instructed. 'Yes,' he said, 'I was – but first I need to verify your statement. You say you were here all evening, in this room?'

'Yes. As you've probably gathered, I don't get about much these days.'

'And you didn't see – sorry, hear – anything unusual?'

Russell shook his head. 'Footsteps on the stairs – music – that sort of thing.'

'Voices?'

'Nothing particular. I had the wireless on for most of the time. Jean – that's the girl who comes in—'

'Jean Tyndall?'

'That's right. Didn't see anyone else all evening. I'd thought Hampton might come down for a chinwag, but of course he didn't.'

'Did you know him well?'

'I don't know about "well". Quite a time, certainly, because he and his wife – she died in November – had been here almost as long as I have, and I came here in 1937. After I lost my sight he used to read me things out of the paper. He was a great one for politics. Self-educated, of course. Had a lot of bees in his bonnet as these types tend to do – don't have the breadth of knowledge, so they lack perspective . . . But a nice enough fellow. Took the death of his wife very hard – really knocked the stuffing out of him.' Russell nodded emphatically, as if he'd finally made up his mind about something. 'I liked him. I shall miss his company. Now,' he added, after a few seconds' contemplative silence, 'let me tell you my story. I was drummed out of the Colonial Service. Bit of a scandal, I'm afraid. Wife upped and left, took the children, and I've not seen any of them since.' He sat back, clearly wanting Stratton to ask for more.

'The scandal – was it a girl?' asked Stratton.

'It was a boy, Inspector.' This was produced like a trump card and uttered with the gleeful candidness of someone who had absolutely nothing left to lose by his honesty. 'Nineteen-twelve, it was. When you –' here, the bristly lower half of his desiccated face contorted in something like a leer – 'were in short trousers.'

'Yes,' said Stratton, 'I was.' He'd been seven in 1912.

'I can always tell the age from the voice.' Russell gave a triumphant crow of laughter. 'Still remember that boy, though. A native, of course – there wouldn't have been half so much fuss if he'd been one of ours. The mother found out and kicked up a hell of a stink – caused a lot of embarrassment all round, so they shipped me back home. But' – his tone became serious – 'there is a point to my telling you this: I know these people, you see. And I can tell you – despite what you may hear to the contrary – that none of them would have killed Hampton. They're here for a better life, not to make trouble, and besides, Hampton was trying to help them.'

'Over the rent, you mean?'

'That's right. I don't know how much you know about the situation here – with housing, I mean.'

'I'm not exactly an expert, no,' said Stratton.

'Hampton bent my ear about it often enough,' said Russell. 'I'm what's known as a controlled tenant, you see. I pay twenty-five shillings a week for this place – have done since 1939, because the law says the landlord can't put my rent up.'

'But . . .' Stratton recalled reading something about this in the newspaper the previous year. 'Haven't they just changed that?'

'Yes, last year. The new Rent Act – but that only applies to houses with a rateable value of more than forty pounds – if they're in London, anyway, not slums like this. Of course a fixed low rent is pretty well guaranteed to turn any place into a slum. If the landlord's not getting a decent return it isn't worth his while to make repairs, so the houses end up falling to pieces. And you can't get a controlled tenant out: in this house there's me, Bill Harkness upstairs, the two Lewis witches and the Tyndalls downstairs, and of course there was Hampton too. Unless we leave of our own accord, there's nothing the landlord can do. Well, nothing legal. He can, of course, make our lives so intolerable that we'll pack our traps and clear off, but – so far – that hasn't happened here. Perlmann's preferred method is to fill the place with whores and Negroes and encourage them to make everyone else's lives a misery by having parties every night with loud music and so forth – not that they need very much encouragement.' Russell chuckled. 'Noisy by nature, I'm afraid.'

'Have you had trouble of that sort here?'

Russell shook his head. 'Perhaps we've just been lucky, but I think Hampton being here had a lot to do with it. Perlmann was very careful not to rent the rooms unfurnished – if you do that you automatically create another controlled tenancy, and of course that's the last thing he wants. Hampton told me the stuff he put in was junk – falling apart, half the time.'

'Did Hampton pay any rent himself?'

'Oh, yes. He told me that Perlmann said he could live here free in exchange for collecting the rents, but that he insisted on paying in order to ensure his controlled status, so Perlmann gave him a bit of money for collecting from the houses he owns in this street.'

'How many?'

'Four. Lots more round about, of course, but Hampton only collected here. The coloured always end up paying more for a room because so few people will accept them.'

'What about the local council?' asked Stratton. 'Won't they house them?'

Russell shook his head. 'Waiting lists are full. In any case, you need proof that you've been resident in a particular locality for five years before they'll even look at you, and most of them around here are less than a year off the boat, so you can see they don't have a lot of choice. And of course with the tarts you can charge pretty well what you like – sky's the limit.'

'Vicky Allardice told me she pays £2 a week for her room.'

'Well she would, wouldn't she? She pays £15. Hampton told me. Conroy and Crockett and the new chap pay a total of £8 – Perlmann couldn't give two hoots about sub-letting, so long as he gets his whack. MacDonald and Royce pay £8 a week too, and so do the Gilchrists, who took over Hampton's flat. Those two no-hopers at the top—'

'The art students – Massingberd and Hartree?'

'No idea of their names. Hampton told me they look like a pair of circus clowns – clothes covered with paint, berets . . .' Russell snorted. 'They pay £10 between them, and Jean pays £1 for a room on this floor that's barely more than a cupboard.'

Stratton did a moment's mental arithmetic. 'So if the controlled tenants were replaced with coloured people—'

'Or prostitutes. Schwartz and tarts, Perlmann calls it.'

'—then he'd make, say, £86 a week instead of £55. And

presumably, he'd get about an extra thirty-odd quid each from all the other houses, would he?'

'Something like that, I should think.'

'So if Hampton was going about telling all these tenants to go to the rent tribunal and Perlmann heard of it, he wouldn't be very popular . . .' Stratton thought for a moment. 'Although uncontrolled tenants, if the landlord finds them wanting, can presumably be booted out fairly easily.'

'A month's notice, as the law stands, and then if they don't leave you can evict them by force. *But*,' Russell leant forward for extra emphasis, 'once that tenant has applied to a rent tribunal for a reduction, ten to one he's given three months' security of tenure, which is renewable each time the three months is up. There's something else you might like to know, too. Hampton told me he'd been told not to bother collecting rents off us controlled tenants.'

'Why?'

'Why do you think? So that he could claim we were in arrears and evict us.'

'Did Perlmann say that to him?'

'Not in so many words, but we knew what his game was. Hampton told him he wouldn't do it and he'd have to have the money whether he wanted it or not.'

'I get the picture. So who's been collecting the rent since Hampton died?'

'Chap called Laskier. Sort of bookkeeper for Perlmann, I think. I imagine that's only a temporary state of affairs, though.'

'And he's been collecting the rent from everyone, has he?'

Russell nodded. 'As far as I know, he has.'

'And have there been any direct threats? Trying to get you to leave, or warning the coloured tenants not to go to the tribunal?'

'Not me. As to the other thing, I don't know. I did hear something one evening last week. Wednesday, I think, or Thursday.'

'What was it?'

'Royce and MacDonald had visitors. Two, I think. I wouldn't have paid much attention, except that they had a dog with them. I heard it growl and it sounded like a big beast. Dogs make all sorts of different noises but this one was vicious, as if it couldn't wait to take a lump out of somebody.'

'Did you hear what was said?'

'I heard one of the Jamaican boys say, 'What do you want?' and then it sounded as if whoever it was pushed them back inside the room – a scuffle, pushing, shoving, all very quick – and I could hear the dog's feet scrabbling on the floor and it was snarling, and then the door slammed shut.'

'Do you think that was Perlmann's doing?'

'Well, I can't think of anyone else.'

'Do you think he could have been responsible for Hampton's death? If Conroy and the others had decided to go to the rent tribunal, and they'd told people about it, then everyone would be getting their rent lowered and Perlmann's income would take a hell of a knock.'

'I don't know. But I'll tell you something – with Hampton out of the way, there'll be a lot more of that business with the dog. You mark my words: for all our talk of liberty and tolerance, we're going to see something very ugly here, very soon. We've spent years spreading ourselves all over the world without so much as a by-your-leave, but when a few thousand harmless Negroes come to our shores, we throw up our hands in horror. That's why they're here, Inspector, and don't you forget it. They're here because we are – or in some cases, were – there; because of the history of this island. Oh, well . . .' Russell sighed. 'Still, I've lived too bloody long already, so I doubt I'll be around to see it.'

CHAPTER FOUR

Both Royce and MacDonald were out at work. Stratton made a mental note to come back and speak to them about the men with the dog, then went back upstairs to ask Conroy if he'd received a similar visit. The Trinidadian, visibly agitated by his persistence, became almost hysterical in his denials, and Stratton, concluding that Russell had been right about the nature of the visit, went down to the basement.

Mrs Tyndall was, Stratton guessed, around forty, although her tired face and general air of defeat made her seem much older. Jean Tyndall, who appeared in the doorway at her mother's shoulder, looked older than her years too. She had a full, ripe figure and was heavily made up with a thick coating of salmon-coloured lipstick and a sticky-looking mound of lacquered curls. This must be, Stratton thought, in imitation of Connie Francis. Not that he'd have known who Connie Francis was but for a conversation with his daughter Monica back in April. Monica, a make-up artist at Ashwood Film Studios, knew all the latest styles and had explained about the Connie Francis thing when he'd complained that her new hairdo looked like a rain-sodden haystack.

The other four Tyndall children were shovelling down sausages and mash to the tinny accompaniment of a pop song from a transistor radio placed in the centre of the table. The basement flat, obviously the largest in the house, had its own kitchen as well as three other rooms. The place smelt of frying and – even in this hot weather – of damp. Stratton noted the dusty bloom of mushroom-coloured spores on the wallpaper between the battered Welsh dresser and the tin bath hanging from its nail. The shared lavatory bowl, which Stratton had glimpsed on the way in through a battered wooden door, was a foetid and seatless horror crouched in the dank space beneath the front steps, an ominous puddle spreading from the base of its cracked pedestal.

The Tyndalls, mother and daughter, confirmed their whereabouts at the time of Hampton's death. Fifteen-year-old Tom volunteered that he'd been at the boys' club in the church hall on Lancaster Road. 'And Mr Tyndall?' asked Stratton. 'Is he here?'

'Pub.' Mrs Tyndall's tone was resigned. 'Walmer Castle, that's where you'll find him.'

'And the evening that Mr Hampton was killed?'

'Same place.' Again, Stratton noted the quiet weariness of a once painful emotion which had, over time, been rubbed smooth. 'Lost his job eighteen months back and hasn't been able to get another. The darkies take them all.'

'That's not fair, Mum.'

'Isn't it?' Mrs Tyndall rounded on her daughter, who was leaning against the sink, arms folded. 'I don't know how you can stick up for them.' Turning back to Stratton, she said, 'If they're not taking jobs, they're poncing off white women. That,' she told Jean, 'is how you'll end up if you don't watch out.'

Jean, who was lighting a cigarette, looked unperturbed. 'Don't be silly, Mum,' she said, in a sort of long-suffering sing-song which suggested a well-rehearsed argument. 'I've told you—'

'And I've told *you* often enough, and so's your dad. She'll end up on the game,' Mrs Tyndall told Stratton. 'On the game with a pack of half-caste brats.'

My Dad says it's the coloureds, thought Stratton, remembering Shirley Maples's statement as he went across the road to find her.

Stratton had noticed, as he'd climbed the stairs at number 19, that the air grew warmer with every flight, but number 24 seemed to be even worse. When he turned the corner to the penultimate flight, the heat that enveloped him was almost suffocating. Mr Maples, who answered his knock, looked about fifty, small, deathly pale and bald – a sweating peeled egg with thick glasses. When Stratton explained the reason for his visit and Mr Maples moved back to let him in, Stratton saw that he dragged a club foot behind him – the reason, he supposed, for asking Shirley to take the rent to Hampton.

The lino in the Mapleses' sitting room was covered in stacks of flat balsa-wood cut-outs in the shapes of penguins in profile, and beside what was clearly Mr Maples's designated armchair was a palette smeared with white paint and a selection of brushes in a jam jar. 'Careful where you step,' said the little man. 'I was just about to make a start. I paint them, you see. It was Mr Hampton got me on to it, in fact – he had a mate with a stall in the market. This chap's got someone who cuts out the shapes, then I paint them, then he collects them and gets them mounted on wheels with a stick to pull them along. Very popular, they are. I used to be a caretaker,' he added, 'but it got too much for me with my leg, and Mr Hampton knew we was hard up . . . Shirley's in her room.' He gestured towards a door from behind which the sound of 'All I have to do is dream' could be heard. 'Plays that soppy record all the time . . . She's a good girl, though,' he added quickly. 'Not like some of them round here.'

Shirley Maples, skinny, nervous and unpainted, with slightly protruding teeth, looked altogether more Stratton's idea of a seventeen-year-old than had Jean Tyndall across the road. She perched on the edge of an armchair, chewing her cuticles and nodding while he took her through her statement. 'That's what happened, yes.'

'And you're sure you didn't see anyone as you went upstairs at number 19?'

Shirley didn't meet his eye, but stared instead at a pile of soon-to-be penguins.

'Did you see anyone?'

'I . . .' Shirley continued to gaze at the wooden shapes as though mesmerised.

'You must tell me, Shirley. It could be very important.'

'There was a man, but . . .' The girl shook her head. 'Will I get into trouble?'

Mr Maples shuffled forward and put his hand on his daughter's shoulder. 'Why didn't you say something?' he asked, giving her a little squeeze, and, to Stratton, 'She won't be in trouble for this, will she?'

'No, but I do need to know who she saw. I also need to know why it wasn't in her original statement.'

'I'm sorry,' said Shirley, in a small voice. 'After I saw Mr Hampton all . . . like he was, I was that upset I couldn't think straight and I just forgot. I mean, I didn't do it on purpose.'

She blinked at Stratton, who, spotting the first sign of tears, said quickly, 'I'm sure you didn't. You'd just had a horrible shock.'

'When I remembered afterwards, I thought it probably didn't matter – I mean, if it was just one of those who live in the house . . .'

'One of those . . . ?'

'Darkies.'

'A man?'

Shirley nodded.

'Did you recognise him?'

'No. I don't know his name or nothing.'

'But you know he lives at number 19?'

'Not exactly. I think I've seen him going in there but I'm not sure.'

'Hard to tell one from another,' said Mr Maples.

My dad says it's the coloureds, thought Stratton. Mr Maples had claimed not to know anything about it, but all the same . . . 'You are telling me the truth about this, are you, Shirley?'

'Yes!' The indignant squeal was, Stratton was sure, genuine.

'So, what did this man look like?'

'Quite tall. I didn't get much of a look at him. He was coming down the stairs as I was about to go up.'

'You didn't see or hear him leave the building?'

'No, but the front door was open when I got there, so I thought somebody must want it like that, and I left it.'

'What was the man's complexion like?'

'Not *dark* dark, more sort of browny . . . Like in that picture.' Shirley got up and went to stand in front of an insipid watercolour of leaves and grasses hanging on the wall beside the window. Stratton spotted the title 'Autumn Hues' beside an indecipherable signature. 'Here,' said the girl, pointing at a leaf which Stratton thought was best described as a coppery burnt umber: Conroy's colouring.

'Can you remember what he was wearing, Shirley?'

The girl screwed up her face in concentration. 'Something quite dark. Not a suit or a jacket, something more . . . soft. Maybe a jumper. I didn't really notice. Are you sure I won't be in any trouble? I promise it was a mistake, me not telling you.'

'Nobody told you not to tell us, did they?'

'Told me not to?' Shirley looked puzzled. 'No. Anyway,' she added, with a visible recovery of confidence, 'if someone had, you know, scared me or something, I wouldn't be telling you now, would I?'

'That's true. Now, unless there's—'

'Yoo-hoo!' The door swung open and a small, ruddy-faced woman appeared, swollen feet in carpet slippers and clad in an overall, a black cat weaving itself around her thick ankles. She was brandishing a string shopping bag full of oranges and talking nineteen to the dozen. 'Mr Hoyt gave me these for Mrs Banks – ever so nice of him – I'll take them up to the hospital tomorr— Oh! I'm so sorry. I didn't know . . .'

'My wife,' explained Maples. 'Elsie, this is Inspector Stratton. He's come to ask Shirley a few more questions about when she found poor Mr Hampton.'

''Orrible thing to happen, 'orrible.' Elsie Maples lowered herself into the armchair that her daughter had just vacated. Settling herself with the cat on her lap, she carried on talking as Shirley and Mr Maples lifted up one leg each and set her heels on the seat of a hard chair positioned opposite. 'Have to do this, you see – it's the weather, makes my legs blow up something chronic so I can't wear nothing but slippers. Stop it, Nigger!' She put her arm underneath the cat's body and lifted it on to her chest. 'He will dig his claws in. Mr Hampton was a lovely man, always so kind to everyone – he'd have given you the shirt off his back, I swear it. Did Norman tell you he found him this work, painting the toys?'

She paused just long enough to draw breath but not long enough for Stratton to get out more than 'I—' before launching into another machine-gun burst of speech.

'He got on with everyone round here, Mr Hampton. Mind you, we get on with them too, don't we, Norm? See these?' She indicated the string bag of oranges which was now reposing on her lap. 'My boss – mornings, I work at a greengrocer down the road – he give 'em to me for our neighbour. Black as my shoe but ever such a nice woman, do anything for you. She's just had a lovely baby boy – four days ago, it was, so she's still up at the hospital – and I thought I'd take them to her tomorrow. It's her first and I took her to the hospital myself when it started because they don't know, do they? Only been here a month or so and they probably just go and have them in the fields back home . . .'

This time, Stratton managed 'I th—' before she started up again.

'We thought these –' here, she patted the oranges – 'would remind her of home. We've got a couple of coloured boys live downstairs too – when they moved in about six months ago I said to Shirley, You stay away from them, because you never know . . . Well, we all saw what happened at number 19, didn't we? Not that my Shirley's anything *like* that Tyndall girl, thank the Lord – we brought her up right – but all the same . . .'

Both Shirley and Mr Maples, who had subsided into chairs one on either side of Elsie, remained deadpan. They'd probably realised long ago, thought Stratton, that trying to shut the woman up was futile. He wondered how on earth Norman had got her to keep quiet for long enough to propose, never mind anything else. Perhaps he'd got a secret supply of chloroform.

'. . . the thing is,' Elsie's voice had dropped to a sibilant whisper, 'a lot of them don't have their wives over here. That's the trouble. There are brothels everywhere round here, quite disgusting. The fact is,' she nodded significantly, 'men need women to keep them in order.' She gave a sidelong glance at Norman, presumably to check that he wasn't about to sneak off to an orgy.

After several minutes of this, Shirley piped up that she was late getting back to work so, having ascertained that she had nothing to add to what she'd already said, Stratton let her go, and then – after eliciting the information that the Maples family had had no difficulties with Perlmann, left himself. Walking down the road, he could almost feel his back bending under the weight of the stares – not only from the groups clustered on the front steps, but from people looking out of windows too, including a row of slatternly-looking white girls who were sitting on one of the larger window sills, dangling their legs in the sunshine. The sudden hush that had fallen when he'd emerged left him in no doubt that the bush telegraph was working overtime with news of his visit.

CHAPTER FIVE

Stratton rounded the corner into Ledbury Road and paused to glance at his watch. Half past two. Time for a word with Mr Perlmann. Perlmann's office, he knew from the information he'd been given, was only a short distance away, in Westbourne Grove.

It was still uncomfortably hot. Being on duty, Stratton couldn't take his jacket off, but compromised by loosening his tie and undoing the top button of his shirt. Looking down the various streets as he walked, he could see that some of the houses were in worse condition even than those in Colville Terrace. He saw doors with planks of wood nailed across them and corrugated iron over the windows, and all manner of rubbish, including tyres and discarded furniture, strewn across the pavements. The few cars he spotted looked as though they'd been either stolen or abandoned. He could hear children playing – the repetitive slash of a skipping rope and the thump of a ball being bounced against the wall, and ahead of him a rent collector, or perhaps a tally man, was knocking on one peeling front door after another.

Through a broken wooden fence he glimpsed a bomb-site full of rubble with nettles poking through the carcasses of two burnt-out vehicles, and beyond, the back of a laundry. The double doors were wide open, revealing a dozen ironing boards set up inside, the flexes of the big metal irons hanging down from the ceiling so that they resembled so many miniature dodgem cars. The female operatives, red-faced and bare-legged, were clustered outside on their break, fanning themselves with their hands and blowing down the necks of their overalls.

Rounding a corner, past a brick wall daubed in both chalk and paint with – again – the letters KBW, he spotted a junk shop. The window was full of dusty trinkets with sun-bleached price tags displayed against a background of curling, faded tissue paper, and a 'closed' sign hanging in the door. He paused for a moment, to look – quite why, he wasn't sure – and a pretty silver bracelet caught his eye. Victorian, he thought, or maybe Edwardian. His wife Jenny, he supposed, would have thought it old-fashioned. Had she not been dead for – oh, Christ – fourteen years now, her tastes might have changed, of course. Time seemed to pass more quickly these days, as if his life, beyond his control, was accelerating away from her with a momentum of its own. It was always a shock to him to realise just how long ago it was that she'd been killed, and he still hadn't entirely got used to the feeling that he was, somehow, leaving her behind – still slightly guilty, as if it were something he could prevent.

He looked again at the bracelet, wishing he had someone

to buy it for. Could he, perhaps, send it to Diana as a welcome-to-California present? She'd have arrived by now – they'd had dinner together over three weeks ago, just before she sailed. He imagined her on the deck of a great liner, leaning on the rail, elegant in a nautical costume, with her blonde hair curled up under a sporty white cap. Except that she wouldn't be alone, would she? Lester Manning, her husband of three months, would be leaning on the rail beside her. Their elbows would be touching and his hand, perhaps, on her arm, as the pair of them watched the coast of England recede into the distance . . .

Stratton turned away from the display, catching sight of his reflection in the dusty window – dishevelled and pouchy-eyed, his broken nose wonkier than ever – as he did so. Yes – he quickly straightened his back – he was still as tall and broad-shouldered as ever, but there was no denying he'd got thicker round the middle, and under his hat his hair, although still as plentiful as ever, was greying at an alarming rate. It was something of a miracle, he thought, that Diana had ever looked his way in the first place. Sending her the bracelet was a ridiculous idea. Not that he posed any sort of threat from 8,000-odd miles away, but that type of gift turning up in the post was – whether or not Diana had told Manning about them being lovers – bound to lead to difficult questions.

Lester Manning was a director Diana had met a couple of years before at Ashwood Studios, where she'd been designing sets for one of his films. How soon after their first encounter the relationship had blossomed into romance,

Stratton didn't know. When Diana had told him about it the previous summer she'd been halting and apologetic. Stratton had listened quietly and refrained from asking questions about when or where or how. He hadn't been surprised. In fact, for a couple of days he'd felt unable to put a name to the emotion he was feeling. Resignation, certainly – he'd been unconsciously schooling himself for the moment ever since they'd first started seeing each other. He'd counted himself lucky – more than lucky – while whatever it was had lasted. Eighteen months earlier, in the low-beamed cottage bedroom in Suffolk where she'd come to visit him during the course of a murder investigation, she'd told him, 'We both know I'm never going to be Mrs Stratton and that we're living on borrowed time.' He'd been shocked to hear it put so baldly, reacting churlishly, but he'd known, at the same time, that she was right.

Her going away to America made it easier, somehow. Manning had been offered work in Hollywood where Diana, he supposed, would also find a job if she could get a permit. When they'd had dinner together that last time, she'd joked about becoming a housewife in Beverly Hills.

Still, he might buy the bracelet anyway, if he happened to be passing when the place was open. He couldn't see the price on the tag, but surely it couldn't be too expensive – not here – and Monica might like it. Yes, he'd do that.

He moved away briskly, keen to leave a clear boundary between himself and the fused mess of memories and emotions. Two days into his new job, his task was to concentrate on the present, not to indulge himself by getting tangled up in the cat's cradle of the past.

Further down the street, he halted beside a poster in the window of the Coin-Op launderette. Put there by the Union Movement – whose office, he noted, was in Kensington Park Road – it advertised a meeting to be addressed by Sir Oswald Mosley: End Coloured Immigration Now. On a stretch of brick wall opposite the shop was daubed, in white paint, 'House Britons Not Blacks'. He recalled reading somewhere that the Union Movement had grown out of the old British Union of Fascists and that its members wanted to turn Europe into a single nation, or something equally implausible. He suddenly thought of the stuff he'd seen on the newsreels about Germany in the 1930s, the slogans and smashed windows. Of course one couldn't make a direct comparison – what happened to the Jews in Germany had been officially directed – but none the less . . .

The entrance to Perlmann's office was in a side street. The office itself was a gloomy basement, reached down a flight of iron-railed stone steps. The door to the place was ajar, so Stratton walked straight into the main room. His immediate impression was one of immense disorder: piles of paper on every surface, cigarette packets with smudged columns of figures scrawled on them, overflowing wastepaper baskets and ashtrays as well as three metal buckets full of shillings presumably collected from gas meters, an adding machine, several half-eaten sandwiches and half-drunk, scummy cups of tea, and, in the middle of it all, a disembowelled typewriter, its ribbon spooled out over the keys. Such furniture as there was – two desks and three chairs – was chipped and shoddy; little better, in fact, than the stuff Perlmann afforded his tenants. Stratton, who'd remembered PC Jellicoe's words about the man driving a Roller and having a mansion, had expected something altogether more impressive. For a moment he thought the place was empty, but then a man scrambled out from underneath one of the desks, muttering to himself in a language Stratton didn't recognise. He coughed to indicate his presence, and the man, who was kneeling on the floor, apparently searching for something, raised his head. He had sleek black hair that flopped forward over his face, sharp, chiselled features, high cheekbones and a slightly hooked nose that gave him the air of a bird of prey, but there was an unmistakable look of strain about his eyes. His suit jacket was hanging on the back of one of the chairs, and the sleeves of his white shirt were rolled up to the elbow. Stratton supposed he must be about thirty, maybe slightly older.

'Yes? Can I help you?' The man got to his feet, and Stratton saw that he was broad-shouldered and almost as tall as he himself was. The accent was definitely foreign – somewhere behind the Iron Curtain, Stratton thought.

'I'm looking for Mr Perlmann.'

'He isn't here.'

'Are you expecting him?'

'No.'

'Where is he?'

'Why do you want to know? If you have something to

say to him, I can give a message.' The tone wasn't hostile but it wasn't helpful either, simply resigned – although to what, Stratton wasn't sure. When he introduced himself and explained the reason for his visit, the man said, 'Danny – Mr Perlmann – he's already spoken to the police.'

'I have no record of a statement being taken.'

'Well, he did speak to someone. I am sorry, but . . .' He spread his hands in a theatrical gesture of helplessness, smiling placatingly as he did so. 'We cannot do more.'

'What is your name?'

'Stefan Laskier. I keep the books here.'

'And where is Mr Perlmann now?'

'He likes to have lunch at the Daquise Restaurant in South Kensington. He is usually there until about three o'clock, and it's . . .' Laskier brought his arm up slightly to glance at his wristwatch and, as he did so, Stratton caught sight of a sequence of numbers written on the inside of his arm, just below his elbow. It took him a second to realise that he was looking at a tattoo.

Laskier saw the direction of his gaze and for a fraction of a second their eyes met. Then Stratton looked away, embarrassed, and Laskier continued, in a louder voice than before, as if trying to drown out what wasn't being said, '. . . it's a quarter past three now, so he'll probably be on his way to the Kenco in Queensway or the Kardomah in the King's Road. He prefers to do business in cafes and restaurants, and then he visits his clubs in the evening.'

As he spoke, a newsreel flickered across Stratton's mind, from the end of the war. Belsen, Buchenwald, Auschwitz.

Open mass graves full of socket-eyed almost-skeletons. The living, scarcely more fleshed than the dead, in striped pyjamas, waiting behind barbed wire . . . This man had survived those things. How old could he have been at the start of the war? Fifteen, Stratton supposed, or sixteen. Twenty-one or two when it ended.

'So,' he said, pulling himself together, 'Mr Perlmann's never in the office?'

'Only for an hour in the morning, to make telephone calls. People know where to find him.' Laskier looked a challenge at Stratton, then, with an air of deliberation, rolled down his sleeves and did up his cuffs.

'Must make things rather complicated for you, surely?'

'Mr Perlmann has an extraordinary mind. He never makes notes because he remembers everything.'

Which, thought Stratton, makes for chaos in the office.

'I am sorry,' Laskier repeated, 'but—'

'What do you know,' Stratton asked, 'about threats made to tenants?'

'Threats?'

'To persuade them not to go to the rent tribunal for a re-evaluation. To get their rent lowered,' he added, by way of explanation.

'I know what it means,' said Laskier. 'Look at this.' He opened a drawer in one of the desks and pulled out a newspaper cutting. Stratton saw that it was from the *Empire News*. '*Mr Perlmann,*' he read, '*is probably London's largest individual landlord for the coloured population . . . He says, "The Government does nothing to house these West Indians when they come over.*

Somebody must. That's why they come to me. I take people as they come. Mind you, some white people do object to the coloured people when they move in. They don't like the way they play jazz records up to 1 a.m. and always loudly. If white tenants complain, I help them to find another place. I give them financial assistance. Last year I gave away £2,000 to help white tenants buy their own homes."'

'Very commendable,' said Stratton drily. 'I suppose he's in business for his health, is he? As well as the good of mankind.'

Laskier shook his head and indicated the newspaper. 'You can see it there. We're giving a service.'

'And you're telling me that he's never threatened anyone. Never offered to set dogs on them or throw them out or—'

Laskier put up his hands in a surrender-like gesture. 'He uses the strong men – strong-arm. All landlords do this. Some tenants don't pay when they should, so . . .' He shrugged. 'And some of the men have dogs, yes. A lot of money – they have to protect it.'

'Yes,' said Stratton. 'He charges very high prices.'

'As you said,' replied Laskier, 'it's a business. We have bills to pay.'

'Bert Hampton wasn't a strong-arm man, though, was he? In fact, he told the coloured tenants that they could apply to the tribunal. I bet Mr Perlmann was none too pleased when he found out about that.'

'He didn't know about this. Mr Perlmann has a lot of properties. He doesn't know what is happening with each one. He is too busy for that. There are some landlords who'll evict tenants if they are behind with the rent, but

Mr Perlmann is a generous man. If someone's in trouble and they can't pay, then he gives them money to help them out.'

'And he doesn't charge them interest?'

'Not the girls.' Laskier's smile looked tired, accepting. 'He's soft-hearted with women.'

A blonde on each arm, thought Stratton, remembering what Jellicoe had said. 'Women like Vicky Allardice, you mean?'

'Vicky . . . ?'

'The whore who lives at 19 Colville Terrace.'

'I know nothing about this.' Laskier's face gave nothing away.

'I understand that a number of your tenants are prostitutes.'

'As far as I know,' said Laskier, 'we don't rent to that sort of girl. In any case, one in a house doesn't count as a brothel. You should be asking the Church Commissioners this question, not us.'

'Why?' asked Stratton, disconcerted.

'They have a vast estate in Paddington – the biggest brothel in Europe.'

'But they have nothing to do with this murder inquiry.'

'Neither do we, Inspector. You have my assurance. And Mr Perlmann has given a substantial donation to the Police Orphanage.'

'Has he indeed?' said Stratton, hoping that this wasn't going to prove to be connected to the absence of any formal statement from the man.

'Yes,' said Laskier, apparently missing the wry tone. 'And he's helped a lot of our compatriots too.'

'Which country?'

'Poland. He's always tried to give them work, help them out with somewhere to live, money and so on.'

'You're very loyal to him,' said Stratton.

'He's a good man.'

'Clearly,' said Stratton. 'A saint, one might almost say.'

'He can't be a saint,' said Laskier, deadpan. 'He's Jewish.'

'How long have you been in this country?'

'Twelve years,' said Laskier. 'Both of us came in 1946. We walked halfway across Europe to get here and spent most of the winter in a resettlement camp in Dumfriesshire.' He grimaced. 'The Poles didn't want to know us because we were Jews, and the Jews didn't want to know us because we were Poles . . .' He shook his head.

Uncertain how to respond to this, Stratton said, 'Well, your English is very good.'

'Thank you.' Laskier's tone was sardonic.

'I shall need to take a formal statement from Mr Perlmann. Perhaps you could let him know.'

Stratton decided to go down to the Kenco place Laskier had mentioned in Queensway, and see if Perlmann was there. Walking down Westbourne Grove towards the junction, he thought about what Laskier had said. He'd seemed genuinely to admire Perlmann . . . He said they'd arrived in Britain together, having walked halfway across Europe, so presumably Perlmann had been in a camp, too – perhaps the same one. An experience like that would forge strong bonds – and from all he'd read about concentration camps, you'd need to know every trick in the book in order to survive.

Judging by what Laskier had said, Perlmann was the type of man who softens the ugly reality of how he earns his living by individual acts of generosity and kindness and is thus able to see himself in a favourable light. Then there was the business about being 'Mr Big' to a coterie of Polish hangers-on – all part of the same thing, thought Stratton: a way of being generous and calculating at the same time, securing their obligation to him by helping them. Presumably Laskier, having arrived in Britain with Perlmann, was the first of these; he certainly seemed to fit the bill as favoured henchman or lieutenant.

As he turned into Queensway, Stratton saw a gleaming navy blue Rolls-Royce speeding away and heard women's voices shouting, 'Hey, Danny!' and 'Take me with you, Danny!' A male arm, a thick glint of gold watch at the wrist and a fat cigar clasped in the hand, waved at them out of the car as it shot off towards Hyde Park, horn blaring. Stratton realised that he'd just missed Perlmann, and that the blurred impression of teased-up blonde hair in the passenger seat meant that somebody had, indeed, been taken with him, even if it wasn't one of the whores who, though not out in force at four o'clock, none the less had a definite presence, parading up and down in their summer frocks, high heels clicking across the hot pavement.

*

Stratton located the Kenco cafe, found a table, and ordered a cup of tea. Spotting a copy of the *Kensington Post* unattended on a nearby chair, he picked it up. Two items caught his eye. The first, headlined '7 accused of stab attack', was an account of a group of coloured men accused of causing grievous bodily harm to 21-year-old fitter George Edward Starkey of Stowe Road, Shepherd's Bush. All of the accused had pleaded not guilty and been given bail. Next to this was an item entitled 'No bail for 9 men on wounding charge' about a group of youths who were charged with unlawfully and maliciously wounding a coloured man called Joseph Welsh with intent to cause grievous bodily harm. Further charges, Stratton read, would be made in connection with serious injuries caused to three other coloured men who were receiving treatment in hospital.

A third item, smaller and further down the page, was headed 'Raid on Cafe'. *Five youths*, read Stratton, *whose ages ranged from 17 to 23 were at London Session on Tuesday found guilty of causing malicious damage to a cafe at Shepherd's Bush owned by a coloured man. They were each conditionally discharged for 12 months, ordered each to pay £40 compensation and to pay 10 guineas towards the cost of the prosecution. Proprietor Samuel Thomas said that the cafe was raided for five minutes by a gang of between 20 and 30 youths. 'It was like an earthquake,' he said, 'I didn't try to stop them because I would have been killed.'*

With that many, thought Stratton, the ones who were caught must have been the ones who were too stupid to leg it in time. All of them local lads – Notting Hill, Shepherd's Bush, Hammersmith and Fulham. Turning to the back of the paper he discovered, glancing through the advertisements for rooms to let, that there were quite a lot which specified 'No coloured', 'Europeans only' or even 'English only'. A moment's mental arithmetic told him that the ratio of these to the non-specific advertisements was approximately one to eight, and a spot more calculation confirmed that advertisements from landlords who positively encouraged black tenants ('all nationalities', 'coloured welcome', and so on) numbered about one in forty. When Stratton thought about it, he supposed that he had, in the past few months, seen signs saying 'No coloured' in the windows of several boarding houses, joining 'No babies', 'No dogs', and – depending on the area – 'No Irish'. Of course, there'd be no guarantee that those who did not elaborate on their preferred sort of tenant would actually take a coloured one – in order to avoid an admission of prejudice, they could simply claim that the room was already taken.

He put down the paper and stared out of the window. Apart from an elderly man shuffling out of the tobacconist's opposite, the only people he could see were the whores, each at her post, radar eyes scanning the street, hair sticky with lacquer, bare-armed and dressed in a frock with a nipped-in waist and pointy-toed shoes. Two more girls appeared and, when they stopped to buy milk from the machine across the road, Stratton saw that one of them was Vicky. Her companion was a few years older, stick-limbed, large-eyed and sharp-featured, with a pile of blonde hair – the roots of which, Stratton noticed, could have done with touching up. He wondered if this were the 'friend' – riffling through the pages of his notebook, he saw that her name was Marion Lockwood – that Vicky had mentioned. If so, she'd be able to confirm Vicky's whereabouts on the evening of Hampton's death.

Stratton paid for his tea and crossed the road to where the two girls were standing, smoking and drinking from the little cartons. Seeing that he was making a beeline for the pair of them, the blonde girl thrust out a hip and said, 'Like a good time, darling? Three pound each, more if you want something—'

At this point Vicky, who'd automatically assumed an expression of coolly licentious promise that belied the dark crescents under her arms and the sheen of sweat leaching through her pore-clogging make-up, stiffened and put a hand on her companion's arm. 'It's that copper. You following me or something?' she asked Stratton. 'What do you want now?'

'Just a bit more information. Who's your friend?'

'Marion. She was with me that day. I told you, remember?'

Marion, who'd clearly been put in the picture about their interview, nodded in affirmation of this. 'We was both here all afternoon. We went shopping and then we had tea in the place down there.' She waved her milk carton in the direction of the Larchwood Cafe.

'What time did you start work?'

Marion looked mulish and said nothing.

'For God's sake,' said Stratton, 'you've just propositioned me.'

'I didn't mean nothing,' she said sulkily.

'It's all right, I'm not going to take you in.'

Marion and Vicky exchanged glances. 'Do you usually work together?' asked Stratton.

'Only if it's slow.'

'But it was slow that night, wasn't it? Vicky said she didn't get her first pick-up until half past eight.'

'I had to go and meet a friend—'

'When was that?'

'About half past six. But I saw Vicky when I came back at about eight o'clock, and we were having a chat when a man stopped to talk to us, so I went with him, and when I got back Vicky was gone. That's right, isn't it, Vick?'

Vicky nodded.

'Fair enough,' said Stratton, making notes. 'Where do you live?' he asked Marion.

'45 Powis Square.'

Remembering the streets that Jellicoe had mentioned, Stratton asked, 'Who's your landlord?'

'Mr Perlmann.'

'Do you work from home?'

Marion shook her head.

'Where, then?'

'In the park sometimes, cars . . .'

Seeing her hesitate, Stratton asked, 'Anywhere else? Don't bugger me about, love. I can easily find out if you're pulling a fast one, and I won't be happy.'

'Hustling gaff in Chepstow Road. This end.'

'Very convenient.' Clearly Marion, unlike Vicky, lived with a boyfriend at least part of the time – the rules being that a man who lived with a prostitute in the place where she actually worked could be prosecuted for living off immoral earnings.

'Does that flat belong to Mr Perlmann too?'

'Yes.'

'Has he ever made any threats to either of you?'

Vicky looked baffled. 'Why would he do that?'

'Do you know about the rent tribunal?'

'What?'

'Mr Hampton didn't explain it to you?'

'Explain what?' Stratton looked at Marion and saw that she was as confused as Vicky.

'That you could go to the tribunal and apply to get your rent lowered.'

Vicky stared at him, incredulous. 'Us? You must be joking.'

'So you don't know anything about it.'

'No, I told you. Anyway, Mr Perlmann's all right. Not stuck-up, like some – takes people as he finds them. Gives you advice, and that. Told me I should get some pictures taken – schoolgirl, French maid, that sort of thing.'

Stratton raised an eyebrow. 'And did you?'

'I might.'

'He likes us,' said Marion. 'And he's cheery – always gives you a wave. I wouldn't say no to a ride in that flash car of his, either.'

CHAPTER SIX

As he made his way back down Queensway, Stratton wondered if Hampton had neglected to tell Vicky about the
rent tribunal because he disapproved of what she did for
a living, or because he thought they wouldn't listen to
someone who was obviously on the game. He thought, too,
about Perlmann advising the whores on how to improve
their business. He imagined that most of them, here as in
the West End, were too lazy or dopey to take the advice,
too given to being stupid over 'boyfriends' who took all
their money and beat them up into the bargain. Did it just
come down to a willingness to pass on tricks learnt for
survival, or was it because he got his kicks from dirty talk
with the girls?

He pulled out his handkerchief to wipe his face. The
combination of the heat and the general grubbiness of the
subject matter made him long for a pint and a cool bath.
It was a quarter to six – he'd lingered in the cafe for longer
than he'd realised. As Matheson said he'd be around until
eight o'clock, he decided to go back to the station via Colville Terrace and see if Royce and MacDonald – who he saw

from his notes worked in, respectively, a laundry and a food processing plant – were home from work.

His visit was almost a replay of what had happened when he'd asked Horace Conroy if he'd been threatened over the business of the rent tribunal. Ernest MacDonald wasn't there, but Jeffrey Royce answered the door with a degree of caution that suggested he had every reason to suspect the worst. Instantly alarmed when Stratton introduced himself, he became even more so when asked about a visit from the men with the dog. He kept reiterating that he and Mac-Donald paid their rent and didn't want any trouble, as if he thought Stratton might be reporting back to Perlmann rather than the police station.

'What type of dog was it?' asked Stratton.

'I don't know about dogs,' said Royce.

'Big? Small?'

'Big. It was a big one.'

'Long hair or short hair?'

'Look man, I don't know.' Royce backed away from him, shaking his head, looking desperate for Stratton to leave.

'Fierce?'

'No – just a dog, you know?' The man was obviously making an effort to keep his voice calm, but his body language – and certainly his eyes – told a different story. Hands before him in a gesture of supplication, he backed away even further. 'Please, man. Please.'

'I'm trying to help you, Mr Royce.'

Royce said nothing, but continued shaking his head, looking as if he'd like to tell him to pull the other one because it had bells on. He was, Stratton noticed, of a similar height to himself – and therefore to Conroy – but definitely a couple of shades darker than the man upstairs, being more molasses than burnt umber. 'I'll leave you in peace,' he said. 'But if you have any trouble – if anyone here has any trouble – telephone the police station and ask for me.' Tearing a page out of his notebook, he scribbled down his name and the number. Royce stared at it, still with an expression of disbelief, thanked him, and, evidently relieved the ordeal was over, closed the door smartly in his face.

Walking back towards Harrow Road, Stratton saw that the pubs had opened their doors and that already the smoke hung in slow, suspended skeins above the drinkers' heads. The people on the doorsteps had gone inside now, and the few children left playing were being called in for tea. He heard a jazzy sort of music and discovered, rounding a corner, that it was issuing from a basement. Peering through the railings and into the area below, he saw through the window that the room had kitchen chairs and tables dotted about and crude murals of palm trees on the walls. As he watched, a coloured man appeared, stepping as lightly as if he were lifted aloft by the beat. The door, which was situated beneath the front steps of the house, was open, and he could smell something pungent which he was fairly sure was marijuana smoke. This, clearly, wasn't the time to investigate, but, thinking that he might have a word with someone back at the station, he made a note of the address.

He'd been walking for about fifteen minutes and was

just about to turn into the Harrow Road, when something else occurred to him. In the time he'd been walking, the streets had well-nigh emptied. Besides no children, there weren't any adults in evidence, either. The only people around in any numbers were young men in groups: some all white, some all black, but never mixed. Several had jostled past him, walking as if they owned the place. Which, seeing that there appeared to be some sort of unofficial curfew in operation, Stratton supposed they did. Both groups had a swagger to them, but there was an aggression, too, among the whites, a predatory atmosphere that told you they weren't just out for a lark. The coloured groups looked purposeful too, but wary. Presumably, Stratton thought, they were travelling together for safety, but also, by being in the streets, making the point that they weren't going to be bullied into staying at home. Stratton thought of the coloured man wiping spittle from his face as he carried on walking down Colville Terrace, and of Horace Conroy watching from the window and lifting his hand to his cheek. Then he remembered what Mr Russell had said and thought, I'm not sure I want to be around to see it, either, because the old man was right. Something was going to happen – and it was a matter not of if, but when.

CHAPTER SEVEN

'I always thought,' said Matheson, swirling the whisky in his glass, 'that Norman Backhouse looked like the type of chap who went around sniffing girls' bicycle saddles when no one was looking.'

This was so unexpected that Stratton, caught in mid-swallow, felt Scotch burning his nasal passages as he choked back a yelp of laughter.

They'd been talking about Stratton's past cases – seriously, up to now, because the Backhouse case, in which the killer's innocent neighbour, Davies, had been wrongfully convicted and hanged, was no laughing matter. 'Of all the murderers I've come into contact with,' Stratton recovered himself swiftly, 'he was the one who really made my skin crawl.'

'I'm not surprised.' Matheson leant back in his chair and put his head on one side. 'And of course you did some work with MI5 during the war, didn't you?'

Stratton opened his mouth, then closed it again. When Matheson had interviewed him, there'd been no mention of what had happened in 1940 and Stratton was officially forbidden to speak about it. Now, seeing his evident alarm,

Matheson said, 'It's all right. Chap I know told me. Jock Anderson.'

'Anderson?' Stratton had no idea who he was talking about.

'Colleague of Charles Forbes-James.'

'Ah.' Forbes-James had committed suicide in 1950, in circumstances which Stratton guessed – but didn't actually know – were to do with his homosexuality. He was sure that Diana, who'd worked for the man, knew more about it than he did, but he'd never asked for information and she'd never volunteered anything. Now Stratton had the sensation of putting his whole mental weight against a door that he wanted to remain firmly closed.

Perhaps Matheson observed something of this, because he said blandly, 'I gather your superiors were most impressed.' As there wasn't much he could say to this without sounding like a self-satisfied twerp, Stratton simply nodded. 'In fact, talking to DS Lamb and some other people, I soon formed the impression that you get on with things, which is what is needed here. I need someone I can trust – your predecessor was rather less use than a wet paper bag in that respect.'

Stratton actually clenched his jaw to keep his mouth from dropping open. The way Lamb had always carried on, Stratton didn't think he'd ever trusted him to sit the right way round on a lavatory, never mind anything else. 'That,' continued Matheson, 'is why I was so keen to snap you up, as it were – you're going to be working on your own for a lot of the time in the next few months. I need someone I can trust to get on with it. The trouble is that the powers-that-be are proving rather difficult when it comes to allocating more manpower to this division. It is, I fear, part of a grand plan to stick their heads in the sand about the race problem. They seem to believe that – despite all evidence to the contrary – if they keep denying it exists, it'll somehow go away. It won't, of course, but there you are.'

Stratton's surprise must have shown, because Matheson took another sip of his drink and continued, 'I don't see any point in being disingenuous about it. We've let them in and now they're here we've got to deal with the consequences, and of course they're entitled to go about their business without being molested, just as much as the next man. A cafe owned by a Jamaican chap was attacked last week – every stick of furniture and every piece of crockery smashed to pieces.'

'Yes,' said Stratton, 'I read about it in the local paper.'

'Then you probably saw the other news too – a coloured man leaving a party with a white girl attacked and beaten about the head so that he needed stitches, and another man tripped up and beaten – he had to have stitches to his leg and suffered severe bruising to his face, apparently inflicted by a youth wielding a lump of wood. Those aren't the only ones, by any means – and in every case, the assailants have made it very clear that they attacked these people solely because of their skin colour. *However*,' Matheson leant forward to emphasise the importance of what he was about to say, 'I have been told – not in so many words, you under-

stand, but message received and understood – to deny that
there is any element of racial conflict in these attacks.'

'But surely,' Stratton began, 'if—'

Matheson held up his hand, palm forward, and continued, 'I see no point in concealing this. I'm sure you've
gathered for yourself that there's a very definite atmosphere
of racial conflict in this area. Some of it, I grant you, is
straightforward hooliganism – young men taking the chance
to make a nuisance of themselves. Some of it is caused by
ignorance on both sides and some by fighting over women
– because a lot of the immigrants are single men – and over
resources such as housing. You've noticed the overcrowding,
no doubt.'

Stratton nodded. 'Pretty grim.'

'It is,' agreed Matheson, 'although, if you look at the
houses, the majority of them are well-built – not like all
those Victorian warrens in the East End. Most of them would
be decent homes if anyone had the money or sense to take
care of them. And of course the area wasn't bombed, so it's
low down on the list when it comes to rebuilding . . . The
landlords are up to all sorts of tricks, and we've had instances
of West Indians who've bought up houses and illegally
evicted the white tenants. Then there's the fact that when
one of them gets a room, all his friends and relations come
to stay. You get cases where one's working nights and one's
on days and they're sharing the bed. Also, there's the fact
that – in Notting Dale at least – you've got families who've
lived in the same place for generation after generation and
they're all related by blood or marriage – kick one and they

all limp. They don't like white strangers from Acton, never mind black ones from God knows how many thousands of miles away.'

'Urban peasants,' said Stratton. 'They don't like outsiders any more than the rural ones.'

'Ah, yes,' said Matheson. 'You grew up in . . . Devon, wasn't it?'

'Yes, sir.'

'It's a lovely part of the world.' Matheson sipped his drink and continued, 'As to what we were saying, it's the younger ones who cause the trouble, but it's tacitly condoned by many of their elders. A great deal of the animosity is due to the fact that a lot of black men live off white prostitutes, and a lot of white men would like to do just that. Nevertheless, there is, shall we say, an "official line", and, for the time being at least, we must stick to it.'

'Isn't that going to be a bit difficult, what with Union Movement meetings and so on? I saw the advertisements.'

' "And so on" is correct – Mosley addressing a meeting is nothing to the White Defence League. Ah, I can see you haven't yet had the pleasure. It's based in Princedale Road and run by a chap called Gleeson. Left the League of Empire Loyalists because it wasn't right-wing enough for him, and thinks Mosley's a kosher fascist and the Jews are behind West Indian immigration. Very keen on Nazi regalia and the like, been holding a lot of rallies recently. But, getting back to the matter in hand, your impressions this afternoon were . . .?'

Stratton gave him a rundown of what he'd seen and

heard, raising the problem of the lack of any formal statement from Perlmann, and his donation to the police fund.

Matheson looked nonplussed. 'I knew about the donation, of course – quite a sizeable one, I believe. Perlmann
seems particularly keen to get on the right side of the right
people . . . You'll rectify the business about the statement
as soon as possible, of course, but in the absence of any clear
evidence that he was involved with Hampton's death, I'm
not sure that there's much we can do.'

'It's entirely possible,' said Stratton, 'that it's nothing to
do with him. I mean, if the coloured tenants could be dis-
suaded from going to the rent tribunal by threats, why kill
Hampton to prove a point?'

'Why indeed?'

'It could be,' said Stratton, 'that there's a lot of other
stuff going on that I'm not yet aware of . . . I'd like some
more information about known local troublemakers, for
example—'

'Half an hour with PC Jellicoe should sort that out, but
if you need to borrow one of the others, have a word with
the station sergeant. I'm sure he can reorganise things –
provided you don't do it too often, of course.'

'I had an encounter with one of Jellicoe's rock buns
earlier on,' said Stratton ruefully.

'Yes, I understand he's not to be trusted with comest-
ibles. However, if you want any information, he's your man
– been here so long he's practically part of the fixtures. It'll
also be handy for you to meet the LCC councillor for North
Kensington – he's a Labour man – and the youth-welfare

officers and people from the Moral Welfare Society and the school care committees, and so on. There's a reception tomorrow evening – just a get-together, really, but I can introduce you to some people who've been trying to do something about the housing problem and generally stop the rot – and I think I can safely promise that rock buns won't be on offer.'

This, thought Stratton, sounded as if it might be worthwhile, although he suspected that the Moral Welfare lot and their ilk were probably the 'bunch of do-gooding women' that Mr Russell feared would treat him 'like a mentally-deficient toddler'. He felt fairly sure that the old chap's anxiety was justified. In his experience, the bank managers' widows and the like who sat on these sorts of voluntary committees were undoubtedly good-hearted but also firmly convinced, despite the narrow confines of their own experience, that they knew exactly what was best for others.

He must have looked a bit dubious because Matheson chuckled. 'I can guess what you're thinking: a bunch of clueless, middle-aged types who've just woken up to the fact that they have rather easy lives and are feeling guilty about it – but they're not all bad, you know. And they do have the right ideas about improving the housing situation and generally—' He broke off in response to a knock on the door. 'Come!'

A flustered-looking young constable stood there, Adam's apple bobbing convulsively. 'What is it, man?'

'A stabbing, sir. Coloured man in Golborne Road, near

the railway line. Died in the ambulance on the way to Saint Charles's.'

'Anyone down there?'

'No, sir. Sorry. Sergeant Matthews says to tell you that he's telephoned the police mortuary and sent Brodie and Dunning down to Golborne Road, but DI Peacock's off sick and he doesn't know—'

Stratton stood up. 'I'll go. Thanks very much for the drink, sir.'

CHAPTER EIGHT

Stratton thought he could picture the part of Golborne Road where the attack had taken place – rotting houses that shook every time a train came past, with the gasworks looming behind them. The young constable had said that so far they had no idea of the dead man's name, and that there were no witnesses except for the woman who'd telephoned half an hour earlier. That would have been – Stratton glanced at his watch – around half past eight, so surely there'd have been a few people about, even in that godforsaken area? There were a couple of pubs down there, after all.

Waiting by the reception desk while someone who didn't know fetched someone who did, Stratton felt himself wilting. He'd been feeling tired, though pleasantly so, relaxed by Matheson's good Scotch and very ready to toddle off home. Really, he'd had no choice but to volunteer – it was important to show willing, especially at this point – but the sense of having to crank himself up again made him feel exhausted.

The 'someone who knew' proved to be a tired and anaemic-

Stratton telephoned the station with the information on the pawn ticket and, seeing that it was now almost ten o'clock, decided to call it a night. He was about to leave the hospital when, passing the entrance to the Casualty department, he spotted Perlmann's bookkeeper, Laskier, in the company of a pretty young redhead. *We don't rent to that sort of girl*, thought Stratton, remembering their conversation that afternoon. In a pig's arse you don't, chum.

The two of them were sitting together, not speaking, in the middle of a bench crammed with waiting outpatients – an anxious-looking woman with a baby, another with a wailing child with a bandage tied round its face, a man with a crutch and another with an ominously bright rash spreading up his neck and across his chin. Laskier's arm was round the girl's shoulders, but there was a stiffness about him which – despite the concern clearly visible on his face – suggested that he did not know her particularly well. The girl herself, slight, with skin almost as pale as the white blouse she wore, looked jumpy and brittle. A man's white handkerchief – Laskier's, presumably – was wrapped round one of her skinny arms, a large bloom of blood seeping through it and down on to her slender hand and thin skirt. Laskier was looking down at his lap, but she was staring straight ahead, eyes huge and smudged with black make-up, helpless but somehow, at the same time, defiant. Laskier must have felt someone's eyes on him, because he raised his head. For a moment his face was blank but then, seeing Stratton approach, he assumed a resigned expression.

'What's happened?'

'Just an accident, Inspector.'

'Fell over, didn't I?' The girl, whose accent was a gentrified Cockney, stared up at him, distrustful and clutching the bandage. Everything about her seemed so fragile that Stratton had the impression of some delicate wild creature caught in a trap, unable to flee.

There being nowhere to sit, Stratton hunkered down so that he wasn't towering above her. 'That looks nasty,' he said. 'What's your name, Miss?'

The girl turned to Laskier, eyes wide with fear. 'You promised,' she said. 'You said you'd never—'

'He didn't,' said Stratton. 'I'm here on another matter entirely. Just happened to be passing on my way out.'

'This is Irene,' said Laskier. He looked, Stratton thought, spent, deep troughs of exhaustion beneath his eyes. 'She fell over in the street and cut her arm. I just happened to be passing –' this was said heavily, in deliberate echo of Stratton – 'and I brought her here.'

'Very thoughtful of you. How old are you, love?'

Irene's voice was barely audible. 'Eighteen.'

'Are you indeed?' Stratton gave Laskier a meaningful look. 'And where do you live?'

'Powis Terrace.'

'One of your tenants, Mr Laskier?'

Laskier, taking his arm from Irene's shoulders and making to stand up, said, 'I don't think I have to—'

Stratton, rising so that he was directly in front of Laskier, said quietly, 'I think you do. It's a simple enough question.'

Looking down at Irene, who shrank away from him, he said, 'What number Powis Terrace?'

'Twelve.' Again, he could hardly hear her.

'And who's your landlord?'

'I don't know.'

'Mr Perlmann is the landlord,' said Laskier.

'Where are your parents?' asked Stratton. 'Do they know you're here?'

Irene shook her head.

'Well,' said Stratton, 'I think they'd like to know, don't you? Are they on the telephone?'

Irene, now staring down at the bandage on her arm, shook her head again.

'I see. Do they live at number twelve?'

This time the head shake was violent and when Irene raised her head, Stratton saw that her face was now a chalky white and she had tears in her eyes. 'Please . . .' the word came out in a terrified whisper.

'OK.' Stratton turned to Laskier. 'What's going on? Having a party, were you? Bit early for things to get out of hand, I'd have thought—'

He was cut off by a shout of 'Miss Palmer!'

Irene got to her feet. Laskier was about to accompany her, when Stratton said, 'She'll manage by herself. Off you go, love.'

They watched while Irene was led away to a cubicle by a bosomy nurse. 'Well?' said Stratton, taking Irene's place on the bench.

'There was no party,' said Laskier. 'I found her in the street.'

'Did you see her fall over?'

'No. She was like that when I found her. Bleeding. She said she'd fallen over.'

'And you believed her?'

'No.'

'Where did you find her?'

'Portobello Road. The corner of Oxford Gardens.'

'What time was that?'

'I think . . . about nine o'clock.'

Stratton glanced at his wristwatch and saw that it was five-and-twenty past. 'Did she say what she was doing there?'

'She said she was going for a walk.'

'On her own?'

Laskier nodded. 'I think she was lost.'

'So close to home? Not very likely, is it?'

'I don't know. I've never seen her before, Inspector. When she told me where she lived, I was surprised, but . . .' Laskier shrugged. 'People come and go – it's difficult to keep track of them.'

'But she lives with one of your tenants.'

'Yes,' said Laskier wearily. 'A Jamaican called Clinton Etheridge. But I only know this because she told me. I think she's run away from home.'

'And where's this Etheridge character now?'

'I have no idea. These girls . . .' Laskier shook his head.

'And she stuck to her story about falling over?'

'Yes.'

'No mention of a punter getting rough with her?'

'No.' Laskier looked thoughtful. 'I can see how it appears to be, Inspector, but I don't think she's selling herself. She doesn't look . . . you know?'

Stratton could see what Laskier meant. If Irene was on the game, she hadn't been doing it for long enough to acquire the patina of use.

'I think she's a nice girl,' said Laskier. 'I was thinking . . . maybe we offer her a job at the club.'

'Club?'

'I'm sorry. I think – thought – you already know this. Maxine's Club. In the West End.'

Stratton thought of the clientele Maxine's attracted: aristocrats, debutantes in fur stoles, mannequins, wealthy businessmen – elegant, assured and debonair. He couldn't imagine a shy working-class girl like Irene, however pretty she was, fitting into such a place. She did, however, strike him as ripe for exploitation, if not by the chap she currently lived with then by someone else. 'What sort of a job?' he asked.

'Waitress.' Laskier looked at him for a moment, and Stratton had a sense of someone unutterably sad as well as very tired. 'Serving drinks to the customers. Nothing more. I would like to help her, if I can. She reminds me of my sister.' Before Stratton could formulate anything approaching a response to this, he added gently, 'Or perhaps I only think she does. I can't remember. A dream, perhaps. But it doesn't matter.'

'I'm sorry,' said Stratton awkwardly. 'I'm sure you'll do

your best for her,' he added, getting to his feet. 'You'll see she gets home all right?'

'Yes.'

At the door of the Casualty department Stratton, turning, saw that Laskier was staring ahead of him, and wondered what the man was seeing. The half-remembered features of a girl who, in a crowd of faceless others, was herded away to be killed? Without knowing why, he felt a deep sense of shame. He attempted, as the train took him home, to rationalise it away – after all, what had happened to Laskier's sister, and probably his whole family, was no fault of his – but it remained with him, inexplicable and impervious to logic or excuse.

CHAPTER NINE

It was gone midnight when Stratton arrived back in Tottenham, so he was surprised to see a light coming from behind his sitting room curtains, as neither of his sisters-in-law – who, since Jenny's death, had taken it in turns to do the housekeeping – would be there so late. Opening the door, he heard Pete's voice call out, 'Hello, Dad!' and a moment later his son, 6 foot 4 in his socks, stood in front of him, filling the hall. 'I've been expecting you for hours. Aunt Doris let me in.'

Since leaving home for the army eight years before, Pete had forgotten or lost his key so many times that Stratton had eventually refused to replace it. 'Well, I wasn't expecting you. You might have phoned or something.'

'Last-minute change of plan,' said Pete airily. 'And I'm afraid I've eaten your supper.' He made a hitch-hiking movement behind him with his thumb, and Stratton saw a plate on the rug beside his armchair, empty but for a leaf of lettuce and a smear of what looked like mustard.

'Looks like you enjoyed it,' said Stratton, taking off his jacket. Having stopped feeling hungry at about the time he spotted Laskier and Irene at the hospital, he didn't really mind, although he wished Pete wouldn't be quite so offhand about things.

'I did, thanks. Anyway, I've got some news. Fancy a drink? I bought some beer.'

Stratton loosened his tie and jerked it over his head. 'Why not?' Although tired, he didn't feel ready for bed yet – too unsettled – and Pete's news, whatever it was, might help to take his mind off things.

He went through to the scullery and splashed his face with water at the sink. 'God, that's better.'

'How's the new job?' Pete lounged against the door of the refrigerator that Stratton had recently bought after Doris and Lilian had joined forces to nag him about it.

'Not sure yet. Tiring, anyway. Pass me that towel, will you?' Pete grabbed a tea towel off the hook behind the kitchen door and chucked it in his direction. 'Not that one!'

'Oh, never mind. Come on, Dad,' Pete dislodged himself enough to open the fridge and take out two bottles of beer. 'We've got something to celebrate.'

Stratton looked up from rubbing his face on the tea towel, which smelt faintly of gravy. 'Have we?'

'I've got an announcement.' Pete wielded the bottle opener with a flourish.

'Oh?' Stratton dropped the tea towel on the draining board. Pete rarely, if ever, told him anything at all about himself and was only slightly more forthcoming to Monica, his elder sister. It wasn't that he expected his son to wear his heart on his sleeve, but a little more information, he'd often felt, would be nice. Relations between them had been strained for some years after Jenny's death, and, wary of arguments as well as respecting privacy, he'd refrained from asking the boy too many questions. Some years ago he'd come to the conclusion that he must have failed Pete, but over time he'd decided, in a cautious, provisional way, that perhaps he might not have done so badly after all. Nowadays the lad (if one could call him that, at 26) seemed fairly contented and hadn't, so far as he knew, got into any serious trouble.

'Yes. Here you go.'

Stratton took the bottle his son had shoved towards his midriff and made a show of looking at it pointedly. Pete gave an exasperated sigh and started yanking open cupboard doors.

'In there.'

'Right.' Pete handed him a glass. 'Now can I tell you?'

Stratton took his time filling his glass, enjoying his son's obvious impatience. 'Fire away, then.'

'I'm getting married.'

'Ah.' Stratton wasn't entirely sure what he'd expected to hear – he'd rather assumed, given the general lack of personal information, that it must be something to do with his career. 'Do I know her?'

'Alison. I brought her here at Easter, remember?'

'Oh, yes.' Pete had been as casual about Alison – Stratton remembered dark curly hair, gorgeous deep brown eyes and generous breasts – as he had about all her predecessors, so Stratton hadn't attached any particular importance to the visit. 'Well, congratulations. She seemed very . . .' Stratton faltered. The truth was that, hair, eyes and breasts excepted, he could remember nothing about Alison except that she'd giggled quite a bit. '. . . nice,' he finished, lamely. 'Lively. Anyway, cheers,' he concluded, raising his glass.

Pete leant forward and clinked his bottle against it. 'Cheers. We're thinking about November. Something fairly quiet.'

'Does the bride's mother know that?' asked Stratton, recalling Jenny's mum's insistence on organising every detail of the proceedings. Not that it had been a particularly fancy wedding – quite a modest affair, in fact. He realised that, at this distance – he'd been married in 1929 – he couldn't remember very much of the actual event at all, except that Jenny had looked beautiful and that, despite his nerves, his speech had gone off all right.

'I think so. Alison's family's not well-off or anything, so it won't be a great big do. I'm leaving it up to her.'

'You've known her for a while, haven't you? Monica told me you were writing to her when you were in Suez, but you never mentioned her to me, so I thought . . . I didn't think anything, really, because you never seemed to be very involved with anyone – any of the others, I mean – and . . . Well, I thought you were playing the field.'

Pete's eyes widened and for a moment Stratton thought he'd offended him. Then he laughed. 'I suppose I was. Or that's what I thought. Bit of a lady's man, you know? But then I realised they kept on giving me the chuck.'

'I did wonder,' said Stratton. 'The ones you brought here,

you never mentioned them afterwards, and you were pretty offhand when I asked, so . . .'

'Yeah.' Pete grinned ruefully. 'But Alison's different.'

'Do you think she'll take to being an army wife? I know my job was difficult for your mother sometimes, but at least we always lived in the same place, and—'

'Actually, Dad, that was the other thing I wanted to talk to you about. I'm thinking of jacking it in.'

'Seriously?' This was even more of a surprise. When Pete had opted to stay in the army after doing his National Service, Stratton had assumed he'd remain there until they retired him.

'Seriously. In fact . . .' Pete looked uncharacteristically diffident, 'I was thinking of joining the police force.'

Stratton blinked. 'Really? I know you were interested at one stage, but when you opted for the army, I thought—'

'So did I. But now, with Alison and everything . . .'

'Everything? She's not . . . ?'

Pete laughed. 'Don't worry, Dad. It's not going to be a shotgun wedding.'

'That's a relief.' It would also be a relief, Stratton thought, if Pete's future didn't involve being posted to Cyprus or Malaya or anywhere else where he stood a good chance of getting his head blown off. 'But it's a big step, you know.'

'Which bit?'

'All of it – getting married and leaving the army, starting a new career. Are you sure about it?'

'I'm sure about Alison, Dad.' This was said quietly, with total sincerity. 'I know I've been a bit of a . . . well, a shit really in the past, but now, with her, you know . . . And you were younger than me when you married Mum, weren't you?'

'Yes,' said Stratton, 'I was – twenty-four. But I knew that marrying her was the best thing that was ever going to happen to me.'

'Yeah.' Pete looked down at his feet, embarrassed. 'Look, Dad,' the words came out in a sort of staccato mumble, 'I'm sorry. About the things I said. You know, after Mum died. It wasn't fair.'

Stratton cleared his throat. 'It's all right,' he said gruffly. He fumbled for his cigarettes, uncertain of what to say. 'Tell you what – let's forget it, shall we?'

'Yeah. Thanks.' There was an awkward pause during which Pete looked at his feet a bit more before adding, 'Long day, eh?'

Stratton rubbed a hand across the back of his neck. 'Still getting my bearings.'

'Bit different from Piccadilly, I should think. Do they give you Wog Money?'

'Give me *what*?'

Pete grinned. 'Wog Money. It's what you get if you're attached to a West Indian regiment. Like a bonus – by way of compensation.'

'No, they bloody well don't,' said Stratton.

'Perhaps they should. The ones in Suez would nick everything they could get their hands on if you gave them half a chance.'

'For Christ's sake . . . You won't get very far in the police force with that sort of attitude.'

'All right, Dad.' Pete held up his hands in a gesture of surrender.

'Yes, well.' Stratton took another gulp of his drink. The last thing he wanted was to have a row with Pete, especially now. In any case, he wasn't exactly sure of his own feelings on the subject – it was all too new for him to have formulated any sort of solid opinion. Besides, he knew damn well that 'that sort of attitude' would not be any sort of bar in the police force; in fact, as far as casual canteen utterance went, it would be just the reverse – and one thing he definitely *did* know was that a bunch of policemen with racialist ideas were going to cause a damn sight more of a problem than there was already. 'They're British citizens, and they're entitled to the same treatment as everyone else.'

'OK, keep your hair on. I didn't mean anything by it.'

Stratton sighed. That had been the problem with his son for as long as he could remember – he'd come out with things that upset people or made them angry, and then claim it was a joke or an innocent remark. Not wanting to end on a sour note, and also feeling that it wouldn't be right, under the circumstances, to go up to bed before he'd finished his beer, especially as Pete was in the process of opening another bottle, he started telling him about Matheson.

'Old school, then? Firm but fair?'

'All that.'

'Sounds like one of the sergeants we had when I did National Service. Some of them were bastards, but this chap ... Oh, he'd stick it to you, all right.' Pete threw back his shoulders and brought one elbow in as if carrying a swagger stick, and bellowed, 'Stratton, you're marching like a donkey wiv an 'ard-on!'

Stratton laughed. 'He said that to you, did he?'

'And the rest. Thing was, I couldn't get the hang of marching, not at first. I don't know why – I was good at PT and everything, always picked for the teams at school – but I just couldn't do it.' Pete shook his head. 'I was all over the place. I used to lose sleep over it – how I was going to let the others down on parade and all that.'

'Did you?' Stratton was surprised again by this admission of weakness, so unlike the Pete he knew. This Alison girl really was having a good effect, he decided.

'Oh, yes. I used to lie there and think about what happened at school . . . There was this gym master, when we were evacuated, he used to make the boys who couldn't vault over the horse stay behind for hours, practising. You know, the fat ones and the feeble types. Every bloody night after school. I don't think there was one of them who ever learnt to do it, but he kept on and on, shouting at them, telling them they were useless . . . We – I mean the rest of us, who could do it – thought it was funny at the time, but then, with the marching thing, I felt terrible about it, how we'd laughed at them.'

'Was that when you had to share premises with that boarding school?'

'Yeah. Load of snobs – called us the Cockney kids. The boys, that was. The teachers just looked down their noses. It was their gym master who did that. Our bloke got called up, I think – anyway, he didn't come with us like the others did.'

Stratton was struck by how little he knew about his children's schooldays. They'd written, of course, but they'd had their own war, out in the country, while he'd been having his in London. 'You never told us they gave you a hard time.' As he said this, Stratton wondered if Pete had actually mentioned it in one of his otherwise uncommunicative letters, and he'd somehow missed it.

'Not particularly.' Pete shrugged. 'Just the usual stuff. Didn't bother me, anyway.' He grinned and held up a fist. 'I could look after myself. And it was good, in a way, mixing with different sorts. Like the army. But this sergeant, he was decent. Really took me under his wing. He'd be shouting at me on the parade ground all morning, but he always had a word afterwards. You know, "Don't worry, lad, you'll get the hang of it." And I did, eventually.'

'Why did you decide to stay in the army?' asked Stratton. He'd often wondered about this, but the opportunity to ask Pete had never, before now, presented itself.

Pete fiddled with his beer bottle for so long that Stratton was about to say he was sorry he'd asked and didn't mean to pry when he said, 'Partly because of blokes like that sergeant, I suppose, but more . . . Well, I was used to it, wasn't I? I mean, it wasn't as if I had a place at some university waiting for me, and even if they bugger you about a bit, you know where you are in the army. What's expected. To be honest, I think I was a bit . . . Well, scared.' He put his fists up to his eyes in a gruesome parody of a crying child. 'Boohoo, the big world outside.' Taking another pull from the bottle he said, 'You know, if I left I'd have to be the new recruit again, somewhere else. Stupid, really.'

'You always seemed pretty sure of yourself,' said Stratton.

'Yeah, well . . . Got to look the part, haven't you? Otherwise people take advantage.'

'I suppose so.' As Stratton said this, he realised that there was no 'suppose' about it. 'Looking the part' was exactly what he'd be doing at Harrow Road until he got the hang of things. And he could see, too, that the army, where it was a virtue not to think, and certainly not to imagine, but just to do what one was told, had a sort of harsh comfort. 'You'll be all right in the big world outside – just takes a bit of getting used to, that's all. I was pretty green when I started police training. I'd never been to London before, and the others used to call me Farmer Giles because of my accent.'

Pete laughed. 'You've never told us that before.'

'Well, you don't want to listen to my old stories. Anyway, I was homesick at first because it was all so different, but then I started to like it, and . . . Well, that's it, really. I suppose,' Stratton added, feeling that something of a more pensive nature was called for, 'it's about feeling that you're where you should be.'

He fell silent, feeling that as philosophical remarks went, this was a pretty lame effort, but Pete surprised him by nodding thoughtfully and saying, 'Yes, you're right. A place where you belong. Here,' he held out his cigarettes. 'Have one of these.'

'Thanks.'

'By the way, Dad, I'm sorry about your girlfriend. Leaving and everything.'

Stratton paid close attention to extracting a cigarette from the packet, and then to the proffered match, before saying, 'Monica told you, did she?'

'Yes.' Pete lit his own cigarette, avoiding his father's eye. 'She said she'd got married and gone to live in America.'

'That's right,' said Stratton. 'Probably for the best, in the long run.'

As he pulled on his pyjamas, he wondered if the guards in the camp who'd tormented Laskier and herded his sister into a gas chamber had felt a similar sense of security and belonging. If he or Pete had been called upon to do something like that, would they have obeyed? He bloody well hoped not. But, he thought as he got into bed, no one could say that they wouldn't, could they? Not if they were honest – unless they'd actually been in that particular situation themselves and refused to cooperate despite whatever threats or blandishments were being offered, of course. It was interesting, Stratton thought as he drifted off to sleep, that nowadays he no longer identified with the heroes in books he read, thinking that if the circumstances were different, he could be like them. Nowadays, he identified with the chaps who'd failed or compromised or turned out to be cowards or let people down . . . It was his age, he supposed. Pete wouldn't think like that. Or Stratton hoped he wouldn't. Not yet, anyway.

CHAPTER TEN

Opening the *Express* the following morning in the bus on the way to work, Stratton was astonished to discover that the killing had already been reported. The victim's name wasn't given – hardly surprising as the poor bastard hadn't been identified yet – but there was a statement from Matheson. *We are satisfied,* Stratton read, with mounting disbelief, *that it was the work of a small group of white teenagers who had only one motive – robbery or attempted robbery of a man who was walking the streets alone. The fact that he happened to be coloured does not, in our view, come into the question.*

'For Christ's sake,' he muttered, louder than he'd intended and causing several people sitting nearby to glare reproachfully. Taking the official line was one thing, but talk about jumping the gun . . . It was true that the doctor at St Charles's – who Stratton had no reason to disbelieve – had found nothing in the corpse's pockets but a pawn ticket, so money or other valuables could well have been stolen from him, but Matheson didn't actually know this, any more than he knew the intentions of the as-yet-unidentified assailants. Stratton wondered if the speed with which he'd acted –

Matheson must have spoken to the journalists very soon after he himself had left Harrow Road for the hospital – was due to pressure from above.

There were still a few pressmen hovering about when he arrived at the police station. 'All leave's been cancelled,' said a gloomy-looking PC Jellicoe. 'I was going to take the wife down to Eastbourne. Been looking forward to putting my feet up for a few days.'

Stratton, suppressing a cartoon image of Jellicoe, trousers rolled up and paddling in the sea with a knotted handkerchief on his head, commiserated. 'Has the pawnbroker come up with an address yet?' he asked.

'Powis Square. Number 45. Name's Clyde Johnson.'

'That sounds familiar.' Stratton leafed through his notebook and discovered that it was the same address Marion Lockwood had given him. 'Hmm . . . What was the item, by the way?'

'A watch. Not a very good one – bloke only give him three-and-six. That was on Monday. I've got the name and address of Mrs Marwood, the woman who called the police. The guv'nor sent a couple of blokes last night to talk to the neighbours, and they had a quick word with her too, but he said to tell you it's all yours.'

Golborne Road – at least the section near the railway where Mrs Marwood lived – was empty but for a woman banging a mat against the wall outside the Earl of Warwick pub and two men peering under the bonnet of an elderly Singer which, apart from the car he was driving, was the only vehicle in sight. The Marwoods' flat was part of a dingy terrace, all cracked skylights, rotting window sills, broken railings with buddleia sprouting between them and peeling paint on the front doors.

Mrs Marwood came to the door in a dressing gown. She was, Stratton thought, about twenty years old. Pale as a wraith, and looked as though she was about to collapse from exhaustion. 'I'm sorry,' she said, when he'd introduced himself. 'I've been up all night with the baby. She's only just gone off, and my husband works nights, so please—'

'Don't worry,' said Stratton, *sotto voce*. 'I'll keep my voice down.'

Susie Marwood tottered into the front room, which was a kitchen, and sat down at the table. The place, although fairly clean, was untidy, its surfaces cluttered with dirty dishes and odds and ends of food.

'I was here with Sandra,' she said, indicating the window, 'walking up and down, trying to get her to settle. I must have had my back to the window, but I heard a noise so I turned round and I saw a coloured man being pushed and shoved by a lot of white boys.'

Stratton looked out of the window and found that he had a clear view of both sides of the Earl of Warwick on the corner diagonally opposite as well as to the street directly opposite with its row of shops that led away from the railway bridge.

'What time was this?'

'About half past eight, I think. Maybe earlier. I'm not really sure.'

'And where exactly were they?'

'Down there. Outside the grocer's. It was shut, obviously.'

'Did you see where any of the men came from?'

Mrs Marwood shook her head. 'I wasn't really paying attention – Sandra was crying, and . . . I'm sorry, Inspector. She never sleeps . . .' She shook her head in helpless despair. 'I barely know what day it is.'

'That's all right, Mrs Marwood. Tell you what, why don't I make you a cup of tea?'

Susie Marwood blinked at him, and for a brief moment her eyes lit up with astonishment. 'I'd have offered,' she said, 'but once I sit down I feel as if I'll never be able to get up again. To be honest, I'm surprised I haven't nodded off talking to you.'

'That's all right,' said Stratton. 'You look as though you could do with one, that's all. Just point me in the direction of the tea caddy, and I'll do the rest.'

'You are good,' she said, as Stratton poured out two cups and set them on the table. 'Joe can't find his way round a kitchen at all. Not that I'd expect him to,' she added hurriedly. 'I shouldn't complain – I've got the loveliest baby in the world. It's just . . .' She tailed off, looking as if she might burst into tears at any moment.

'My wife was just the same,' said Stratton, 'when we had our two.' As he said it, he wondered if that had actually been the case. There must have been some times when Monica and Pete had refused to go to sleep – he remembered waking in the night on the odd occasion – but Jenny had always dealt with it. And of course she'd had her sisters, whose children were that bit older, to help her . . . Susie Marwood, he guessed, didn't have that sort of support.

'How many men were there?' he asked.

'I'm not sure. Six or seven. They were all round him, barging him, and one of them pushed him so he fell down against the wall.'

'Were they making a noise?'

'They were shouting – I had the window open because it was hot, so I could hear.'

'Did you hear *what* they were shouting?'

'Some of it. "You black so-and-so," and worse. It was quite loud.'

'Did anyone come out of the pub to see what was happening?'

'Not that I saw.'

'What happened after the man was pushed?'

'Well, they were crowding round him, sort of jostling, all arms and legs, pushing and shoving. One of them had a wooden stick in his hand, and another had a bit of railing, or that's what it looked like, anyway . . . And then they all stepped back and I saw that the coloured man was lying on the pavement, and then I saw these two girls—'

'Were they there before?'

'I don't know – I mean, I didn't see them. At first I thought they must be with the boys, but then one of them turned round and saw them, and he shouted, "That's a black man's whore." One of the girls ran away and the other girl stood there for a second and then she ran away too, and the boys chased them.'

'All the boys ran after them at once?'

'I suppose so. Some of them were quicker – I was watching the girls, so I didn't notice.'

'Which direction did they go?' asked Stratton.

'That way.' She pointed towards the railway bridge. 'None of them stayed behind, though, because when I looked back at the coloured man he was lying – well, sort of half-lying, half-sitting – there, and there wasn't anyone with him. I couldn't see any blood, but he wasn't moving and I couldn't see no one coming to help him, so I went out to the telephone box. I couldn't leave the baby and it was difficult to make myself understood because she was crying. By the time the ambulance came there was quite a crowd, and then the police arrived so I told them what I'd seen. And I spoke to them again, after, and they told me the man died. Joe said I shouldn't of got involved, but the bloke was just lying there and I couldn't pretend I never saw it, could I?'

'No, love,' said Stratton. 'You did the right thing. Did you see anyone trying to rob the man? Going through his pockets, or anything like that?'

'No. It all happened so quick, and then they all just stepped away from him. I don't know about afterwards though – there were so many people there, and Sandra was crying . . .'

'Can you describe what the men looked like?'

'Quite young. Teenagers, or not much more, anyway. Some of them were wearing the Teddy boy stuff – the longer jackets. The rest just looked ordinary. Brown hair – one of them had black hair – but they were moving about very fast, so it was only an impression, really.'

'You didn't recognise any of them?'

Mrs Marwood shook her head. 'As far as I know, I've never seen them before in my life.'

'What about the two girls?'

'Never seen them before, either. One was about the same age as the men, I think – the other one looked a bit older, but she was quite tarted up. Blonde hair, done up at the back, high heels, dark-coloured dress, sleeveless, with a full skirt . . . The younger one just had a blouse and skirt – they were both quite slim, but she looked more like a kid, if you know what I mean. Reddish hair. The other one's hair looked as if it might have been dyed, but I don't think hers was.'

'What colour were the blouse and skirt?'

'White blouse, nothing very fancy . . . The skirt was blue, blue-grey.'

Stratton thought of Irene, sitting with Laskier in the hospital. 'And her hair was red?'

'Yes. But more pale. I mean, not too dark. I'm sorry I can't be more exact about it, but . . . It was like a nightmare. That poor man . . .'

Stratton stood up. 'Thank you. You've been very helpful.' Mrs Marwood smiled wanly. 'Don't worry,' he added, 'I'll see myself out . . . Leave you in peace.'

Stratton closed the door as quietly as he could and tiptoed down the stairs. Just as he was about to open the front door, he heard a baby's high, insistent wail.

CHAPTER ELEVEN

Stratton got in the car and took out his notebook. Mrs Marwood had telephoned the station at just before half past eight, and Laskier had said he'd found Irene on the corner of Portobello Road and Oxford Gardens at about nine o'clock. If she was trying to get back home to Powis Terrace that would make sense, but then why hadn't anyone seen her? Cursing his still incomplete knowledge of his new patch, and feeling like a fool, he pulled his *A to Z* guide out of his pocket and discovered that she could have gone down Kensal Road and turned onto Ladbroke Grove. Laskier had said he thought she was lost – and if she'd been attacked she'd certainly have been scared and confused . . .

Telling himself it was all just supposition, he went to the call box and dialled the number for Perlmann's office. Perlmann himself would have to wait, but he needed to know how to get into Johnson's flat at 45 Powis Square. On discovering that (a) there was a caretaker on the premises who held keys and (b) Irene had got home safely, he told Laskier he'd phone him the following morning, thanked him, and hung up.

Powis Square was just as tatty as Colville Terrace and the other surrounding streets, its clutter of dustbins swarming with clouds of flies in the morning heat. Such grass as there was was scrubby and brown from lack of rain and strewn with dog turds, litter and broken glass that glinted in the bright sunlight. The trees round about, sooty-leaved and necklaced with flabby rings of yellow fungus, looked as though they were being slowly poisoned. Several lengths of broken-down chain-link fence suggested that the 'Trespassers Will Be Prosecuted' notices fixed to poles at either end were routinely ignored.

On hearing the purpose of his visit the caretaker, Mr Richards, ancient and, despite the heat, clad in a heavy three-piece suit, said, 'Well, it's one less of 'em, I suppose.'

'Did you know Mr Johnson well?' Stratton asked, as Richards fumbled with the key on the landing outside the room.

Richards shook his head. Close to, his breath smelt stale, as though it had been inside his body for a long time. 'Didn't even know that was his name. Ding-Dong, they called him.'

'Who did?'

'His friends.'

'Did he have a lot of friends?'

'Just the odd one or two, come to see him.'

'Do you know them?'

'No, I don't, and I don't bloody want to neither. Shouting all the time, playing music and making a racket till all hours . . . But you want to ask her upstairs about him. He used to roll for her. You know,' he added, 'hide somewhere and rob the punters while they were . . .' He put his hand in the crook of the opposite elbow and gestured with his fist.

'I know what rolling means, thank you,' said Stratton. 'The woman upstairs – what's her name?'

'Gloria. That's what she calls herself, anyway. Don't suppose it's anything of the sort. Dirty whore, she is, going with coloureds.'

Johnson's room was similar to those of Conroy, Royce and the others at Colville Terrace – with rickety old furniture, peeling wallpaper and an offcut of threadbare carpet in the middle of the floor. There was a light film of dust over the few surfaces, and the only thing in the place that looked to be of any value was a record player. Richards, standing in the doorway, surveyed it grimly. 'This used to be a respectable neighbourhood. Decent. I'm glad my wife isn't here to see what it's come to. You want to try living next to 'em! The papers go on about people like me having colour prejudice, but they're prejudiced against the working class of this country. The way they put it, anyone would think we're a dirty, shiftless lot who were dragged up in brothels and we've no right to complain about anything.'

Revolting as Richards was, Stratton had to concede that he had a point: people who wrote for newspapers and spoke in Parliament certainly didn't live round here. He thanked the man, told him he'd be down for a list of the people in the house and, closing the door firmly in his face, had a look around. There wasn't much to examine: some items of clothing, a few creased photographs and a cheap suitcase, inside which was a packet of tea, a tin of condensed milk, a bag of sugar, a teapot, a cup and a half-empty bottle of rum. Stratton imagined Johnson waving goodbye to the people in the photographs and stepping up the gangway of the boat with the suitcase in his hand, full of hope. The dustpan and brush beneath the chair suggested an attempt to keep things up to scratch. Stratton wondered if this was in response to a parting injunction from the fearsome-looking matron clad in what looked like her Sunday best – but otherwise the place was, he thought, the typically stale and cheerless room of a single man living away from home and family. The discovery of a passport and papers told him that Johnson had been 26, hailed from Jamaica, and that he was registered at the labour exchange and receiving benefits of £6 a week. This – if what Conroy, Royce and the others were paying was anything to go by – would have done little more than cover his rent. As he obviously hadn't managed to find a job it was little wonder if he'd gone into business with Gloria upstairs. As he pocketed the documents, he thought that if 'Gloria' didn't turn out to be Marion Lockwood, then he'd eat his hat, and hers as well, if she had one.

Marion, rather to Stratton's surprise, was dressed in a blouse and skirt. She looked as though she'd had a rough night. Leaning against the door frame, she blinked at him, puffy-eyed, and said, 'You again. What do you want?'

'I'm here to ask some questions about Mr Johnson, your neighbour downstairs.'

'What about him?'

'I'm afraid he was attacked last night, badly. He died on the way to hospital.'

'Ohhh . . .' No surprise or shock registered on her face. She looked, Stratton thought, as though this were one more inconvenience in a life that was already full of them. 'Well, I don't know anything about it.'

'When did you last see him?'

Marion shrugged. 'Couple of days ago?'

'Are you asking me or telling me?'

'Dunno. It's nothing to do with me.'

'Sure about that, are you, Gloria?'

Marion's eyes flickered from side to side. ''S just a hustling name.'

'So I gathered. I also gather that Mr Johnson – who you knew as Ding-Dong – used to roll for you.'

'Not me.' This time she stared him brazenly in the face, eyes as hard as marbles. 'I barely knew the bloke.'

'Was he your pimp too?'

'No!' The indignation, Stratton thought, was genuine.

'Who is?'

'No one.'

'You don't live with anyone?'

'Nope.'

Stratton raised an eyebrow. 'You better tell the bloke you don't live with to clear out, in case I decide to come back with a warrant. Do you know if Ding-Dong had any relatives in Britain?'

'No idea. I told you, I barely knew him.'

'What about friends?'

'Well, I'm sure he's got some, but I don't know who they are.'

Mrs Marwood had said that one of the women she'd seen had been wearing a dark-coloured dress and had dyed blonde hair. Marion's hair was dyed, all right – it looked like straw, and the roots looked almost black in contrast with the rest of it – but he couldn't remember what she'd been wearing when he'd seen her in Queensway in the afternoon. Something with a pattern, he thought. Sleeveless, as Mrs Marwood had said, but paler . . . Easy enough to change, though.

'What were you doing last night?'

'What time?'

'From when I saw you in Queensway.' Stratton took out his notebook.

'Well, I was out with Vicky early on, wasn't I?' She shrugged. 'Hustling.'

'Did you do a lot of business?'

'Wasn't bad.'

'So, you were travelling between Queensway and . . . where was it?' Stratton flipped through his notebook. 'Chepstow Road.'

'Mostly, yeah.'

'And Ding-Dong was at Chepstow Road, was he?'

'No, I *told* you.'

'So he wasn't there that evening.'

'No. He was supposed to meet me earlier, but he never turned up.'

'So he *did* roll for you?'

'I didn't say that. He was just meeting me, that's all.'

'Why? Was he a punter?'

'No!' Again, the momentary indignation seemed real. 'Look, it was just for a drink, all right? About half past seven. It's a bit slow around then – picks up again later on.'

'When he didn't turn up, did you ask anyone where he was?'

'No.' Marion shrugged.

'What did you do?'

'Well, I just carried on, didn't I? Got back here . . . I don't know. About one, I think.'

'So you had no idea where Ding-Dong was or what he was doing?'

'No, I told you.' Pushing herself away from the door frame with a visible effort she added, in a wheedling tone, 'I don't suppose you've got a fag, have you?'

Stratton went downstairs, collected a scribbled list of the inhabitants of 45 Powis Square from Richards – there appeared to be twelve people living there, although not all of the names were given in full – and drove back to Harrow Road, wondering how much of what Marion Lockwood had told him was true.

CHAPTER TWELVE

'KBW?' repeated PC Jellicoe. 'Stands for Keep Britain White. You'll see it all over the place round here.'

The office chair creaked alarmingly as the portly policeman leant back, arms folded over the blue serge dome of his stomach. 'Now, I've been checking up on Marion Lockwood. List of convictions for soliciting as long as your arm. Johnson's been in trouble too. Got pulled in with a bunch of others when we raided one of the shebeens. He was let off with a caution, but a couple of them got sentenced for possession of drugs.'

'Do you know who Johnson's associates are?' asked Stratton.

'I don't, but I know a man who might, and he should just be coming off his lunch break.' Jellicoe, whose back was to the door, tipped his chair so far back that he was in serious danger of ending up flat on his arse, and bellowed, 'Dobbsy!'

PC Dobbs, when he appeared, was a morose-looking individual who appeared to be suffering from fallen arches. Initially inclined to be monosyllabic, he only perked up after coaxing from Jellicoe and some mendacious second-hand flattery on Stratton's part – 'DS Matheson tells me you know your way around better than anyone.'

'Well, I don't know all the names,' said Dobbs, now clearly concerned that he wouldn't live up to his billing, 'but there's a chap called Clinton Etheridge he used to go about with.'

'I've heard that name before.' Stratton checked his notebook. 'Lives with a girl called Irene Palmer in Powis Terrace.'

'Don't know anything about any Irene Palmer,' Dobbs looked affronted, as though she should have asked his permission before moving in, 'but that's where he lives. Slippery as an eel, he is. We're pretty sure he's poncing off at least one of the girls, but we've never had the evidence to do him for it.'

'Was Johnson a pimp too?'

'Not so far as I know, but we did have a complaint about that girl Lockwood – bloke said he'd been robbed. She might have done it herself, of course, but Johnson lives in the same house and I've seen them about together, so it could have been him.'

'What happened?'

'Nothing. The bloke's been with her at Chepstow Road, then he gets round the corner and finds his money's gone, so he spots me and starts shouting about it, insisting I go back with him, and of course I find her all on her tod, ready to go out again, and she says she doesn't know what he's talking about and she's never seen him before in her life. She's opened up her handbag and shown me her purse.

There's only a bob in it and this bloke's talking about how she's pinched thirty quid off him. She's calling him all the names, telling me to look under the mattress if I don't believe her ... By this time the bloke's getting cold feet about his missus finding out if it came to court – so he says he must have made a mistake, and that was that.'

'What about gangs? Teddy boys and the like?' Stratton relayed the descriptions, such as they were, that Mrs Marwood had given him of Johnson's attackers. 'A list of known troublemakers – white ones – would be very useful.'

'There's plenty just out to make trouble,' said Dobbs, 'but there's a very nasty bunch that hang around that White Defence League place in Princedale Road. I don't hold with all these coloureds coming over here myself, but that Gleeson who runs the place is a gold-plated bastard, and there's a young bloke called Eddy Knight who's there a lot, handing out leaflets and that, and—'

'Whoa!' Stratton held up a hand. 'Could you write all this down for me? Of course,' he added hurriedly, seeing that Dobbs was looking pointedly at his wristwatch, 'I'll talk to the station sergeant about changing the roster for this afternoon.'

Wonderful, he thought, as he left PC Dobbs happily taking the weight off his feet. I haven't been in the place four days and I'm about to piss off the very bloke I really need to keep sweet.

Sergeant Matthews, who seemed resigned rather than annoyed about Dobbs's absence from the duty roster, agreed to get someone to fetch details, including statements, of all the cases in the past six months which had involved fights between black and white men.

Stratton spent the next couple of hours familiarising himself with a depressing litany of prejudice and irrationality, while Dobbs, opposite him, made a great performance of scratching his head and licking the end of his pencil. Exactly as DS Matheson had said, the assailants had made it abundantly clear that they attacked their victims precisely because of their skin colour. Various reasons were advanced for their dislike – *I don't like the way they behave with women, they're dirty, you can't get a job because a black man'll work cheaper* . . . The odd thing about this last complaint was that, judging from the employment records he'd been reading, every single one of them had been in work since the day they'd finished school. Shop assistants, plumber's mates, window cleaners, machinists, £8 a week, £9 a week, £10 a week . . . Not bad, considering that hardly any of them were old enough for National Service. Every one of them lived at home, and assuming that what they handed over to Mum each week was a fraction of what Johnson and Co. forked out on rent, they had spending money that would, when Stratton was their age, have exceeded his wildest dreams.

Breaking off to eat, he managed to persuade the hair-netted harridan who was mopping the canteen floor to produce a late lunch. This, when the plate was banged grudgingly down on the table, turned out to be an enormous lump of corned beef and a salad composed of a single slice of beetroot and a leaf of lettuce with a very thoroughly boiled egg on top of it.

On his return to the office, he found that PC Dobbs had finished writing and was gazing into space. His vacant expression, which didn't change when Stratton entered, gave him an unexpected pang of nostalgia for Arliss at West End Central, whose incompetence had remained a station legend long after his retirement. Thinking that as he'd got Dobbs for the rest of the day he might as well make use of him, he announced that they were going to pay a visit to the White Defence League. It hadn't been mentioned in any of the documents he'd read, but without any obvious leads, it seemed as good a place as any to start making enquiries. Pocketing Dobbs's list – an exhaustive catalogue of names beginning with Eddy Knight's, some with addresses written beside them in tipsy capitals – he led the way to the car.

The headquarters of the White Defence League turned out to be a shopfront, with the name of the organisation in large capital letters picked out in white on a black background. On either side of the name was a thick cross with a circle around it, which Stratton supposed must be their symbol. Two solid panels at the bottom of the window advertised something called *The Black and White News* at 6d, and the glass was covered with a grille, behind which he could see six posters, all with the same legend:

KEEP BRITAIN WHITE
STOP COLOURED IMMIGRATION
JOIN THE WHITE DEFENCE LEAGUE

Beside them was an appeal to 'The white people of Notting Hill' accusing the new immigrants of: Increasing the Housing Shortage; Spreading Disease; Promoting Vice; Costing a huge sum in National Assistance; Endangering the employment of British workers, and Producing a Half-Breed Population, and demanding that they be shipped back home at once.

Stratton rang the bell as instructed by the sign on the door. Immediately a loud and furious barking started up – not from directly behind the door, but somewhere above. A split second after that, the door was opened by a man who must, surely, have been waiting in a pre-sprinting position in the narrow hallway. 'John Gleeson,' he said, voice raised in competition with the racket from upstairs, which had now been augmented by curses and yells of 'Shut up!'. 'How may I help you?'

'Inspector Stratton,' said Stratton equally loudly. 'CID, from Harrow Road.' Gleeson's handshake was a firm downward tug. 'We're here,' Stratton continued, 'because a coloured man called Clyde Johnson was stabbed last night in Golborne Road by white youths, and died on the way to hospital.'

'I read about it this morning, in the newspaper.' Gleeson's voice was cultured and slightly high-pitched. Thirty-five or so and beefy, with thinning hair, he possessed the broad forehead and heroically square jaw of the man of action and the ardent eyes of the zealot. Stratton wouldn't have minded betting that he believed his looks to be the physical manifestation of his Aryan destiny, strength of will and the whole spurious caboodle. The effect was, however, slightly marred by the fact that he was shod in a pair of mangy carpet slippers.

'It's certainly regrettable,' he said, in a bland tone that suggested he thought it was anything but. 'I'm afraid I don't have any knowledge of the incident, but if you'd like to come in . . . Don't worry,' he added, as Stratton peered apprehensively upwards, 'the dog can't get down here – and even if he could, he wouldn't hurt a fly.'

Stratton doubted this. The dog hadn't stopped barking. The continued shouting from the man above seemed to be having the effect of encouraging it rather than the opposite, and a series of thumps and rattles suggested that it was hurling itself against the door he could see at the top of the stairs. *It sounded vicious*, old Mr Russell had said. *As if it couldn't wait to take a lump out of somebody*.

'What sort of dog is it?'

'German shepherd.'

Stratton saw Dobbs give an almost imperceptible lift of eyes and chin which indicated 'Wouldn't you bleeding know?' as clearly as if he'd actually said it. Gleeson must have caught it too, because he said, 'It's a guard dog. We're entitled to protect ourselves.'

The place was sparsely furnished with a desk, a couple of hard chairs and a few displays of books with titles such as *Blood and Soil* and *Land and Destiny*. The walls were decorated with photographs of Gleeson in what looked remarkably like the uniform worn by Hitler's Brownshirts, but with the cross-and-circle symbol on the armband. Seeing where

Stratton was looking, Gleeson raised his chin slightly, as if about to give a Nazi salute.

'As I told you,' said Gleeson at normal volume, the barking having subsided, 'I know nothing of the matter. This organisation does not condone violence. I personally abhor the use of force.' There was a great deal more of this, during which Stratton got the sense that he was hearing the official version of the White Defence League creed, especially the flourishes about 'getting a square deal for the Negro in his own country'. Phrases from the statements he'd been reading: *We gave the nigger a belting . . . a good larruping . . . We steamed into him and done him up . . .* jabbed at his memory in aggressive counterpoint to what Gleeson was saying. 'It's all very well,' the man continued, 'for those who don't have to live cheek-by-jowl with them to talk about giving them a warm welcome. They don't live in fear that their homes will be sold over their heads to coloured people who will drive them out in order to house their friends and relatives. They don't feel resentment when they see the Negro with his smart clothes and flashy car—'

'Be that as it may,' said Stratton, 'what I'm interested in is what you and your colleagues were doing yesterday evening.'

'I was here,' said Gleeson. 'Writing an article.' He gestured towards a newspaper lying on the desk. Stratton saw that it was a copy of *The Black and White News*, and that the main headline was 'The Coloured Invasion'.

'I see,' said Stratton, feeling that he couldn't take much more of this. 'Was anyone with you?'

'I was here all evening, by myself. I took the dog out for a walk at about ten o'clock, and then I went to bed.'

'What about your colleague Mr Knight? Where was he?'

'I have no idea. You'll have to ask him.'

'Is he upstairs?'

Sensing that Gleeson was about to deny this, Stratton said, 'Someone is. Unless that dog of yours can talk as well as bark.'

Gleeson sighed heavily. 'I'll fetch him. Whatever you may think, Inspector, we believe in the democratic process.'

Stratton looked over at the photograph of Gleeson in his Brownshirt uniform. 'Really?'

'Yes,' said Gleeson with controlled exasperation. '*Really*. We are merely reflecting the views of a sizeable – very sizeable, I may say – percentage of the population. They may not be those who write for the newspapers or speak in Parliament, but their voices deserve to be heard. We don't set out to make trouble.'

'But,' said Stratton, 'you've clearly *had* trouble. You said you got the dog for protection.'

'Yes, to prevent trouble.'

'So you *haven't* had any?'

'Not yet, no. But it's coming, Inspector. It's bound to. The people of this country won't stand for what's happening.'

Eddy Knight, when he appeared a few minutes later, was a strikingly handsome man who looked to be in his early twenties, quite as heroically square-jawed as Gleeson, with high cheekbones, dark-brown eyes and thick, caramel-coloured hair. He might, Stratton thought, have been a film star – pin-up boy for the white race – but his voice, a Cockney whine, shattered the illusion. 'I don't know nothing about any bloke called Johnson.'

'Where were you yesterday evening?'

'At the pub with me mates.'

'All evening?'

'From about seven o'clock.'

'Which pub, and which mates?'

'The General Smuts.'

'It's on the White City Estate, sir,' said Dobbs.

Knight gave him a scornful look. 'Yeah, course it is.'

'And the names of your friends?'

Knight counted them off on his fingers. 'Ronnie Mills, Gordon Baxter, Fred Larby, Tony Pearson . . . I think that's all.'

'What time did you leave?'

'Closing time.'

'And then?'

'Then I went home.'

'Where's home?'

Knight reeled off an address on the White City Estate, which was a sprawl of boxy brick council blocks a couple of miles down the road.

'Why aren't you at work?' asked Stratton.

'Starting a new job next week.'

'Where's that, then?'

'Whitham's on Shepherd's Bush Road. It's a hardware shop.'

'How long were you unemployed?'

'Couple of weeks.'

'Why did you leave your last job?'

'Didn't like working with blacks, did I?'

'What are you doing here?'

'Helping Mr Gleeson.'

'Eddy is an active member of the League,' put in Gleeson, who'd been hovering proprietorially during this exchange.

'Dog handler, is he?'

'He sometimes exercises the dog, yes.'

'Walk it up Colville Terrace do you, Eddy? Take it into coloured people's homes so you can threaten them?'

'I don't know what you're talking about.'

'You may not, Mr Gleeson,' said Stratton, 'but I think Eddy does, don't you, Eddy? After all, if you've not been in work it'd be an easy way to earn some cash, wouldn't it?'

'I don't work for Jews,' said Knight.

'Who said anything about Jews?'

'You didn't have to,' said Gleeson. 'Everybody knows what Perlmann's up to.'

'My uncle worked for him,' added Knight, 'and look what happened.'

'Who's your uncle?'

'Bert Hampton. Got murdered in cold blood by a bunch of niggers after the rent money and your lot haven't done nothing about it.'

'I take it you have proof of this.'

'Don't need no proof. It's obvious.'

*

'God Almighty,' groaned Stratton, easing himself gingerly into the uncomfortably hot car and immediately winding down the window. As if being sweaty and dispirited wasn't enough, he also felt, in some irrational and not-quite-definable way, contaminated. Further questions to both Gleeson and Knight had been met with repeated assurances that neither man knew anything about Johnson's murder and a lot of other guff about how they abhorred violence and would never dream of condoning such a thing, never mind actually taking part in it, etc., etc., and Stratton hadn't believed a word.

'Well,' said Dobbs with gloomy satisfaction. 'That's democracy for you.'

Surprised, Stratton asked, 'Would you prefer something else?'

'Hitlerism, you mean? No, I bloody well wouldn't. But what I mean is, they're entitled to say what they think, aren't they?'

'Yes, they are.' Except, thought Stratton, that they hadn't – not even the half of it.

CHAPTER THIRTEEN

'What a splendid idea!'

The Honourable Mrs Virginia Rutherford had so much of the girls' boarding school about her that Stratton couldn't quite believe she hadn't said that it was a 'wizard', or even a 'ripping' idea. Not that he had any notion of what the idea actually was – the noise level in the room made it impossible to hear anyone who wasn't standing right next to you. Whatever it was had been proposed by a fat, earnest-looking individual in a crumpled suit, who'd been introduced as Malcolm Watson, councillor for North Kensington. His voice was quiet, whereas the Hon. Virginia had the sort of jolly bray that would have carried across a hockey field. She was a large, untidy woman of forty-five or thereabouts, almost as tall as he was, with broad shoulders already stooped from a lifetime of trying to make herself seem smaller. Her clothes, though undoubtedly expensive, were decorated with a lot of fussy details that seemed to emphasise, rather than diminish, her size. She was friendly in a clumsy, self-mocking way that made Stratton think she must have been teased a good deal in the dorm and decided that pre-emptive measures were the best form of defence. He had not, as yet, been able to discover her reason for being at the gathering, which was taking place in a drab function room in a building of tattered Edwardian grandeur near the town hall. Various attempts had been made to give the place a festive air – potted palms scattered about the perimeter and coloured streamers hanging from the handful of subfusc oil paintings that adorned the walls. There was a table equipped with various bottles and another, next to it, with plates of what Stratton thought were probably fish- and meatpaste sandwiches and bowls of potato crisps. White-jacketed waiters were weaving their way through the crush proffering trays with glasses of sherry and – to Stratton's relief – half-pints of beer.

Watson started talking again. Stratton, momentarily dropping the pretence of being able to hear, allowed his eyes to wander round the room. Although two of the three large windows were open, the lack of any sort of breeze meant the place was like a Turkish bath. Watson, Stratton noted, was having a particularly bad time. There were twin pouches of sweat under his eyes, more sweat was trickling down from among the thin wisps of reddish hair on the top of his head, and he kept pushing back his glasses, which slid repeatedly down his nose.

'We're going to make it a social occasion,' the Hon. Virginia was saying. 'We're having it in a proper local place – a basement club – so that we can meet people on their home turf, as it were. Really get below the surface, see everyone behaving naturally, just as they normally do.' She sounded like an anthropologist enthusing about some just-discovered far-flung tribe. 'I've said I'll look after the refreshments. What do you think, Inspector?'

She turned to Stratton, mouth momentarily open. She had a smear of lipstick on her top teeth and he found the sight of it oddly touching. 'An excellent idea,' he said, wondering what it was he'd just endorsed. Some sort of party, by the sound of it. Letting his eyes roam about the room once more, he noted that the ratio of male-to-female was about fifty-fifty, with the talkers tending to be men and the listeners, women. In the last hour, he'd been introduced to a fair few of them by Matheson. The men seemed to be mostly youth-welfare officers, NSPCC workers and the like, and the women, members of voluntary committees. Stratton spotted Matheson himself in the company of one from – he was pretty sure – the Family Welfare Association. Both of them were paying close attention to the chap from – he thought – the probation service.

Catching the words 'rent tribunal', Stratton leant forward and strained his ears to hear what was being said. 'Do you realise,' said Watson, 'that Mr Perlmann owns a hundred and forty-seven properties in the area? He gets the money to buy them by charging these exorbitant rents, of course, and the conditions are terrible – people living like animals – but it's an uphill struggle getting them to the tribunals and the Council won't act unless the complaint is brought by the tenant himself. I suppose one could try reasoning with the likes of Mr Perlmann, although I can't imagine there's much of a "better nature" there to appeal to.'

The Hon. Virginia, who had acquired a large pink blotch on both cheeks during this speech, said, 'As a matter of fact, I do know Mr Perlmann. Not well, of course,' she added hastily, 'but my husband is a member of his club. I'm going along there after this, to meet him. Perhaps you gentlemen would like to come with me?'

'I hardly think that would be appropriate,' said Watson. 'For someone in my position, I mean.' Stratton thought he detected a wistful note in the man's voice, which provoked a memory of something said to him years ago by Colonel Forbes-James: 'These principled Socialist types are all the same – give them lunch at the Ritz and they'll eat out of your hand.'

'Yes,' said Stratton, 'I can see that might be a bit awkward . . .' On the other hand, he was buggered if he was going to pass up an opportunity to view Perlmann in his natural surroundings. 'But,' he finished, 'I'd like to come, if I may.'

'Oh, *yes*.' The Hon. Virginia's pinkness, now apparently due to pleasure rather than unease, had spread to reach her ears. 'I'll ask DS Matheson if he'd like to join us, shall I?' she added.

Watson's attention was claimed by a brisk, unsmiling woman from the Marriage Guidance Council with a very tight and – judging by the faint ammoniac fumes emanating from her head – very recent perm. Turning away from the two of them, the Hon. Virginia said conspiratorially, 'I'm rather new to all this, as I expect you've gathered. But it is so wonderful to feel that one might be able to make a difference to people's lives.'

Not only people's lives, thought Stratton; her own, too. He felt drawn to her – not by any physical attraction, but by how open and guileless she was.

'It's like this super idea of Mr Watson's,' she was saying rather breathlessly, 'for a get-together with our coloured friends. I mean, it's all very well to say, "Love thy neighbour," but one has to get to know him first, doesn't one? Of course, it won't solve the problem of overcrowding, or –' she lowered her voice – 'the immorality – brothels and girls on the streets and so forth – but all the same . . .'

Listening to her talk, Stratton found himself imagining what her life must have been like and thought he could see why someone like her would be drawn towards the oppressed, and especially oppressed outsiders. Noblesse oblige must be part of it, but also, he imagined, a desire to be freed from the shackles of her upbringing.

Suddenly she gave a little cry and, sticking out a hand, caught the arm of a woman who was making her way past them. 'Here's someone you absolutely must meet, Inspector!'

'Hello, Mrs Rutherford.'

'This is Mrs Jones, Inspector. She does the most wonderful work on the Care Committee, and—'

The rest of the sentence was lost in a roar of laughter from somewhere behind him. The Hon. Virginia carried on talking animatedly, but even when the laughter died down, Stratton wasn't taking in the words. Mrs Jones had deep brown, almond-shaped eyes with long lashes, and waves of black hair that framed an oval face with a fresh, slightly suntanned complexion. She wore a simple frock of a creamy-yellow colour, which perfectly suited her slender curves, but then, Stratton thought, anything would have suited her. Conscious that not only was he staring at her but he hadn't actually spoken yet, he put out his hand. 'Ted Stratton, from Harrow Road Station. Pleased to meet you.'

'Fenella Jones.' She wore no gloves, and her palm felt soft and cool against his. He wanted it to stay there forever.

Forcing himself to let go of her, he said, 'That's an unusual name.' Oh, God. What an idiot! She must have heard that hundreds, if not thousands, of times.

Her smile, which had been in place before, but in a sociable, pleased-to-meet-you sort of way, widened into warm intimacy. She's just being polite, he told himself, and anyway, she's married. The Hon. Virginia had just said as much, hadn't she?

'. . . so I think my mother must have seen it in a book or something and persuaded my father – he died when I was quite young, so I never had a chance to ask him about it . . .' Stratton was too busy watching her eyes and mouth to get more than the gist of this. She had a London accent – not Cockney or plummily ruling class, but somewhere in the middle. His gaze must have made her self-conscious, because, still talking, she put her left hand up to brush an imaginary hair from her cheek, and Stratton saw that she wore no ring. '. . . but I don't remember his ever calling me by my full name, just "Fen", which made me feel like a sheepdog or something.'

But you're lovely, Stratton wanted to say. Instead – because she'd stopped talking and was now looking at him with slight perplexity – he said, 'I've never—' just at the same time as she said, 'I'm sorry—'

The Hon. Virginia, whose existence Stratton had entirely forgotten, cut in here with, 'Well, I'm sure you two will have heaps to talk about, and there's someone I really *must* speak to, so . . .' She tailed off and disappeared into the crowd.

Fenella laughed – a proper laugh, not a social trill. 'Oh dear. What were you going to say?'

'Just . . .' Stratton, who was experiencing some difficulty breathing properly – which must surely be due to the heat of the room – pulled himself together. 'Just that I've never seen anybody who looked less like a sheepdog. I should know,' he added. 'I was brought up on a farm.'

'Oh.' Clearly embarrassed, Fenella said, 'I'm sorry. I wasn't . . . you know, fishing.'

'I didn't think you were,' said Stratton, feeling fractionally more in control of the situation. 'But it's true.'

'Well, thank you. It's nice of you to say so.'

There was a short, awkward pause and then Stratton said, 'What is it you do? It's so noisy in here that I'm afraid I didn't entirely catch what Mrs Rutherford was saying when she introduced us.'

'I'm on the Care Committee – that's how I know Virginia. It's a bit of a mixed bag, really. A lot of the time it's rather like being with Universal Aunts – you know, escorting children about the place, visiting pensioners, and so on – except that it's voluntary, and of course I'm not trained or anything, although I was a teacher before I married. I haven't been at it all that long, so I'm still finding my feet, really.'

'But you enjoy it?'

'Oh, yes. Well, so far, anyway. It probably sounds rather silly to . . . well, to someone like you, but it's nice to feel one's being useful, even in a small way. After my husband died . . .' The last words reverberated round Stratton's head, temporarily blocking out the rest of what she was saying. It hadn't occurred to him that she might be a widow. She'd given the information quite matter-of-factly, so he supposed that it must have been a while since her husband had died . . . The fine lines he could see about her eyes and mouth suggested that she might be in her mid or even late forties, although she didn't look it.

Making himself focus on what she was saying, he caught the words, '. . . and now that our son is grown up, it's really—'

At that point, someone jostled past Fenella so that, for a moment, he felt a charge like a small electrical shock as her body bumped against his.

'I am sorry, Inspector.'

'Ted, please.'

'Ted, then.' Fenella looked down at her glass. 'Good job it was empty.'

'Would you like another?' His own glass was empty, too, but the last thing he wanted to do at this point was to get into the time-wasting rigmarole of trying to catch a waiter's eye, or – worse – having to make his way through the crowd to the drinks table, which would mean leaving her to be buttonholed by somebody else.

'Heavens, no. I don't really know why I accepted this one – I've never liked sherry much. Virginia's much more sensible – always opts for orange squash, and doesn't give a hoot what anyone thinks. But what about you? Would you like another drink?'

'No, thanks,' said Stratton, hastily. 'I'm fine. You were saying . . . ?'

'I think,' Fenella gave him a delightfully impish smile which made him feel breathless again, 'that I've told you quite enough about myself, and it's your turn.'

'I'm finding my feet too. Harrow Road's a new posting for me. I was in the West End before . . .' He carried on talking for another minute or so, while she listened, apparently with interest. '. . . and so,' he concluded, 'I ended up here.'

'Do you think you're going to like it?'

'Well, it's certainly different. One gets used to things, I suppose, and people . . .' He talked a bit more, hoping like hell that he was presenting himself as reasonable and conscientious, without seeming dull, and again she seemed to be following, keeping her eyes on his and looking generally engaged.

'Did you grow up in the West Country?' she asked.

'Devon. I know,' said Stratton, 'there's still a touch of the oo-arr.'

'I rather like it.'

Feeling ridiculously pleased by this, Stratton said, 'That's just as well, because I don't suppose I'll ever get rid of it now.'

'Did you try? At first, I mean?'

'Not really. They used to call me Farmer Giles.' How strange, he thought. The only person he'd ever said that to was Jenny, and now here he was, twice in two days. 'I married a London girl, and she used to laugh about it – it was much stronger then, of course. I never made any effort to change it – not consciously, anyway – it just wore off over the years.' Then, on impulse, because he thought he'd seen an almost imperceptible – very possibly imaginary – flicker of a frown pass across Fenella's face, he added, 'She died, unfortunately. During the war.'

'I'm sorry.'

'These things happen. Well, you know, of course. Your husband. . .'

'Yes . . .' Fenella looked down at her feet. 'They do.'

There was another, even more awkward silence, and then Fenella put a gentle hand on his arm, the pressure there for just a moment, then gone. Meeting her eye once more, he saw that her expression was one of calm seriousness. 'It's terrible,' she said, 'if you marry someone, and you're happy – not necessarily all the time, because one couldn't be – but you know what I mean, and you can't imagine not being with that person, not growing old with them . . . and then they're gone and everything changes. And of course one gets used to them not actually being around, and with not being the person you were when you were with them, and after a while – quite a long while, in my case – you stop feeling like half of something with the other bit missing. I'm probably not saying this very well, but—'

'Found you at last!' The Hon. Virginia reappeared, trailing in her wake a youngish, heavily bearded man who, on being introduced, started talking nineteen to the dozen about the excellent progress made by some society or other, punctuating himself with assertive jabs of his pipe, so that Stratton and Fenella found themselves inching away as far as they could without actually crashing into the people standing behind them. Fenella suddenly said that she was terribly sorry to interrupt but she really had to be going. The Hon. Virginia, apparently taking her cue from this, said that they ought to go too, or her husband would be wondering where she'd got to.

Leaving the pipe chap to find someone else to talk at, Stratton led the way, with a lot of 'Excuse me' and 'If I might just . . .' to the door. At this point the Hon. Virginia said, 'Oh, crikey, I've forgotten Mr Matheson!' and doubled back into the crowd, so that he found himself alone with Fenella in the comparative peace of the wood-panelled landing.

'Goodness, wasn't it hot in there?' Fenella was, he noticed, looking slightly flushed, fanning the air in front of her face with her hand.

Banishing a sudden and discomfiting image of himself, face like a tomato, hair all over the place and tie askew, he said, 'Yes, wasn't it?'

Fenella glanced around her and then back at him, looking as if she'd been about to say something but thought better of it.

'Look—' he started, at the same time as she began with, 'Well, it's been very nice—'

After a few seconds of false starts on both sides, Stratton said, 'About what you were saying, before – I thought you expressed it very well. Very well indeed, in fact. And,' he gabbled, as a hoot of laughter from somewhere near the doorway told him that the Hon. Virginia was about to bear down on them, 'I wondered if you might like to go out to dinner some time.'

'Here we are!' The Hon. Virginia bustled up, accompanied by DS Matheson. Patting her hair back into place with a large, white-gloved hand, she said, 'All set?'

The two women proceeded downstairs to the cloakroom, Stratton following with Matheson. As Fenella hadn't answered his question, he wondered if she might be going to make a polite pretence, given that the Hon. Virginia had been honking away just behind her, of not having heard it. She said nothing as he helped her on with her coat – the same creamy-yellow and simple design as the frock – and, standing behind her, he was just gearing himself up for an urbane and inconsequential goodbye when she turned round, gave him a big smile, and said, 'Thank you. I'd love to have dinner with you.'

'How can I contact you?' Stratton asked, as they went down the front steps slightly behind the other two.

'I'm in the directory. C. H. Jones – I'm afraid I haven't got round to changing it.'

'Can we drop you anywhere, Fenella?' asked the Hon. Virginia, indicating the black Daimler saloon waiting at the kerb.

'Heavens, no. I only live round the corner, and it's still light. Besides, I could do with a breath of fresh air.'

As the chauffeur bore them away, Stratton turned to wave at Fenella as she crossed the road. It was the first time he'd had a clear view of her legs – which, he noted with satisfaction, were quite as nice as the rest of her.

CHAPTER FOURTEEN

In nightclub terms, it was fairly early when they arrived at Maxine's, and Stratton was surprised to find it so busy. Standing in a corner with Matheson – 'I'll introduce you in a moment. Get the lie of the land first, eh?' – he sipped his drink and took stock of the place. The decor was plush, with plenty of gilt and velvet, extravagant floral displays, a large and well-supplied bar and a special area for dancing. The place was, as far as he could see, one very large room, with various recessed doors leading off it. Pretty mannequins, each with a fashionable expression of camel-like hauteur, were stationed here and there – rather, Stratton thought, in the manner of the potted palms at the previous do. Most of them were being engaged in conversation, and, in a couple of cases, discreetly pawed, by various of the male clientele. All of these seemed to be thirty-five or older – sometimes considerably well-heeled and, to judge by the ringing voices that rose effortlessly over the music, well-bred. Stratton had a sudden memory of being called, as a young policeman, to a disturbance in a club in a grand house somewhere off Piccadilly. He couldn't remember what had happened, but

he did have a vivid recollection of a group of red-faced Eton-
ians, egged on by the whores, squirting each other with
soda siphons and quaffing champagne straight from the
bottle. He wondered if any of them were here now; still,
after more than thirty years, insulated from life by money
and privilege.

'That's Perlmann, over there.' Matheson nodded in the
direction of a short, plump chap of perhaps forty with a
receding hairline and small, expressive hands. He was seated
in an alcove with several women who seemed to be hanging
on to his every word. His shark-skin suit, a fraction too tight,
and general air of brash dynamism made Stratton think of
American gangster films he'd seen before the war. He could
hear nothing of what was being said, but the bursts of
feminine laughter that punctuated it sounded genuine
enough. 'This place is named after his wife, although I don't
think she comes in very often. I'll introduce you to him in
a moment.'

The Hon. Virginia joined them, bringing with her a man
who she announced, rather breathlessly, as 'my husband,
Giles Rutherford'.

Rutherford, Stratton noted immediately, was well-built,
a fair bit younger than his wife, and had good looks that
were showing signs of being eroded by dissipation. His handshake was perfunctory and his 'pleased to meet you' a bored,
rapid drawl. He remained with them just as long as the
minimum standard of politeness required, then wandered
off to cut in on one of the mannequins. If his wife minded
this, she gave no immediate sign of it. A few moments later,

Matheson was claimed by an old buffer called Wuffy or Wuggy or some other upper-class nursery mispronunciation. The Hon. Virginia carried on talking with determined animation on the subject of the Care Committee for about thirty seconds, then said, 'You seemed rather taken with Mrs Jones, Inspector.'

Stratton, disconcerted by the abrupt change of tack and the sudden shrewdness of her gaze, said, 'Yes. She seemed very nice. Very . . . charming.'

'She is. Quite a "hit" with the chaps. I've often wondered how that would feel.' This was said wistfully, and with such a complete lack of self-pity that Stratton, lost for words, would have been unable to produce a gallant lie. For a moment he wondered if she'd had too much sherry, then remembered Fenella's remark about the orange squash. He was saved from having to reply by Perlmann, who suddenly bobbed up beside him like a cork, enveloping Stratton in a cloud of eau-de-cologne, beaming and patting the Hon. Virginia on the bottom. Far from being offended by this, she surprised Stratton by giving a girlish giggle.

'Danny, you are terrible.'

'I am, aren't I? You look beautiful as always, Virginia. Now, aren't you going to introduce me to your friend?' Perlmann's voice was slightly high-pitched, and his accent similar to Laskier's but with more careful and emphatic pronunciation, the longer words broken into distinct syllables.

'This is Inspector Stratton, from the station at Harrow Road. I hope you don't mind—'

'Not at all! Don't worry, dear lady.' Shaking hands with Stratton, Perlmann said, 'Danny Perlmann. Pleased to meet you. You came to the office, I think? Stefan told me.'

'Yes,' said Stratton, feeling on the back foot. 'Yesterday morning.'

'And he mentioned poor Mr Johnson, of course. Very unfortunate. But now is not the time, I think?'

Stratton, who could sense waves of inquisitiveness coming off the Hon. Virginia, agreed hastily.

'A sad business,' said Perlmann, 'but for now . . . I see you have a drink, which is good – although we have champagne, if you would prefer—'

'Thanks,' said Stratton, 'but I'm fine with beer.'

'Good, good . . . And we have beautiful ladies. I can introduce you.' Perlmann winked.

'That's very kind,' said Stratton, 'but I'm quite happy just looking.'

Perlmann eyed him for a moment, then said, 'You are clever, I think. Stefan said you were, and he's never wrong about these things.'

'Funny,' said Stratton. 'He said that about you too.'

'Did he?' Perlmann laughed. 'Then there is proof that he is never wrong. But you know, Inspector, there is something I never understand about the English. They think that if a man is clever he must be cold, and if he is . . .' he put his hand over his heart, 'then he must be stupid. It is ridiculous. I do not think that you are a cold person, Inspector.'

'Well,' said Stratton, 'I do my best.'

'So English!' Perlmann laughed again, this time uproariously, as though Stratton had made a great joke. There was, Stratton thought, something of the showman about him, as though he were playing the part of himself. 'You do your best. And Virginia does her best too, don't you, my dear?' He rolled his eyes lasciviously, and – once more to Stratton's surprise – the Hon. Virginia coloured with pleasure. Surely, he thought, she ought to disapprove of Perlmann, and yet here she was, clearly enjoying his attentions. It was true that the man was an outsider – not 'one of us' – but he'd done well for himself, hadn't he? And done it at the expense of the very people she was trying to help. She obviously found his brashness exciting.

A commotion in the doorway made them all look round. Stratton saw a chap in his twenties, dressed in scruffy, paint-splashed clothing and waving a champagne bottle which he appeared to have swiped from a waiter. Flanking him were two black men of a similar age, one of whom looked distinctly uncomfortable. Seeing them, the Hon. Virginia gave a little jump as though she'd just been goosed and murmuring 'Do excuse me', set off towards them.

'Michael Duffy. He's Viscount Standon's son, but,' Perlmann rolled his eyes, 'he plays at being an artist. I'd buy one of his paintings myself, but . . .' He waved a dismissive hand.

'No good?'

'Always the same – naked men. If they were women, that would be a different matter. And his clothes . . .' Perlmann looked repulsed. 'I don't understand this. When he has such a birthright – to be a lord, when his father dies! He should be proud of it, not ...' Perlmann shook his head, then gestured as though he were throwing handfuls of something into the air. 'Pff! To wear rags and live like a peasant ...'

'Perhaps,' said Stratton, 'he's trying to shock.'

'But why? What does he have to prove? Any bastard can live in a slum!' For a second Stratton glimpsed the raw edge of a genuine, long-held anger, and then it was smoothed over as Perlmann shrugged and said affably, 'But I know his father – we do some business – so every so often Michael comes here, and sometimes he brings his friends. Why not?'

'Mrs Rutherford seems quite taken with him.'

'Ach, it's the schwartzers she likes.'

Stratton watched as the Hon. Virginia drew the black men aside. One of them was dressed in a flashy suit and jazzy tie. He seemed to be at ease and enjoying himself. The other, whose complexion was several shades paler, appeared to be hanging back rather, and wore clothes that were quietly smart, as if, Stratton thought, he were trying to merge into the background. He and Perlmann were too far away to hear what the Hon. Virginia was saying to the pair of them, but she was delivering it in a manner that was almost grotesquely coquettish.

'Do you know them?'

Perlmann shrugged. 'Could be anybody. I don't mind – I take people as they come. You see that?' He laughed. 'What can you expect? Her husband can't be bothered with her.' He gestured towards Rutherford, who was thoroughly occupied in flirting with a very attractive blonde. 'He married her for her money, I think. I like Virginia. She is a nice woman but unfortunately she is one of these English upper-class ladies who look like a horse dressed in curtains.'

This was such an accurate description that Stratton laughed in spite of himself.

'Ah – you agree? But a very nice horse. A thoroughbred, naturally – the daughter of a viscount. I tell you something, Inspector, when I first came to this country I couldn't understand a word of English. Stefan, he also couldn't understand, so we learnt as quick as we could . . . But when we reached London, we couldn't understand the Cockneys because they don't pronounce any consonants, and we couldn't understand the smart people because they don't pronounce anything else. Only the people in the middle. Stefan and I, we still joke about this.'

'I often have difficulty with the smart people myself,' said Stratton. 'Is Mrs Perlmann here? I should like to meet her. And Mrs Laskier, of course,' he added as an afterthought.

'I named this club after my wife,' said Perlmann, 'but she prefers to spend her time at home.' He shrugged. 'Different interests, you know? And Lola's not here now.' His face seemed to close up as he said this, and Stratton had the impression of a shutter coming down.

Before he could respond, the two of them were joined by the Wuffy-or-possibly-Wuggy chap and another plummy-voiced, red-faced type called Hamilton, both of whom, after introducing themselves, ignored Stratton completely. The music had changed from lilting strings to something distractingly bouncy with a singer who injected growls and yelps of 'Oooowee!' and 'She's awwwwlright' into the proceedings, which made the conversation difficult to hear. He made a polite pretence of listening while concentrating on what was happening on the other side of the room. A man and a girl were dancing to the music. She – considerably younger than he – was jigging about quite prettily, smiling and tossing her head. His movements made Stratton think of someone writhing while impaled on a spike, though whether the expression on his face was agony or ecstasy, he could not tell. Both, perhaps?

The Hon. Virginia was still being skittish with the black chaps, although now she had competition from a couple of others – women rather older than the mannequins, who looked as though they might well be the wives of members. One of the men was responding in kind, and the other looked even more uncomfortable than before. Michael Duffy, who seemed to have been edged out of the conversation, was looking annoyed at having his prize exhibits appropriated. Serve him right, thought Stratton.

The music changed again, this time to something Stratton recognised – 'Smoke Gets in Your Eyes', performed against a background of tumbling plinky notes and yearning violins by one of those crooners with sincere and velvet tones – and a glance in the opposite direction showed him that Rutherford and the blonde girl were now indulging in what one of his old colleagues had memorably described as 'a dry fuck on a dance floor'. If the Hon. Virginia had noticed this, she wasn't showing it.

The sight of the two of them – *'I of course replied/ Something deep inside/ Cannot be denied'* – sent him into a reverie about Fenella Jones, only interrupted by Perlmann's calling for champagne, which he proceeded to press on everybody but did not take for himself.

A moment later Stefan Laskier appeared with a small bottle of what seemed to be fizzy water and presented it to Perlmann, who took it and inspected it carefully before cracking the seal, removing the lid, and raising it to his lips. If either of the others thought this odd, they gave no indication of it – whether from good manners or simple lack of curiosity, Stratton wasn't sure. At that point someone hailed Perlmann from the other end of the room and he departed, clutching the bottle and tailed by the others.

'Who are the men with Mrs Rutherford?' Stratton asked.

Laskier, who looked even more exhausted and dejected than when Stratton had seen him at the hospital, gazed at him blankly for a moment, then said, 'I don't know the one on the right, but the more . . . flamboyant one, on the left, is Clinton Etheridge – I think I told you about him, Inspector.'

'He's the one who lives with Irene Palmer?'

'Yes.'

'And I understand he's a friend of Clyde Johnson, who – as you know – was killed last night. He was attacked not far from where you say you found Miss Palmer.'

'I told you the truth, Inspector. We have many tenants – how can we know everything about them?'

'I don't suppose you can,' said Stratton and then, to change the subject, 'Quite a place you've got here.'

'Yes.' Laskier surveyed the noisy crowd, the corners of

his mouth turned down. For a long moment his eyes rested on Rutherford and the girl. The record being almost finished, they were glued together, mouth to mouth, she with her back arched and he with a hand on each buttock, pushing her into his crotch. 'Half of London comes here at Danny's expense.'

'They pay, don't they?'

'Some of them. But Danny's too generous with them – champagne, drinks . . . food, very often. Banquets, where anyone can help himself. Dinner parties at his home. He keeps boxes of chocolates to give their wives. I tell him to stop, we can't afford it – he tells me it doesn't matter. Danny wants all these top-drawer people to accept him. To be . . . *regarded* by them. Respectable like them. He dreams of a knighthood.'

'You're joking.'

Laskier shook his head slowly. 'I'm not. Danny thinks that as long as he keeps behaving like this, these people will accept him. He doesn't understand. They'll eat his food, drink his champagne, of course – but he'll never be one of them. He's got no more chance than those schwartzers.'

After a few more minutes, Stratton told Laskier he'd be in to see Perlmann in the morning and left him standing in the middle of the room, quite still and quite alone, as people ebbed and flowed around him. The Hon. Virginia seemed to have disappeared, but he found Matheson and said goodnight, and then looked around for Perlmann. Eventually, he spotted him at the side of the room, chatting volubly to someone who was hidden in one of the recesses, and made his way through the now dense crowd towards him.

Just as he managed to squeeze his way around a knot of chatterers, Perlmann disappeared behind the recess and Stratton saw that he was going through a door with, in front of him, Clinton Etheridge. The door – marked 'Private' – closed behind them and Stratton made his way back through the crowd and out into the fresh air of the street.

CHAPTER FIFTEEN

Even at nine o'clock in the morning with the windows wide open, the station was like an oven.

'That's last night's little lot,' said PC Jellicoe. Neatly arranged in a line on the table in front of him were a length of iron railing, two knives, a table leg and a starting handle, all tagged with labels. 'We've got eight downstairs – six white, two coloured. PC Fleetwood's up at Saint Charles's having his face stitched – got hit by some kids throwing bottles. And as if that wasn't enough, a bunch of Teddy boys tried to run a coloured bloke down in a car and managed to crash into a wall, so two of them are in hospital as well, along with the poor darkie who got clobbered with *that* –' Jellicoe indicated the starting handle. 'We're a bit short-handed, what with all this going on, but we've got a couple of blokes doing house-to-house enquiries about Clyde Johnson . . . oh, and Dr McNally says can you telephone him about the post-mortem. Cup of tea?'

'. . . time of death was recorded by the ambulance men as 8.56 p.m.,' Dr McNally reeled off his notes in a staccato

Scottish accent. 'A single stab-wound to the heart, approximately five and a half inches long. Most of the bleeding would have been internal, and such blood as there is on the clothing belongs to the victim. There are no—'

'Can you slow down a bit?' Stratton mopped his face with his handkerchief before wedging the receiver more firmly under his chin. 'I'm trying to take notes.'

'Sorry,' said McNally. Stratton had a mental picture of his elongated, austere frame seated amid the grisly mementoes in his office: booze-hardened livers and abortions floating in jars, stockings used to strangle their owners, rapists' trouser buttons and the like. In the fifteen or so years they'd known each other, the pathologist had built up a museum of the things, arranging them with as much care as a housewife might a prized collection of china animals or holiday souvenirs. 'There isn't much more,' he continued. 'No defensive wounds to the hands, some bruising to the arms and torso, which would be consistent with his having been pushed about and hit by several people, as I understand there was quite a gang involved. Last meal was fish and chips, consumed about an hour prior to death, no alcohol . . . I think that's about it. I'll send you the report.'

'Thanks. You did the PM on Herbert Hampton a couple of weeks ago, didn't you?'

'That's right. Wait a minute.' Stratton heard several dull thuds down the line, as though heavy textbooks were being moved. 'Here we are. What about it?'

'Could it have been a similar weapon?'

'Similar, yes . . .' McNally sounded cautious. 'I couldn't

say more than that, you understand. Lots of these hooligans carrying knives nowadays ... Enjoying your new job, are you?'

'Never a dull moment. We had more trouble here last night.'

'Aye,' said McNally. 'And it'll get worse before it gets better.'

'That,' said Stratton, thinking of what old Mr Russell had said, 'is what I'm afraid of.'

'These tribunals are against the landlords,' said Perlmann, with an air of injured innocence. 'I tell you, Inspector, when these councillors and the people on the committees have got their publicity and the other things they want, they'll all disappear – pfft!' – he mimed a cloud of smoke with his hands, 'but the schwartzers will still be here and I'll still be the only one prepared to rent them houses to live in.' Shiny with sweat, wearing sinister-looking dark glasses and seated in his office at a desk heaped haphazardly with papers, he flipped through a pile of letters as he talked, giving each a cursory glance before tossing it aside. Laskier, seated behind the other desk, was muttering over an adding machine.

'Ach, it doesn't matter,' said Perlmann, tossing a letter over his shoulder.

'Do you think Mrs Rutherford wants publicity?' asked Stratton.

'As I told you, Inspector, Virginia is a nice woman whose husband ignores her. She has money, and that makes her feel guilty, so she tries to make herself feel better. Also, she is not beautiful, and – like any woman – she would like some attention, so . . .' Perlmann shrugged. 'One cannot blame her for that.'

So far, Stratton had got no further forward with his enquiries about Hampton's death than he had with Laskier, and he sensed that he wasn't going to – Perlmann had flatly denied any shenanigans over the rent collection, and was only eager to discuss his own grievances, so his statement was more a formality than any actual use. 'Look at this,' he said, pointing at a jumble of broken padlocks lying on the desk. 'The man who empties the gas meters finds this every week. The tenants break them and steal the money. Five or six of these we replace, every week.'

Feeling that this could go on for some time, Stratton said, 'Did you know Clyde Johnson?'

'Only the name – Stefan told me. It's terrible, but I'm afraid I cannot help you.'

'But you know his friend Clinton Etheridge?'

'Etheridge?'

'I saw you with him last night, at your club. You were going into a room marked "Private".'

Perlmann thought – or appeared to think – for a moment. 'Ach, yes. But I did not know him before he spoke to me. He wanted to complain about his flat. He said it was too small, so I have offered him a bigger one – no extra money – with its own kitchen and bathroom. I like to help people if I can.'

Stratton saw, out of the corner of his eye, that Laskier

had looked up from his calculations and was staring at Perlmann, face furrowed in exasperation.

Driving to Powis Terrace, Stratton wondered if Etheridge
had threatened to go to the rent tribunal and been bought
off with the promise of a better place to live. If so, then
judging from the expression on Laskier's face, it was news
to him – and, presumably, worrying news, because Perlmann
couldn't hope to buy off all his tenants in such a way. Unless,
of course, he had Etheridge lined up to do something else
for him. Stratton wondered what that might be, and what
else Perlmann might not have told Laskier. Secrets were a
lot easier to keep if you didn't share them – perhaps, Stratton
thought, Perlmann had learnt the hard way not to rely on
anybody but himself.

The place seemed peaceful enough – shops open, groups
of children running about the streets, stockingless housewives in carpet slippers gossiping in pairs, tradesmen and
workmen going about their business in shirtsleeves. Stratton
parked the car and climbed the cracked front steps of
number 12. The hall and stairs were, if anything, in worse
shape than the house he'd visited in Colville Terrace. He
skirted the pail of water balanced precariously on the por-
table oil stove on the landing, and knocked on the door.

There was no answer, but when he turned the knob the
door moved slightly, as if it wasn't locked but something
was blocking it from the other side. He put his ear to the
wood and thought he heard a faint – very faint – sob. Stratton
put his shoulder to the door and gave it a hard shove. There

was a second's resistance, followed by a splintering noise and then the door gave, precipitating him into the room over the remains of a kitchen chair. It was empty but for Irene, who was cowering behind the remaining chair on the far side of the table, her face buried in the checked gingham of the cloth. He put the broken chair to one side and closed the door behind him.

CHAPTER SIXTEEN

'Miss Palmer?'

Irene raised her head fractionally, so that Stratton saw the two enormous greeny-gold eyes framed with spider's-leg lashes beneath the mop of pale red hair, and the dusting of freckles across her nose. She was wearing a short-sleeved jersey, with the bandage around her arm clearly visible, and she was just short of shaking with fear.

But for the table and chairs, the room was bare of furniture except for a shelf holding a small collection of crockery and tinned food, and a paraffin stove in the corner. The only ornament Stratton could see was a bunch of paper flowers in a jam jar on the cast-iron mantelshelf. He crouched down beside the girl. 'There's no need to worry, Miss Palmer. It's Inspector Stratton from Harrow Road. We met at Saint Charles's Hospital – you were with Mr Laskier. Do you remember?'

Irene nodded. She looked as though she were about to faint.

'Mr Laskier said he'd found you in a confused state on the corner of Portobello Road and Oxford Gardens, and you told him you'd gone for a walk, got lost and fallen over, and that you live here with a man called Clinton Etheridge. You told *me* that you were eighteen and your parents didn't know where you were. Now, you may or may not be eighteen, but I'm definitely too old to be sitting on the floor, so let's get up, shall we?' Rising, he went to take Irene's arm, but she flinched away from him and scrambled to her feet unaided. 'Come on.' He patted the seat of the chair. 'Much more comfortable.' Gingerly, and keeping her distance, Irene sat down. Whatever she is, Stratton thought, she's not a street girl. 'I think,' he said aloud, 'that you're what they call a mystery. Not been here long, have you?'

She blinked and shook her head.

'But you come from London.'

She nodded.

'You're not eighteen, are you?'

'Yes.' The word came out in a hoarse whisper.

'Yes, you are or yes, you aren't?'

'I am.'

'I believe you – for the time being, at least. Want a cigarette?' Stratton proffered his packet of Churchman's.

'Thanks.' Her hand snaked out and took one quickly, as though she was afraid he'd snatch them away.

He lit a match for her. 'Who are you afraid of, love?'

'I'm not.'

'Usually barricade the door and pretend to be out, do you?'

More head-shaking.

'Is it Etheridge?'

'No-o.' This was said with a hint of a smile, so that she looked and sounded like a child to whom an adult has said something deliberately preposterous.

'Where is he, by the way?'

'I don't know. He went out.'

'I see. Is it your family that you're afraid of? Mr Laskier thinks you've run away from home, and I think he's right.'

'No.' Hands shaking, and definitely no smile this time, Irene fiddled distractedly with the cigarette and did not meet his eye.

'Well, it's obviously *somebody* . . . Of course!' Stratton slapped his forehead with his palm in a parody of revelation. 'It's the people who attacked you two days ago. The gang of boys on Golborne Road. Do they know you live here?'

'No, they don't – they didn't – I don't know what you're talking about.'

'Irene—'

'No!' Irene took a deep breath, trying to steady herself.

'Irene, I'm trying to help you. If—'

'No! I wasn't in Golborne Road.'

'A witness gave a description of a girl who sounds very much like you, who was there when Mr Johnson was attacked.'

'I don't know anything about it.'

'The witness said there were two girls who were chased away by the gang.'

'I told you, it wasn't me.' Irene stood up abruptly, sending her chair clattering to the floor. 'It's like Mr Laskier said. I fell over, and—'

'Fell over because you were running away?'

'No!' She was shouting now, gulping back tears. 'I wasn't! I—'

'Irene?' The door was flung open and a black man – not Etheridge – stood on the threshold. 'Are you OK? What's happened here?'

'Detective Inspector Stratton. I was just talking to Miss Palmer. You are . . .?'

'My name is Royston Walker. I live upstairs.' As he spoke, Stratton recognised him as the chap who'd been with Michael Duffy and Etheridge in Maxine's the previous evening. Close to, he was tall, well-built, and smartly but soberly dressed in a suit and tie. Walker, who was staring at him – not, Stratton thought, with active dislike, but certainly with suspicion – gave no sign of having seen him before. His voice was deep and rich and he sounded far more educated than either Royce or Conroy and didn't seem in the least bothered at being in the presence of a policeman. 'I was passing and I thought Irene might be in some trouble.' Stratton wondered if he meant trouble with Etheridge and, if so, whether it had happened before.

'I see,' he said. 'If I might have a word with you outside?'

Irene stared as Stratton thanked her for her time, and, taking Walker by the elbow, steered him onto the landing. 'I live upstairs,' Walker murmured. 'It's better she doesn't hear.'

Mystified, Stratton followed him up to a freshly painted and spotlessly clean room on the top floor of the house.

'Please,' said Walker, indicating the solitary armchair and seating himself on the edge of the bed.

'Thanks,' said Stratton. 'I saw you last night. At Mr Perlmann's club.'

'Oh?' Walker looked suspicious again.

'There's nothing wrong with your being there,' said Stratton hastily. 'I noticed you, that's all. With Mr Etheridge. You didn't look as though you were enjoying yourself very much.'

'I wasn't.'

'Why not?'

Walker sighed. 'Etheridge introduced me to Michael Duffy, and they were going to this place – Maxine's – and asked me to come, so I went along. Etheridge likes Duffy because he thinks he can get something out of him—'

'Such as?'

'An introduction to a bunch of rich women who will fawn on him. Duffy certainly likes Etheridge.' Walker screwed up his face in disgust. 'I don't enjoy being paraded around like a circus animal. I don't mean,' Walker added quickly, 'that Duffy isn't kind – he's been a great help to a lot of people, standing bail and other things, but the trouble is, he thinks all of this,' he made an encompassing gesture with his hands, 'is romantic.'

'He's not alone in that,' said Stratton, thinking of the Hon. Virginia Rutherford. 'Is Etheridge a homosexual?'

Walker shook his head. 'He's happy to play up to Duffy if he'll gain by it, but he likes girls. You know he's a ponce?'

'We suspected it,' said Stratton, surprised by his directness.

'Not Irene – at least, not yet – but there's another girl who works for him.'

'Do you know her?'

Walker shook his head. 'I've seen her, that's all. The two of them. He told us—'

'Us?'

'Duffy. He seemed to like the idea.' Walker looked scornful.

'Did he tell you her name?'

Walker shook his head. 'Blonde girl. That's all I know.'

'Why are you telling me this?'

'I feel sorry for Irene. She's young, and she doesn't have anybody to look after her.'

'Except Etheridge.'

'Who will put her on the streets. We're not all the same, you know, any more than you are. We don't all talk like dis, man.' The last few words were spoken in an exaggerated West Indian accent. 'Most of the people here,' he gestured towards the window, 'are people I wouldn't associate with back home. Etheridge, for example.'

'Why not?'

'He was a labourer, and then a seaman. What? You think we can be ruled by the British and not have a class system? It's not so different to yours. Birth is important, education, money . . . And colour, of course.'

'Colour?' echoed Stratton, feeling stupid.

'The lighter your skin, the better it is. Better jobs, better status – unless you have money. I tried explaining this to

Duffy, but he wasn't interested because that doesn't fit his bill, to hear that coloured people prefer lighter to darker. I'm lighter, as you can see, and a qualified engineer. I had a skilled job back home, but here . . .' He slapped his palms on his knees. 'The Mother Country! We know all about you – we grow up learning far more about England than we do about our own country – but you know nothing about us, and you don't want to.'

'Do you have a job?' asked Stratton.

'Oh, yes.' Walker's tone was sardonic. 'Machine minder – anyone could do it. I borrowed and saved to come here, and that's all I can get. I took it because I wasn't going to go to the National Assistance Board and have people say I'd come here to get a free ride. But I can't tell my family what sort of job it is, or how I am living, so I tell lies in my letters. My father came here to fight in the war, and he encouraged me to come. If he saw how it is now in this country . . .' Walker shook his head, baffled. 'I can't afford to go home – can't afford the money, or to disappoint my family. They would think it was my fault, that I didn't try hard enough.' He gave Stratton a wry smile, adding, 'I'm too old for my mother to beat my backside, but . . .' before shaking his head again, and standing up to look out of the window at the grubby street below. 'I'm so tired with it all.'

'I'm sorry,' said Stratton. As responses went, it was pretty lame, but he felt he had to say something. 'I can see that it must be very difficult for you.'

Walker didn't turn round. 'You see people come here,' he said, 'and after a while, when they learn how it is, you see this bewildered look on their faces, because they don't understand – because it wasn't supposed to be like this. But you know when they come to write home they're going to tell lies, too, because it's too much for them to say what it's really like.'

Stratton thought of what Laskier had said about Perlmann thinking that if he played the game, 'they' would accept him. He wondered why Walker had chosen to unburden himself – sympathetic though Stratton was, there wasn't anything he could actually do. His concern for Irene seemed genuine, but he was speaking for himself as well. Stratton could understand the man's need to impress upon him that he was an educated person, middle-class and well-spoken – that he had worth. 'Do you think,' he addressed Walker's back, 'that you could keep an eye on Irene? Maybe go down and have a chat with her? She's obviously frightened. I don't know why, but my asking questions isn't helping. We got off on the wrong foot, me bashing through the door like that, so I can't blame her for not wanting to talk to me.'

Walker turned, frowning. 'And you want me to tell you what she says?'

'I'm not asking you to break a confidence unless you think she's in danger.'

Walker angled his head to one side, then said, 'OK.'

'I don't suppose you have any idea of where Etheridge might be?'

'Irene didn't tell you?'

'Said she didn't know.'

'Well, I don't know either, but I'd guess that he's with the other girl, or he's at the club.'

'Club?'

'It's in a basement on Colville Road.'

'Do you know which number?'

'No, but it shouldn't be hard to find. Etheridge started it a few months ago, with the boy who was killed.'

'Johnson? Did you know him?'

'No. I suppose he may have come here sometimes, visiting, but I never saw him.'

But Irene might have seen him, thought Stratton. She might have known him. And Johnson – otherwise known as Ding-Dong – had rolled for Gloria, hadn't he? And Gloria was blonde, and a blonde had been seen with a redhead when Johnson was attacked . . . 'It's possible,' he said aloud, 'that Irene may be in danger from the gang who attacked Johnson. That's why, if she does say anything, I'd like to know about it.'

Shaking hands with Walker, he added awkwardly, 'What you were saying – I hope that things improve. I'm sure they will, given time.'

Driving round to Colville Road, Stratton reflected that he wasn't at all sure of any such thing.

CHAPTER SEVENTEEN

As Walker had said, the club wasn't difficult to spot. There were wooden crates of empties stacked in the area, and the basement door was open, with music issuing from it '*Darling, you send me, I know you send me . . .*' against a background of Woo-oo-oo's.

It looked as though two rooms had been knocked into one large one, furnished with assorted second-hand chairs and sofas, as well as a long table laid out as a makeshift bar and beside it, a record player. He spotted an old gas bracket secured to one wall – unused, judging from the unshaded bulb, the sagging, frayed electrical wiring and the grimy Bakelite switch beside the door.

Hearing a familiar whooping laugh coming from behind a curtain made of multi-coloured plastic strips at the back, he went through and found Etheridge in the company of the Hon. Virginia in a small kitchen-cum-storeroom. Etheridge was dressed as flamboyantly as he had been at the club – even, Stratton noted, wearing several rings on his fingers. He didn't look at all pleased to see Stratton, and, after confirming his name, shut up like a clam. The Hon. Virginia, on the other hand, had the breathless composure of someone who'd just missed being discovered in a compromising position. Not all that compromising, as she was fully dressed and in an outfit that suggested she might be about to open a church fete, but all the same she had a definite air of speedy readjustment and there was an excited, even feverish, look in her eyes.

'We're preparing for that party I told you about, Inspector. Look!' She pulled a bottle wrapped in tissue paper from one of several cardboard boxes on the floor. 'We've managed to get some authentic West Indian rum. We would invite you, Inspector . . .' The look on Etheridge's face clearly said that *he* wouldn't, 'but it might be off-putting to some of the guests. You see, it was felt that we need to invite everybody, and some of them are, you know . . .'

'Some of them are pimps?' said Stratton, looking squarely at Etheridge, who gave him a sullen stare in return.

'Well . . . yes, actually.' The Hon. Virginia coloured slightly. 'We decided that we'll never manage to solve any problems unless we bring people together, and that includes the, er, rougher element. Clinton's been making enquiries, and about the girls too. As I say, we do feel it's important to include everyone. We've got our local MP coming as well, and some others from the House of Commons – it's a bit of a fact-finding tour for them, to meet the local community.'

'Very commendable,' said Stratton. 'Just remember to count your fingers after you shake hands, won't you?' Etheridge glared at him.

The Hon. Virginia gave an embarrassed laugh and said uncertainly, 'I'm sure you don't mean that, Inspector.'

'When is this party, anyway?'

'Tomorrow evening.'

'That soon?' said Stratton, wondering if Fenella Jones would be present.

'Best to strike while the iron's hot,' said the Hon. Virginia, her eyes shining. 'Especially with all this trouble.' I'll bet she hasn't had this much fun since the war, Stratton thought. 'We need community leaders,' she went on, giving Etheridge a big smile. 'People who can get things done.'

Or, thought Stratton uncharitably, people who can sit on their arses while things get done for them by people like you. 'On the subject of getting things done,' he said, 'I'd like a word with Mr Etheridge, if I may.'

'Of course! I must be off in any case.'

Quite deliberately, and challenging Stratton with a look as he did so, Etheridge kissed her on the cheek. 'I'll see you later.'

When she'd gone, Etheridge shook his head and smirked in a way that made Stratton yearn to punch him. Instead he raised a quizzical eyebrow – don't fuck with me, chum, I know what you are – and said, in a neutral tone, 'Mrs Rutherford appears to be enjoying herself.'

'Yeah . . .'

Stratton braced himself for the smart, knowing remark, but it never came. Instead Etheridge said, 'She will do it all – she and these other white people. We won't learn to organise things ourself in this country if white people do it for us, tell us how bad it is and they understand what we feelin'.'

This was so not what Stratton expected to hear that it brought him up short, unsure how to respond. Etheridge was right. The Hon. Virginia was clearly well-intentioned and – equally clearly – hungering for new experience, but she was also grabbing the chance for a demonstration of merit. Stratton felt positive that there was an attraction in being able to claim that she was one of a very few who truly understood how black people thought and felt. Something told him that there was going to be a great deal more of that sort of thing in the future, and that people like Etheridge would use it to their advantage. 'But you're happy to go along with it?' he asked.

Etheridge shrugged. 'Coloured man got no chance in this country.'

'So you're going to play both sides against the middle? I saw you with Mrs Rutherford at Mr Perlmann's club last night. Did she know that you had a chat with him privately, later on?' Etheridge stared at him through narrowed eyes, but said nothing. 'Well?' Stratton prompted. 'What were you talking about?'

'My flat. I said I need somewhere bigger. He said he'd fix it up. You can't arrest me for that.'

'I have no intention of arresting you. I just need to ask you some questions about your friend Clyde Johnson.'

'He was killed. By white men like you.'

Ignoring this last bit, Stratton said, 'We want to catch them.' Etheridge made no attempt to hide his disbelief at this statement. 'When was the last time you saw him?'

'Couple of days ago. He was here – we were moving furniture.'

'The same day he was killed?'

Etheridge nodded. 'In the afternoon. He left about five o'clock. I went home, then I came back here at eight to open up.'

'Did Johnson say where he was going?'

'No.'

'Have you any idea?'

Etheridge shook his head.

'Did he have a job of any kind?'

'Couldn't get a job. Neither of us. That's why we have to hustle.'

'OK. Does this place have a licence?'

'Don't need one. Don't serve alcohol. Mrs Rutherford brought this –' he pointed to the cardboard boxes on the floor – 'for the party.'

Stratton was about to ask about the empty beer bottles he'd seen outside, when there was a shout of 'Cooo-eee!' from the front and the click-clack of high-heels. 'Darling!'

Etheridge shot past him into the main room, and Stratton followed. He was just quick enough to see an uncomprehending Marion Lockwood, otherwise known as Gloria, pressing a wad of notes on Etheridge, who muttered something and tried to stuff them back into the gaping mouth of the handbag that hung from her wrist.

Looking up, and taking in the situation in a flash, Gloria smiled politely and said, 'Clinton lent me some money, didn't he? I'm just paying it back.'

Stratton lounged in the doorway, hands in his pockets. 'Go on, Gloria, pull the other one.'

'It's true,' said Gloria automatically, 'on my life.' Etheridge, who'd reared away from her as if he'd been stung, nodded in confirmation.

'Really?' said Stratton. At that point, the last few 'Woo-oo-oo's' faded out, and for a moment there was silence but for the rhythmic scratching of the record player's needle.

'I think that's enough music for the time being.' Stratton ambled over and turned it off. He took the disc off the spindle and threw it, with a flick of his wrist, to Etheridge, so that it sliced, spinning, through the air. Etheridge, shocked, the whites of his eyes like peeled eggs, caught it just in time.

Leaning against the wall near the front door, Stratton took his time about lighting a cigarette, before saying to Gloria, 'Tell you what. Either you can tell me where you were at the time Johnson was killed, or I'll nick the pair of you.'

'I've told you already.' Gloria stared at him with bullet-eyed defiance.

'That was the truth, was it?'

'Yes. On my life.'

'I was inclined to believe you the first time, but I've just remembered something one of the ambulance men said about your pal Ding-Dong.'

'So?'

'He said your name. The ambulance man thought it was "Glory" – a reference to the hereafter, he thought. But it wasn't, was it? It was "Gloria". That suggests to me that he was telling the bloke to talk to you because you'd witnessed it.'

Gloria shook her head.

'No? Then you won't mind if your boyfriend here goes down for poncing? I don't imagine that being pinched will make much difference to you, but –' here, he turned to Etheridge, who was staring at the pair of them with barely concealed fury – 'ponces don't have a very good time in prison, for some reason. And your important new friend isn't aware of your occupation, is she? She might be rather upset if she found out.'

'What are you talking about?' demanded Gloria. 'What new friend?'

'I'm sure,' said Stratton smoothly, 'that Mr Etheridge will tell you all about it in his own good time. Well?'

'I want to know about this new friend,' repeated Gloria. 'Who is she?'

'It's no one important,' said Etheridge, whose face, throughout this exchange, had the anguished look of one making rapid mental calculations to determine the least bad course of action.

'He just said she was! "Important new friend", he said.'

'I'll explain later.'

'He'll explain just as soon as you've told me where you were,' said Stratton. 'Otherwise, I'm afraid you're going to have quite a wait.'

Etheridge looked from Stratton to Gloria and back again. 'Tell him, darling.'

'Why should I?' Gloria crossed her arms defiantly.

'Please, Gloria.' Etheridge moved back to Gloria and put a hand on her arm. 'Just tell him, and I'll explain.'

Gloria shook him off, then poked about in her handbag for cigarettes, frowning as she weighed up the situation. After a moment, she lit up, gave a sigh of resignation and said, 'All right. We was in Golborne Road.'

'We?'

'Me and Irene. She's Ding-Dong's girlfriend – Irene Palmer.'

'Johnson's girlfriend?' Stratton looked pointedly at Etheridge, who suddenly became fascinated by the record in his hands.

Gloria nodded. 'We weren't with Ding-Dong – we just walked into it.'

'Why were you there?'

'We had a meal in one of the cafes, just the two of us. We hadn't arranged to meet him.'

'Which cafe?'

'Astley's. Near the railway bridge.'

'Why there and not Queensway?' asked Stratton. 'Isn't that more convenient for you?'

Gloria shrugged. 'Fancied a change.'

'How long have you known Irene?'

'Only met her a couple of times. She's not been here long, and she don't know too many people, so Ding-Dong said why didn't we go out, girls together sort of thing, you know, just friendly, and . . .'

'. . . And you could show her the ropes,' supplied Stratton.

'I never said that.' Gloria sounded indignant. 'Irene's not, you know . . .'

'. . . On the game?'

'No, she ain't.'

She ain't *yet* was more like it, Stratton thought. He imagined Etheridge telling Ding-Dong to tell Gloria to persuade Irene that they needed money and that the whole thing was a piece of cake and she'd be stupid not to when it was so simple . . . And of course she might be more persuadable if she didn't have the sordid reality of the Bayswater Road right under her nose – hence the choice of venue. He wondered what lie Etheridge had told Irene to explain both Gloria and why she had to pretend to be Johnson's girl. It must have been a pretty good one because, judging from Irene's reaction when he'd mentioned Etheridge, she'd believed it. But then again, she didn't have anywhere else to go, did she?

'What time did you leave the restaurant?'

'Half past eight, near enough, then we walked down the road a little bit, and that's when we saw the boys.'

'How far down the road?'

'About half the parade. Astley's is right at the end, away from the bridge.'

'And you were walking towards it, were you?'

'Yes. We'd passed about seven or eight shops, and they was all outside a shop with green paint. I don't know what shop it was because there was shutters over the window.'

'What were they doing?'

'Well, at first it looked like they was just talking, so I didn't think nothing of it, but then they started having a go at Ding-Dong. Not that we knew it *was* Ding-Dong, not at first.'

'When did you realise?'

'When I saw the suit. It's got these thick red stripes, sort of shiny. You never saw anything like it. Told me his aunt made it for him.' Gloria's face brightened momentarily, then fell. 'He was ever so proud of it – used to get the dead needle with me when I told him she must be colour-blind. I mean,' she added, forlornly, 'he looked like a bleeding deckchair.'

'What was he doing there, do you know?'

'Dunno. Free country, ain't it?'

'Not meeting you? I'd say that's the most likely explanation. Going to give the new girl a masterclass in rolling, were you?'

'No, we weren't. We was going to have a drink, if you want the truth.'

'With Ding-Dong?'

'No! Look, he might have decided to come up and meet us, I don't know. He was just *there*.'

'Just dropped out of the sky, I suppose,' said Stratton. 'Did you see any weapons?'

'One bloke had a bit of wood, like a chair leg or something, and I saw a flash of something that could have been a knife, but I wouldn't swear to it because it all happened so quick, and then we were legging it.'

'Why did you run?'

'Because we thought we'd be next. When they saw us, they started yelling about us being black men's whores and a lot more like that, so I ran for it and so did Irene. I thought she was behind me, but when I stopped she wasn't there.'

'Where was that?'

'Outside the station – Ladbroke Grove. There was people about, so I thought I'd be safe . . . The blokes weren't there, and neither was Irene.'

'Did you go back to see if she was all right?'

'I couldn't, could I? They was going to do me.'

'Did you recognise any of the men?'

'No.' This was swift, decisive and, Stratton surprised himself by thinking, truthful.

'But they knew who you were.'

Gloria shrugged again. 'Maybe they've seen me around.'

'Would you be able to identify any of them if you saw them again?'

'Dunno. I could give it a try, I suppose. You should ask Irene.'

'Does she know them?'

'Dunno that either. But she recognised one of them.'

'How do you know?'

'She was walking along beside me, and when we got close she suddenly stopped. Then she said something – a name. It sounded like Johnny or Tommy, but I'm not sure because just when she said it one of them turns round and sees us and starts shouting.'

'Why didn't you call the police?'

'What, go into a call box so they could catch us?'

'Afterwards.'

'I was scared, wasn't I?'

'Did you see anyone chasing them?'

'What, after the ones that were chasing us?' Gloria looked at him as though he was mad. 'I was running, all right? I wasn't going to turn round and have a look, was I?' Dropping what was left of her cigarette on the concrete floor, she ground it out with one pointy-toed shoe. 'Happy now?'

'Yes, thanks. Now, if I could just have a word with Mr Etheridge in private . . .' He stood back to indicate that Gloria should leave. 'I shan't keep him for more than a minute.'

Through the window, Stratton watched Gloria's backside, clad in a tight-fitting black skirt, wiggle as she climbed up the steps to the pavement. Etheridge caught him looking, and the two men stared at each other in a second's uncomfortable complicity before Stratton said, 'Was she talking about the same Irene Palmer who lives with you at number 12 Powis Terrace?'

'Yes.'

'Gloria said she said a name – Johnny or Tommy. Do you know who that could be?'

'No.'

'Aren't you curious?'

'Her business.'

'I see. Just out of interest, when were you going to tell Gloria and Irene about each other? Or were you planning to let them work it out for themselves and hope they got used to it?'

'You know how it is, man.' Etheridge shrugged. 'You run around, keep them sweet, and Gloria . . .' He shook his head, looking every inch the henpecked husband. 'She always shouting for something.'

That, thought Stratton, was the truly strange thing about the ponce/whore relationship. True, Etheridge could bash

Gloria if she didn't bring home enough money, but she was the one who earned it, so he was dependent on her just as much as any housewife depended on her husband. Etheridge might be exploiting what limited opportunities he had to hand, but underneath the flashy clothes and the bravado he was powerless.

At the door, Stratton gestured at the crates of empties. 'If you don't have a licence, you'd better get those out of sight sharpish,' he said.

Etheridge looked at him, surprised. 'Thanks, man.'

Stratton nodded curtly and went up the steps to the pavement. Gloria was waiting at the top, lounging against the railings, cigarette between her lips. Her habitual pose, Stratton thought. She couldn't help looking as though she was touting for business. Four or five years ago, she'd probably been just like Irene. Stratton could easily guess at the combination of circumstances that had delivered her – and was in the process of delivering Irene – to Etheridge. It would be drearily familiar from hundreds of stories just like it told by girls who'd ended up on the streets.

Jenny's voice came to him so clearly that he jumped: *You can't be responsible for the world, Ted.*

'You all right?' Gloria was looking at him curiously.

'Fine, thanks.' Jerking his head towards the basement steps, he added, 'Get on with you.'

'Oh, ta very much,' said Gloria sarcastically, and, straightening up with a blatant wiggle, she click-clacked back downstairs to Etheridge.

CHAPTER EIGHTEEN

Watching Gloria descend the steps, Stratton found himself, for about the fiftieth time that day, thinking about Fenella. It wasn't in any particular way – well, not if you didn't count imagining what she might look like naked – but it seemed to be colouring all his thoughts. That morning, on his way to work, he'd even found himself looking at the cartoons page in the *Daily Express* and wondering if George and Gaye Gambol ever had sex. It was, he'd decided, unlikely – for one thing they slept in separate beds, and for another, the only time George ever seemed to touch Gaye was to help zip up her frock.

Telling himself that it was hardly likely to come to that – in all probability Fenella had only accepted his invitation to dinner because she couldn't think of a polite way to refuse – he drove back to Powis Terrace. He'd definitely have to wait until this evening before he telephoned her, in any case. He certainly wasn't going to do it from the station, where anyone could walk in on him, and a public call box seemed too exposed, somehow. Besides which, you could never be sure that some idiot wouldn't start banging on the glass and telling you to hurry up.

As he skirted the unwashed milk bottles and ersatz cooking equipment on the landing, Stratton heard yelps of laughter coming from Irene and Etheridge's room. The noise stopped abruptly when he banged on the door and called, 'DI Stratton – can I come in?'

Walker answered the door, a pot of glue in his hand. Behind him, Irene was sitting on the remaining chair, holding two pieces of the smashed one in an improvised vice. There were more glued pieces lying on the small table. 'You'll have a job with that,' said Stratton.

'I can do it,' said Walker. 'My dad was a carpenter. I used to help him in his shop.' He looked serious, but Stratton could tell that he'd been enjoying the work, much as he himself did when faced with a tricky practical task – not to mention having the opportunity to impress a pretty girl by the doing of it. By the sound of it, Irene was enjoying herself too – or rather, she had been. Now she looked fearful.

'Need a hand?'

Walker shook his head. 'We have to wait for the glue to set before I can do anything else.'

'Well,' said Stratton, 'perhaps I could have a word with your assistant here while it does.'

'You want me to go?' Walker cast an anxious look at Irene, who was wide-eyed and seemed ready to bolt from the room.

'That's up to Irene,' said Stratton.

Her eyes flitted from Stratton to Walker and back again. 'I'd like him to stay.'

'Fair enough,' said Stratton. 'Why don't you give that –' he indicated the pieces of wood she was holding – 'to Mr Walker.'

Irene stared at them for a second, as if she'd forgotten what they were, then handed them over, careful not to disturb the join. Walker took them and retreated a few paces, his discomfort obvious. He already knows what I'm about to say, Stratton thought, or he's guessed.

'Now,' he said, 'I'm afraid I need to ask you again about where you were when Mr Johnson was attacked in Golborne Road.' Irene opened her mouth, but he held up a hand. 'You told Mr Laskier that you'd gone out for a walk, and you told both of us that you'd fallen over and hurt yourself, but that wasn't true, was it? I've just been speaking to a friend of yours called Gloria, and she says that the two of you were in Golborne Road at the time Mr Johnson was attacked, and that you recognised one of the men who assaulted him.'

'If she says that, she's lying!' Irene burst out fiercely. 'She's always trying to make trouble. Clinton said—' She stopped as abruptly as she'd started, and looked up at Stratton in confusion.

'Mr Etheridge was present when Gloria spoke to me,' said Stratton gently. 'He seemed to think she was telling the truth.'

Irene gazed at him in bewilderment.

'They told you not to say anything, didn't they? It's all right,' he added, seeing the alarm in her eyes. 'I'm not asking you to tell tales, but I do need to know what happened. After all,' he added, 'we can't just let people go about attacking each other and getting away with it, can we?'

Stratton had the impression that Walker, who was standing slightly behind him, wanted to say something, and, turning his head, saw that he was gazing at Irene intently. 'I'm sure Mr Walker would agree with me,' he said firmly.

'I . . .' Irene didn't look directly at Stratton. Her gaze hovering somewhere between the two men's shoulders, she cleared her throat and said, 'I was there. With Gloria. When it happened, I mean.'

'The men attacking Mr Johnson knew you, didn't they? Gloria said they called you names.'

'Well, I don't know about her, but I've never seen them before. They were shouting at us, though. I don't know what it was – I was just trying to get away. We both were.'

'And your injury? How did that happen?'

'I tripped, and one of them grabbed me from behind and then I felt a pain in my arm and there was blood. I was on the ground and they were all round me, and I couldn't see what was going on, but then one of them said "Leave it" and they ran off.'

'Where was that?'

'Near the corner of Golborne Road, I think. I mean, I wasn't thinking about where I was going – just to get away in case they changed their minds, but my arm was hurting . . . I couldn't see Gloria anywhere, and I didn't know what to do. Then Mr Laskier came and asked me if I was all right, and I just told him the first thing I could think of.'

'Did you see anyone chasing the men?'

Irene looked bewildered. 'Chasing *them*? No.'

'Can you describe any of them?'

'Not really. They were just, you know, ordinary. Not old, but . . .'

'Older than you?'

'A bit, I think. Most of them.' Irene frowned, trying to remember. 'A couple of them had the Tony Curtis hairstyle, with a quiff, and one of them – I think he was a bit older than the others – had a drape jacket. You know, long, like a Teddy boy. Some of them had trousers, but a couple had jeans . . . I can't think of anything else.'

'What about their faces?' asked Stratton. 'Did you notice anything particular?'

Irene shook her head. 'I only noticed the legs and feet because I was on the ground. They just looked the same as lots of people, really. And,' she added, thoughtfully, 'when people are angry and shouting like that, they don't look like themselves, do they? They look like animals.'

Struck by this, Stratton said, 'But you don't know what they looked like when they weren't angry, do you? Unless you *did* recognise them, of course.'

'No.' Irene shook her head emphatically. 'Honest, I didn't.'

'Gloria said you mentioned a name – Johnny or Tommy.'

'I never!' Irene leant forward. 'I told you, she's lying.'

'But she wasn't lying about the pair of you being in Golborne Road, was she?' said Stratton gently. 'And – until just now – you were.'

'Yes.' Irene shifted uncomfortably, not looking him in the eye. 'But I didn't know who they were.'

'So why would Gloria say you did?'

'She wants to make trouble!' Irene's eyes blazed. 'She doesn't like me. It's all, "I'll be your friend, Irene. I'll help you." At first I thought she meant it and it was nice to have a friend because I didn't hardly know anyone, but then I found out it was all put on.'

'Why do you think she's putting it on?'

'Because of Clinton, of course.' Irene's tone was that of a child explaining some piece of playground lore to a kindly but uncomprehending adult. 'That's why I had to pretend I was Ding-Dong's girlfriend.'

'I'm sorry,' said Stratton. 'Why don't you spell it out for me, love?'

Irene sighed. 'When Clinton first came to London he didn't know anybody. He said Gloria was one of the few people who was friendly – helped him find a room and all that – but the problem was that she was, you know . . . *stuck* on him, and he didn't feel the same about her. She'd get jealous if he took other girls out, and he didn't want to upset her because she'd been nice to him, so he said to me to pretend to be Ding-Dong's girl and then she wouldn't get the needle.' All this was said with total sincerity, but she must have seen something on the listeners' faces, because she said, in a hurt voice, 'You do believe me, don't you?'

Ignoring this – and deliberately not looking at Walker – Stratton asked, 'Does Gloria know you live here?'

'No.'

'Isn't that a bit difficult? I mean, if she comes to visit?'

'She doesn't know Clinton lives here. He tells her he moves around – staying with friends and that.'

'And she believes him?'

'I suppose so. She never said she didn't.'

'I see,' said Stratton. 'So when you were in Golborne Road and you said the name Johnny or Tommy, that was . . . ?'

'I didn't say anything! Well, I might have done, because I was that scared I don't remember what I said, but I don't know who those men were.'

'You're sure about that, are you?'

'Yes! I've never seen them before.' She stared at him as if willing him to believe her. 'And I didn't even realise it was Ding-Dong until we heard about it later. I told you, Gloria's making it up because she's jealous of any woman that Clinton even looks at, and . . .' She faltered, frowning, as if something had just occurred to her, then said, 'Why are you looking at me like that?'

'Like what?' asked Stratton, who hadn't realised he was looking like anything.

'Both of you.' Irene had shrunk back in her chair, arms rigid at her sides, hands grasping the seat on either side of her thighs. She looked unbearably young and vulnerable. 'Like you're sorry for me. Well,' she added, like a truculent child, 'you needn't be, because I can look after myself.'

'I don't think that's entirely true, is it?'

'Well, I've got Clinton to look after me.'

For the first time, Walker spoke. 'No, Irene. You haven't. Clinton Etheridge is only interested in looking after himself.'

Glancing at him, Stratton saw that his face showed no anger, only compassion.

'You ought to be on his side,' Irene retorted fiercely.

'Whether you believe it or not,' said Walker softly, 'I'm on your side, Irene.'

'Then you must be on his, too,' said Irene. 'Because he loves me. This man was trying to make me go to a club with him – we were in a cafe, arguing about it – but Clinton wouldn't let him. He just appeared out of nowhere and told the man to leave me alone. I had no money or anything, and he was so kind to me . . . He didn't try to, you know . . . He brought me back here and said I could stay as long as I want.'

'And that was just after you ran away from home, was it?' asked Stratton.

'Yes,' said Irene defiantly. 'Clinton's the only one in my life who's been nice to me, other than my dad, and he's dead.'

'Was that why you left home?'

'Sort of, but . . .' Irene dropped her head and started picking at something on her skirt. 'It was more when my mum got married again.' The words came out in a hurried mumble. 'I hate him.'

'Your stepfather?'

'Yeah.' Irene twisted her head to one side, avoiding eye contact with either him or Walker, and began fiddling with her hair, winding a strand of red gold round and round her finger. 'I think she'd started seeing him when Dad was in hospital before he died. He was always trying to get me on my own. I was only thirteen when he started.'

Stratton glanced at Walker. His face was impassive, the eyes opaque. Wishing there was a policewoman present, he asked, 'Was he interfering with you?'

'Yes. I tried to tell her, but as soon as I started she jumped down my throat and called me a liar. She did that before I'd even said it – like she knew what I was going to say. She said I was sly – making things up. Then she told him in front of me and he said it was because she'd spoiled me when I was a kid, but all the time he's looking at me when she can't see, as if he knows he's won or something. I'm not lying, honest I'm not.'

'I know.' While she'd been talking, a familiar sensation had descended upon Stratton, one that he always felt when he heard versions of this story: sadness coupled with the weary resignation of knowing there was bugger all he could do about it. He couldn't turn the clock back and undo the damage, and in the very rare instances where these things came anywhere near a court it would come down to the child's word against the parents. 'When did you run away?' he asked.

'About six weeks ago.'

That would make it the beginning of July – in other words, about a year since she'd left school. Stratton sighed. 'You're not eighteen, are you?'

Irene shook her head.

'What's your parents' address?'

She shrank back in her chair. 'You ain't sending me back

there. I won't go – you can't make me – and anyway, they don't want to know me.'

'What makes you say that?'

'I wrote to Mum to say I was all right, and she wrote back saying she'd heard I was living with a black man and it was disgusting. She said she was ashamed with people knowing about it and I'd let them all down and she never wanted to see me again. Besides . . .' here, Irene's eyes filled with tears. 'I'm happy here. Clinton loves me, and I love him.'

Stratton looked sideways at Walker, who was staring resolutely at the floor, his discomfort palpable. Why did I start this? he thought. It's not part of the case and even if she is underage, I'm not about to frogmarch her back to her family, or to hand her over to a bunch of welfare people who'll send her back labelled 'imbecile' or 'juvenile delinquent' or something else that will make damn sure no one ever listens to her. Stifling the treacherous thought that he almost certainly wouldn't have been taking such an interest if she weren't so appealing and pretty, he said, 'I'm not saying Etheridge doesn't love you, Irene. Now, what's your parents' address?'

'You ain't—'

'There's no reason why I should contact them,' said Stratton soothingly. 'And if you don't tell me, Irene, I can easily find the information elsewhere.'

'All right,' said Irene sulkily. 'It's the White City Estate. Number 16 in Durban House.'

Producing his notebook, Stratton jotted this down. 'And you've been living here for six weeks, have you?'

''Bout that.'

'Well, how long do you think it's going to be before Gloria finds out you're living with Etheridge – if she hasn't already?'

Irene sniffed. 'I don't care if she does. He wants me, not her, and this is *our* home.' She looked around the sparsely furnished room in a forlorn parody of housewifely pride. 'You know what Gloria does for a living, don't you?'

Irene gave him a scornful look. 'I wasn't born yesterday.'

'She gives the money to Etheridge.'

Stratton saw shock flash across her face for an instant before she rallied, saying, with weak defiance, 'Well, if she wants to give him money, that's her lookout.'

'He's living off her, Irene. Him and you.'

'I know that.' She hadn't, thought Stratton. 'But it's only because no one'll give him a job. It isn't fair.'

Stratton, remembering Walker's words earlier, thought there was more than a grain of truth in this last bit, although he wondered how hard Etheridge had actually tried to find work. 'I realise it can be difficult,' he said, 'but you have to realise that she's not giving him all that money without expecting something in return.'

'You mean he . . .?' Irene stopped, shaking her head violently as if to rid herself of the image of Etheridge and Gloria together. 'It's not true.'

'He never spends nights away from you?'

'Only when he sleeps at the club.'

Stratton raised an eyebrow. 'Really? And how often does he do that?'

'Two or three times a week, when they're busy. It's

because he doesn't like to wake me up – he's always back in the morning . . .' Faltering, she said, 'I still don't believe you. You're just saying it because you're trying to spoil everything,' she finished childishly. 'He loves me, I know he does. When I was sitting in that cafe, I didn't have any money left and I didn't know what to do –'

'– and you were very vulnerable,' finished Stratton. 'You'd run away from a bad situation at home, and he was kind to you – no one's denying that. But it's not a fairytale, Irene. Etheridge lied to Gloria about you, didn't he?'

Irene's smooth forehead crenellated in a frown. 'Yes, but that was different.'

'So he's capable of lying to Gloria but not to you?'

Irene opened her mouth to reply, then shut it again. Turning to Walker, she said, 'You know Clinton. Why don't you tell him it's not true?'

Walker, who was still looking down at the floor, didn't move, and the silence in the room seemed to thicken. Watching the realisation creep across Irene's face, Stratton had the sensation of having smashed something precious. Not that it was entirely his fault – her stepfather had begun it and Etheridge was simply the next step in a process that would lead, inexorably, to disappointment. There were plenty of older, worldlier women, he thought, who'd wilfully deceived themselves over men with far less excuse than poor Irene.

'He wants to marry me.' Irene sounded uncertain. 'He said.'

Walker cleared his throat. His voice, when it came,

seemed to rise from somewhere deep inside him. 'You think he doesn't tell Gloria the same thing?'

Irene recoiled as if she'd been hit. 'But she's a pro! Clinton wouldn't marry her.'

'Maybe he wouldn't,' said Walker. 'But he doesn't mind taking her money, does he? And,' he added, 'he won't mind taking yours either.'

'Why can't you let me alone?' cried Irene. 'Both of you!'

'Because,' said Stratton, 'we don't want you to end up like Gloria.' Deciding to take a chance, he continued, 'The evening Mr Johnson was killed, you and Gloria had a meal in a cafe in Golborne Road, didn't you?'

'Ye-es.' Irene looked mystified.

'What did you talk about?'

'Ermm . . .' Irene coloured. 'I can't remember.'

'Oh, I think you can. "It's easy money – three pounds for a short time. You'll soon get used to it, and you'd never be short of offers, pretty girl like you. You could buy yourself new clothes – anything you wanted – find yourself a nice flat . . ." Was that how it went?' The expression on Irene's face told him he'd hit home. 'Of course,' he continued, 'Gloria thought you were Ding-Dong's girl, didn't she, so I'm guessing that Etheridge asked him to ask her to have a word with you, and you have a nice cosy chat, and just as you're getting used to the idea along comes Ding-Dong and tells you what a smart move you're making, and suddenly it feels as if it's all your idea and you're a very clever girl. You're not the first one it's happened to, love, and you certainly won't be the last. I know,' he added, 'that you must be feeling a bit mixed up at the moment –' The look on Irene's face told him this was as masterly an understatement as he was ever likely to make – 'and, judging by your behaviour this morning, I'd say that something has made you very, very frightened about being here by yourself.' Again, Irene's face provided ample confirmation of this. 'Are you absolutely sure that you didn't recognise any of the men who attacked Mr Johnson?'

'N-no.'

'Have they threatened you? Is that why you don't want to tell me?' Blinking rapidly, Irene shook her head. 'Is it someone from the White City Estate?'

'No – honest – it's just I don't like being on my own, that's all.'

'Really? It looked like a bit more than that to me. Do you know someone called Eddy Knight?'

'I don't know none of them.'

'None of who?'

'None of the people you're talking about.'

'Eddy Knight lives on the White City Estate.'

'It's big. Lots of people live there.'

Stratton produced his notebook and leafed through it until he found the notes from his conversation with Knight. 'What about Ronnie Mills? Do you know him?'

Irene shook her head.

Stratton produced PC Dobbs's list from his other pocket and checked it. 'He lives on the estate too, and so does Gordon Baxter. What about him?'

Another headshake, lower this time, so that her eyes were obscured by a curtain of hair.

'Fred Larby?'

Another headshake. Now Stratton was looking at the crown of her head.

'Tony Pearson?'

Irene jerked her head up. 'No!' The word came out as a cross between a sob and a scream. 'I don't know a single one and I never saw them and I don't know nothing about any of it! Why can't you just leave me alone?'

CHAPTER NINETEEN

Seeing that there was nothing to be gained by staying and feeling like a bully, Stratton patted Irene awkwardly on one heaving shoulder and withdrew. Walker, looking reproachful, followed him onto the landing. 'She's too frightened,' he said in a low voice.

'I know. It's no good, and I shouldn't have kept on at her like that. But she does need to get away from here. It's all right,' he added quickly, seeing the alarm on the other's face, 'I'm not going to try and send her back to her mum, and I'm not going to say anything, either, or she'll end up in a Remand Home and that won't do her any good at all.'

'So what can you do?'

'Your landlord, Perlmann – his manager, Laskier, told me he was willing to offer her a job at Maxine's.'

'That club?' Walker looked disdainful. 'All those old men . . .' He shook his head. 'It's no better than what she has now. Besides, she told me about this – that man offered her the job, and she said no. You know what she said? That Etheridge would be vexed so she didn't tell him.'

'But it would get her away from him, wouldn't it? And Laskier might offer her a place to live as well.'

Walker stared at him in disbelief. 'He's no different to Etheridge.'

'I know what you're saying,' said Stratton, 'but I believe you're wrong.'

Walker's eyebrows almost disappeared into his hairline. 'You trust him?'

Stratton surprised himself by saying, firmly, 'Yes, I do. And I'm not on his payroll, if that's what you're worried about. I'm doing this because I want to help Irene, and I think that Laskier does too, so you might suggest she gets in touch with him. She won't listen to me. If she doesn't have his telephone number, she can go to the office. It's on the corner of Westbourne Grove and Monmouth Road. I honestly think – at the moment, at least – that this is the best way to get her out of here.'

Walker peered at him through narrowed eyes. Realising that the man was trying to decide whether or not to believe him, Stratton said, 'And what's more, it would get Irene away from whatever it is that's frightening her – because it's obvious that something, or some*one*, is scaring her out of her wits. And,' he added, 'if it's the people I think it is, then the longer she stays here, the more danger she's going to be in.'

The General Smuts pub was on Bloemfontein Road. Apart from that one, all the roads on the White City estate were named after Commonwealth Countries – South Africa,

Australia, Canada and New Zealand. The blocks of flats were rectangular brick structures, either facing the road or standing at ninety-degree angles to it, and most of these had names associated with the Commonwealth too. Besides the one where Irene had lived, which was called Durban, there were Auckland, Brisbane, Canberra, and a lot more besides. The pub, a square brick building with two bay windows on either side of its front door, was designed in a similar style to the flats.

As it was quarter to one, Stratton decided he might as well combine his visit with something to eat. Having bitten through the stale crust of a withered pork pie and encountered a gluey, grey filling, he wished he hadn't bothered. The plate – which, like his glass, was none too clean – sat on the sticky bar before him between puddles of ale and overflowing ashtrays. To his left, a row of grim-faced men sucked on pints and divided their time between staring into space and marking the racing pages in a manner that suggested they were already resigned to losing their money. The stout barman, trousers almost up to his armpits and a grimy towel slung over his shoulder, was leaning against the side of the cash register, apparently stupefied by the fog of cigarette smoke and inertia that hung over the room.

Pushing away the remains of his lunch, Stratton ambled over and introduced himself. On hearing who he was, the barman's sleepy eyes opened wide for a moment, and he scrambled upright, hands held up in a placatory gesture. 'Guv'nor's upstairs. I'll fetch him.'

Stratton waited, aware of the barrage of hostile stares from the drinkers at the bar. The man closest to him belched loudly, and, ramming his hat onto his head with the flat of his hand, slid off his stool and made for the door.

'Arthur Norris. How can I help?' The publican, who had a face like a Victoria plum with grog blossoms, wrung his hands together in a show of obsequiousness while the barman, who'd followed him downstairs, waddled about making half-hearted swipes at the slops on the counter with his filthy towel.

'I'd like to ask you about a group of young men who were drinking in here the evening before last.'

Norris looked dubious. 'I'll do my best, but we get a lot in here in the evenings, and I don't know everybody.'

Sensing that he was about to be met with a show of helpful non-cooperation, Stratton said, 'I realise that, but at least three of them live locally: Eddy Knight, Gordon Baxter and Ronnie Mills.'

'They come in regular, but I couldn't say the last time I saw them – don't know if it was this week even.'

'That's a pity.' Leaning casually against the bar, Stratton added, 'Because if we find out you've been lying to us, you'll lose your licence. You wouldn't want that to happen, would you?'

As expected, this worked like a charm on the landlord's memory. 'You had me there for a moment, Inspector, but I've remembered now. As I said, it's difficult with so many faces . . . But they was all here, with a couple of others –

don't know them, they've only been in three or four times
– but they had a few drinks.'

'What time was this?'

'Early on, I think it was – I wasn't down here all the time,
but I know they come in around seven, something like that.'
Turning to the barman, he said, 'You was here, Alf.'

Alf, who'd been listening, looked alarmed at being put
on the spot and said, 'You want to ask Paddy about that.'

'Who's Paddy?' asked Stratton.

'Our potman,' said Norris. 'He's out the back.'

'I'll fetch him, shall I?' Alf threw down his towel and
bustled off without waiting for an answer.

Stratton took out his notebook. 'Paddy who?'

Norris looked nonplussed. 'I don't rightly know. Come
to think of it, I don't know if Paddy's his real name, only
he's Irish, see, and they're all called that, aren't they? The
wife'll have a note of it, though. For the books,' he added
virtuously.

'Paddy', who was ushered in by Alf about thirty seconds
later, was a sallow, undersized man with a limp who turned
out to be called Joseph O'Driscoll. He had the wary look of
someone long used to being a target for bullies. 'There were
five or six of them here,' he said, after a nod from Norris.
'Out for trouble, they were. I was collecting the empties I
was, and one of them stuck out his leg and tripped me up.
Five glasses, all smashed. When I asked him what the fuck
he'd done it for, he starts giving out about it was for being
an Irish bastard.'

Norris laughed, but Stratton noticed that his colour had intensified to a lurid maroon. 'Just a bit of horseplay.'

Oh, really? thought Stratton, looking at O'Driscoll, whose face was white and pinched with suppressed anger. 'Which one was it?' he asked.

'That was Eddy Knight did that,' said Alf, bolder now. 'He's always taking the mickey out of him.'

'Do you know the others who were with Knight?'

'There's the two that you said,' said Alf, 'but most of the others are regulars. Don't know the names, though.'

'One of them's called Johnny,' said O'Driscoll. 'I heard them say it.'

'All the same age?'

'I'd say so.'

'How long did they stay?'

'I know they was gone by quarter past eight,' said Alf, 'because we run out of fags behind the bar so I went out the back for more and I saw the clock in the passage. When I come back, the table was empty.'

'They got into a van,' said O'Driscoll. 'Green delivery van, with the two doors at the back. They all piled in except the one that tripped me. I saw them through the window at the front there.' Stratton noted this down. He hadn't seen anything in the results of the house-to-house enquiries from Golborne Road about a green van, but that didn't mean it hadn't been there.

'And Eddy Knight, where did he go?'

'Came back inside.'

'Did he?' Alf looked surprised. 'I never see him.'

'He was in the corner there, sitting on the bench.' O'Driscoll indicated an old-fashioned wooden settle with high sides.

'Oh, then I wouldn't. And,' said Alf, excusing his lack of observation, 'a whole crowd come in straight after – rushed off my feet, I was.'

'How long did he stay?' asked Stratton.

'Closing time, almost,' said O'Driscoll. 'About twenty past ten a man came in and spoke to him.'

'Did you recognise the man?'

'Never seen him before. Older than the rest, and he'd be dressed in a fancy suit. Smart, and he'd a big car outside.'

'What sort of car?'

'A rich man's car. Bentley, Daimler . . .'

'Bentley, it was,' interrupted Norris. 'I'd gone upstairs for a moment and I saw it out the window.'

'Colour?'

'Black or dark blue,' said O'Driscoll. 'Hard to tell.'

'Then what happened?'

'The driver didn't stop for a drink. He just talked to your man in the corner, and then they left.'

'Together?'

O'Driscoll nodded. 'In the car.'

'Which direction?'

'That way.' He pointed to the left.

'And when the main group left, before, which way did they go?'

'The same.'

'Did you hear them say anything about where they were going?'

'The only thing one of them said was they were going to find some niggers.'

'Which one said that?'

'He'd be the dark-haired one – that modern style the young ones wear now.'

'Did he – did any of them – say anything else about that?'

'No, they just laughed.'

'Probably a joke,' put in the landlord. 'They're friendly enough, those boys.'

'Did they have any weapons on them?' Stratton asked O'Driscoll. 'Knives, anything like that?'

'Not that I could see,' said the Irishman.

'We don't have anything like that here,' put in Norris. 'I wouldn't stand for it.'

'Do you ever have coloured people coming in?'

'Not here. Got their own places, haven't they? I've nothing against them, of course,' he added hurriedly. 'Live and let live, I say, long as they behave themselves.'

'Sounds as if your customers wouldn't like it if they did come in,' said Stratton.

'This is a friendly house,' said Norris. 'We never have any trouble – do we, lads?'

Alf nodded in vigorous agreement. O'Driscoll, Stratton noticed, wasn't nearly so certain.

CHAPTER TWENTY

'So,' said Matheson, 'we've got Eddy Knight, Ronnie Mills and Gordon Baxter, all from the White City Estate, in the General Smuts pub, along with Tony Pearson and Fred Larby and possibly one or two others. And then there's the matter of whoever came to fetch them in the delivery van and the chap who came for Knight later on.'

'Unlikely that he gave him a lift home,' said Stratton, 'seeing as it can't be more than two minutes' walk, and he'd been hanging around in the pub by himself for a couple of hours.'

'But not drawing attention to himself by buying a drink or giving the Irish chap a hard time of it,' concluded Matheson. 'It's not much to go on, but it's a start, and of course there's the matter of the witness who may have recognised one of them during the assault on Johnson.'

'She denies it,' said Stratton, 'but according to the other girl, she may have said either "Johnny" or "Tommy". Knight didn't mention either of those names when I asked who was with him at the pub, but then he only mentioned four others – so that's five including him – and the potman said there were six or seven of them. There's a Johnny and a Tommy on PC Dobbs's list of known troublemakers.' Scanning the list of names again, he said, 'Thinking about it, Ronnie sounds quite a lot like Johnny, so Mills might be a possibility, although the witness denies that she knows him . . . I'll look into the other two first, though.'

'Good idea,' said Matheson. 'Anything more on Hampton?'

'Not yet, sir.'

'Pity. The last thing we want is to give the impression that we're concentrating on this case to the detriment of the other.'

'I'm beginning to wonder, sir, if the two aren't connected – tit for tat, as it were.'

'One of ours, one of theirs, you mean?' Matheson rubbed his chin wearily. 'Bloody hell! That's all we need. Things are bad enough at the moment without us stirring them up for no good reason, so for Christ's sake let's try and get a bit more corroboration before we start hauling people in. Just remember: we're sitting on a bloody big powder keg and the last thing we want is for it to blow up in our faces.'

Mr Williams's knuckles had a raw, purplish appearance, much like the skinned rabbits that hung from hooks on the rack behind his head and the scraps of meat he was feeding into the large mincer at the back of his shop. 'Tommy?' He straightened up and wiped his hands on the pink-stained front of his striped apron. He shook his head so that his florid jowls wobbled and a stub of pencil fell from its perch behind one large red ear and plopped into a bowl of liver on the counter. Retrieving it, he said, 'He's not here now.' The accent was faintly Welsh, so that 'here' came out as 'yere'.

'Where is he?'

'In Wales. His grandfather died, see, and we went to the funeral. I'm his uncle,' he added. 'He stayed behind – helping his grandmother on the farm, see?'

'When was this?'

'Last week. He'll be back on Monday. Not in trouble, is he? Tommy's a bit of a tearaway, but he's a good worker.'

'No, you're all right.' Stratton made a hasty note in his book. 'Can you tell me where Arthur's Timber Yard is?'

'Left out of the shop, and right at the end, and you're there. After Johnny Andrews, are you? I've told Tommy to keep away from him. He's been up on a charge before now – stole a car, see? But you'll know all about that.'

Outside, Stratton checked PC Dobbs's list. Against Johnny Andrews's name, he'd written an address in Bramley Road and *TDA, 6 months' conditional discharge.*

Andrews was a skinny youth of about seventeen with acne crusting his cheeks and chin. Stratton found him leaning against the freshly sawn ends of a pile of planks, smoking, his clothes covered by an oversized brown warehouseman's coat. Clearly nervous, he reluctantly admitted that he'd been in the General Smuts with the others, and left with them in the car. 'But they dropped me off, see?'

'Who was in the van?'

'All of them from the pub except Eddy.'

'Names?'

'Tony Pearson, Fred Larby, Gordon Baxter,' Andrews counted them off on his fingers. 'Ronnie Mills, me . . . I think that's the lot.'

'And who was driving?'

'Tommy Halliwell.'

Stratton jotted down the new name. 'Was he in the pub with you?'

Andrews shook his head.

'Does the vehicle belong to him?'

'Dunno.'

'What colour was it?'

'Green. I never seen it before, though.'

'Do you know where Tommy Halliwell lives?'

'Near the pub, I think. Don't know him that well.'

'On the estate?'

'That's right. Heard him saying something about how he lives near Eddy.'

'Where did they drop you?'

'Silchester Road, near the Baths.'

'Why did they drop you off?'

'Wanted to see my fiancée.'

'And did you?'

'Yes. She lives round there. You can ask her, if you like. Ask her mum and dad, an' all. Went to fetch her, didn't I?'

'What time was that?'

'About half past eight. You ask Pat.'

'That's your fiancée, is it?'

'Yes.' Andrews felt in his coat pocket, produced a wallet

and showed Stratton a photograph of a pretty, round-faced girl. 'Pat Moorehead. They live on Treadgold Street.' As Stratton was jotting this down, Andrews continued, 'I don't know where they went after, but I don't want no more trouble.'

'Why did you think there might be trouble?'

'The niggers. They're always taking liberties with us. The other day a pair of them done up one of my friends for no reason at all. I'm not going to get lumbered with that.'

'You mean, if your mates were out to get their own back?'

Andrews pressed his weight into the wood. 'Look, I don't know nothing about it. But this is our place, right? My family's been here for years. Me and Pat'll get married in Saint Clement's Church, just like our mum and dad did, and their mums and dads before them.'

Stratton walked past St Clement's Church, which was on the corner of Treadgold Street, on the way to see Pat's mother. Mrs Moorehead, as round-faced as her daughter, with neat, pink-rinsed curls, stuck her head out of her front window, the white net curtain framing it like a bridal veil. She confirmed that Andrews had, indeed, come to fetch her daughter at about half past eight. Reassuring her that her potential son-in-law wasn't in any trouble, Stratton made his way back to the station to find an address for Tommy Halliwell.

On the off-chance that Tommy's parents might have a telephone, Stratton tried the book and was pleased to discover that there was a listing for Halliwell at Canberra

House on the White City Estate. Dobbs, who was pensively chewing on one of PC Jellicoe's rock buns as if it were a particularly solid form of cud, shook his head at the mention of Halliwell's name. 'Pretty sure I've not come across him, sir, but I'll check.' Levering himself out of his chair with a sigh, he shuffled out of the office.

Five minutes later he was back, shaking his head. 'Must have kept his nose clean, because there's nothing in the records.' Sighing, he subsided back into his chair and, with an expression of grim determination, broke off another piece of the rock bun.

Twenty years ago, Stratton thought, Mrs Halliwell might have been strikingly attractive, but the passage of time had hardened her eyes and turned her skin the colour and texture of cuttlefish. Smoking irritably as she guarded her front door, she informed Stratton, with ill-concealed relish, that her son wasn't in.

'Do you know where he is?'

'He's out.' Her mouth closed in a firm line. Give me strength, thought Stratton.

'Out where?'

'Out working.' Eyes narrowed in suspicion, she added, 'What you want him for, anyway?'

Ignoring this, Stratton said, 'Where does he work?'

'He's a labourer for the North Thames Gas. Could be anywhere.'

'When's he likely to be back?'

'Don't know.'

'Does he work Saturdays?'

'Just the mornings.'

Making a note to come back early the following after-noon, Stratton said, 'Does he have a van or a car?'

'Nope.'

'Does he have a driving licence?'

'Yes. Got it two months ago, when he turned eighteen.'

'Do you know where he was the evening before last?'

Without so much as a second's pause, she shot back, 'Here, wasn't he?'

'Was he?'

'Yes, he bleedin' was. Here, with me and his dad.'

'Can anyone else confirm that?'

'You saying you don't believe me? Because we've had it up to here with you lot. Always had it in for him. First sign of trouble and you're round here. "Where is he? What's he been up to—" '

'Mrs Halliwell,' said Stratton firmly, 'this isn't just a matter of a few broken windows. I'm conducting an inquiry into a serious assault on a man who later died, and it's important you tell me the truth, because if we find out that—'

'You won't find out nothing! I'm telling you, he was here with us all the time. Now, if that's all you've come for, you've got it, haven't you?'

CHAPTER TWENTY-ONE

A burst of raucous laughter made Stratton look up from riffling through the station's telephone book for Fenella Jones's number.

'Don't I, though?' The speaker, a thick-set type of around thirty whose name, he thought, was PC Brodie, had been regaling some of the younger coppers with tales of his sexual exploits, most of it, thankfully, in hushed tones. A group of them, centred around PC Dobbs, who didn't seem to have moved since Stratton had gone out to talk to Mrs Halliwell, were taking the weight off their feet, slurping tea and lobbing bits of PC Jellicoe's rock buns at each other. 'Done my National Service in the Far East,' Brodie continued, 'and they had all sorts of girls there – Chinks, Eurasians, Wogs, the lot. Lovely, they were – dirt cheap and *very* obliging, if you know what I mean.'

'When was that?' asked Stratton.

'Forty-eight, sir. Beginning of the Malaya emergency.'

'Sounds as though you enjoyed yourself.' Stratton looked pointedly at his watch before reapplying himself to the list of names and addresses. At this mild rebuke, the group got up, slowly and resentfully, and began buttoning up their tunics, talking among themselves.

'Anyone know how Fleetwood's doing?'

'How do you think? You didn't see the state of him – great gash all down his face, poor sod. I tell you, I'm bloody glad I'm going home.'

'I don't know – be a chance to get stuck in.'

'We ought to leave them to it. Let them fight it out.'

'If the Government would just do their job and stop them coming over in the first place . . .'

Deciding he'd had enough for one day, Stratton went to find the Duty Sergeant and see if anyone could be spared the following morning for a house-to-house enquiry about a green delivery van in Golborne Road at the time Johnson was attacked, then went home.

Hesitating outside the gate at Lansdowne Road, Stratton took the scrap of paper on which he'd written Fenella's telephone number out of his trouser pocket. Several times, on the bus, he'd put his hand in to check that it was still there, and now he saw that the pencilled digits were faint and smudged. Still legible, though.

He looked at the house, imagining himself picking up the phone, talking to her . . . He put his hand on the gate, then stopped. Supposing she knocked him back? No, he'd save it for a bit. He needed to prepare himself – get a breath of fresh air and separate himself from the day. Besides, he'd been neglecting the allotment, and, what with the hot weather, the plants would be parched – if they weren't dead already. He ought to go and see what could be salvaged. After all, there was still plenty of light.

'Didn't expect to see you up here.'

Stratton's brother-in-law Donald was busy watering the rows of wilting leeks and spinach, the lowering evening sun glinting on the speckled dome of his bald head and his shirtsleeves rolled up to show thickly freckled arms. Three-year-old Tim was tottering down the rows behind his grandfather, concentrating hard on what Stratton guessed must be an imaginary watering can.

'Bit late for him to be out, isn't it?'

Don straightened up, one hand rubbing his back. 'He's not sleeping. I thought I'd get him out from under Doris's feet for a bit. It's too hot, and he's missing his mum.'

'How's she doing?' Stratton asked, feeling guilty. His niece, Madeleine, was in hospital, having had her appendix removed.

'She's fine. Doris went to see her this afternoon – says she'll be out in a couple of days. Geoff's away on one of his business trips, so Tim'll be staying with us till she gets her strength back.'

Tim lurched over to Stratton and, wrapping one arm round his leg, opened his palm to offer a very squashed raspberry. Judging by the state of his face, he'd already consumed quite a few of them himself. 'That for me?'

Tim nodded solemnly. 'They're nice.'

Stratton popped the raspberry into his mouth. 'So they are.'

'Grandpa said the lettuces went wrong.'

'It does look that way,' said Stratton, glancing at the row of plants which had exploded upwards in a whoosh of skinny, pale leaves. 'Never mind,' he said ruffling the boy's hair. 'We don't have to eat them.'

'Thought you might be too busy to get here,' said Don.

'I am a bit.'

'You look done in. Why don't you sit down? Ground's dry enough, and anyway, I'm nearly finished.'

'Thanks.' Stratton sank down gratefully. After weeks of no rain the earth around the plot was rock hard, the scuffed grass turning brown. Tim sat down beside him and began rummaging through his jacket pockets. 'Remind me to buy you a pint.'

'That's all right – we eat the stuff too, don't we? How's it going?'

Stratton grimaced.

'That bad, eh?'

'Bloody awful.'

'Go on.'

Stratton spent the next few minutes recounting the week's events, while Don pulled up weeds and Tim amused himself by aligning Stratton's notebook, wallet, handkerchief, cigarettes, matches and keys in a row at his feet.

'Know what that reminds me of?'

'Which bit?'

'Your Honourable Mrs Rutherford. Makes me think of all those books where posh Socialist types forsake their families to go and live with the proles, then come back and write about how they've got no table manners and don't give a hoot about politics.'

'Left Book Club stuff, you mean? George Orwell?'

'Not just that. There was one written by a bloke who went to live in Stepney or somewhere, and some woman who became a char for about five minutes . . .'

'I don't suppose Mrs Rutherford'll write about it.'

'No, but it's the same thing, isn't it? Slum it for a bit and – in her case – play Lady Bountiful, and dine out on it afterwards. It's not going to make a blind bit of difference to anything – and none of those people in the thirties and forties wanted it to, not really. I mean,' Donald picked up an enamel bowl and began harvesting their last crop of peas, 'all that tosh about the dignity of labour and the dictatorship of the proletariat was just *ideas*. They'd have been horrified if the Revolution had actually happened here, because whatever they may have said, that lot believed they were born to rule, and they still do. The Revolution's never going to happen because – as you've just said – the workers aren't ever going to unite because they all hate each other's guts. They don't want outsiders muscling in on their jobs – or their homes or their women.'

'I'm not interested in a Revolution,' said Stratton. 'I just want them to stop kicking each other's heads in.'

'You'll be lucky. But coming back to your Mrs Rutherford – whether she writes about it or not, it's just like when all those la-di-da types used to go on about how spontaneous and carefree the working classes were. Now they've started saying it about the coloureds.' Putting on a whinnying aristocratic tone – not actually very far from the Hon. Virginia's own – he added, 'My dear, they have so much vitality . . .'

'She's a nice woman,' Stratton protested. 'And I don't know about you, but right now I've got about as much vitality as a suet pudding.'

'Ah,' said Donald, 'but you don't count. You're a figure of authority.'

Stratton mouthed 'Piss off' over Tim's head.

'Well, you are, aren't you? And I don't doubt she's a nice woman, but if she's got any sense she'll leave well alone,' said Donald, throwing the last of the peas into the bowl and plonking himself down beside Tim, who immediately stretched out a hand to the pile of fat green pods. 'All right, but not too many or you'll get a bellyache and I'll catch it from your grandma.'

The two men smoked in companionable silence for a few minutes while Tim crammed peas into his mouth.

'Basically,' Donald leant back on his elbows and blew smoke at the sky, 'it comes down to the same thing – we're all from different tribes.'

'Here comes a stranger,' murmured Stratton. 'Let's chuck a brick at him.'

'Talking of strangers,' said Don, removing the bowl of pea pods from Tim's view, 'Doris said Pete was here a couple of days ago.'

'Yes, he was. He's getting married.'

'Oh?'

'She's called Alison. He brought her home at Easter, but I had no idea it was that serious.'

'What's she like?'

'To be honest, I don't really know. Lovely looking, and she seems to be a good influence on him. He says he wants to leave the army too.'

'And do what?'

'Join the police.'

'Following in father's footsteps, eh?' Donald broke into song: '*I don't know where he's going, But when he gets there I'll be glad, I'm following in Father's footsteps – Yes! I'm following me dear old Dad!*'

'Put a sock in it.' Stratton flicked a pea pod at him.

'Well, good luck to him. Sounds like he's found the right girl, anyway. How's Monica? We've not seen her for a while.'

'Neither have I. She's been busy working on a film about Tommy Steele's life.'

'His *life*? He can't be more than twenty-one.'

'I don't suppose he is, but it's for the fans, isn't it? Monica says he's a nice kid. Comes from Bermondsey, she said.'

'There you are – it's that old working class vitality again.' He started to croon, in a slurred, American-style drone, '*Well, I never felt more like singing the blues—*'

'For God's sake – you'll frighten the boy.'

'No, I won't. Look at him.' Stratton leant forward to peer past Donald's knees and saw that Tim was spread out like a starfish, fast asleep. 'I don't understand all that stuff.' Don scrambled to his feet, brushing the backs of his trousers.

'Leaping in the air and wriggling about – and you can't make out half the words.'

'We're old,' said Stratton. 'We're not meant to understand it.'

'God knows what music'll be like by the time he's our age.' Don nodded at Tim. 'Oh, well. Come on chum, let's give you a heave-ho.'

The child murmured something as Don picked him up. Seeing their faces close together Stratton thought how alike they looked – Tim couldn't have got his sandy hair and the pale skin on which clusters of freckles were beginning to emerge like spots on a Dalmatian puppy from anyone else but his grandfather. Following the pair of them down the path to the road, he found himself wondering who his future grandchildren would take after. It was interesting that his news about Pete hadn't prompted a question from Don about Monica's personal life. When he considered this, Stratton realised that no one had asked about that for quite some time. It seemed that without ever having been officially informed that Monica and her friend Marion were a couple, the rest of the family had accepted that marriage and children weren't on the cards for her . . . And they'd long ago given up asking him about himself.

He said goodbye to Don and Tim outside his front gate. His resolve to telephone Fenella there and then wavered when he caught sight of an envelope on the mat with Diana's handwriting and a foreign stamp. Perhaps he should read it first and then call Fenella, or should he call first? Or maybe he ought to give it a miss tonight and call her tomorrow.

After all, she might be out. Fully aware that he was making excuses, Stratton went upstairs to take off his jacket and tie. He took his time about washing his hands and face and combing water through his hair, wondering why it was that the idea of telephoning Fenella on the same evening as reading Diana's letter seemed so distasteful. After all, he was no longer involved with Diana, so where was the problem? And what the bloody hell was the matter with him? Usually he just got on with things, and now here he was, dithering like some elderly spinster trying to choose a wedding present.

Feeling that he must do something, he went down to the scullery to see what Lilian (it was her turn) had left for his dinner. Lilian had never been any great shakes when it came to cooking, and in the year since Reg's death she'd definitely got worse. Telling himself he shouldn't complain – it was very kind of her and Doris to look after him in the way they had, unfailingly, since Jenny's death – he whisked the cloth from the dishes, uncovering three slices of spam arranged around a bit of salad and some cold rice pudding for after. Wishing he'd brought back some of the raspberries from the allotment, he took the whole thing through to the kitchen where he made himself a cup of tea, cut some bread and sat down at the table.

Spent the entire voyage feeling ghastly . . . travelling on the train was a hoot . . . absolutely in my element with a whole house to decorate . . . Lester says it's hotter here than in Ceylon, which I don't think can possibly be right, but he insists it's so . . . Ceylon? Of course, Manning's last British film had been a Second

World War thing set in a POW camp, the success of which had led to the offer from Hollywood. Diana had said something about it being done abroad, hadn't she? *L has already started work on a film. It's a romantic comedy and I think it sounds awful, but L seems happy enough. I'm sure it will be all right, just silly nerves on my part, & of course I haven't said anything . . . People have parties all the time here, and the head of the studio has invited us to the Sands Hotel (Las Vegas!) to see Frank Sinatra . . . Thank you for everything, Edward. You will always mean so much to me . . . Good luck, my dearest. You, more than anyone I know, deserve to be happy, as I am with L.*

Stratton put down the letter. His plate, with its spam and salad, was untouched, but he didn't want it now. There was a finality about Diana's last words that made him wistful but, at the same time, warmed his heart. As to whether anyone 'deserved' to be happy – in that way or in any other – he didn't know, but he was going to have a damn good try. He would telephone Fenella. Not tonight, but tomorrow. He felt, in an absurd, almost chest-bursting way that he knew he'd never be able to articulate, that Diana – like Jenny before her – had given him her blessing.

CHAPTER TWENTY-TWO

Stratton decided to look in on Irene on his way to the station. He could hear the sounds of the Saturday market in Portobello Road as soon as he emerged from Ladbroke Grove Station. With the sunshine and blue sky, the vivid impression of colour and bustle and noise made him forget, for a moment, the rusting railings, crumbling garden walls and peeling shopfronts that surrounded the place, and reminded him of exotic foreign bazaars seen in films. It didn't look like England at all. Close to, he could pick out vivid African head cloths, alongside chiffon scarves concealing curlers. Pork pie hats and, once, a Sikh turban, behind stalls stacked with everything from vegetables to bric-a-brac, the uneven pavements were piled high with wooden fruit boxes, and women were pawing through heaps of rancid second-hand clothing and misshapen shoes. The jostling was good-natured, white and black housewives with prams and bags of shopping were chatting to each other, and nobody was arguing. What a pity, thought Stratton, as he made his way through the crowd, that it couldn't be like this all the time.

He paused in the grimy hallway at Powis Terrace to help a young mother who was attempting to negotiate the stairs with a bawling toddler and a pram in which a furious, red-faced baby was wedged with bags of groceries. What with the yelling of the children and the clatter and scrape of the wheels on the stairs, Stratton hadn't registered the noise from above until they'd manoeuvred the pram safely onto the landing, knocking over half a dozen empty milk bottles in the process.

'Thanks, mister,' said the woman, who was already, at barely nine o'clock, whey-faced with exhaustion. Grimacing in the direction of the shouts – which were coming, Stratton now realised, from Etheridge and Irene's rooms – she added, in a voice hollow with resignation, 'I'll never get him off to sleep with that lot going on. I tell you, we've never had a moment's peace since we moved in.' As she unlocked the door and shoved the pram through it, Stratton caught a glimpse of the single room where they lived. Pervaded with the smell of soaking nappies, every surface, including the bed and most of the floor, was strewn with a jumble of clothing, crockery and broken toys.

On the landing, Stratton stood for a moment, listening intently. He could hear Etheridge's voice, loud and accusing, and a quieter male voice, whose words he could not catch.

'What happen to "all of we is brothers together"?' Etheridge was shouting. 'Tell me that! Don't fuck with me, man – where she gone?'

Stratton knocked on the door. There was silence for a second, before it was jerked open and Etheridge's head appeared. 'What you—' he began, then turned abruptly away to mutter something.

Walker was sitting at the table, but on seeing Stratton he jumped to his feet, looking alarmed. Of Irene there was no sign, and the evidence of female occupation that Stratton had seen before – talcum powder and cosmetics on the mantelshelf, a pair of stockings hanging on a clothes horse – was gone. 'Everything all right?' he asked. 'I came to see how Miss Palmer was doing.'

'She not 'ere,' said Etheridge shortly. 'I don't know where she gone.'

'I see.' Deliberately not looking in Walker's direction, Stratton said, 'Well, in that case, I'll leave you to it. Might be a good idea to keep the noise down, though – there's a lady with a small baby next door, and I think she'd appreciate a bit of hush.'

When Walker caught up with him a few minutes later, Stratton could see that one side of his face was puffed and turning shiny from a bruise.

'She's gone?'

'Yesterday – while he was out. The Jew offered her a room and a job in that club, like you said.'

'Where's the room?'

'Above the club, he told her. Came to fetch her in his car while Etheridge was out. Neighbours staring out of the windows . . .' Walker shook his head.

'It's better than sending her back home,' said Stratton firmly. 'And I think Mr Laskier will look after her.' Seeing

Walker's frown, he added, 'He said that Irene reminded him of his sister.'

'Oh?' The monosyllable was loaded with disbelief.

'I think,' said Stratton, 'that his sister may have died in the war. In a concentration camp.'

Walker's frown deepened. 'If things happen to people – bad things – they don't care any more. They're just out for themselves, like Clinton.'

'I know. But I think Laskier's different.'

'Well, I hope so. Irene . . . She's a nice girl.'

'Don't worry,' said Stratton. 'I shall be keeping an eye on her.' Tapping the side of his face, he said, 'Was that Etheridge?'

'Yes. He thinks I'm after Irene myself.'

'But you didn't tell him anything?'

Walker shook his head. 'Better for him to think that. I can look after myself. And he'll find out where she's gone soon enough.'

This, thought Stratton afterwards, was undoubtedly true but somehow he didn't think that Etheridge would pursue Irene if he thought that she had, effectively, been poached by someone higher up the food chain. It was entirely possible that Gloria would get wind of it and, putting two and two together, give Etheridge a piece of her mind . . . Not that it would stop him finding other fish to fry, of course, but it would mean that in all probability he'd leave Irene alone . . .

As it was close by, Stratton decided to see if Laskier was

in his office and walked round to Westbourne Grove. The basement door was opened by one of the largest men that Stratton had ever seen. Several inches taller than his own 6 foot 3, he was built like a brick shithouse, with colossal feet, hands like shovels, and an unstable look in his eye that suggested he might attack without warning. He made a rumbling noise like a cement mixer, then said in gravelly, heavily accented English, 'Mr Perlmann no here. Play tennis.'

Blinking at the grotesque image of the portly Perlmann bulging in a tennis shirt and shorts, Stratton said, 'It's Mr Laskier I want.'

'What is it, Jan?' Laskier appeared and, murmuring something to the big man in what Stratton supposed must be Polish, ushered him inside. The disorder he'd noticed on his two previous visits seemed to have got worse. Now there were piles of papers on the floor as well as the other surfaces, and a third man, almost as big as Jan, with thick curly hair and shoulders that made Stratton think of a bison, was sitting with his feet up on one of the desks, staring at him with barely concealed hostility. A large, hairy Alsatian sprawled by his chair. It didn't move when Stratton walked in, but followed his progress across the room from under flickering eyebrows. Laskier, who looked – if it were possible – even more tired than he had before, gave the pair of them a despairing glance.

'Can I have a word with you in private?'

'If you wish.' Laskier turned to the two men and said something else in Polish, whereupon they left, taking the dog with them.

'Who were they?'

'They collect the rent, help with the houses . . .'

'Perlmann's charity cases?'

'He helps them, yes. Jan – the one who came to the door – he isn't quite right here.' Laskier tapped his temple. 'Something happened in the war. An injury on his head. Danny finds some small jobs for him to do, to make him feel as if he is useful.'

'Poor chap. How's Irene doing?'

'Mr Walker told you, did he? She's getting settled into the flat. The manageress lives up there, so she's not on her own.'

'That's good. What about Etheridge?'

Laskier frowned. 'What about him?'

'What's his position with Perlmann?'

Laskier sighed. 'I asked Danny about the new flat he'd promised and he told me it was a favour because Etheridge had been collecting rent for him. I had not known this.'

'Was that to stop him going to the Rent Tribunal?'

'I have no idea. Danny is impulsive, Inspector. He makes arrangements and he doesn't remember to tell me.'

'Would Etheridge have tried to stop Hampton encouraging people to go to the Tribunal? Warned him off?'

'Danny would never ask him to do something like that.'

'You really are loyal to him, aren't you?'

Laskier stared at him. 'He saved my life,' he said shortly. 'Anything else you want?'

'Do you know about this party that Etheridge and Mrs Rutherford are planning?'

Laskier shrugged. 'I heard something. It's not important.'

'Not important that Etheridge is working for Mr Perlmann and cosying up with the Rent Tribunals lot at the same time?'

'Danny doesn't think so.'

'What do you think?'

'Ach . . .' Laskier shook his head. 'What I think . . . I think it's complicated. Do you know, Inspector, that Virginia Rutherford's father was one of the men who gave Danny a start in this business?'

Stratton recalled Perlmann saying that Mrs Rutherford was the daughter of an earl. 'How do you mean?'

'Please, Inspector, sit down. Long story, if you want to hear . . .' Waving him towards the chair recently vacated by one of the Poles, Laskier dragged another one over to the other side of the desk and sat down facing him, arms on the table. 'You know how the houses here were built in the time of Queen Victoria?'

'Yes,' said Stratton, puzzled. 'I'm aware of that.'

'Then you know also they were built on land owned by the smart families, aristocrats like Mrs Rutherford's father, yes?'

'Yes,' said Stratton, wondering where this was leading.

'So those families,' continued Laskier, getting into his stride, 'gave a lease of one hundred years to a builder: and they took a payment of ground rent. It's good business for the builder, he sells the houses on, makes his money – houses for big families, rich, with servants to look after them.' Laskier made an expansive gesture with his hands. 'And then,' Laskier brought his hands together, 'everything got small again. Smaller families, smaller money, servants gone and people with more money move away, so the houses are split up, the leases sold on, sublet, sublet, until – by the time it's one hundred years later – it's a big tangle and nobody makes a profit any more. The houses haven't been looked after for years, so it's expensive to fix them, and now the ground rent is . . . pfft! So small it is barely worth the trouble to make the collection. So, these original owners, what do they do? They sell. It's a mess – poor families, prostitutes, criminals, Negroes – they don't want to have an association with that sort of people, so . . . goodbye.' Laskier pushed his hair back from his face and, as he did so, Stratton caught sight of a long puckered scar, white against the sallow skin of his forehead.

'And that's where you come in, is it?' he asked.

Laskier nodded. 'Danny asked me to help him set up a company to buy houses. Then he'd buy the tenants out and sell the property for a higher price within the week.'

'Where did he get the money?'

'Inspector,' Laskier wagged his head, 'if you want to succeed in property you do not need money – all you need is to know people who can get hold of money. There are always people willing to lend if you offer to pay a little extra. We found a solicitor with the use of some trust funds. As long as they receive a good rate of interest, the trustees don't mind how the money is invested. They don't ask – why should they?'

'How did you find the solicitor?'

'The estate agent who was selling the properties introduced him to Danny. This is why I am telling you, Inspector. The first properties Danny purchased were houses that belonged to Virginia Rutherford's father, and some of the money he borrowed to buy them was from family's trust funds, including hers.'

'So,' said Stratton, making sure he'd got it clear, 'Perlmann used Mrs Rutherford's family's money to buy their estate from them.'

'That's right.' Laskier described a circle in the air with one finger. 'Ver-ry neat. A small part of the estate, of course. At first Danny had only four houses – more later, and from other estates too. Mortgage one hundred per cent at a nice high rate of interest so Mrs Rutherford and her family got a good return on their money. They weren't doing us favours, you know. You look surprised, Inspector.'

'I am. Surely Mrs Rutherford wouldn't have—'

'You think she knew about it? The money was held in trust until she was married – which was not so many years ago – so she had the interest, but not the capital sum. And as long as the interest was coming – money in the bank – why ask questions?'

'But—'

'Before you can ask a question, Inspector, you have to know what the question is. Mrs Rutherford's family is rich. She feels guilty about this, that she has – in her pocket, at least – good luck while others have bad luck but she doesn't question where the money comes from, because it is simply *there* and it has always been there, and always will be there.

How can she have any idea of what the world is like? Do you think a woman like that knows anything about money except for how to spend it?' Laskier leant forward, sunken eyes glittering so that he seemed more hawkish than ever, hands gripping the edge of the table like the claws of a bird of prey about to strike. 'You think she has any idea that a world could exist where men were so hungry – so desperate – that we ate shit in order to survive?'

CHAPTER TWENTY-THREE

Walking towards Harrow Road in the bright sunshine, Stratton reflected that while he could see what Laskier meant about the Hon. Virginia being naive, what the two men had been through was something that most people would struggle to imagine. To be reduced to eating excrement in order to stay alive . . . Feeling the stirrings of nausea, he deliberately kept his eyes averted from the piles of white, crumbling dog turds scattered round the bases of the trees along the pavement.

More than that, though, it was the pain in Laskier's eyes that stayed with him. He thought of Perlmann, flipping aside the pile of letters and saying, 'Nothing matters.' In those situations, so bad that the unthinkable became the obvious solution, morals were a luxury.

For no logical reason – or anyway, no reason that he could properly justify, even to himself – Stratton decided to take a quick detour and see if he could buy the silver bracelet he'd seen in the shop on his first visit to Colville Terrace. It wasn't as though he was thinking of presenting it to Fenella, or anything like that. She might not care for such things, and as they had yet to make plans for dinner, it was definitely jumping the gun . . . But it was nice to buy a present for someone, and he'd enjoy doing it – and anyway, he could always give it to Monica.

The interior of the shop was dark. The elderly and shrivelled proprietor – who, despite the weather, was wearing a woollen waistcoat and knitted fingerless gloves – emerged from a jumble of furniture and what might have been surgical appliances stacked haphazardly at the rear. The transaction conducted – ten and six – Stratton peered out through the dusty window while the old man rooted about the capacious drawers of a vast antique writing desk for a jewellery box. Broken glass glittered on the tarmac further down the road, and, craning his neck, Stratton saw that it came from smashed windows on the first floors of two of the buildings opposite.

'Last night, that was.' Strings of thick white saliva shone at the corners of the wizened mouth. 'Gang of hooligans.'

'Seems pretty peaceful now,' said Stratton, thinking of the market down the road.

'Now it does, but you wait.' The old man nodded his head with a prophetic emphasis that reminded him of old Mr Russell and repeated, with gloomy satisfaction, 'You wait.'

Returning to the station, Stratton realised that Laskier's account of Perlmann's business had omitted a big chunk of the story. There must have been several staging posts between his arrival in London and acquiring the houses.

The black market, he guessed, remembering the spivs on Wardour Street after the war with their suitcases full of cheap watches, nylons and bottles of coloured water, and then – another guess – renting flats in his own name and subletting to prostitutes for far more money. He knew little about financial dealings but supposed that, if the lender were greedy enough and the borrower prepared to pay extra interest, it was possible to get an unsecured loan. His own mortgage would be paid off next year – the house in Lansdowne Road had been bought in 1934, when Monica and Pete were small. He'd be the first one in his family to own a house. His brother Dick, like their father before him, rented the farm, going every quarter to pay at the estate office. He wasn't at all sure that he'd have thought of taking out a mortgage himself if it hadn't been for the influence of Jenny's father, who'd been, in a small way, a speculative builder of flats in Tottenham, and he'd certainly had a few sleepless nights over it . . . As to Perlmann, he supposed you had to admire the sheer brass neck of the thing, if nothing else. He increased his pace. He needed to stop wasting time and find out how they'd got on with the enquiries about the green van in Golborne Road, and then he needed to talk to Tommy Halliwell.

'I wouldn't climb over her to get to you, Dobbsy.'

PC Jellicoe, Dobbs and several of the others were staring, with some relish, at an array of recently confiscated pornographic photographs which, for no good reason that Stratton could see, had been placed on display alongside the previous night's haul of assorted weapons. They appeared to consist of matronly-looking women offering their breasts or buttocks to the camera with expressions of housewifely satisfaction, as though dishing up a particularly fine Sunday roast. They weren't – to his eyes, at least – even faintly erotic.

'I'd give her one, sir,' said one of the younger coppers. He looked, Stratton thought, barely old enough to shave, never mind anything else.

'I'll give you one round the ear if you don't clear off,' retorted Jellicoe. 'You've no business in here.'

'I'm meant to be here, sir. Duty Sergeant said I was to speak to Inspector Stratton, sir. Information about the van on Golborne Road.'

'Fair enough,' said Jellicoe. 'He's right here. Say what you've got to say, then scram.'

Stratton perched on a corner of the nearest desk and took out his notebook. 'Fire away.'

'We went house-to-house this morning, sir,' The lad's cockiness was replaced, now, with eagerness to impress. 'There's a man who lives above the hardware shop. That's next to the grocer's where the attack took place, sir. He said he was looking out of the window when the ambulance came, and he saw a green van parked on the opposite side of the road.'

'So that would be when? Quarter to nine?'

'About then, sir, nearest he could say. He said the van wasn't there the following morning.'

The van being there made sense, thought Stratton. If the

gang had chased after Irene and Gloria, they might have decided it best not to return immediately.

'Did he say which way it was facing?'

'Away from the bridge, sir.'

'Did anyone else notice it?'

'Bloke who was coming out of the pub—'

'That's the Earl of Warwick?'

'Yes, sir. He was with his mate. They saw Johnson lying on the pavement, and Mrs Marwood when she come out of the telephone box with the baby, and they saw the van. He lives on the other side of the railway bridge and he said he was pretty sure it didn't belong to anyone local, or he'd have recognised it.'

'But he said it was green, did he?'

'Yes, sir. Green, and no windows at the back. He thought it was a Bedford.'

'Thank you . . .'

'Illingworth, sir.'

'Thank you, Illingworth.'

'Now scram,' said PC Jellicoe, as Illingworth's eyes strayed towards the photographs on the table, 'before you stunt your growth.'

Mrs Halliwell had said that her son worked only on Saturday mornings, so there was, Stratton thought, a good chance – after he'd had some lunch – of catching him at home, or, failing that, in the General Smuts pub.

Deciding he'd prefer to try his luck in one of the local cafes rather than risk a repeat visit to the canteen, he was walking past the front desk when he saw, standing in the sunlight that streamed in through the open front doors, the unmistakable – and even more attractive than he'd remembered – form of Fenella Jones.

CHAPTER TWENTY-FOUR

The sun was shining on her hair and outlining the profile of her figure, slender in a pale green, fitted dress. Stratton was all too aware that not only was he staring at her but that he felt as breathless as if he'd just been thumped in the solar plexus, and seriously doubted his ability to speak. Do something, he urged himself. Say something. Don't just bloody stand there with your mouth open.

She'd seen him now, and she was smiling, walking towards him. She was saying something, but, too intent on her face, on her lips, he hadn't picked it up . . . For Christ's sake, you fucking idiot, talk to her!

'Hello,' he said lamely.

'Hello, Inspector.'

She was still smiling, looking expectant. What the hell was wrong with him? What did he think she was going to do – bite him? Keeping his eyes firmly on her face, he said, 'I'm glad I've run into you. I've been meaning to telephone, but the last couple of days have been rather . . .' Realising it sounded like an excuse, and might not be taken the right way, he stopped in confusion.

'Heavens, don't apologise. I've been following it in the newspaper. All this fighting . . .'

Feeling relieved, Stratton said, 'It does keep us on our toes,' then thought, before he'd got even half the words out, that it was a thoroughly stupid thing to say. 'What are you—' He stopped: what are you doing here sounded like some sort of accusation, but he couldn't think of a polite way to phrase it. 'I mean . . .'

'Why am I here?' God, her mouth was beautiful. 'A mix-up, really. I was supposed to collect a child, but apparently someone else has taken him, so I'm surplus to requirements.'

Now or never, thought Stratton. 'In that case, I don't suppose you'd care to join me for a bite of lunch? I thought I'd try one of the cafes.'

Fenella looked taken aback. 'Aren't you busy? On duty, I mean?'

'I am, but –' Stratton laughed to show it wasn't a rebuke, 'they do let us stop to eat.'

'Of course, but . . . Well, yes, I'd love to. If it's not putting you out, that is.'

'Not at all.'

'She ran away from home a few months ago. She's only thirteen, but I don't think the mother can want her back all that much, because she didn't report it. The father's left, apparently, and there are three other children, all much younger, and she's expecting another, so I suppose she's got her hands full.'

They found a rather nice and very quiet cafe a few streets

away from the station, where they sat eating surprisingly pleasant sandwiches beneath a colourful mural of a Venetian canal. It looked, Stratton thought, a damn sight better than the smelly Grand Union round the corner: lots of gondolas and stripy poles sticking out of the nice blue water, and not a dead cat or a used contraceptive in sight. He made a conscious decision to stay with safe, work-related topics of conversation and not – unless Fenella were to lead the way – to stray into the arena of the personal. In the middle of the working day it felt wrong and besides there would, he very much hoped, be plenty of time for that on future occasions. 'Do you know why the girl ran away?' he asked.

'She made all sorts of wild accusations about being raped by a gang of boys, but when she was asked for details she came up with another story, about how the mother's new boyfriend had interfered with her . . .' Fenella sighed. 'I say it's a story, but actually I think it's quite likely to be the truth, although no one seems to believe it. Why on earth anyone thinks it's a good idea to send her back home, I don't know – but of course there's nothing else to be done with her, unless she turns out to be pregnant. And if it's the mother's boyfriend's baby and the mother knows it . . . I hate to think what's going to happen.'

Struck by her matter-of-factness, Stratton said, 'I suppose you've seen quite a lot of this sort of thing.'

Fenella shook her head. 'I've led a very sheltered life, Inspector—'

'Ted.'

'Sorry, Ted. My father was a JP for a time, and I remember

overhearing the odd snatches of conversation about young people who'd come up before him, but it wasn't . . . Oh, dear. I was going to say they weren't people like us, but that sounds horribly like snobbery. It's that I never connected them with us, or with any of the people I knew.'

'I know what you mean. But lots of kids go through a difficult phase, and they're not all from broken homes,' said Stratton, thinking of his nephew, Johnny, who'd managed, by the skin of his teeth, to avoid ending up in borstal.

'Yes, I suppose that's true. But I've got a lot to learn. I still spend quite a lot of time trying not to make judgements or show that I'm shocked. And I still shock myself when I hear myself asking the sorts of questions I'd never have imagined . . .'

'Such as?'

Adopting a prim, official tone, Fenella said, ' "Is he the father of all three of your children?" And *he* never seems to be married to her. I've found that husbands are in rather short supply, especially in Notting Dale. I suppose,' she added, 'that you must think me very naive.'

'Not really,' said Stratton. 'It's one thing tutting over those sorts of things when they're at arm's length in the newspapers but quite different when you're dealing with people face to face on a daily basis. I came across a situation recently like the one you were talking about before. This particular girl is a bit older, but she said she was thirteen when her stepfather started his tricks. She ran away too, after a few years, and ended up living with a chap who wanted to put her on the streets.'

'What happened?'

'Well, she was adamant that she didn't want to return home, so we found her a job and another place to live.'

Fenella raised her eyebrows. 'The police did? Shouldn't they have sent her back home?'

'It wasn't official – and, as you just said, home isn't always the best place. Believe it or not, her landlord agreed to help.'

'*Really?*'

'They're not all monsters, you know. At least, not all the time.'

'I suppose not, but one does hear such awful stories . . .'

'Are you going to this shindig this evening?'

'Councillor Watson's party, you mean? Yes. Are you?'

Stratton shook his head. 'Not invited. Don't want a policeman putting a damper on things . . . Mrs Rutherford told me about it. It should be interesting.'

'Yes, I suppose so.'

'You sound dubious.'

Fenella fiddled with her coffee cup for a moment, then said, 'It's probably silly – and I'm sure it *is* good idea, in principle – but I'm worried that it's going to be terribly awkward and we might end up offending people without meaning to. Virginia – Mrs Rutherford – thinks it's really going to break the ice, but I keep imagining a whole roomful of people trying terrifically hard to be friendly and natural and nice to one another but not having the foggiest idea what to say and everyone as stiff as boards . . . That sounds terribly negative, doesn't it? But I suppose I've never been all that keen on parties, really – or not that sort of party, anyway.'

'I know what you mean,' said Stratton. 'I'm sure they have the best of motives. Have you known Mrs Rutherford long?'

'About a year. We were new girls together, really – although she'd grown up doing charity work, helping her mother.'

'*Noblesse oblige*,' said Stratton.

'Definitely,' said Fenella. A sudden, impish smile lighting up her face, she added, 'You'll probably think me awful for saying this, but one of the reasons I feel so uneasy about this wretched party is that I keep remembering something my great aunt told me. She and my grandmother had both been in service, but Grandma had married rather well and didn't like being reminded . . . Great Aunt Phoebe never married – she'd started when she was twelve and gone all the way up till she became a housekeeper, and when she retired she came to live with us. One of the stories she used to tell was about the servants' ball at Christmas, when she'd worked in one of these huge places, about how the countess or whoever she was had to have the first waltz with the butler, and how all the house guests tried to make conversation with the staff and had absolutely no idea what to say to them. Oh, dear. I hope you don't think I'm being catty, but there's just, you know . . .'

'I know you don't mean it unkindly,' said Stratton. 'I take it you haven't mentioned any of this to Mrs Rutherford.'

Fenella laughed. 'If I told her my grandmother and great aunt were in service she'd be terribly embarrassed. But I shouldn't laugh. My family never did anything for charity, unless you count knitting horrible tea cosies and things to sell at the church bazaar.'

Stratton imagined a suburban background with tennis courts, laurel hedges and tidy nature. 'We didn't do much either,' he said, 'apart from the harvest festival and a few shillings for the mission.'

'Ah, yes,' said Fenella. 'Farmer Giles.'

'You remembered,' said Stratton, feeling ridiculously pleased.

'Of course,' said Fenella lightly. 'But coming back to this event tonight, I really do hope it succeeds, for Virginia's sake if nothing else. It's the way she's put her heart and soul into it. She's such a good, decent person.'

'Yes,' said Stratton, remembering what he'd seen at Maxine's and guessing Fenella had witnessed something similar, 'but not a very happy one.'

Fenella stared into her cup for a moment, then said thoughtfully, 'I don't think she's ever been loved. She told me once that her mother had said – when she came out – that at least she had money, so somebody would be bound to marry her. And then she said that nobody had, even for that.'

'Until Rutherford came along,' said Stratton. 'I've met him.'

'She's never really talked about him, but when I met him . . . Well, one could see: he doesn't take any notice of her, does he?'

'He certainly didn't seem to. He was behaving like a . . . As if she wasn't even in the room. She didn't appear to be taking any more notice of him than he was of her, but—'

'That doesn't mean she didn't mind,' said Fenella, with sudden vehemence. 'I'm sorry, I just don't like to think of people laughing at her. It isn't fair.'

'I wasn't,' protested Stratton. 'I didn't mean to—'

'I know,' said Fenella. 'I didn't think *you* were laughing at her. It's just that it's humiliating, having your husband eyeing every other woman in the room.' She flushed and started fiddling with her cup again, turning it round and round in the saucer. 'And I *am* sorry – I've said far too much.'

Unsure whether she meant she'd said too much about the Hon. Virginia, or about the last bit, which must have been – however unlikely it seemed – an allusion to her own marriage, Stratton couldn't think of anything to say in response. Feeling in his pocket for cigarettes, his fingers encountered the small jewel case with the bracelet inside. On impulse, he fished it out and slid it across the table. Fenella let go of her cup and stared at it for a moment. When she raised her eyes, they were puzzled and slightly nervous.

'I bought it this morning,' said Stratton. What the bloody hell am I doing? he thought. She'll think I've gone off my rocker. 'Have a look.'

Fenella opened the box, but made no move to touch the bracelet. 'It's very pretty,' she said, 'but I don't—'

'Why don't you try it on?'

'But . . . Isn't it for someone?'

'It's for you, if you'd like it.'

Now, she was looking actually alarmed. Oh, God, why had he done it? 'I don't want anything . . . in exchange,' he said. 'That is, apart from your company, which,' he continued in a rush, 'I'm enjoying very much. To be honest, I don't really know why I bought it. I saw it a few days ago, and when I went past the shop again it was still there, in the window, so . . . I'm not in the habit of just buying jewellery on a whim – or buying anything, really – but it caught my eye and I just . . .' Just what, exactly? The process, step by step, of the thoughts and feelings that had culminated in buying the bracelet were too complex and unwieldy for any neat explanation, but, sitting there in front of Fenella, he knew why he'd bought it, all right: because he was lonely. In essence, it was as simple as that. 'I'm not explaining this very well, am I?'

'Not really,' said Fenella. She still hadn't touched the bracelet.

'I promise I'm not going to try and pounce on you, or anything like that. When I first saw it, sitting in that window, I hadn't even met you. I just looked at it, and I thought it was a long time since I'd bought a present – for a woman, I mean. Look, I'm sorry. It was a stupid thing to do. I didn't mean to offend you.'

'I'm not offended.' For a moment, Stratton couldn't read the expression on Fenella's face – and then she smiled. It wasn't a nervous smile, but the wide, intimate one he'd seen before. Holding out her wrist, she said, 'Why don't you put it on and we'll see how it looks?'

CHAPTER TWENTY-FIVE

Turning the car into the White City Estate, Stratton found himself resting his elbow on the open window, singing 'The Wild Colonial Boy' and feeling, for the first time since he'd arrived at Harrow Road, uncomplicatedly happy. Despite – or possibly because of – that daft business with the bracelet, the chance meeting with Fenella had gone off better than he could have hoped. She had not only kept the thing – and left still wearing it – but she'd also agreed to have dinner with him next week and, when they'd parted company outside the cafe, given him a swift and very discreet peck on the cheek.

Still singing, Stratton pulled up outside Canberra House, 'At the early age of seventeen, He left his native home; And to Australia's sunny shores, he was inclined to roam . . .' and started up the stairwell. 'He robbed the rich to feed the poor, He stabbed James MacIlroy; A terror to Australia was the wild— Christ!' A man charged round the bend in the stairs above him and thundered past in a blur, knocking him with his shoulder and catching him off balance so that he fell hard against the wall. Swearing, he righted himself and, in doing so, saw above him, for just a second before they disappeared from view, a pair of over-made-up eyes and a black bouffant that looked remarkably like Mrs Halliwell's.

Realising that she must have been looking out of the window and seen him coming, Stratton raced back downstairs after Thomas Halliwell. Spotting him sprinting across the grass some two hundred yards away, heading for Wormwood Scrubs prison and the enormous stretch of parkland beyond, he gave chase, cursing himself for his inattention.

A minute later he realised with a shock that Halliwell – being far younger and a hell of a lot fitter – was getting away from him. He forced himself to speed up but, after another minute or so, sweating like a pig with bursting lungs and burning leg muscles, he was about to give up when Halliwell, running past a clump of trees, tripped on a root and sprawled, a tangle of lanky limbs, on the parched grass.

Clutching the stitch in his side, Stratton managed to get to him just as he was struggling to his feet, and brought him down with a violent lunge to the knees (although, as he admitted to himself afterwards, the reason it worked had a lot more to do with his weight than any rugby-playing finesse). Pinning Halliwell to the ground with one knee in the small of his back, Stratton, whose arms felt as if they'd been torn out of their sockets, concentrated on breathing rather than speaking. After a moment he managed, between deep, rasping gulps of air, to get out, 'What's your name?'

'Mind your own business!' Halliwell began to struggle, catching Stratton a sharp blow in the eye with his elbow.

'Name!' Stratton gasped. Jesus, his lungs were on fire.

'Take your hands off me, or I'll have you for assault!'

'I said, name!' When was the last time he'd chased someone? He couldn't actually remember. Christ, what had happened to him? He was falling apart.

'Fuck off!'

Stratton gave him a clip round the ear with his free hand, making him yelp. 'Listen, son, I'm too old for this, all right?'

'He's got Tommy.'

Spotting a pair of grubby plimsolls and grey, baggy socks in front of his face, Stratton looked up sharply to find that he was being stared at by eight pairs of shrewd young eyes. A group of boys aged nine or ten were standing in front of them. Judging from the fact that one was clutching a tennis ball, another, a bat, and a third, what looked like three sawn-off broom handles, they were on their way to, or possibly from, an improvised game of cricket. Wonderful, thought Stratton. As if this wasn't enough of a shambles already – now he was in a fucking Ealing Comedy.

'What you doing with Tommy, Mister?' asked the one holding the bat.

'I'm a policeman,' said Stratton, trying to control his ragged breathing. 'Now scram.'

'Where's your uniform, then?' said the one with the stumps.

'He don't look like a policeman to me.' The one with the bat narrowed his eyes. 'He looks like that bloke what used to—'

'Wait a minute,' said Stratton, sensing, with a growing

feeling of unreality, that he was about to be compared to some swivel-eyed local pederast. Digging his knee even more firmly into Tommy's back, and using one hand to pin him down by his scrawny neck – he could feel the vibrations of suppressed laughter through his palm – he used the other hand to feel inside his jacket for his warrant card.

'It can't be,' said another, with authority. 'My dad said he's in prison.'

'*My* dad said he should be hanged,' said someone else.

'*My* dad said they should cut off his—'

'Here,' said Stratton, dragging out his warrant card and holding it up. 'I'm arresting him, and I'll arrest you lot too if you don't clear off.'

The boys goggled at him for a moment and then, as Tommy gave a gurgle of laughter, broke their line and ran, whooping, across the grass.

'I don't know what you've got to laugh about, *Tommy*. Those kids just identified you, and I saw your mum looking over the banisters when you came down the stairs like the Charge of the Light Brigade.'

'What d'you want to ask me for, then?'

'Less of it!' Stratton would have dearly liked to clobber him again, but, seeing in his mind's eye an image of himself taking revenge on Halliwell for witnessing his humiliation at the hands of the children, thought better of it. Nevertheless, it was all very well for Matheson to talk about powder kegs and not stirring things up, but he was buggered if he was chasing this bunch of toerags round the manor all on his tod, never mind having to contend with gangs of vigilante brats while he was at it. 'I'm taking you in.'

'Whaffor?'

'Because I want you for a fucking sunbeam. You know damn well what for because your mummy told you about my visit, didn't she? Now, for the third time of asking: What. Is. Your. Name?'

'Tom Halliwell.'

'That's more like it. In case Mummy didn't pass this on, I am DI Stratton from the Harrow Road nick.' Stratton took out his handkerchief and mopped his brow.

'*Are* you arresting me?'

'No, I'm not. I'm asking you – very nicely – to accompany me. Now, are you going to come quietly? Because if you don't I shall be forced to conclude that you're as guilty as sin and before you know it –' he grabbed a handful of Halliwell's hair and jerked his head sharply upwards so that he was looking in the direction of Wormwood Scrubs – 'you'll find yourself doing time in there with all the other slag.'

'All right. All right! Please, you're hurting me. If I promise, will you let go? It's like my mum said, I ain't done nothing.'

'Fair enough. As long as you understand.' Stratton took his knee off Halliwell's back. As the boy scrambled to his feet, he got an impression of a mop of brown hair and the protruding wrists, elbows and knees of one who hadn't yet filled out – before, quick as a flash and before Stratton could grab him, the lad shoved him hard in the chest and took off in the same direction as the children.

Stratton, too tired even to attempt to catch him, watched him go. Chastened, the happy feeling of an hour or so before entirely evaporated, he hobbled wearily back to his car, mopping the dirt from his hands with his handkerchief. As he climbed into the driving seat he looked up at the top floor of Canberra House just in time to see Mrs Halliwell disappearing behind a net curtain, her face a hard mask of triumph.

CHAPTER TWENTY-SIX

'The mother had obviously tipped him off, sir. But we've got a witness saying that there was a green van parked near the Earl of Warwick, where the attack on Johnson took place, and a lad who was in the General Smuts with the others says that Halliwell was the driver.'

'Halliwell was with them, was he?' asked Matheson.

'No, he came to collect them from the pub.' Stratton, aware of the dishevelled appearance he must present, had wanted to clean up a bit before reporting the debacle to his superior. Unfortunately, Matheson had been at the front desk when he arrived which meant that he was forced to explain himself within earshot of the desk sergeant, Curtis, who wasn't even bothering to pretend to be occupied with anything else. So far, Matheson's face hadn't indicated that he'd seen anything amiss, so perhaps the damage wasn't as bad as it felt. 'The witness, Johnny Andrews, says he got into the van with the others but they dropped him off at Silchester Road, so they were going in the direction of the Golborne Road. Andrews said he went to see his fiancée who lives nearby, and the girl's mother has confirmed that he was there to pick her up at around half past eight. I don't see any reason to disbelieve her – unlike Halliwell's mother, who was uncooperative from the start and obviously lying through her teeth. She seems to believe that the police have got it in for her son. I'm not sure why, because according to PC Dobbs there's no record of him ever being brought in for anything. However, I'd say the fact that he scarpered as soon as he saw me is fairly conclusive – and I don't see that we can get much further without bringing them all in, sir. If I'm right, and Halliwell was involved, then we need to do that before he warns his pals.'

'Fair enough,' said Matheson. Glancing at Stratton's legs, he added, in a neutral tone, 'Bit of a struggle, was there?'

Following his gaze, Stratton saw that not only were there grass stains on his trousers, but that there was an L-shaped tear just below his right knee, with a flap of material, three inches or thereabouts, hanging down loose. 'Something like that, sir. Not so fast as I used to be, I'm afraid.' He hoped Matheson wasn't going to ask any more questions because he was buggered if he was going to mention the business with the children. The desk sergeant had now been joined by PC Illingworth, who was staring at him with unconcealed curiosity – if it ever got round the station that a gang of kids had mistaken him for the neighbourhood pervert, he'd never live it down.

'You've got the makings of a nice shiner there,' observed Matheson. 'Why don't you give me a list, and I'll put things in motion while you go and sort yourself out?' Clapping Stratton on the back he added, in a lower voice, 'These things happen.'

It was obvious that this was meant kindly, but Stratton couldn't help feeling that, nevertheless, he'd gone down several notches in his new boss's estimation.

The relevant details having been noted down by a smirking Sergeant Curtis, Stratton trudged off to inspect his bruise in the lavatory's few inches of flyblown mirror. Halliwell's elbow must have caught him square in the eye, because he looked as though he'd gone three rounds with Freddie Mills. What an idiot he'd been to let go of the lad! After all these years . . . Barely a week in the place and already he was the object of derision – and it was no one's fault but his own. Shaking his head, he turned away from the basin and began examining his trouser legs. Beneath the tear was a two-inch gash that had bled copiously down his shin and into his sock. He was looking around for something to mop it up with – his handkerchief was a sodden ball, the hard toilet paper didn't absorb anything, and he could hardly take down the roller towel – when PC Jellicoe's head appeared round the door.

'Heard you'd had a bit of bother, sir.' The tone was cheerfully solicitous. I'll bet you did, thought Stratton. 'Deary me,' Jellicoe clicked his tongue sympathetically at the ripped material. 'You *have* been in the wars. I'm sure one of the policewomen could put a few stitches in that, just till you get home.'

Pushing away a nightmare vision of standing in his underpants in front of a crowd of sniggering coppers while some scornful Amazon sewed up his trousers, Stratton said, 'Thanks, but I'd rather keep them on.'

'I'm sure she could do it while you're wearing them, sir,' said Jellicoe. 'I don't think you've had the pleasure of our Miss Jenner yet, have you? Dab hand with a needle, she is.'

'All right,' said Stratton, with bad grace, 'but fetch me a bottle of Dettol and some cotton wool first, will you? And if there's any Elastoplast, I'll have that too.' He was damned if he was going to have Miss Jenner pawing at his bare leg as well as his trousers.

'Yes, sir. And I'll put a cup of tea on your desk. Don't mind my saying so, sir, but you look as if you could do with one.'

Our Miss Jenner turned out to be sweet-faced, with dimples and a halo of fluffy blonde curls, and looked so young that Stratton thought she must be just out of school. He sat in a chair, drinking the tea that Jellicoe had provided for him, while she knelt beside his outstretched leg and, in total silence with her eyes very firmly on her work, executed a deft repair. Jellicoe, who, though sympathetic, was clearly enjoying his role in the drama, stood guard at the door, shooing away any potential gawpers. Leaning back in his chair, Stratton clasped a towel full of ice that Jellicoe had procured from the canteen's refrigerator to his black eye. He'd just have to hope that Illingworth and the others had now been sent out to bring in Knight and his chums, and that the excitement generated by so doing – and, God willing, their subsequent arrests for Johnson's killing by himself – would put paid to any fun at his expense and win him his spurs.

CHAPTER TWENTY-SEVEN

'I ain't done nothing.' Stratton glanced at his watch – a quarter to six – then at PC Dobbs, who was leaning against the grimy wall of the interview room, arms folded, staring stonily ahead. Stratton couldn't blame him. They'd had three hours of this, first with Mills, Baxter and Pearson – Knight and Halliwell were yet to be located – and now with Fred Larby, who, slouched in the chair on the other side of the table, had his hands in his trouser pockets and the cock-sure look of one who has decided that he can afford to brazen things out. Like the others before him, he'd admitted to being in the General Smuts but nothing more. His story, like theirs, was that Halliwell had picked them up in the van – nobody seemed to know who it belonged to – and taken them to a party in St Ervan's Road, off the Golborne Road, dropping Johnny Andrews on the way. None of them could remember the number of the house where the party was supposed to have taken place, nor the name of the person who gave it, each claiming that he was a friend of one of the others, but all of them had insisted, repeatedly, that they had remained there for the rest of the evening.

Leaving Larby to stare insolently at Dobbs, Stratton went to find the station sergeant and see how he was getting on with the witnesses. Matthews had been none too pleased about the idea of a series of hastily convened identity parades, but Matheson had agreed that Susie Marwood, Irene and – supposing they managed to track her down on Bayswater Road – Gloria could be brought in to see if they recognised anyone.

'Not going too well, I'm afraid,' said Matthews with grim satisfaction. 'It's obvious that Mrs M. doesn't have a clue – she's just picked out Illingworth.'

'Who was she supposed to be picking?'

'Baxter. Neither of the whores recognised him either.'

As Baxter was a nondescript-looking lad with absolutely nothing to distinguish him from anybody else, Stratton wasn't particularly surprised by this. 'So they're both here, are they?'

Matthews nodded. 'Don't worry, I've kept 'em separate, like you said. The redhead—'

'Irene Palmer, you mean?'

'That's the one. Can't have been on the game long, or we'd know her. We've had the other one in here more times than you've had hot dinners. She's in the charge room with Miss Galloway, and the Palmer girl's in there,' he jerked his thumb at the door behind him, 'with Miss Jenner. Can't get a peep out of her – just keeps on shaking her head. The other one *thinks* she recognised Mills, but she won't swear to it.'

'What about Mrs Marwood?'

'She dithered over Mills but she wasn't sure either.'

Mills, Stratton recalled, was only fractionally more distinctive than Baxter. Being more filled out – or perhaps just more thickset – he might fit Irene's description of being 'a bit older than the others'. Also, he was the only one to be wearing a drape jacket, which was something else she'd mentioned. Maybe, Stratton thought, she'd recognised him but been too frightened to say so.

'What about Pearson?' he asked.

'They're bringing him up now.' As he spoke, Tony Pearson appeared, escorted by Jellicoe. He had black hair done in what Irene had described as a 'Tony Curtis' style – although the resemblance ended there because the attempt at a fashionably sullen expression was undermined by the open mouth and adenoidal breathing. Thinking that this, at least, would be memorable, and recalling Larby's chocolate-coloured mole positioned just above his upper lip, Stratton reassured himself that, although Susie Marwood had been too far away to pick up on either, Gloria – or possibly Irene – must have noticed them.

This brief flare of optimism was swiftly replaced by incredulity when a line of young constables appeared, dressed in hastily assembled mufti. A lot of it was, to say the least, seasonally unsuitable – Wellington boots, two flat caps and even an army greatcoat, while one sported a waistcoat decorated with a fob watch on a chain, and another a bowler hat. Clearly, someone had been raiding the station's lost property box. 'Hold it,' said Stratton, incredulous. Taking

Matthews aside, he asked, 'Did the other line-ups look like this lot?'

'It's having to do it at the last minute, sir.' Matthews sounded thoroughly unrepentant. 'They can't keep wearing the same things, and you've asked for four different lots with the same witnesses. Makes it very difficult.'

'They look like something out of a pantomime. And for Christ's sake tell me you haven't been using the same people each time.'

Matthews gave him a reproachful look. 'Couldn't do that, sir – it wouldn't be right.'

Noting that Illingworth, at least, was not among the gathered constables, Stratton said, 'Well, that's something, anyway.' Motioning Jellicoe to take Pearson through to the yard, he went down the line, removed the caps, the bowler and – to the relief of its wearer, who looked ready to faint – the greatcoat. Several of them, he noticed, barely managed to conceal their grins at the sight of the bruise emerging around his eye. 'Right,' he said. 'That's more like it.'

'Are you going to come and have a look, sir?'

Stratton shook his head. 'You get going, and then you can do another one for Larby. I'll be in the office.'

After about half an hour Matthews appeared, looking disappointed. 'Well?' said Stratton.

'Mrs Marwood's prepared to identify Pearson, and the Lockwood girl identified both Pearson and Larby.'

'Excellent,' said Stratton. Matthews eyed him sourly. 'Now we're getting somewhere. What about Miss Palmer?'

'Same thing – shakes her head, won't talk.'

'Do you think she recognised anyone?'

'Couldn't say, sir,' said Matthews blandly. 'You're not going to want any more people bringing in this afternoon, are you?' He made it sound as if Stratton had thoughtlessly arranged a tea party.

'No,' said Stratton. 'But I'd like a word with this lot of witnesses before they go.'

'Sorry, sir, I didn't realise. I've sent them home.'

'Give me strength,' muttered Stratton. 'Separately, I hope.'

'I made sure of it, sir,' said Matthews virtuously.

'That's something to be grateful for, anyway.' As Walker had said in the morning, Etheridge was bound to find out where Irene was, but not, he hoped, too soon – and Gloria would have been able to winkle it out of her in no time at all.

'I take it you want to hang on to Mills and the rest of them, sir?'

'Of course I do,' snapped Stratton. 'Anything on Knight or Halliwell yet?'

'No, sir.'

'Let me know as soon as there is, will you?'

'Yes, sir. Now, *if* you don't mind,' Matthews assumed a martyred expression, 'it's not exactly quiet out there . . .'

Jellicoe appeared a moment later. 'Which one do you want first, sir?'

'Pearson, I think.' At the initial interview, Pearson, whose answers had been laboured rather than pat, had struck him as the dullard of the group. He was also, at just seventeen, the youngest.

'Right you are. How's the eye, sir?'

'Not too bad, thanks. Did you watch the line-ups?'

'Yes, sir, all of them.'

'Irene Palmer – the girl with the red hair – how did she seem?'

'Frightened, sir. Shaking, she was. Eyes like saucers, and she never said a word. Tell you the truth, I felt quite sorry for her.'

'Do you think she recognised anybody?'

'Hard to tell, sir. She was sort of hiding behind her hair, and she's barely given any of them a look before she's started shaking her head, but it's possible.'

'Anyone in particular?'

'Mills, perhaps. But I couldn't be sure, sir.'

That would make sense, thought Stratton, as he followed Jellicoe to the interview room. Mills lived on the White City Estate, and Ronnie did sound a bit like Johnny or Tommy. Baxter, though, also lived on the estate. Pearson's address was Bramley Road, same as Johnny Andrews, and Larby lived in the council flats on Portland Road, which, from what Stratton could remember of the area, was pretty close by . . .

Pearson's breathing was now audible and stertorous – the product, Stratton hoped, of mounting anxiety. 'Two of the witnesses identified you as being one of the men who attacked Clyde Johnson on Golborne Road,' he said flatly. 'You were there, chum. What have you got to say now?'

Pearson's eyes darted round the room, as if searching for an escape route. 'I never done it.'

'But you were in Golborne Road.'

'I never said that.'

'No, you didn't. But someone else – or rather, two someone elses – have said it. That's two witnesses to the fact that you and the rest of your pals attacked Johnson in Golborne Road, and then there's the fact that he's dead and you killed him. They'll probably go easy with you because you're under eighteen but – unless, of course, you decide to cooperate, and provided I decide to put in a good word – you'll be going down for a bloody long time, so you might as well forget about—'

'It wasn't me!' Pearson's face was now the colour of lemonade.

'Who was it, then?'

'I don't know – I didn't see.'

'So you *were* there?'

'Yeah, but I never done anything.'

'Why couldn't you see? Did you have your eyes shut?'

'Course not.'

'Well, then, you *could* see, couldn't you? Don't fuck about with me, son. I want to hear it from the beginning.'

'Well, we was in the General Smuts.'

'And who was there with you?'

'Eddy, and then Ronnie, Gordon, Johnny and Fred. And

Tommy Halliwell came to pick us up in the van, like I told you.'

'Whose van was it?'

'Dunno. I never seen it before. He must have had it off some bloke.'

'Stolen it, you mean?'

'I never said that. He could have borrowed it.'

'Why?'

'Why what?'

'Why would he borrow it to pick you up?'

'To take us to that party.'

Stratton sighed flamboyantly. 'Don't waste my time, son. We had all that about the party on the first go round, and I didn't believe it then either.'

'No.' Pearson leant forward earnestly. 'We was going to a party, but we never went.'

'Why not?'

Now he looked confused. 'We was talking in the pub, and Eddy was saying about his uncle – you know, how the niggers done him up – and he said we ought to even things up a bit.'

'One of the witnesses in the pub overheard you saying . . .' Stratton flicked through his notebook until he found the interview with O'Driscoll. ' "We're going to go and find some niggers." '

'Yes, but it weren't my idea. I just went along with them. Eddy was saying about his uncle, and we was just talking – the usual . . . I don't remember.'

'Eddy said you should go off and kill a coloured man, did he?'

'It weren't like that. Just that we should, you know . . .'

'Not until you tell me, I don't.'

'He meant we should go and get one. Give him a scare.'

'Any particular one?'

Pearson looked nonplussed and shook his head.

'So why did you pick up Johnson?'

'I dunno, really. I mean, he was there, strutting along as if he owned the road, and we'd had some others slinging milk bottles at the van before, shouting at us an' that.'

'Who was sitting in the front with Halliwell?'

'Fred and Ronnie.'

'So you were at the back with Baxter?'

'Yes, and Johnny Andrews, till we dropped him off.'

'So you couldn't see these people throwing milk bottles?'

'No, but I could hear 'em all right.'

'And you couldn't see Johnson?'

'Not till I got out, no.'

'But you just said . . .' Stratton motioned to Jellicoe, who was taking notes, and read out, "He was strutting along as if he owned the road." '

'Yeah. Well, Ronnie said that.'

'What did he say exactly?'

Pearson's brow furrowed in thought. 'He said, "Look at that black cunt, strutting along as if he owned the road." '

'Then what happened?'

'We all got out.'

'Why didn't Knight go with you?'

'He had to meet a bloke.'

'What bloke?'

'Dunno. Just some bloke.'

'Any idea why?'

'Just said he had to talk to him about something.'

'Were you carrying a knife?'

Pearson shook his head. 'Niggers carry knives.'

'Well,' Stratton sat back and folded his arms, 'Clyde Johnson certainly didn't stab himself, so one of you must have had one – unless you took it off him, of course.'

'We never.'

'I thought you said you couldn't see what happened.'

'No, but—'

'But if you could see well enough to know that nobody took a knife from Johnson, you must have been able to see who it was that stabbed him.'

'I didn't. We all steamed into him and gave him a whacking, but I never saw any knife.'

'Did Johnson have a knife on him?'

'Not that I could see.'

'Were you carrying a weapon?' Holding up a forefinger to forestall Pearson, who was already shaking his head, Stratton added, 'Remember, we have witnesses.'

'There was bits of wood an' that at the back of the van, so I took one of them.'

'That's more like it,' said Stratton. 'What did the others have?'

'I think Fred had some wood, and Millsie had a bit of iron.'

'What about Baxter and Halliwell?'

'I don't know. I suppose they got something, too. Out of the van, I mean.'

'Do you know who put the stuff in there?'

'Nothing to do with me.'

'What about the girls? Did you recognise them?'

'Never seen them before.'

'Somebody did, didn't they?' Pearson looked uncertain. 'Come off it,' Stratton continued. 'You were chasing them, calling them names.'

'Yeah, but . . .' Pearson shrugged. 'That was just because the others were doing it, you know. And they shouldn't go with coloureds. It's wrong isn't it? You get a lot of half-castes running around.'

'How do you know those girls go with coloureds?'

'I told you, someone said. I don't know who, because everyone was shouting – next minute we was all just running after the girls.'

'Which way?'

'Over the railway bridge, towards Portobello.'

'Then what happened?'

'One of them took a tumble, so we all stopped. That was just by the corner of Portobello Road.'

'What did you do?'

'Nothing. Someone said we should leave it, so we did.'

'Do you know who said it?'

'Millsie or Tommy, I think because they was right behind me. But,' he added virtuously, 'I'd never hit a woman, even if she was going with a nigger.'

CHAPTER TWENTY-EIGHT

By ten o'clock, Stratton had four statements that, to all intents and purposes, matched each other. Faced with a combination of threats, coercion and – as with Pearson – some slight distortion of the facts, first Larby, then Baxter and finally Mills had admitted to taking part in the attack on Johnson. PC Jellicoe, having wedged his bulk behind a typewriter in the office, was bashing out copies with two thudding fingers, and Stratton, exhausted, was inspecting the results. They'd got about halfway through when Sergeant Vokes, who'd replaced Curtis on the desk, appeared and handed him a slip of paper.

'Telephone call from DS Matheson, sir. He says to give him a ring and let him know how it's going.'

'Where is he?'

'At home, sir.'

'Are you sure about this?'

'Yes, sir. The number's written down there. He said you're to call him any time, sir.'

'He always likes to be kept in the picture,' said Jellicoe helpfully, when Vokes had departed.

'Bit late, though.' In all his years at West End Central, Stratton had never once telephoned DS Lamb at home and he had a strong suspicion that, had he done so, he'd have spent the remainder of his career on point duty. 'You're absolutely sure, are you?'

'Yes, sir. And you've got good news for him, haven't you?'

'Of sorts,' said Stratton. 'We've not managed to collar Knight or Halliwell yet, remember.'

'No, sir. In spite of your best efforts.'

Stratton groaned. 'Thanks for reminding me. I feel as if I've been run over by a bus.'

'I'll be honest with you, sir.' Jellicoe paused to take a swig of his tea. 'When you come in this afternoon looking like you did, I thought, well . . .' He made a disparaging face. 'But then, seeing you downstairs with that lot – lovely job, that was.'

'Thanks,' said Stratton, surprised. 'I'm not sure that Matthews would agree, though.'

'You don't want to worry about him,' said Jellicoe. 'He's been here near as long as I have, and he thinks he's running the show. Why don't you give the guv'nor a ring, sir, and I'll see if I can't get the canteen to rustle up a couple of sandwiches?'

'There's still a lot we don't know, sir, but it's a start.'

Matheson, Stratton thought, must have been sitting on top of the telephone, because he'd picked it up on the first ring, and had seemed more than happy to listen to the details. Stratton pictured him sitting in a leather armchair

in a room decorated in the beef and holly colours favoured
by gentlemen's clubs, surrounded by brass artefacts, with
a Labrador at his feet and his wife, an unimagined blur,
somewhere in the background.

'But you haven't charged them with anything,' said
Matheson, when Stratton had finished explaining the events
of the day.

'No, sir. I thought it best to wait until I'd spoken to you.'

'Fair enough. I take it the parents are aware of what's
going on? You said that Pearson and Larby are both under
eighteen.'

'That's right, sir. They were both at home, so the parents
know what's going on, and Mills's and Baxter's families
have been informed. I understand there wasn't much difficulty – they all agreed to come in voluntarily . . . I get the
impression that they thought if they kept their story straight
– the original story, I mean, about the party – they'd get
away with it because the two girls wouldn't say anything.
Certainly, according to what I've been told, none of the
parents seemed very concerned about it.'

Matheson grunted in a way that suggested he wasn't
surprised by this, then said, 'Were these all on Dobbs's list
of troublemakers?'

'All except Larby and Halliwell, sir.'

'Any previous?'

'Not for this type of thing, except for Knight. He was
bound over after an incident at one of the White Defence
League's political meetings back in March. Baxter – he's
twenty-one, currently a sheet metal worker at an outfit in

Latimer Road – he was fined thirty shillings for stealing ten gallons of petrol last year . . .' Stratton paused to leaf through his notes. 'Pearson's been taken in for questioning a few times but never charged with anything, but Mills was given eighteen months' probation last summer for loitering with intent. He's nineteen – managed a year's National Service before he and the army parted on bad terms. Earlier records show persistent truancy from school . . . They sent him to an LCC residential place in Surrey for a couple of years – eighteen different jobs in the two and a half years between leaving and being called up . . .'

'What's he doing now?'

'Currently unemployed and drawing national assistance,' read Stratton.

'Department of No Surprises,' said Matheson. 'And that goes for all of it. Right, then – we haven't enough for manslaughter. Charge them with malicious wounding and then we can hang on to them until Monday and see if we can't get hold of the other two in the meantime.'

'Yes, sir.'

'That's it, then. I expect you'll be glad to get home tonight, won't you?'

'Yes, sir.'

'I'll let you get on with it, then. Be sure to let me know if there are any developments before you leave won't you? Oh, and Stratton?'

'Yes, sir?'

'Well done.'

CHAPTER TWENTY-NINE

By the time they'd finished charging Mills and the others, it was nearly half past eleven and Stratton, whose head was now throbbing rhythmically after spending the afternoon and evening in smoky rooms with no ventilation, felt punch-drunk with exhaustion. He had just put his hat on to go home when Sergeant Vokes appeared, looking flustered. 'Sorry, sir, but there's been a serious disturbance. Big party in Colville Road, and there's mayhem – crowds of people, and they're throwing petrol bombs and all sorts—'

'Hang on,' said Stratton. 'Colville Road? What number?'

'Thirty-seven, sir.'

Etheridge's club, thought Stratton. 'Do you know who's involved?'

'We're a bit confused, sir. It's usually a coloured club, but when PC Leonards called it in he said there were respectable people in there and—'

'Councillor Watson's party.'

'I don't know about that, sir, but we've sent reinforcements and the fire brigade's on its way, and the ambulance. I know you're not on duty, sir, but DI Culshaw's had to go down to another incident in Bramley Road – there's a fight going on down there with the coloureds and a house is on fire, and we've just had a report of a big gang gathered under the railway arches at Latimer Road, all set to lynch the first darkie they see, and there's another lot smashing windows in Oxford Gardens, so—'

'Whoa! It's all right – I'll go.'

Vokes's relief was evident. 'Thank you, sir. It's just . . . Well, I don't know what to expect next. Your driver'll be right outside, sir.'

The driver was a hare-eyed young copper called Dunning who looked even more unnerved than Vokes had. 'I've just come back from Latimer Road tube, sir,' he said, as they sped along, bell clanging. It was a bright night, with a full moon surrounded by grape-coloured sky, and Harrow Road seemed peaceful enough. Shutters down, curtains drawn and everyone tucked up in bed.

'It's murder down there, sir. They're throwing things through the windows and the coloureds are fighting back, chucking milk bottles at them. I've never seen anything like it.'

'Let's concentrate on the matter in hand, shall we?' said Stratton grimly, images of Fenella crowding his mind. It sounded as if there was a full-scale battle going on, and if she were in the middle of it she might have been hurt, or assaulted, or . . . The way things had been going in the past few weeks, not to mention that business in Nottingham last weekend – and it being the August bank holiday – he should have guessed that something like this might happen. Councillor Watson's bloody soirée was sheer provocation, and, in a situation like the one Vokes had described, all those well-meaning types were going to be about as useful as tits on a billiard ball. As for Etheridge . . . Stratton shook his head in frustration. He should have seen it coming. He should have warned Fenella not to go anywhere near the place, warned Mrs Rutherford . . .

'I'd wind up your window, sir,' said Dunning, as they turned into Ledbury Road and a car shot past them, men hanging out of the windows. Stratton caught a glimpse of clenched fists and contorted faces and heard a shout of 'Niggers out!' before the car disappeared. It was followed by a hail of stones and bricks, one of which hit the bonnet of their Austin 90 with a colossal bang, making them rear back, arms across their faces. Dunning lost control of the wheel and the car slewed sideways, clipping a couple of dustbins which clanged onto the pavement, spewing rubbish and scattering a group of teenagers and younger kids who were milling around the open door of one of the houses. They laughed and shouted as another car full of men drove past, yelling and gesticulating. Stratton could hear more bells now, fire engines and other police cars round the corner. Further up the street, more dustbins were overturned in the middle of the road, with a motorcycle parked halfway across so that Dunning had to steer round it. Their progress was slower now, because the pool of bystanders on the corner of Colville Terrace had spilled from the pavement into the road. They paid little attention either to the siren or to

Dunning sounding his horn, but stood there placidly, talking among themselves, breaking off to look up and down the street as though they were waiting for a parade to pass. All were white, their skins a grey-mauve colour in the light of the street lamps. Cautiously winding down his window again, Stratton looked up and saw that there were coloured men and women standing behind their closed windows, unmoving and, he thought, silent.

Dunning nosed the Austin 90 slowly through the crowd. They'd got some way down Colville Terrace when Stratton spotted an elderly man. Dressed, despite the hot weather, in an overcoat and muffler, he was taking a small, snuff-coloured terrier for a walk, apparently oblivious to the chaos around him. Stratton was about to ask Dunning to pull over so that he could tell the man to go home when the car stopped so suddenly that Stratton was thrown forward in his seat. Looking up, he saw that two coloured men were running hell for leather from the corner of Colville Road a few hundred yards away with a gang of white men streaming after them, a charge of solid, roaring bodies. The one in front, head thrown back and teeth bared, was brandishing what looked like a tyre iron, and others flailed lengths of wood or swung bicycle chains. The car shook from side to side as they surged past, banging against the sides, closely pursued by five or six policemen, truncheons held aloft, blowing their whistles.

Stratton twisted round in his seat to see both coloured men haring up the steps of a house at the end of the street and plunging through the front door. The gang, who'd been joined by a bunch of teenagers on scooters from Ledbury Road, jeered from the pavement and threw things at the windows. One man picked up a child's tricycle from beside the dustbins and, lifting it above his head, was about to hurl it through the front window when two coppers jumped on him, knocking him to the ground. The crowd surged around them, shouting and throwing whatever missiles came to hand, while the other policemen tried to fight their way through to help their colleagues.

Stratton's attention was abruptly drawn back to Colville Road by the whoomphing noise of an explosion and the sound of shattering glass. 'Get moving,' he shouted at Dunning, who was staring ahead of him, apparently in a state of shock. Turning round, he could see that the people from the end of the street, as well as the bystanders on the corner, were running back towards them to see what was happening. More people must have joined them, because a moment after Dunning had started the car, they were penned in by a sea of bodies and unable to move anywhere.

'Hang on,' he said to the young policeman, whose face was ashen, 'I'll see if I can get some help. In the meantime, try and move forward as best you can.' With some difficulty, he managed to shove open the door of the Austin 90 enough to extricate himself, and began pushing his way through the press of people to the end of Colville Road. A line of harassed-looking policemen, legs braced and truncheons at the ready, were almost nose to nose with the milling crowd. Periodically, bricks, stones and milk bottles thrown from the back rained down on them and the bonnet of the car he could see just behind them. As Stratton pushed his way through to the front, he saw that one of them already had blood running down his chin.

'Sorry, sir,' said PC Coxon, as Stratton slid towards him between two Teddy boys, 'You can't— Oh, it's you, sir. Are you all right?'

'Just about,' Stratton panted. 'The car's stuck back there with Dunning.'

'Won't be long, sir. Got to get the darkies out first before this lot lynches 'em.'

'Where?'

'In the car, sir. They've nearly turned it over twice.'

Stratton stood on tiptoe to look at the car. It was a Hillman Minx, ringed by police who were holding back a surging crowd. Inside four coloured men were cowering, their arms over their faces, and beyond it, smoke belched from a building. Seeing it, the last vestige of hope he'd been unconsciously clinging to, which admitted the possibility of it being another house, with another party, vanished: it was the house he'd visited yesterday. Through the smoke he could see a single fire engine and the bulky, purposeful forms of firemen busying themselves with hoses. There were other people too, men and women straggling unsteadily across the road in ones and twos, silhouettes outlined in the bright flames of a car which was blazing away behind them.

'Watch it, sir!' Coxon grabbed his jacket and pulled him out of the way of what looked like a flying bundle of burning rags. A second later there was a crash of glass on the pavement behind them and several women screamed. 'Petrol bomb,' said Coxon. 'In a bottle. We've had a couple of those. That's what did that car up there – straight through the window. There was a bloke in it, an' all – never seen anyone move so fast in my life.'

'Bloody hell . . . Listen, I need to get down the other end. Who's in charge?'

Coxon looked confused. 'You, sir.'

'Before I got here.'

'I don't know, sir.'

'Do you know if there's a radio car back there?'

'I'm sorry, sir, I don't. It's been so—'

'I understand.'

'Shall I help you, sir? To get through, I mean.'

Resisting the temptation to say that he wasn't in his dotage yet, Stratton contented himself with, 'I think you've got your work cut out here, son. Make sure Dunning's all right, won't you?'

'Yes, sir.'

'Good.' Stratton clapped him on the shoulder. 'Best of luck, then.'

It took him several minutes to battle his way round to the rear end of the Hillman and out through the thinning crowd, and the effort left him doubled over on the pavement, coughing.

When he recovered enough to stand up straight, he could see that the firemen were attempting – apparently without the help of the police – to herd people away from the burning house. One or two were standing uncertainly on the pavement. They'd definitely been at Watson's party, he thought, eyeing their ruined evening clothes. Two ambulance men with a stretcher hurried past in front of the burning car. On the other side of the car Stratton could see skirmishing figures, alternately illuminated by the blaze and swallowed by the shadows. He looked again at the dishevelled party-goers. Dazed, bleeding and uncomprehending, they reminded him of the casualties he'd dealt with in the Blitz. He didn't recognise any of them but there was a strong possibility, he thought, that one of them might know where Fenella—

'Sir!' A young policeman, arms spread wide as if trying to herd a flock of sheep into a pen, said, 'You can't come up here, sir, there's been an incident.'

Stratton whipped out his warrant card. 'Stratton. And you are?'

'Colbert, sir.'

'Who's the senior officer?'

'Sergeant Parker, sir, only he's in the ambulance. Got hit by a brick, sir.'

'Where is the ambulance?'

'Just round the corner, sir, in Lonsdale Road.'

As he spoke, a figure detached itself from the others and staggered towards them. Stratton recognised him as Duffy, the artist from Maxine's. His face was dirty and bloodied, and he had a large glass of something in one hand and was gesticulating wildly with the other. 'Is there a radio car here?'

'Yes, sir. That's in Lonsdale Road too.' Duffy lurched between the two of them, stood swaying for a moment, his hand reaching for Colbert's arm and then, sinking to his knees, vomited noisily on the pavement. As he did so, a savage roar went up from the crowd around the car. Stratton turned to see that it was moving off down Colville Terrace in a hail of bricks and bottles, with those in front pushing and shoving to get out of its way while, all around, truncheons flailed in the air, clashing with stakes and bicycle chains as the line of police struggled to hold back the throng.

'Escort this man to safety, Colbert, then get onto the station and tell Sergeant Vokes we need more men.'

'None to spare, sir,' said Colbert, hauling Duffy to his feet. 'Sergeant Parker asked, and they're all down at Latimer Road. DS Matheson's been contacted, sir.'

'That's something, anyway.' Stratton left him to it and started towards the burning house. Despite the firemen's best efforts, smoke was billowing up from the basement. On top of the portico a coloured woman, who appeared to be wearing only a slip, was screaming, the flicker of flames clearly visible in the window behind her, while below, a fireman steadied a ladder against one of the pillars while another began to climb. One of the partygoers, her face, arms and the pale material of her evening dress filthy with soot, was being escorted up the basement steps by a man with his arm round her shoulders. Another, with blood on the front of his shirt and a stupefied expression on his grimy face, was being led away by a member of the ambulance crew.

One of the firemen rushed to intercept him. He was about Stratton's own age, grim-faced and craggy. 'You shouldn't be here, mate. It's not safe.'

'DI Stratton. Who's in charge?'

'I am, for what it's worth. Hale.' Removing his glove, Hale extended his hand. 'We're getting everyone out as fast as we can but frankly, the place is a fucking tinderbox.'

'The wiring?' said Stratton, remembering what he'd seen.

'Buggered.'

'How many more to come?'

'No idea. Place was heaving. Party in the basement and Christ knows how many in the rooms upstairs. We'd have been here quicker but for—' He jerked his thumb towards the mêlée at the junction with Colville Terrace. 'We've just come from Bramley Road – no idea when the others'll get here.' He shook his head in disgust. 'What a shambles. It was easier during the war – I mean, we had the odd looter, but we never had to deal with all this malarkey. You look like you've had a time of it, an' all.'

Stratton, who'd forgotten about his black eye, put a hand up to his face. 'Yes – we're not doing a lot better,' he added as PC Coxon came weaving towards them, blood streaming down his cheek, guided by another policeman.

'Fuck me,' muttered the fireman. 'Bunch of fucking hooligans we got here. Right, better get on.'

'Best of luck,' said Stratton.

'Thanks, mate. We're all going to need it.'

They'd need to make sure everyone in the building was safe. Tugging his notebook out of his jacket pocket, Stratton turned back to the fire. More partygoers were stumbling up to street level through the smoke. Among them, Stratton spotted a fat chap in a lounge suit that he was pretty sure was Councillor Watson, head down and trousers torn, hobbling with his arm round the shoulders of another. He was about to go and ask for the names of those at the party when he saw, emerging from the haze, the unmistakable figure of Fenella, who appeared to be propping up ... no, he wasn't wrong, it definitely was, so they really *had* invited everybody – Marion Lockwood, also known as Gloria.

CHAPTER THIRTY

Stratton dashed across to help them onto the pavement. Apart from the smuts on her face and clothes, Fenella seemed – thank God – to be all right. Gloria's dress, which was filthy, had been torn away at the right shoulder, revealing the grimy straps of underwear, and Stratton could see blood beneath the coating of dirt on her skin. She was tottering crab-like, the heel of one shoe snapped in half, her elaborate hairdo sagging to one side and her face smudged and tear-streaked. She was trying to push Fenella away and shouting at her. 'Let me go! I've got to find him.'

'What's going on?' asked Stratton. 'Find who?'

'Oh,' said Gloria, 'it's *you*. You tell her – I've got to find Clinton.'

'No, you haven't,' said Stratton. 'The firemen'll do that.'

'But I've got to,' Gloria wailed. 'I couldn't see him – he's in there – I don't know where he went. Get off me!' she shouted at Fenella.

'Just be grateful you're safe,' said Stratton brusquely. 'Your boyfriend'll be out in a minute—'

'You don't know that!'

'No, I don't – but if he's in trouble, the firemen'll be able to help him better than you can. In the meantime, you need to get those cuts looked at.'

'Leave me alone!' Gloria spat at him. 'And you,' she said to Fenella, giving her a shove, 'just fuck off, will you?'

Before Stratton could move or even speak, Fenella's free hand shot out and slapped Gloria across the face. 'Pull yourself together! You're coming with me to the ambulance, and that's that. The firemen have got enough to do without you interfering, you stupid girl.'

'You listen to Mrs Jones,' said Stratton, taking hold of Gloria's other arm. 'Come on. Ambulance. Now!'

'Where did you learn that?' asked Stratton, once Gloria, a blanket round her shoulders, was being ministered to by a repressively sensible nurse. Several people who looked as if they might have been important were milling around near the ambulance, and a trio of coloured men were sitting, ignored, on the edge of the pavement. Noting the slings and bandages and general air of bewilderment, Stratton presumed all were from the party – the crisis having unmixed the gathering and returned it, as it were, to its separate ingredients. All, however, were draped in shawls or coats – in one case, an eiderdown – which must have been loaned by people in the nearby houses. A couple of elderly ladies in candlewick dressing gowns and hairnets were distributing tea. Behind them shuffled an old man, pyjama legs visible beneath his mackintosh. Stratton watched as he bent down to touch the shoulder of one of the black men huddled on the pavement, pulling a half bottle of what looked like Scotch from his pocket.

'I was an ARP warden during the war,' said Fenella, accepting a jam jar of tea. 'Ooh, that's hot. Jeepers, what's happened to your eye?'

'Spot of bother earlier on.' Stratton took the jam jar from her and balanced it on the top of a wall. 'Let it cool a bit. I can't imagine you dealt with too many hysterical prostitutes when you were an ARP warden, did you?'

'Is that what she is? I did wonder.'

Stratton nodded. 'The chap she was worried about isn't her boyfriend, he's her pimp. Can you tell me what happened?'

'I was hoping that you might be able to tell me.'

'We don't exactly know at the moment. All I got was a report of a petrol bomb.'

'So that's what came through the window.'

'Was there any disturbance before that?'

'Not that I heard. But it was all quite noisy, with music and people chatting and everything – in fact, it was going rather better than I'd thought it would. It was jolly awkward at first. We – I mean Councillor Watson and all the others – were all sort of standing about in a bunch, watching our hosts, or I suppose they were our hosts, drinking and dancing and so on . . .'

'And smoking marijuana?'

'Yes, that as well. They started showing Councillor Watson and some other people how to roll the cigarettes, and after that it all got quite merry, you know . . .'

'I can just imagine,' said Stratton wryly.

'I had a long conversation with a man named Etheridge who seemed to be in charge of things. Very charming, and extremely interesting – he was telling me about his childhood and how difficult he's finding it to—'

'That girl you brought upstairs,' Stratton interrupted. 'Etheridge was the one she was shouting about.'

'Oh. You mean that he is . . .'

'Yes, he is.'

'Heavens. I wonder if Virginia – Mrs Rutherford – knows that.'

'She doesn't,' said Stratton. 'In fact, I was surprised to see Gloria tonight.'

'That's her name, is it?'

'Only for business purposes. What happened then?'

'Well, after that I talked to a couple of other people, and then there was the sound of glass smashing when somebody threw the bomb through the window, and then there was a bang and everyone sort of fell backwards. I was standing at the back, near the table where the drinks were, and several people landed on top of me. By the time we'd all got disentangled, the lights had gone out and there was smoke and everything was in a terrible mess with broken bottles. People were screaming and blundering about trying to get out, but someone near me said we ought to stay put because there were so many people in the room, and it would cause a panic. People near me had been hurt but you couldn't actually get to anybody because the room was too full of bodies and smoke and it was dark. And then the curtains caught fire and everyone screamed and then it was just . . .' Fenella shook her head. 'Chaos. I don't know how long it was before the fire engine came. The girl, Gloria, she came blundering past me – trod on my hand, in fact – shouting out something. I suppose it must have been Mr Etheridge's name.'

'I see. Would you mind staying with Gloria for a bit? I'd get someone to take you home, but we can't really spare—'

'Don't worry about me.' Fenella put a hand on his arm. 'You need to get back to work.'

'Yes, I'd better go and—' A great crash from round the corner made them both flinch. 'You'll be all right, will you? If I don't see you—'

'I told you, I'll be fine. And if there's anything I can do to help – I can't imagine how, but if there is – you can count on me. I do mean that.' She smiled and squeezed his arm and, looking down, Stratton saw that she was still wearing the bracelet. 'Keep safe, won't you?'

CHAPTER THIRTY-ONE

Running back round the corner into Colville Road, Stratton bumped straight into PC Colbert coming the other way. 'More trouble, sir,' he panted, as a crowd of men thundered past them towards Colville Terrace, pursued by a posse of constables. They jumped back as a dustbin arced across the road and landed with a clang a few yards away, its contents spilling onto the pavement. Stratton could make out, through the acrid smoke drifting down the road, a line of smashed ground-floor windows and a carpet of broken glass sparkling beneath the street lamps.

'Your car got through, sir,' Colbert shouted above the din of shouts and running feet. 'It's further down and the reinforcements are here, but you need to come, sir.'

'Where?'

'Down there. It's those blokes from the White Defence League.'

'Christ, that's all we need. Listen, I need you to start taking statements from anyone who was at the party, before they disperse. Make sure you get a note of the names of anyone who was there. You can start down there, by the ambulance.'

Stratton ran back down the road. A Black Maria had now arrived and men were being loaded inside. Beyond, the flames seemed to be out, and he supposed that the firemen must have the thing under reasonable control, because two of them were playing a hose on the carcass of the car that had been on fire. Now it was smouldering, thick gouts of black smoke rolling off its tyres. Eyes watering, he dodged past the parabola of water and came to a halt, wheezing, in front of a dark-coloured Rolls-Royce which was slewed across the road. A sudden blast of light – for a moment, Stratton thought it was another petrol bomb, then realised it was the magnesium flare of a cameraman on the other side of the car – lit up Danny Perlmann, still in dark glasses, his face like putty, emerging from the passenger door. Turning slightly, Stratton caught sight of a crowd on the pavement to his left. He was sure they hadn't been there earlier; thirty or so people, old and young, white and coloured, had appeared out of thin air. They stood, silent, some with their arms folded, concentrating intently, and Stratton was reminded of the men you sometimes saw bunched outside the windows of Radio Rentals watching the football.

Another flare went off, this time illuminating something further up the street: John Gleeson, resplendent in his ersatz brownshirt uniform, marching at the head of a cohort of ten or so young men, their faces set and implacable. PC Coxon appeared at his side with several other constables, all out of breath. 'Managed to chase them off, sir. Other end of the street's clear.'

'Someone down there?'

'Two, with some of the new blokes, sir.'

'Well, let's hope they can deal with any trouble. You need to go and head that lot off sharpish. Take anyone you can find – just don't let them get down here.'

'Right you are, sir.'

Laskier, taut-faced behind the wheel of the Roller, was leaning across to Perlmann as he stood with the passenger door held in front of him like a shield. As Stratton approached, he could hear Laskier speaking urgently in Polish. Close to, he could see sweat running down the sides of Perlmann's face.

'Please get back in the car, Mr Perlmann.'

'It's my house. It belongs to me.' One fat hand, holding the tattered stump of a thick cigar, stabbed feebly at his chest, and Stratton noticed the tremor in the fingers. 'They have their fucking party at my house.'

'I'm sorry, Mr Perlmann, but there's nothing you can do here.'

'I try to help them, and they—'

Whatever he meant to say was cut off by yells and the clatter of truncheons on dustbin lids as a scuffle broke out down the road. 'Do you want to see this country ruined by niggers and Jews?' Gleeson was shouting. 'Are you going to stand by and let foreigners take over?'

'Come on, Mr Perlmann.' Stratton put a hand on his shoulder. 'It's not safe here.'

Perlmann's entire body seemed to be quivering. He turned away from Stratton and stared down the road to where Gleeson was now struggling between two constables who were trying to drag him away. Around them, his supporters were fighting a running battle with the rest of the policemen as they tried to drive them down towards Westbourne Grove. Stratton could make out nothing of Perlmann's expression behind the dark glasses. He thought of the pictures he'd seen on Pathé News before the war – Kristallnacht – and wondered what was going through the man's mind.

Muttering something to himself, Perlmann ducked his head and began to struggle back into the car. Stratton put out a hand to help him, but he pushed it away. His movements were jagged and effortful and, by the time he was seated, he was breathing heavily. Stratton bent down, one hand on the top of the door. 'You'll have to go past them, I'm afraid,' he said. 'You should be all right if you put your foot down.' Laskier, who was staring straight ahead, seemed not to have heard him. 'You need to leave now,' said Stratton, louder this time, 'before there's any more trouble.'

Laskier turned to him, his face wooden. 'Bastards,' he muttered. 'Bastards.'

'Stefan! Musimy się stąd wydostać.' Perlmann's words came out as a gasp. 'Start the fucking car.'

CHAPTER THIRTY-TWO

As Stratton watched the tail lights of the Rolls disappear down the road, someone plucked at his sleeve. Looking down, he saw the wizened face of a tiny woman, a headscarf tied tightly under her chin.

'Can I help you?'

'The copper down there told me to talk to you.' Her voice sounded rusty, as if it wasn't much used. 'I saw them, see.'

'Saw who?'

'The ones who did it. I live across the way, there.' She pointed a quivering finger at the house opposite number thirty-seven. 'They come by in a van.'

'When was this?'

'About ten past eleven. I was woken up before by the party and the noise down the street and I didn't drop off again – it's not so easy when you're old – so I got up to fetch myself a little something. I was on the landing, see, waiting for the milk to heat, and I was looking out of the window.'

'What did you see?'

'This van. It was stopped in the middle of the road, and two boys got out. I couldn't see well, but they had something in their hands and they threw it down the area.'

'They stopped the van outside number 37, did they?'

'Yes. And they went right up to the railings.'

'Then what?'

'Then they threw what they'd got in their hands, then they ran back to the van and off they went. We heard the bang straight after, and we come out and saw the smoke and all the people come piling up the stairs. One of my neighbours, Mr Patterson, he come with me to call the police. We had to go right to Pembridge Crescent before we found a box that was working.'

'Can you describe the two boys?'

'Just boys – young men, I suppose you'd say. Too far away for me to see properly. The van was one of them with two doors at the back. A green one.'

A fireman appeared at Stratton's elbow as he was taking down the lady's name. 'My guv'nor needs a word, sir. Could you follow me, please?'

The basement of number 37 was a dripping, blackened horror, the tattered remnants of the curtains hanging like rags at each side of the shattered front window. Following the beam of the fireman's torch, Stratton trod carefully, trying to avoid the puddles and sharp edges of the charred furniture, the remains of bottles and glasses crunching beneath his feet. 'Through here, sir.' The fireman conducted him out through the storeroom, one gloved hand shoving aside the fused clump of soot-crusted plastic which was all that remained of the floor-length brightly-coloured strips that had separated the front and back rooms, and out into the garden.

Someone, at some point, had obviously made an attempt

to clear the space immediately outside the rear of the house, which was a small concrete yard. Ducking under the washing line which was strung across it, Stratton followed the fireman up a couple of steps onto scuffed earth. Bare of grass, it was strewn with newspapers and the torn and trampled remains of clothing, including several nappies. 'It's all right, sir, the fire didn't get out here, but you need to mind where you step. This way.' The fireman pointed his torch at a hole in the rickety planks of the wooden fence. Scrambling through after him into the next garden, Stratton spotted three shadowy figures bending down on the far side of a large clump of nettles. As one of them detached itself and came towards him – 'Over here – careful how you go' – he saw that it was Hale.

Hale's torch played along the ground, picking out a pile of tin cans and next to them a woman's shoe, covered in some sort of shiny material. It looked, Stratton thought, boat-like, too large for a woman. The next thing he saw was a hand clad in a white glove, the bare arm, a coral bracelet about the wrist, outstretched as if grasping for something. He felt his heart plummet as Hale stood back to reveal a woman lying on her stomach, the head turned to one side. Most of the visible profile was obscured by a bloody, tangled mass of hair, but from what he could see of the face, the large limbs and thick trunk clad in an elaborate frock, the skirt of which, made stiff by petticoats, stood proud of her legs, Stratton was in no doubt that he was looking at the body of the Honourable Virginia Rutherford.

CHAPTER THIRTY-THREE

The two ambulance men with Hale shook their heads. 'Nothing we can do for her, I'm afraid.'

'Did you find her here?' asked Stratton.

Hale nodded. 'Few minutes ago.'

Stratton looked at his watch. 'Say twenty to one?'

'Sounds about right,' said Hale. 'I didn't think we should move her. The fire didn't do this. And – before you ask – we haven't touched a thing.'

Stratton straightened up. 'Can you stay here while I get hold of the station?'

'I see,' said DS Matheson grimly. 'And you're absolutely sure of who it is, are you?'

'Yes, sir.'

'Right. Better see if we can't track down the husband. Do you know if he was at the party?'

'No idea. Haven't seen him, but the firemen were directing everyone round to the ambulances.'

'I'll send someone to find out. That lot,' Matheson gestured towards Gleeson and his followers, who were being pushed into a Black Maria, 'can be sorted out back at the station. God knows what they're going to do with them all – they're dealing with two van loads from Latimer Road already, as well as a bunch from Bramley Road. Going to be a real bugger's muddle sorting it all out.'

If he'd been roused from sleep, Matheson gave no sign of it, but looked as neat and alert as he had every other time Stratton had seen him. The road was quiet now, but for the activity around the fire engine and a few stragglers who were being herded away by a group of weary constables. Stratton knew exactly how they felt. He stood, numb and exhausted, while Matheson gave orders.

'You look all in, man. Let's go and sit down for a moment.'

'Yes, sir, but I think I should—'

'Nothing we can do for Mrs Rutherford until the medico comes,' said Matheson, 'and I want to know what's been happening.' Leading the way back to his car, he motioned to Stratton to sit in the passenger seat and, leaning on the door frame, palmed a hip flask. 'Here.'

Stratton stared at the flat leather-covered bottle. 'Sir, I—'

'Drink it, man. That's an order.'

'Yes, sir.' He took a gulp and shuddered as the Scotch burnt its way down.

'Again,' said Matheson.

Stratton complied. 'I've got a witness who says the fire was started by two men in a green van.'

'Was it indeed? Cigarette?'

'Thank you, sir. The lady said it was one of those with two doors at the back.'

Matheson raised his eyebrows.

'If I'd managed to get hold of that little toerag this afternoon . . .'

Matheson put a hand on Stratton's shoulder. 'No registration, I suppose.'

'No, sir, but maybe one of the other neighbours . . . I'm betting that there were a few other people looking out of their windows.'

'What about Mrs Rutherford?'

'Looks like a very severe blow to the head, but what she might have been doing in the next-door garden is anybody's guess. If she'd gone outside for a breath of air, why not just step out of the back door? Believe me, sir, those gardens aren't places you'd want to linger. I can't imagine why you'd go to the bother of scrambling through a hole in the fence.'

'Unless she was *with* somebody.'

Stratton frowned, thinking of Mrs Rutherford with her mannish hands, her ungainly, graceless movements and ridiculous frock. The suggestion that she might have slunk away from the party like some lovestruck teenager intent on a fumble in the shadows seemed absurd. Matheson cut across his thoughts, 'She did seem to be rather keen on those coloured fellows at the nightclub.'

'Well, one of them was certainly present. Clinton Etheridge.' Recalling the Hon. Virginia's skittish behaviour of the previous morning and the feverish look in her eyes, Stratton added, 'It's possible, I suppose, but if they had planned a tryst of some sort, you'd think they could have waited.'

'Perhaps it was on the spur of the moment,' said Matheson. 'The moonlight, the heat, the excitement, the thrill of concealment, a spot too much to drink . . .'

'You haven't seen the garden, sir. Also,' said Stratton, remembering what Fenella had told him at the town hall, 'Mrs Rutherford's teetotal.'

'Sometimes people act out of character, especially when they're in unfamiliar company. I can't believe, incidentally, that alcohol was the only thing on offer.'

'Marijuana was mentioned, sir.'

'Well, there you are. Only conjecture, of course. I don't suppose you've had time to speak to anyone from the next-door house yet?'

'Afraid not, sir.'

'Hardly surprising. You might have a word now – I can't imagine they've managed to sleep through all this. I'll send someone to fetch you when the pathologist arrives.'

Number 35 had been evacuated, and its inhabitants had been given shelter, *en masse*, across the road. The basement kitchen was crowded to bursting with adults and children clad in various combinations of nightclothes, shawls and coats. The men, both white and coloured, had settled round the table on an assortment of battered chairs to drink rum, while the women, drooping around the edges of the room, jiggled infants in blankets and swatted ineffectually at the grizzling toddlers clustered about their legs. It didn't take Stratton long to establish that, of the thirteen inhabitants of number 35, none had been present at the party or seen anything untoward in the street outside or the back garden. None of them seemed very bothered by what had happened, and the women seemed only interested in knowing when they could go home and put the children back to bed. The white men were defensive, with a lot of 'It was people from outside, nothing to do with us.' The coloured men seemed to accept this, or at least they didn't dissent, except one, who banged his glass on the table and challenged them, 'Raas! If I could get a good job back home and I had the money to get there, you think I'd stay?' but the others seemed sunk under a pall of resignation, not willing to talk about the situation. Watching him, Stratton felt as if all the sufferings of the men's race was on their shoulders and that he, Stratton, was in some way responsible. He was more relieved than he'd have cared to admit when Dunning appeared to tell him that Dr McNally was waiting for him outside.

CHAPTER THIRTY-FOUR

'Could it have been an accident?' asked Stratton.

'Hard to see how.' McNally glanced back at Mrs Rutherford's body, which now, decorously covered by a canvas sheet, lay beneath bright arc lamps, with the stretcher placed ready beside it. 'Judging from what I've seen of this place, it would be pretty easy to trip over, but unless one were very unlucky . . .' He shook his head. 'You haven't moved anything out of the way, have you?'

'Would I?' Stratton gave the pathologist what he hoped was a look of injured innocence.

'*You* might not, but you said she was found by some firemen, and—'

'And they assured me that they'd left everything as it was.'

'Having trampled all over the garden.'

'Be fair,' said Stratton. 'They didn't know they were going to find a body.'

'I suppose not,' said McNally grudgingly. 'If it was a blow to the head, you'd need a fair amount of force. Yes,' he held up a hand, 'before you ask, it could have been a well-nourished woman. I don't suppose you found anything that looks as if it could have been used to bash her with, did you?'

'We've not had the chance to look,' said Stratton. 'As you may be aware, there's been rather a lot going on round here tonight.'

'So I gather,' said McNally drily. 'I'm looking forward to reading all about it in tomorrow's paper. In the meantime, there's not much more I can do.'

'Can you give me an idea of how long she's been dead?'

McNally pursed his lips in what Stratton privately thought of as his 'not angry, but disappointed' face, but that was clearly as much for form's sake as anything else, because he said, decisively, 'Not more than a couple of hours.'

'She was found at about twenty to one, so . . . ?'

'I'm not saying definitely, but she might still have been alive at eleven o'clock, although not much later. That's not official, of course. Now, if that's all . . .'

Remembering his conversation with Matheson, Stratton said, 'She'd not been interfered with, had she?'

'Not that I could see. Certainly no signs of violence or forced entry – underclothing wasn't disturbed. Again, it's not official, but as far as I can tell without getting her on the slab, she appears to have been lying down when she received the blow . . . Which is another reason for thinking that it *was* a blow and not the result of a fall. I didn't notice any signs that she'd been fending someone off, but I shan't know that for sure until I can examine her properly.'

'So it might not have been against her will.'

'Ah. You want me to look for signs of recent activity in that department, do you?'

'Yes, please.'

'Fair enough. We'll get her squared away, then.'

When McNally and the stretcher bearers had left, Stratton and Dunning repositioned the arc lamps for a look around the garden, but found nothing except more nettles interspersed with mounds of earth mixed up with bricks and rubble from some long-ago building work. Stratton doubted that the garden was used much, if at all, even by the children. Beside the back entrance to the house was an outside lavatory which appeared to have no door and directly in front of it lay the stiff grey body of a dead rat. Looking up and down the row, he could see only the snaggled tops of wooden fences and the silhouettes of trees.

Matheson appeared, accompanied by Hale. 'All done?'

'As much as we can, sir. Did everyone get out all right in the end?' he asked the fireman.

'Yes,' said Hale. 'A few casualties – minor injuries, so far as I'm aware, but no fatalities. At least, not from the fire.'

'Sergeant Parker's been taken to Casualty,' said Matheson, 'so I'm leaving Sergeant Lasson in charge. Most of those at the party have been patched up and gone home, but I think we've got most of the names and PC Colbert's been taking statements. It seems that Mr Rutherford was at the party, but he appears to have left before the incident because no one saw him afterwards.'

'Does he know yet, sir?'

'No. I'm assuming he'll be home by now, so I'd like you to go and break the bad news to him. There were a number of journalists crawling around the place, and one doesn't know what they might have picked up. We'll need a formal identification, of course, but that can be done in the morning. Incidentally, a couple of people mentioned that they'd seen the Rutherfords arguing,' said Matheson.

'Any reason given?'

'No – and of course I didn't tell them why I was asking – just the usual stuff about needing to account for everyone.'

'I'll ask Rutherford.'

'Yes, you might do that. And when you're finished, Dunning can drive you home. No point in you hanging around.'

Colville Road was quiet and almost deserted now, but for the fire engine and the line of policemen at each end. The pavements were littered with the aftermath of the fighting – broken glass, dotted here and there with bricks, lengths of railing, torn clothes and slews of trampled rubbish spilt from the dustbins. Walking along with Dunning, Stratton spotted a set of knuckledusters and a trilby hat and, catching his foot in something, looked down and saw that it was a brassiere.

The Austin 90 had several dents in the side doors but was otherwise intact. Stratton climbed into the passenger seat. 'I take it you know where we're going?'

'Belgravia, sir.'

No surprises there, thought Stratton, wondering if the

Rutherfords had been brought to Colville Road by a chauffeur and, if so, what had happened to him.

As they turned off Grosvenor Place and into Belgravia, Stratton, who'd been lost in thoughts about Fenella and how she'd still been wearing his bracelet, even though she couldn't have had any idea of seeing him, suddenly noticed how peaceful it was. A different country, here – calm, quiet and ordered, with all the inhabitants fast asleep with no idea of what had been happening just a few miles away across Hyde Park.

Except, apparently, Giles Rutherford. 'Looks like he's still awake, sir,' said Dunning, as they pulled up in front of a smartly appointed building. An expensive-looking car was parked outside and lights shone in the first-floor windows. The house, a five-storey affair in the middle of a terrace, was not dissimilar in architectural style to those in the streets they'd just come from, but the difference in condition was extraordinary: not a chip in the paintwork, a dustbin or a piece of litter in sight. You wouldn't dare, thought Stratton, as he crossed the pavement to ring the bell.

He wasn't sure who he'd thought was going to answer the door – some sort of flunkey, perhaps, or a maid – but after some muffled thumping noises from within, Rutherford himself appeared. His hair was ruffled and his clothes, an open-necked shirt with the sleeves rolled up and half-untucked from his trousers, looked dishevelled. His face, Stratton thought, looked pinker and puffier than he remembered it, and he was clutching a brandy balloon in one hand.

He peered owlishly at Stratton for a moment, then put a finger to his lips. 'Sssh. Don't want to wake the neighbours. My wife's friends, you know.'

Stratton's heart sank. The words were slurred, and Rutherford swayed as he led the way upstairs, losing his balance on the turn so that Stratton braced himself in case he fell backwards. 'Don't want the staff to hear.' Lurching against the door frame of the sitting room, he indicated, gesturing widely with the brandy glass and spilling some of the contents onto a handsome Chinese rug, that Stratton should take a seat. 'What can I get you?'

'Nothing for me, thanks.' All the furnishings, from the writing desk in the corner to the pieces of fancy porcelain on the mantelpiece, looked as if they had been inherited rather than bought: heirlooms from Virginia Rutherford's family, presumably. Rutherford made it across the room with some difficulty, fetching up in front of the fireplace, and, after much fumbling in his pockets and ineffectual scraping with matches, lit a cigarette. 'Wife's not home yet. Don't suppose you've brought her back from the party, have you?'

'No, sir,' said Stratton. 'I'm a police officer. DI Stratton, sir, CID, from Harrow Road.'

Rutherford considered this for a moment, tucking in his chin and rocking backwards on his heels. 'Wouldn't be playing a joke on me, would you?'

'No, sir.'

Rutherford raised his eyebrows until they all but disappeared beneath the messy thatch of his hair. 'Are you really a policeman? Because –' as Rutherford's eyes focused on his face his expression tautened into suspicion – 'you look like you've been in a punch-up.'

'Just a spot of bother, sir,' said Stratton.

'I'm not surprised.' Rutherford chuckled. 'Dangerous game, going about pretending to be an officer of the law.'

Sighing, Stratton felt in his jacket and produced his warrant card.

Rutherford squinted at it for a moment then, handing it back, said, 'In that case, you might be able to tell me what's been going on, and what the hell my wife thinks she's up to. That is,' he took a swig of brandy, 'if you have any idea. Of course, you may not, but . . .' staring moodily into his glass, he finished, 'I don't know. I don't know at all.'

'Is there any particular reason why you think she's been up to something?' asked Stratton cautiously.

'She would insist on going to that bloody party. I told her it wasn't right, hanging about with all those . . .'

'Those . . .?'

'Those . . . people. That Etheridge, sniffing round her skirts. I know that type.'

I'll bet you do, thought Stratton.

'Out for what they can get. It's not just him, it's all those others as well, after money for this scheme or that scheme, and of course they're all,' he elongated the word sarcastically, 'good causes. Virginia hasn't a clue how to say no.' Rutherford put his glass carefully on the mantelpiece then leant forward, rubbing the fingers and thumb of one hand together. 'Easy money.'

'But you agreed to accompany her.'

'I told her she wasn't going anywhere like that on her own.'

'Did you have an argument?'

'We certainly had an exchange of views.'

'And at the party itself?'

Rutherford's eyes narrowed, and he seemed to snap into sobriety. 'What's all this about? Has something happened to Virginia?'

'Yes, Mr Rutherford. Perhaps you should sit down.' Rutherford nodded and, one hand cupping his brandy glass, subsided onto the sofa. 'I'm afraid that your wife – Virginia – is dead. Her body was found about an hour and a half ago in the back garden of number 35 Colville Road – next door to where the party was taking place.'

'*What?* What do you mean, *dead*? She can't be dead.'

'We're not entirely sure about how it happened at the moment, sir. She appears to have suffered a blow to the head.'

'And she's . . .' Rutherford looked at him wonderingly, 'dead, is she? I mean, you're sure?'

'I'm afraid so, sir. I'm very sorry.'

'So what . . . I mean, what do I . . . what happens now?'

'Well, sir, tomorrow morning we'll need you to make an identification.'

'You mean it might be somebody else?'

'I'm afraid it's just a formality, sir. Someone will collect you and take you to the police mortuary. At the moment

– if you're feeling up to it, that is – I'd like you to take me through your movements last night.'

Lighting another cigarette – he appeared to have forgotten the one already smouldering in the ashtray on the mantelpiece – Rutherford said, 'What do you want to know?'

Stratton took out his notebook. 'What time did you leave the party, sir?'

'About a quarter past eleven.'

'And Mrs Rutherford didn't want to accompany you?'

'I couldn't find her. Besides, I'd had enough.'

'And you weren't aware of any disturbance?'

'Disturbance? Is that when . . .?'

'As I said, sir, we're not sure yet.' Stratton gave a brief outline of the events of the evening while Rutherford got up to replenish his glass and paced up and down in front of the fireplace. Finally, he said, 'I knew it was asking for trouble, going to that bloody party. I told her not to, but she wouldn't listen. I suppose one of the coloureds must have done it.'

'Not necessarily, sir.'

'Not necessarily,' echoed Rutherford, sarcastically. 'For God's sake, man, who else would have done it?'

'It's our job to find that out, sir. Did you come straight home after the party?'

'What the bloody hell's that got to do with it?'

'We have to ask, sir,' said Stratton pacifically. 'I appreciate that you've had a shock, Sir, but if you could try to remember . . .'

Rutherford paced again, pausing to pick up the second

smouldering cigarette and light a third from it before dropping it back into the ashtray. 'I went to see a friend.' He made a little-boy-caught-out face – clearly a practised look which Stratton imagined had served him well in the past. At the moment, however, it made him look grotesquely shifty. 'I shouldn't have, but . . .' Seeming to register that a policeman wasn't quite the right recipient for his contrite charm, he shifted abruptly into an ingratiating man-to-man tone. 'Look, if you want the truth, I was bloody angry. I went to see April because I thought she'd calm me down.'

'Who's April?'

'April Scott. Lives at Bryanston Mews in Marylebone.'

'How did you get there?'

'I drove.'

'Is Miss Scott a close friend, sir?'

Rutherford ran a hand through his hair. 'No point disguising it, I suppose. I've known her – that is, I've been seeing her – for a few months.'

'Can I ask if Mrs Rutherford was aware of this arrangement?'

'Virginia? I've no idea. It would have been extremely poor form to draw her attention to it.'

You mean, thought Stratton, that as long as you didn't rub her nose in the fact that you've got a mistress, you were doing the decent thing. 'I'm sorry, sir,' he said blandly, 'but I don't quite understand.' Rutherford's expression told him that this was only to be expected from one of his class. 'Are you saying that she was ignorant of Miss Scott's existence, or that she was indifferent to it?'

'I have no idea,' Rutherford repeated. 'I've told you, the matter was never discussed. My relations with my wife were perfectly cordial, Inspector. Now, if that's all, she has just died, and—'

'Not quite, sir. How long did you spend with Miss Scott?'

'I don't remember.'

'One hour? Two?'

'A couple of hours, I suppose. The house was dark when I came back.'

'And the staff? How many do you have?'

'Housekeeper lives upstairs, and she'd gone to bed. The chauffeur had the night off – he doesn't live on the premises – and there's a woman who comes in.'

'Names?'

'The housekeeper is Mrs Boyce, and the chauffeur's name is Logan. I don't know the name of the woman who does.'

'Right.' Stratton jotted this down. 'And what did you do when you got home?'

'Checked to see if Virginia was back – which, obviously, she wasn't, so I thought I'd wait up for her. I came in here and had a drink.'

'And you've been here ever since, have you?'

'Yes. The television was finished, so . . .' Rutherford shrugged. 'I had another drink, and . . . Well, I was waiting.'

Stratton made a mental note to check the television schedules. The epilogue, he thought, went off air at around midnight. Aloud, he said, 'That's fine, sir. We will, however, need to speak to Miss Scott, so if you could give me the details . . .'

Rutherford did so with bad grace, adding, 'I assume you'll be discreet about this.'

'I'll do my best, sir,' Stratton assumed an expression of compliant obsequiousness, 'but in the circumstances there will have to be a public inquest, and while I understand your wish to keep certain matters private, it may not be possible . . . You may,' he added, getting to his feet, 'wish to have a quiet word with members of Mrs Rutherford's family.' That's one in the eye for you, sunshine, he thought as he held out his hand. Rutherford took it for barely a second before dropping it. 'I think that's everything – for the moment, at least.'

Rutherford sank onto the sofa. 'You can see yourself out, can't you?'

CHAPTER THIRTY-FIVE

'Look at that.' PC Illingworth, who was drinking tea and looking through a pile of newspapers with a couple of the other young coppers, held up the *News of the World*. Most of the front page was taken up with two photographs. One showed a horrified housewife frozen in mid-scream as policemen struggled to bundle two young men into a Black Maria. In the other a wounded policeman, clutching his face, was being supported by two of his colleagues while an elegantly dressed young woman looked on. Stratton wondered if she'd been at the party. He'd bought a copy of the *Sunday Express* on the way into work, but seen no direct reference either to the party or to Mrs Rutherford. This, he supposed, was something to be thankful for – provided, of course, that the other papers hadn't mentioned it either.

'*Screaming women,*' read Illingworth with relish, '*helmetless policemen . . . this was London at midnight in the struggle to clear the streets.* Listen to this: *Two hundred people clashed . . . riots spread like lightning . . . Police cars and Black Marias swooped in . . . Squads of men were sent out almost continuously to different trouble spots . . . Housewives joined in the throng, shouting and waving their arms. Bottles began sailing through the air. Stones were thrown from windows. A boy of ten was hit in the mouth with a broken bottle and an elderly woman was knocked flying by the mob.* Blimey.'

PC Dobbs, who was busy tagging a pile of knuckle-dusters, coshes and various improvised weapons, said, 'It's on all the front pages. This lot –' he pointed to the jumble on the desk '– is our biggest haul yet.'

The station had an oddly festive atmosphere, with the sort of relaxed jollity that was usually only in evidence at Christmas time. In the corridor outside the office, there was a steady stream of tramping feet from cells to charge room and back again, and the hubbub coming from the foyer told him that the desk sergeant was still up to his eyes dealing with the various relatives of the people who'd been brought in. Picking up another paper, Illingworth read out the headlines in a declamatory tone: '*RACE RIOT IN LONDON: Truncheons out as violence flares on a Saturday night in Notting Hill. Knife-and-club mob battles with police.* Looks like we missed all the fun.' 'Look on the bright side,' said Stratton. 'You'll probably miss more tonight.'

'Let's hope not.' Jellicoe stuck his head round the door. 'We're full up as it is.'

'Just my luck.' Illingworth carried on complaining. 'I'm not on nights till next week. They had dogs down at Bramley Road and everything.'

'Yes, and five coppers ended up in Casualty,' said Jellicoe. 'One of them had his head split open, so you just be thankful that you were tucked up safe in bed.'

'What's the tally?' asked Stratton.

'There's twelve in the cells at Shepherd's Bush,' said Jellicoe, 'and we've got twenty-three – plus your lot from yesterday, of course.'

Stratton massaged his temples. 'I need to speak to Matheson about them – we think the same van might have been used last night, and there were people from the White Defence League goose-stepping about all over the place. You haven't got Eddy Knight downstairs by any chance, have you?'

'Sorry. He's not at Shepherd's Bush either. Gleeson is, though.'

'I saw Gleeson,' said Stratton. 'I didn't see Knight, but I'll bet he was there somewhere. He struck me as someone who wouldn't be able to resist the chance to prance about in his Nazi get-up. You're all right hanging onto Baxter and Co. for the moment, aren't you?'

'No skin off my nose,' said Jellicoe. 'Matthews might not be too happy about it, though.'

'I can't help that.' It hadn't been Stratton's intention to antagonise the station sergeant any further, but there was fuck all he could do about it. He was aching all over and dog-tired, having dragged himself out of bed after only four hours' sleep. He knew what he must look like. He'd got a shock when he'd gone to shave, seeing his face, grey with fatigue in the bathroom mirror, the blackened eye staring back at him. A smooth chin and a clean shirt hadn't gone nearly as far as they might in counteracting the impression of an ageing heavy who'd lost an argument. He'd spent a couple of hours wearily sifting through the statements from the partygoers taken the previous night, and had come up with what he hoped was a definitive list, together with a note of who'd been treated *in situ* and who'd been taken to hospital. Fenella's statement was among them. Reading it, he saw that Colbert had noted the time at five-and-twenty to one. He hoped she'd been able to get home soon afterwards – he'd telephone her when he had a moment to himself and find out. Feeling a quiet pleasure at the memory of their lunch together and her parting words to him, he returned to the list he'd compiled. Councillor Watson had clearly cast his invitations far and wide: there were two members of Parliament, a pop singer and two well-known jazz musicians among them. None had given statements, and Stratton imagined that, having removed themselves from imminent danger in the club, they'd got out of the area as swiftly as possible.

'At least,' said Jellicoe, who'd been studying the paper over Illingworth's shoulder, 'they aren't trying to pretend that this one isn't a race riot.'

'Don't think anyone would buy it this time,' said Stratton.

'Doesn't look like they bought it last time either,' said Illingworth, holding up a front page which read: *RACE VIOLENCE GROWS*.

'People aren't stupid,' said Jellicoe. 'And,' he added, gesturing at the newspapers, 'you'd best get rid of that lot before Matheson comes back. He said to tell you he went to take Rutherford to identify his missus,' he told Stratton. 'I'd have come in earlier, but I haven't had a minute. He's got someone over there taking statements from the staff as well, and a bunch have gone out to start re-interviewing all the people from that party about Mrs Rutherford. He says he'll talk to the MPs himself, sir.' Blimey, thought Stratton. Talk about quick off the mark – had the man actually managed to get any sleep? 'The other thing,' Jellicoe sounded apologetic, 'is that he's not made any statement to the press about Mrs R and he's made it clear that if anybody breathes a word to a journalist – I'm sure you wouldn't dream of it, sir, but I have to pass it on – he'll have their guts for garters.'

As the statements from the partygoers had been taken before the discovery of Mrs Rutherford's body, no one had particular reason to mention her and, apart from Gloria, they didn't. Gloria's statement, which was short and otherwise uninformative, was also the only one to mention Etheridge. Stratton was wondering what had happened to him. Perhaps Duffy had taken him home – or rather, if Duffy's state was anything to go by, he'd taken Duffy. Glancing over at the front page of the *Sunday Times* – *MIDNIGHT RIOT IN LONDON: Fighting rocks trouble district*, he was considering this in a weary sort of way when the telephone rang. 'For you, sir. A Mrs Perlmann. Putting you through . . .'

'Hello? Hello?'

'Good morning, madam.'

'Is that Detective Inspector Stratton?'

'Yes, Mrs Perlmann, it is. I understand you wish to speak to me.'

'It's my husband who wishes to speak to you, Inspector.'

Stratton had assumed that Mrs Perlmann would have an accent similar to her husband's, but this lady sounded crisply English. 'He says it's urgent.'

'Can you put him on the line?'

'I'm afraid that's not possible.'

'Then perhaps he could telephone later?' asked Stratton, mystified.

'He's in hospital.' Mrs Perlmann sounded exasperated. 'That's why he can't get to a telephone.'

'Was he injured?'

'Injured?'

'Last night.'

'No, Inspector. He had a heart attack this morning. I've only just been allowed in to see him, and he won't talk about anything except how he wants to see you. The doctors haven't said so but it's serious, and Danny knows it, which is why he keeps . . .' She faltered, her voice thickened with tears, then stopped.

'Where is he?' asked Stratton.

'Edgware General. Please, Inspector – as soon as you can.'

CHAPTER THIRTY-SIX

Danny Perlmann looked terrible. His face was a greyish-yellow, with a clamminess that made the skin look like wet dough, his breathing was shallow and laboured, and the vitality Stratton had noticed was entirely gone. Tucked severely into a hospital bed and screened off from the rest of the ward, he fell back on the pillows after only a token attempt to sit up when Stratton appeared, and looked as though he might die at any moment.

'He's had a serious coronary,' the matron had hissed in disgust when Stratton showed his warrant card. 'I can let you have five minutes –' she'd picked up the watch hanging from her bosom and glared at it to indicate the exactness of the amount – 'but that's it.'

'How are you feeling?' asked Stratton.

'Bloody hell.' His voice was low, and getting the words out was clearly an effort. 'Those bastards.'

'The White Defence League? Did they give you any more trouble?'

'They tried, but the police stop them. I'm a foreigner,' Perlmann added matter-of-factly. 'The White Defence League don't like me. Tell me to go back home. They say, "Go back where you come from," but you know, Inspector, I can't go back. Even if I wanted to, I couldn't go.' He spoke in a rush, his normally fluent English breaking up. 'I come from Lvov. In 1918, when I was born, Lvov was in Poland. When I was young man, it was in Poland. Now – after the war – it's part of the Soviet Union. So tell me, how can I go back to a place that doesn't exist? And even here . . . You know, Inspector, all these years I have been in this country, and they won't make me a British citizen. I don't understand. My wife is British. British and Polish fight on the same side in the war. I'm as good as any of them, but now I learned that they turn down my application again.' Stratton nodded, remembering what Laskier had said in the nightclub – *Danny wants all these top-drawer people to accept him . . . He dreams of a knighthood*. He had no idea what he was supposed to say. Surely Perlmann hadn't asked to see him because he thought that he, Stratton, had the power to change anyone's mind? 'That man,' Perlmann continued, 'that Watson—'

'Councillor Watson?'

'Yes, him. That party, last night, I want to tell him . . .'

'Is that why you were there, to speak to him? Do you think it's something to do with him, why you were turned down?'

'Yes. He makes trouble for me, so I want to ask him why. Stefan try to tell me . . . waste of time, but I thought . . .' He made a weak flapping motion with one pudgy hand, 'Ach, stupid. What happened when we left, Inspector? More trouble?' Stratton hesitated. 'Yes, more trouble. I can see from your face.'

'I'm afraid . . .' Stratton began explaining, first about the petrol bombs and then about Mrs Rutherford. '. . . and of course,' he concluded, 'there'll be an investigation, and I'm sure—'

'No . . .' Perlmann reached out and grabbed his arm. 'No . . .' There were beads of sweat on his forehead.

'I'm sorry, Mr Perlmann. I know she was a friend of yours.'

Perlmann's grip on Stratton's arm increased and Stratton had the impression that every ounce of strength in the man's body was going into his fingers. 'Tell my wife I need to talk to Stefan. It's important. Tell her Stefan must come . . .'

'I'll tell her, but I'm not sure he'll be allowed to see you today,' said Stratton.

'He must. I can't . . .' Perlmann gave up with a slight shake of his head. Whether it was because it was too complicated to explain or whether the effort required to get the words out was too much, Stratton wasn't sure. 'Would you like me to fetch a nurse?' he asked.

'No.' The thick fingers were like pincers on his arm. 'I want to tell you . . . Stefan, he is good. A good man. His wife, Lola, she was there in the war. Different camp – place called Majdanek – so we did not know her then but later, when we come here . . . She's dead. From six months. It was too much. She couldn't . . .' Stratton saw the film of tears in Perlmann's eyes.

'Did she commit suicide?' he asked gently.

'She hanged herself. She pinned a note here,' Perlmann tapped his chest with one hand, 'written in Polish. *Stefan, I am sorry.*' I tell you this because Stefan will not speak. He tell me, I don't know why I thought I could protect her. You can't protect from the past, even if you share it. He said they never talk about it. He said . . .' Perlmann paused to catch his breath. 'Only once they talk. He said to her how it's different now – he told me she was angry when he says this. She said the world does not change – if someone thinks so then he's a fool – that it can happen again. Lola can't sleep, she won't go outside and when she does, always with food in her pockets . . . She thinks when Stefan goes out, someone will take him – that she will never see him again.' Perlmann's breathing was now alarmingly laboured. Between gasps, he whispered, 'He is a good man. He trusts you. Help him.'

'I understand,' Stratton assured him, hoping it sounded like the truth.

'He doesn't know . . .' Perlmann tailed off, not looking at Stratton any more. In fact, his eyes no longer seemed to be focused on anything.

'I'm going to call a nurse,' said Stratton, 'So . . .' He looked down at Perlmann's hand, which was still clamped round his arm, and for some reason he thought of Monica grasping his little finger when she was a baby. As tenderly as he could, he detached the gripping fingers and was about to go and find a nurse when Perlmann spoke again. At first Stratton heard only fragments of words – Polish, he thought, not

English. Suddenly, in a hoarse but clear whisper, Perlmann said, 'I ate shit, but I never ate German shit.'

'I understand,' Stratton repeated, and stepped outside the screens.

CHAPTER THIRTY-SEVEN

April Scott's flat in Bryanston Mews was a luxurious affair. On two floors above a garage, it had been done up to the nines with shutters and window boxes of tumbling pink and red geraniums. No expense had been spared inside either – and there was more than a touch, Stratton thought, of Hollywood: a thick, rose-coloured carpet, leopard skin, tumbling cushions, all the latest gadgets. His lack of sleep and the battered appearance he knew he presented made him feel shabbier than ever. Going upstairs to the toilet, he peered into one of the bedrooms and saw a vast bed with a canopy over it, an oval mirror inset in the middle of the pleated silk. Through the half-open door of a white and gold fitted cupboard he spotted a mink coat on a hanger. Miss Scott was clearly not a girl who came cheap.

When Stratton looked at her, the words *poule de luxe* appeared in his mind. He wasn't sure of their precise meaning, but they were certainly appropriate. Golden-haired, manicured and undeniably gorgeous, she was evidently as expensively maintained as the flat. She was also disarmingly friendly, very bright and extremely self-assured, with a slight accent that Stratton couldn't quite place but which slipped out now and again despite her best efforts to hide it.

She'd insisted on making him a cup of coffee – 'I've got a new type of machine – imported from Italy – just wait till you taste it!' – and, his cursory glance round the upper floor completed, Stratton sat in the sunny window watching a chauffeur in shirtsleeves polishing an Alvis on the cobbles. He pictured Perlmann as he'd left him, lying supine in his hospital bed while nurses bustled about him, and thought of his conversation with Maxine Perlmann, who'd been feverishly pacing the corridor outside the ward and who'd pounced on him the moment he'd emerged. Perhaps ten years younger than her husband, she was slender and long-legged, with a delicate pink-and-white beauty. An English rose, Stratton had thought, surprised: despite the accent he'd heard on the phone, he'd somehow expected someone more foreign-looking.

She'd looked askance at his eye, but said only, 'Danny thinks he's dying.'

'Yes,' Stratton had agreed cautiously, 'and he's clearly not well, but that doesn't necessarily mean—'

'What do you think?'

'People recover from heart attacks, Mrs Perlmann,' he'd said authoritatively.

'He went to see a specialist and they gave him some heart pills, but I never thought ... He always said there was nothing to worry about. You know,' she added with a wan smile, 'that specialist died a couple of months ago – a heart attack. When Danny heard about it he couldn't stop laughing. I've never seen him laugh so much.' A smile, bright with the happiness of the memory, had flickered momentarily across her face.

'Do you think they'll let me see him now?'

'I'd leave it a bit if I were you. The nurses were with him when I left.'

'Why? What's—'

'Just routine,' Stratton had said soothingly. 'He says he needs to speak to Stefan Laskier.'

'Stefan? For business – *now*?' She'd blown out her lips in exasperation.

'He was very insistent, Mrs Perlmann.'

'That's what's done this. The worrying, rushing about the place, staying out all night every night. The war – what he went through – weakened his heart, and all of this is making it worse. What did he want to talk to you about, anyway?'

'He was worried about the trouble last night. I think I managed to put his mind at rest.' Stratton's main aim in saying this had been to avoid alarming Mrs Perlmann who, he felt, had enough on her plate already with worrying about her husband. Thinking about it now, he still had no real idea what it was that Perlmann had been trying to tell him, and – more importantly – why. No wonder Laskier always looked so unhappy, thought Stratton. Ever since Perlmann had told him, he'd had the picture in his mind of the hanging woman, feet dangling uselessly, and the note – he imagined a pathetically small scrap of paper, curled at the edges – pinned to her clothing. What about her family?

Had she known, or been able to find out, what had happened to them? Did Laskier and Perlmann know what had happened to theirs, or had there come a point when they realised that there was simply no way that they could have survived? *Lola can't sleep, won't go outside . . . She thinks when Stefan goes out, someone will take him – that she will never see him again.* The enormity of it was too much to think about in any rational way. There weren't words – or, if there were, Stratton did not know them.

He tried to concentrate on remembering what else Perlmann had said. *He doesn't know . . .* What didn't Laskier know? It was after he'd broken the news of Mrs Rutherford's death that Perlmann had insisted that he must see Laskier, so maybe it had to do with that. Laskier had said that Mrs Rutherford – or anyway her family – had lent Perlmann money. Perhaps that was something to do with it. And Laskier had said something about Perlmann doing deals and forgetting to mention them afterwards . . .

While April Scott fussed with coffee cups, Stratton took another look around the room: fancy furniture upholstered in green and gold, and a huge golden harp standing in one corner. He had no idea whether you could actually get a tune out of the thing, but it certainly looked as if it might have cost a bit. Had Rutherford paid for it? Perhaps Fenella had been wrong and he *did* have money of his own . . . Otherwise, all of this – plus, presumably, the running costs, which wouldn't be cheap – must have been paid for by his wife, without her knowledge.

April passed a cup and seated herself opposite him,

fluffing out her skirt and making sure that he had ample opportunity to admire her legs. 'How can I help, Inspector?'

Keeping his eyes fixed firmly on her face – as if that wasn't quite distracting enough – Stratton said, 'I take it you've heard about Mrs Rutherford?'

'Yes. It's very sad.' Her aura of self-assurance seemed, somehow, to have crystallised so that, for a moment, she appeared to him like a ventriloquist's dummy: bright and alert but devoid of expression, the beautiful features hard and shiny. Rutherford, he thought, had primed her for this conversation. Did she, he wondered, hope to become – after a suitable interval – the man's next wife? Somehow, he doubted that Rutherford, however infatuated, would consider marrying a woman without money, and he'd lay a bet that April's only assets were her looks.

'Mr Rutherford says he came to see you last night. What time was that?'

April rearranged her legs, then gave him an up-from-under look that he was sure came straight out of a film magazine. Finally, she said, 'Well, I'm not entirely sure. I think it must have been about half past ten.'

'Why?'

She turned her head sideways and started playing with the bracelet she was wearing on her right wrist. It was made of gold chain and had a heavy-looking medallion attached to it. Stratton found himself wondering whether it was a present from Rutherford and, if so, whether it was inscribed. Sensing the direction of his gaze, she flashed him a tight smile. 'I don't understand.'

'What makes you think it was half past ten, Miss Scott?'

'Well, you know . . .' The smile became more intimate. 'It was Saturday night, and, to be honest, I'm not usually at home.' She paused, fiddling with the bracelet again, allowing him to imagine an infinity of glamorous possibilities. 'I washed my hair, and listened to some music . . .' She gestured towards several long-playing records scattered about the carpet beside the record player. Cocking his head, he read: *The King & I*, *Salad Days*, *The Boyfriend*. All musicals, and, he thought, several years old – Rutherford's taste, perhaps, rather than hers. There was some classical music too – Vivaldi and Bach. Rutherford definitely hadn't seemed the type for those, he thought. Perhaps April was going in for a spot of self-improvement. 'I didn't really notice what time it was,' she said now. 'I wasn't expecting to see Giles.'

'Does he often turn up without making an appointment?'

His choice of words had been deliberate, meant to be insulting, but April remained unruffled. 'He'd told me he had to go to some function or other. To be honest, it sounded pretty boring, and I wasn't really paying much attention. I'd assumed he'd be there all evening, so . . .' She shrugged.

'You didn't make other plans?'

April twiddled the bracelet a bit more, then said, 'I thought it would be nice to have an evening to myself.'

She's confident, Stratton thought. She knows she's protected. 'What did you do when he was here?'

She gave him a saucy smile. 'What do you think, Inspector?'

Two can play at that game, thought Stratton. In his most

courteous tone, he said, 'You spent the entire time fucking, did you?'

For a moment April's eyes opened wide in surprise, but she covered it well, saying, with a little giggle, 'Not quite all the time. We had a drink, and he said he was hungry, so I made him some bacon and eggs.' She reached for her handbag, a large, cream-coloured leather affair standing on the carpet beside her chair, and, removing a compact, began powdering her nose.

'Did you talk at all?'

April looked up from the hand-mirror. 'Well, of course.'

'What about?'

Inspecting her face once more, she said complacently, 'Giles said that the party was dull so he'd come to see me instead.'

'What else did he say?'

'I don't really remember.' She dropped the compact back into the handbag and closed it with an expensive-sounding snap. 'Nothing very important.'

'When did he leave?'

April looked vaguely round the room, then said, 'About midnight?'

'Are you asking me or telling me, Miss Scott?'

'Oh . . .' She tried the saucy smile again. 'I can't really remember. We'd had some champagne, you know . . .'

'How much?'

'I'm not sure. A bottle, I suppose.'

'Did he seem drunk to you?'

'I wouldn't say so. He was a bit fed up.'

'Why?'

'Just about the party. He said that his . . . that Mrs Rutherford had wanted him to go with her, but the whole thing was a washout.'

'And at that point you didn't know anything about the party, where it was, or . . .'

'Not then. He told me later, when he telephoned.'

'When was that?'

'About a quarter to three, I think. He woke me up.'

Just after I'd left him, thought Stratton. 'And how did he seem then?'

'Well, he was very upset and he'd been drinking. He wanted to come over but I told him not to. I didn't think,' she added, primly, 'that it would be right.' And, thought Stratton, you were worried about how it would look if anyone found out. 'He told me about the fighting, too. I was a bit surprised when he said he'd gone to a party in Notting Hill. I mean, it's not exactly a nice area, is it?'

'Not like this,' said Stratton. April Scott, he guessed, was very keen on – and shrewd at – feathering her own nest, and not very much interested in things that didn't pertain directly to herself. 'Does Rutherford own this place?'

April looked down at the bracelet, contenting herself, this time, with merely turning her wrist so that it slipped round a bit, then said, 'I don't know.'

'Oh,' said Stratton genially, 'I think you do – clever girl like you. I can't believe you haven't made it your business to find out. And,' he added thoughtfully, 'because you are such a clever girl, you'll certainly know that it'd be the work of . . . oh, ten minutes or so . . . for me to find out, and you'll also know –' here he widened his eyes and nodded for emphasis – 'that lying to the police is not a good idea and can get you into *lots* and *lots* of trouble, no matter who your friends are.'

April stared at him imperiously for a moment, then, seeing that this wasn't going to work, said, 'This flat belongs to a man called Danny Perlmann.'

'Really?' Whatever Stratton had been expecting, it wasn't that. Now all sorts of possibilities swam into his head. 'And do you know Mr Perlmann?'

April tossed her head. 'I wouldn't say that. I've met him.'

'Oh? Where?'

'I can't exactly remember.'

'I'm sure you can if you try.' Stratton sat back and crossed his arms. 'And if you're going to keep me waiting, I'll have another cup of that delicious coffee.'

The implication that he wasn't going to move until he got what he wanted did the trick. 'At his club.' April was staring at him now with barely concealed hatred. 'Maxine's.'

'Anywhere else?'

She hesitated a fraction of a second too long before replying. 'I don't think so.'

'Here, for instance?'

'Well . . . Giles may have brought him here a few times.'

'Why? Was it a *ménage à trois*?'

'They were playing cards,' snapped April. 'There were other people as well.'

'Gambling?'

'I didn't say that.'

'You didn't have to. So Rutherford pays rent to Perlmann, does he?'

'I suppose so.'

Stratton rose. 'Thank you, Miss Scott. You've been most helpful.'

Turning at the front door, Stratton stuck out his hand. When April Scott responded in kind, he held onto her firmly and, using his other hand, grabbed the medallion on the chain round her wrist and turned it over while she yelped in indignation and tried to squirm free. '*To gorgeous April from Danny. 12.8.58,*' he read aloud. 'Looks as if the flat isn't the only thing round here that's owned by Mr Perlmann. Does Mr Rutherford pay rent for you as well?'

The last thing he saw was her open mouth, pink, clean and outraged – like a cat's, he thought. Without bothering to wait for a reply, he clattered down the stairs and out into the street. 'He doesn't know!' April shouted frenziedly after him. 'Danny doesn't know!'

CHAPTER THIRTY-EIGHT

'It was pretty strange, sir. Perlmann was talking about how he'd not been given British citizenship, and he told me about Laskier's wife who committed suicide six months ago. I think Mrs Perlmann's right and he believes he's dying. He's definitely trying to protect Laskier from something, but I'm not sure what. It could be to do with the Rutherfords – when I told him what had happened to Mrs R he demanded to see Laskier at once – but I think it's something bigger than that. Oh, and Giles Rutherford's been playing around with Perlmann's mistress, April Scott. And on that subject, I'm not at all sure that she's telling the truth about Rutherford being there last night.'

'You think he *wasn't* there?' asked Matheson. Standing in his office, sipping a cup of coffee, he looked as neat and spry as usual.

'I think he probably *was* there at some point,' said Stratton cautiously. 'It's the timing I'm wondering about.'

'The new statements ought to help us there,' said Matheson. 'At least, if it was before all the rumpus. He must have said goodbye to someone at the party before taking his leave.'

'I suppose so,' said Stratton. 'I think the only reason he admitted that he'd gone to see Miss Scott was because I'd caught him on the hop – he realised he needed some sort of alibi but he wasn't sober enough to come up with anything else on the spur of the moment . . . Which, I have to say, suggests that if he did have anything to do with his wife's death it wasn't premeditated. I don't think it's anything to do with Perlmann, by the way – I mean, Virginia Rutherford's death isn't. I think that may have caused problems for him rather than the other way round.'

'But you say Rutherford was seeing Miss Scott behind his back?'

'Yes, but I'm pretty sure Perlmann isn't aware of it. Miss Scott made a point of telling me that. I think that Giles Rutherford enjoys the good things in life and he doesn't care too much if they happen to belong to other people, but I can't see why he'd have killed his wife. Unless he has money of his own – the general opinion seems to be against – it would be tantamount to killing the goose that laid the golden eggs.'

'Unless she was going to remove the source of the golden eggs by divorcing him – or he'd spent a lot of her money without her knowledge and was about to be found out.'

'Possible,' said Stratton. 'What was Rutherford like this morning?'

'Well, he'd obviously got a sore head,' said Matheson, 'and he did seem pretty upset, although I had the impression he felt more sorry for himself than his wife. Said a couple of times that it was just his luck that it should have happened.'

'His bad luck, you mean?'

'Definitely. The implication was that she'd failed him. He said that she hadn't been herself recently, and . . .' Matheson wagged his head significantly, 'he also admitted he'd left the party because she was – as he put it – making a fool of herself with Etheridge.'

'Well, we know that she was keen on him, sir. We saw that at the nightclub. Rutherford didn't seem to be paying much attention at the time, but that might have been a deliberate ploy.'

'Yes,' said Matheson thoughtfully, 'it might. But the "bad luck" business suggests that he sees his wife's death as a bad thing – for him at least.'

There was a knock on the door. 'Sorry to disturb, sir,' said PC Dunning. 'Telephone call for DI Stratton. It's an Irish bloke, sir. Says it's urgent but won't give his name or talk to anyone else.'

Picking up the receiver with a surge of hope, Stratton could hear the faint sound of chatter and the rattle of glasses in the background. 'Inspector Stratton?'

'Speaking. Can I help you?'

'O'Driscoll, sir, from the pub. It's about that car.'

'Hello, Joseph. The green van?' said Stratton. 'Tell me.'

'No, sir. The other.'

'The Bentley?'

'That's the one. I thought you'd like to know. I saw it again last night.'

'You're sure it was the same one?'

'Sure as I can be, sir. It's like Mr Norris told you, we don't see too many cars like that around here. I couldn't swear it was the same man driving, but I think so. He'd two other fellows with him – one beside him and one in the back.'

'What time was this?'

'After closing time.'

'So . . . eleven or thereabouts?'

'Must have been a while after eleven, sir. I'd been clearing up for quite a time – we'd had a busy night of it. I was out at the back emptying some rubbish when I saw the car.'

'So where was it?'

'Driving down Australia Road, sir.'

'Can you describe any of the people?'

'Not really, sir. I'm pretty sure they were all men, but it was too dark to see what they looked like. But the colour's either dark blue or black – I saw that when they went under a street lamp, and the first two letters of the registration – P and then F.'

Stratton put down the receiver and sat at his desk trying to picture the car that had been parked outside the Rutherfords' house. There'd hardly been any other cars in the street at the time. When he'd asked Rutherford how he'd got to April Scott's, he'd said 'I drove', so presumably he'd left the same way he'd arrived and parked the car in the street outside the house. He jumped up and stuck his head out of the door. 'Dunning!'

The young constable appeared at the double. 'Sir?'

'Last night, the car outside the Rutherfords' house – what sort was it?'

'Bentley, sir. Dark blue one.'

'Find out the model and registration of Rutherford's car, would you?'

'Yes, sir. And there was another phone call just now, sir. Woman called Gloria wants to speak to you. She was speaking from a public box – says it's about the woman who got killed last night and it's urgent and you know where to find her, sir.'

CHAPTER THIRTY-NINE

The attic room was stifling and smelt of dusty fabric. There was dust, too, on the scratched Jacobean-style table and the petals of the faded plastic flowers on the mantelpiece. The smeared windows offered only a view of a series of gardens choked with rubbish and the backs of other houses, and the damp stains on the walls and ceiling suggested that you might need to put out more than one bucket when it rained. Gloria had made the effort to brighten the place up by tacking covers torn from *Picturegoer* magazine to the walls. Stratton looked round at images of Joan Collins, Kim Novak and Diana Dors. *Do you copy the stars?* he read. *Then turn to page 12. I feel sorry for Johnnie Ray by the girl who sang with him. You're so wrong about me says Ava Gardner. Inside, colour pictures of Laurie London, Dirk Bogarde and Doris Day.*

Gloria looked terrible. Chalk white, with blue-grey smudges beneath her eyes, she had her right arm in a sling. She must be right-handed, Stratton thought – the shaky attempt to add some glamour with a dash of red lipstick made her look like a ghoul that had forgotten to wipe its mouth.

'They had to put stitches in,' she said. 'I was waiting for over an hour.' Evidently realising what was on his mind, she added, 'You're not exactly an oil painting yourself.'

'I know,' said Stratton. 'What was it you wanted to tell me?'

'Do you know if Clinton's all right?'

'Clinton Etheridge?'

'Yes. Do you know where he is?'

''Fraid not. You said it was urgent, Gloria – about a woman who got killed. What's going on?'

'I'm worried about him, that's all.'

'You'd better not be telling me you've brought me down here just for that, or—'

'No, please.' Gloria put a hand on his arm. Close to, she smelt stale and sickly. 'I'm just worried about him, that's all. I don't know what's happened, and I thought . . . I don't know what I thought. And there is something about the woman last night. I never said when the copper asked me because I didn't realise – well, no one did, did they? Only afterwards.'

'Which woman are you talking about?'

'Her in the garden. Can I have a cigarette?'

'Here.' Stratton took out his packet of Churchman's and lit one for her, then one for himself. 'What woman in the garden?'

'You know,' said Gloria, exhaling an impatient stream of smoke. 'The dead one.'

'How do you know about that?'

'Bloody hell.' Rolling her eyes at him, she added, 'Every-one knows.'

'Who's everyone?'

'Everyone in Colville Road, at any rate. Got eyes, haven't they? I've got a friend lives next door to the house. She saw you lot in the garden. She said they put things round so you couldn't see, but she got a good look before that, with all them lamps and stuff, and she said the woman's frock was like something Alma Cogan would wear and you couldn't miss it if you tried.'

'And when did she tell you this?'

'She didn't. When I come out of the hospital I went down to Dot's, the all-night caff on Westbourne Park Road.'

'Why didn't you go home?'

Gloria sighed. 'I was looking for Clinton. Didn't find him, but I saw this girl I know, and she said she was down that way and my friend told her, and then she told me, and described the frock and everything, I knew it couldn't be no one else. It's that posh woman, Mrs Rutherford, who helped to organise the party. Clinton's "important new friend", you called her – he told me who she was after you'd gone.'

'OK,' said Stratton. 'What about her?'

'Well . . .' Gloria's confidence seemed to desert her and she subsided awkwardly onto the room's single, sagging armchair, wincing as her right shoulder came into contact with the back. 'I only found out about the party after you went to see Clinton. What with you talking about his new friend, and then I saw all them bottles out the back, I asked him straight out what was going on and he tells me that him and his friend on the council and Lady Muck are having a party and they've got all these politicians and famous people coming.' She flicked ash peevishly at the floorboards. 'I asked Clinton when he'd been planning to tell me about it, and he got the needle and said it wasn't nothing to do with me and I'm not invited.'

Interesting, thought Stratton, given that meeting the local flora and fauna was supposed to be the object of the exercise. At least, it was according to the Hon. Virginia and Mr Watson. Etheridge, clearly, had his own agenda, and it wasn't one that involved Gloria.

'So,' she continued, dredging up the word with a sigh, 'come the evening, I go out as usual, but after a couple of hours I thought I'd go and see. I mean, I was fed up – all this about his new friend and famous people . . . It's like, my money's good enough for him but I'm not, so he wants to go on the batter with a load of posh birds. Half of me's thinking he's pulling a fast one and he's got something else going on, and I wanted to know what he was up to, see? He said he was just hustling and if it wasn't for the fact he could get money out of this woman he wouldn't have anything to do with her. Anyway, come half past ten I'd had enough, so I go down to Colville Road to see this woman for myself. There's a party, like Clinton said, so I thought, I'm going in – why shouldn't I?'

'You didn't notice all the disturbance?'

Gloria shrugged. 'More people about than usual, but no one give me any trouble and anyway, I wasn't bothering about that, I just want to find out what Clinton's up to, don't I? So I get there, and there's lots of people and music and I thought, well, he's obviously having me on about all these politicians, because they wouldn't . . .' Here Gloria faltered and paid great attention to her cigarette.

'We know there were drugs on the premises, Gloria. This is a murder inquiry – we're not interested in anything else.'

'Oh, all right,' said Gloria. 'Well, as soon as I went in the place I could tell they'd been smoking weed from the smell. Then I spot my friend Vicky who I work with—'

'Vicky Allardice from Colville Terrace?'

Gloria nodded. 'You've met her. Anyway, she's dancing with this fat bloke who's mad keen to be her best friend, if you know what I mean, and she says he's the MP for Hammersmith or somewhere. So I've asked her what she's doing there and she says she was invited – her and Terri and Rita and a couple of the other girls, and when I look round the room I can see some of their boyfriends as well. Anyway, Vicky says it's all a big laugh, and she tells me how at the start these MPs and people are in one corner being all stiff and polite and staring at them like they're in a zoo or something, and then Sporty – that's Rita's boyfriend, he's this big Jamaican bloke – he goes up to this woman who looks like a duchess and offers her some draw. Vicky said she almost wet herself but she had a smoke and she's going, 'Ooh, how nice!' like it's a tea party. I wondered if that was Clinton's friend so I asked Vicky a bit more and Vicky said she was wearing this great big frock and she looked like a horse . . . Clinton had said that too – the horse thing – when we was arguing, so I thought, OK, that must be Mrs Rutherford, but Vicky said she must have gone because she couldn't see her anywhere. Then I asked Vicky if she'd seen Clinton but she hadn't and nor had anyone else. Anyway,' Gloria leant forward, immersed now in her narrative, 'there was plenty to drink so I helped myself and had a look round. I couldn't see Clinton, but I saw a couple of friends of his, Charlie and Tony, and they said they didn't know where he was – or if they did they weren't saying.'

'And this was what time?' asked Stratton.

'Dunno.' Gloria pulled a face, thinking. 'About eleven, I suppose. I spent quite a long time with Sporty and this la-di-da sort with pearls on who was getting all hot and bothered just being around him. I felt so angry with Clinton that I wanted to say to her, you wouldn't think he was so wonderful if he put you on the game, love, because that's all they're good for. I had another drink then, and I went into the little room they've got at the back. It's usually a storeroom, but Clinton had tidied it up and there were people in there chatting. Then I spotted there was someone in the garden so I went for a look.'

'Wasn't it dark?'

'Yes, but they'd propped the door open for air and there was light coming out the window, so you could see a bit. Anyway, I saw her. Vicky was right about the big frock – I saw the skirt first, all sticking out and bright blue with stuff stuck on it. I'd have gone out there, but then I saw she wasn't talking to Clinton, but some other bloke.'

'What did he look like?'

'Well, he was white for a start. About thirty-five, I'd say. Must have been really gorgeous when he was younger. Light-ish hair, sort of pinky tanned face, linen suit, stripy open-necked shirt, nice gold watch . . .'

'Tall? Short?'

'Quite tall, I think. I noticed he was only a little bit taller than her but she struck me as being more like a man than a woman, really. Reminded me of a bloke who used to come and see me: brought his own frock and apron and wanted to dust the place and be called Muriel while he was doing it.'

It had to have been Virginia Rutherford, thought Stratton. Apart from the description of the dress, she had to be, he reckoned, around 5 foot 10 or 11 in height plus she'd been wearing shoes with heels which would bring her up to, say, six foot. Rutherford was a similar height to himself which would make him, as Gloria had said, only a little bit taller. 'Did you hear him say anything?'

'Oh, yes. They were having a right old ding-dong.'

'What about?'

Gloria frowned. 'I'm not really sure. I didn't catch all of it, but at one point he said something about why was she being so high and mighty. Anyway, I'm listening to this and thinking Clinton's got to be somewhere round the place when someone comes up behind me and grabs my arm, and it's him. "What the hell do you think you're doing?" an' all this and he's dragged me off up the garden—'

'So you went past the man and the woman?'

'Straight past, but they never noticed, just carried on arguing.'

'Did Etheridge know they were there?'

'He wasn't paying no attention – too busy trying to get me away from his nice posh friends so I don't ruin his chances. And it's pitch black once you get away from the little bit of light outside the house. I can't see a bloody thing and I feel like I've twisted my ankle and I'm yelling for Clinton to stop, only he won't let go. He's going on about how I'm going to wreck everything and I'm saying, "Oh, so I'm not good enough for your smart new friends? Let's just ask them whose money it was they think bought you that flash suit and them rings." Then I said—' Gloria's eyes flashed with the memory of it '—I said, "Those posh birds going to get that for you, are they? You want to remember which side your bread's buttered, you do." Course, now he's realised I'm not going to take any shit off him, he's trying to calm me down and he's going, "Come on, man, you've seen how she looks," so I said, "Yeah, but it doesn't stop you fancying her money, does it?" And by now I'm screaming at him, "Did you fuck her?" and all this, and he's doing his nut trying to get me to shut up.'

I'll bet he was, thought Stratton. He'd already lost one potential source of income that day in the form of Irene, and now here was Gloria, tanked up and yelling her tits off, threatening another. 'Do you think the man and woman heard you?'

'I don't know. I never looked to see if they were still there.'

'What about the people in the house?'

'I doubt it. That music was bloody loud and from what I saw they were all, you know . . .'

'So what happened then?'

'Well, Clinton's telling me he never laid a hand on her and I should shut up and go home because I'm drunk – but I can't have been all that drunk because otherwise I wouldn't remember any of it, would I? Anyway, then I've calmed down and said I'll go home and he's saying he's sorry and he'll explain everything, and then we go back to the house.'

'Were the man and woman there then, when you went back inside?'

'Well, two people come past us, and I thought it was them because I heard the woman's dress make a rustling noise, but I couldn't see their faces or nothing.'

'Which direction were they going? Towards the house or into the garden?'

'Into the garden.'

'And you think it was the two you saw before?'

'Well, I never saw anyone else come out. Not that I was really paying attention, but you know, out of the corner of my eye . . . Anyway, I never got the chance to have another look because suddenly there's this bang and all the lights go out and everybody's screaming. I'm knocked off my feet and Clinton's disappeared and I'm thinking he must be dead or something—'

'Were you inside the house when this happened, or out-side?'

'Just outside. I'm trying to pick myself up off the ground and there's people all over the place—'

'People running into the garden?'

'Yeah, lots of them. I'm fighting my way past all these people to get back into the house because I'm thinking Clinton's in there, only I can't find him. And then there's another explosion right in front of me, and I'm down on the floor and I can feel this blood and I still can't see him . . . Then this woman comes and helps me and she keeps saying, "You've got to come with me," but I'm still looking for Clinton. I don't want to go till I know he's all right, but I can't see him.' Gloria shook her head and flicked the end of her cigarette towards the tiny grate. 'You know the rest – you saw me. Are you sure you don't know what happened to him, Mr Stratton?'

'He wasn't taken to hospital, Gloria. If he had been, I'd know about it.'

'But if he'd been hit on the head and lost his memory, or . . . I don't know!' Gloria burst into noisy tears and, as she clearly had no handkerchief, Stratton offered his.

'Thanks. I've been so worried.' She blew her nose violently, mopped awkwardly and ineffectually at her face, then started crying again. The worst thing about such moments, Stratton always found, was having to sympathise with distress while, at the same time, determining its level of authenticity, and this was no different. Now, he said, 'I can understand why you're upset, Gloria, but I can't believe it hasn't occurred to you that there's another reason why Etheridge might have disappeared.'

'He didn't do it,' said Gloria, shoulders heaving, 'if that's what you mean.'

'How do you know? And don't bother telling me it's because he'd never hurt a fly.'

Gloria blew her nose again and stared at him reproachfully. 'I wasn't going to. If he was hoping to get something off her, he'd be pretty stupid to do her in, wouldn't he? But,' she added, glaring at him, 'that ain't going to stop you lot fitting him up for it, is it? Clinton always says a coloured man's got no chance in this country, and he's right.'

CHAPTER FORTY

On his way back to the station, Stratton reflected that Gloria had been brave, if foolish, to return to the burning house to look for Etheridge. Had the circumstances been reversed, he very much doubted that Etheridge would have done the same for her. She seemed to have very few illusions about the sort of man he was – he wondered briefly how much she'd known, or guessed, about Irene – but then he supposed that her expectations of men must be pretty low.

She was right, however, when she said that there was no reason for Etheridge to kill Mrs Rutherford. Alive, she was – potentially, at least – worth a great deal to him; dead, she was worth nothing. But then, it seemed to him that she was worth more alive to Giles Rutherford too, and very possibly to Perlmann.

An elderly tomato sandwich was all the canteen could offer at such a late hour by way of lunch. He carried it into the office, where Dunning had left a note on his desk: *Car owned by Mr G. Rutherford is Bentley 'R' type Continental. Colour blue, registration PFY 340.* O'Driscoll had said that the first two letters of the registration were P and F.

If the man Gloria had seen arguing with Mrs Rutherford just before the explosion was her husband – and it certainly sounded like him – then he couldn't have left the party at half past ten or a quarter to eleven, as he claimed, and he certainly couldn't have been at April Scott's flat at either of those times. Moving aside the curling remains of his lunch, Stratton jotted down some estimates of times and distances:

Colville Road to White City Estate = 2.5m (approx 15 mins drive but depends on where Bentley was parked in Notting Hill – may have taken longer due to disturbance)

Bentley spotted by O'Driscoll 'quite a while after 11 p.m.'

How long spent on White City Est and doing what? N.B. Both Knight and Halliwell live there.

White City Estate to Bryanston Mews = 4.5 to 5m (approx 15–20 mins drive)

GR says he was with AS for 'a couple of hours' – she confirmed but gave time of arrival at abt 10.30 p.m.

Bryanston Mews to Lower Belgrave St = 1.5 to 2m (approx 10 mins drive)

I arrive Lower Belgrave St at approx 2 a.m. & leave 30–40 mins later. GR claimed to have been there since around midnight ('TV was finished')

AS says GR phoned her at 2.45 a.m. and told her Mrs R was dead

If Rutherford had done all of that, Stratton thought, he'd been a very busy boy indeed, and – supposing that he'd returned home shortly before Stratton had arrived at 2 a.m. – he could only have been at April Scott's flat for an hour and a half at most, as it didn't seem possible that he could have arrived there very much before midnight. And while Gloria was prepared to dash into danger for her man, Stratton was fairly sure that April Scott was more interested in looking after number one. He was also willing to bet that whatever she'd told him, she'd been angry and alarmed when Rutherford had suddenly appeared; a little well-organised diversion was one thing, but unexpected arrivals in the middle of the night, quite another.

If she was dismayed to see him again so soon, April Scott covered it well. Stratton had been half hoping that he might find Giles Rutherford with her, but she was alone. He noticed she'd taken the bracelet off, and that the plush front room was less tidy than it had been that morning. There were more records scattered across the thick pink carpet, items of clothing draped over chairs and cups and ashtrays on the surfaces. There was an enormous spray of red roses in a vase on the mantelpiece, and the largest box of chocolates Stratton had ever seen lay on the sofa, lid off.

'Had visitors?'

'Just a girlfriend.' April leant over and rested her arms on the low back of an armchair, displaying her cleavage to best advantage. Stratton doubted that someone like her would have any actual female friends – she was too pretty and too predatory for that – but she might, he thought, have female *allies*: other girls who lived on their wits with an eye on the main chance. They were not, he thought, the sorts of relationships where flowers and chocolates were exchanged – quite apart from anything else, these woman were takers of gifts, not givers.

Without waiting to be asked, Stratton sat down on the sofa and helped himself to one of the chocolates. 'Very cosy. Bring you these, did she? And –' mouth full, he nodded at the roses – 'those?' Seeing her hesitate, he continued, 'Very good friends you must have . . . Unless, of course, they're from Rutherford?' Still, she said nothing. 'A thank you present, perhaps, for keeping the nasty policeman off his back.'

April stuck out her chin and said, 'I don't know what you mean.'

'Oh, I think you do. But as you said, you weren't really sure what time Rutherford arrived here, so you might have made a mistake.'

'I didn't.' The angle of April's chin looked more determined than ever.

'Really?' Stratton dug into the chocolates again. 'I must say, these are delicious. Must have cost a packet. And the roses too – magnificent – but you do need to decide which way to jump, love. I mean,' Stratton settled back and crossed his legs, 'obviously, with Mrs Rutherford being who she is, there's bound to be a lot about all this in the newspapers. If Mr Rutherford is arrested, which I have to say is looking likelier by the minute, well, you'll be in the papers, too. Photos, I shouldn't wonder. And that's going to make Mr Perlmann look rather foolish, isn't it? There *he* is, paying for this lovely flat in good faith, and all these beautiful things, and there *you* are, carrying on behind his back.' He paused to look around the room. 'Be a shame to lose all this, wouldn't it?' Stratton had banked on the fact that nobody'd told April about the heart attack and judging from the look on her face, he'd been right.

'Of course,' he continued, 'you may be banking on the fact that now Mrs Rutherford's no longer with us you'll be able to take her place. I imagine that Rutherford has promised you something along those lines in return for backing up his story, but personally, I wouldn't recommend becoming the next Mrs Rutherford – not unless you're an unusual sort of girl who enjoys prison visiting. Besides which – in case you hadn't realised – Rutherford may *look* wealthy, but the money's all on her side, not his. If, on the other hand,' Stratton paused to select another chocolate, 'because obviously it's important to consider everything – you were just hopping into bed with Rutherford out of the kindness of your heart and what you *actually* want is for Danny to divorce his wife and make you the next Mrs Perlmann, then giving Rutherford an alibi is a sure way to do yourself out of what promises to be a very cushy number.' Sensing that April, who was now bolt upright, arms crossed protectively over her bosom and staring at him pop-eyed, was about to speak, he held up a finger to forestall her. 'The *other* thing you need to consider is that we now have an independent witness who saw Rutherford at the party at eleven o'clock, which is half an hour *after* you claim he arrived here. We have another witness who saw him somewhere else even later than that, and as both these claims are verifiable, you're going to end up being branded a liar as well as a whore. I can see,' Stratton picked out another chocolate and held it up for inspection, 'that it must be a bit of a facer. Of course if you decide to tell me the truth now, we might be prepared to try and keep your name out of it, and you can always explain how Rutherford tried to get you to lie on his behalf. You never know your luck – Mr Perlmann might even be sympathetic. You might end up like a pig in clover and, if that's the case, I hope it keeps fine for you. But – and it's a very big "but" indeed – you might end up screwed either way. I mean that only in the financial sense, of course, because you've already been screwed either way in the other sense, haven't you, darling?'

Popping the chocolate into his mouth, Stratton stretched both arms expansively over the back of the sofa and looked at April, his head cocked on one side. While he'd been talking, her expression had run the gamut from outrage to confusion. Looking at her now, he could almost see the cash register behind her eyes. 'Whenever you're ready,' he said. 'Unless you'd like me to explain all that again.'

'No,' said April, sullenly. 'I'll tell you.'

CHAPTER FORTY-ONE

There was no flashy leg-crossing this time – April sat primly, knees together, on the edge of the seat and smoothed down her skirt while Stratton took out his notebook. 'Off you go, then.'

'I suppose he arrived at about a quarter to one.'

'You suppose, or you're sure?'

'I was asleep. When I said I wasn't expecting him, that was true. The doorbell woke me. I looked at the clock on my bedside table and I can't remember the exact time, but it was about then. When I let him in, he said about the party – you know, being dull – and he asked me for a drink, so I got him one.'

'Did you have the impression he'd been drinking before he arrived?'

'Well, he'd been to a party, hadn't he?'

'It doesn't necessarily follow.'

April considered this, then said, 'He wasn't slurring his words or anything. He seemed more . . . unsettled.'

'How did he look?'

April considered this, then said, 'Untidy. His hair and his clothes. From the explosion, I suppose.'

'Did he say anything about that?'

'Only when he phoned me later. When he arrived, I said something about what on earth had he been doing but he wouldn't tell me. He just kept saying he wanted a drink, and then he went up to the bathroom. I went to get the bottle and the glasses, and I took them upstairs—'

'You told me you had champagne. Was that what he asked for?'

'No, but I didn't have anything else.'

'Really?'

'Yes, really. Danny doesn't drink.'

'Go on.'

'Well, Giles came out of the bathroom after a while, and he said he was sorry for disturbing me and why didn't I go back to bed—'

'Was he dressed?'

'Yes. He was rubbing his hair with a towel—'

'Did he have a bath, or just a wash?'

'He didn't have a bath. He must have washed in the basin, because it was dirty.'

'What kind of dirt?'

April looked puzzled. 'Just . . . you know. There was a tidemark.'

'Earth?'

'I don't know. I don't think so. Just a grey mark.'

'Had he washed his hair?'

April shook her head. 'Not properly, anyway. He hadn't

used any shampoo. I think it was just wet at the front from where he'd washed his face.'

'What did he say after that?'

'Not very much. I'd got into bed, and I was sitting up and he sat down on the edge of the bed and had a drink and held my hand . . .' April sighed. 'I didn't really feel like talking to him after he'd just barged in like that. I mean, what if Danny had been here?'

'Did you say that?'

'Yes. He said he was sorry, but he'd had a bad evening and he was fed up and wanted to see me, and he kept stroking my arm and trying to kiss me. I told him to get off because I wasn't interested . . . I suppose we must have argued about it for a bit, and he drank the rest of the champagne – I only had one glass – and then he said he'd better get home because Virginia would be wondering where he'd got to. So I said, "Good idea," or something like that.'

'He definitely said his wife would be wondering where he'd got to, did he?' asked Stratton.

'Yes. I'd asked him – before, I mean – if he'd left the party without her, and he said something about how he wasn't going to stay and watch her making herself ridiculous.'

'Did he say why she was making herself ridiculous?'

'No – and I wasn't interested. To be honest, I just wanted him to go.'

'And when did he go?'

'Quite soon after that. He was only here for about half an hour.'

'So that would have been about a quarter past one?'

'Yes. I saw him out and went back to bed.'

'You said he telephoned you at about a quarter to three. Is that true?'

'Yes. That happened exactly as I told you.'

'How much do you know about Mr Rutherford's financial affairs?'

'I don't know anything. He didn't talk to me about those things.'

'What about when he was here with Mr Perlmann – or were you lying about that?'

'No, I wasn't. Danny did bring him here sometimes, to play cards. That's how we met.'

'And did they talk about business then?'

'I suppose so.' April sounded dismissive. 'They mentioned property, solicitors . . . I don't know, things like that. It wasn't anything to do with me.' This came out almost as a whine. 'I didn't pay attention.'

'Perhaps you should, next time.' Stratton tucked his notebook back into his jacket. 'You never know, you might learn something to your advantage.' April's beautiful painted eyes bulged with fury, but she said nothing. 'Did Rutherford bring you the flowers and chocolates himself, or did he send them?'

'Sent them.'

'Who delivered them?'

'A man. I don't know him.'

'Someone from the flower shop? Have a job finding one open on a Sunday. Or a shop that sells boxes of chocolates, come to that.' As he spoke, Stratton heard Laskier's voice in his head: *Perlmann keeps boxes of chocolates to give their wives* ... The club had been well stocked with flowers too, hadn't it? Perlmann, of course, was in hospital, but presumably there'd have been somebody else at the club willing to give them to him.

'I don't know! I didn't ask him.'

'But he said they were from Rutherford?'

'Yes.'

'Describe him.'

'Tall,' said April without hesitation. 'Very big – huge, in fact – with a foreign accent, but I don't know what it was.'

'Was it anything like Danny Perlmann's accent?'

'A bit, I suppose. Yes.'

Stratton assumed it was the giant, Jan. 'Thank you.' He rose. 'That's all for the time being, Miss Scott.' April accompanied him to the door, tight-lipped, shoulders hunched.

'I'm sure you've made the right decision,' he said, 'but don't think about going anywhere, will you? We'll need to talk to you again. Thank you for your cooperation – and thanks for the chocolates. They really were delicious.'

He could feel April glaring at his back as he went down the stairs.

CHAPTER FORTY-TWO

Stratton got into the car, wincing at the heat of the leather seat, then wound down both front windows, loosened his tie and lit a cigarette. It was just gone half past four, and he couldn't be more than ten minutes' drive from the Rutherfords' house in Lower Belgrave Street. Definitely worth a try, he thought.

The door was opened by a neatly dressed middle-aged woman, greying hair swept back from her face. 'Mrs Boyce?' Seeing her eyes widen at the sight of his black eye, he quickly held up his warrant card. 'DI Stratton, from Harrow Road Station. Is Mr Rutherford here?'

'I'm afraid not.'

'When do you expect him back?'

'I'm afraid he didn't mention a time.' The house-keeper's voice was deliberately and politely neutral, and she seemed composed enough, but a reddened, slightly rabbity look about her eyes and nose told him that she'd been crying.

'Did he say where he was going?'

'I'm afraid I don't know.'

'Not to worry,' said Stratton cheerfully. 'I take it that you are aware of what's happened?'

'Yes.' For a second Mrs Boyce's careful expression of professional courtesy wavered. 'Mrs Rutherford,' she said, not meeting his eye. 'Yes, Mr Rutherford told me.'

'Quite a nasty shock, I imagine,' said Stratton. 'Perhaps, as I'm here, we might have a quick word?'

'With me?' The housekeeper looked bewildered. 'I spoke to the police this morning.'

'I'm in charge of this investigation, Mrs Boyce, and I'd like to talk to everyone connected with Mrs Rutherford,' said Stratton gently. 'Much better to do it here . . .' He stopped, leaving the words 'than down at the station' hanging in the air between them.

'Do you take sugar, Inspector?'

'No, thanks.' Stratton smiled encouragingly. 'Gave it up during the war.'

'I think a lot of people did,' said Mrs Boyce. Sitting at the table in her basement kitchen, away from the eyes of the street with a cup of tea, she was already more relaxed.

'Were you here then?'

She shook her head. 'The family had the London house shut up for the duration.'

'When you say "family",' asked Stratton, 'whose family do you mean?'

'Mrs Rutherford's,' said the housekeeper sharply. 'Her father – you know he's the Viscount Purbeck?'

'No.' Stratton made a note. 'I didn't.'

'Well, he is.'

'So he's still alive?'

Mrs Boyce nodded. 'Ninety-four years old. Lady Purbeck died a couple of years ago. The estate's in Herefordshire – there were a lot of staff there until the war, but it's pretty well shut up now. The only son was killed at El Alamein so when Lord Purbeck dies the title will be extinct. He gave Mrs Rutherford this house when she married.'

'When was that?'

'The summer of 1953. Just after the Coronation.'

'And you worked for the family before, did you?'

'Yes. I started as a parlourmaid in 1924.' As she stared critically at her cup and saucer and made a minute adjustment to her spoon Stratton imagined, in her mind's eye, the long vista of years filled with polished furniture, beaten carpets, laid fires and perfectly ironed piles of snowy laundry. 'Not many left like me now.'

'No,' Stratton agreed, wondering if she'd stayed for lack of a better offer, or if there was some tragedy that had overturned her hopes for a future in a home of her own. The 'Mrs', he was fairly sure, was an old-fashioned courtesy. 'Your loyalty does you credit,' he said.

Mrs Boyce ducked her head and made another adjustment, this time to the embroidered cloth on the carefully presented tray, then took a lace-edged handkerchief from the sleeve of her dress and dabbed at her eyes. 'Forgive me, Inspector. As you say, it's a shock.'

'I'm sure it is,' said Stratton. 'After all, you'd known her since she was quite young, hadn't you?'

'Yes. I came here with her when she married. She was always very kind, Inspector – thoughtful, even as a child. She was our favourite – the staff, I mean. We were all so fond—' She broke off, shaking her head in distress at her tears, lips pressed together in a quivering line.

'Perhaps,' said Stratton, 'you could tell me something about her? It always helps, when someone dies in . . . well, let's say *unusual circumstances* . . . if we can build up a picture of what they were like. From the people who knew them best, I mean. You needn't worry,' he added. 'Anything you tell me about Mrs Rutherford will be treated in the strictest confidence.'

'Well,' Mrs Boyce leant forward with an air of disclosure, 'she didn't have an easy time of it. Lady Purbeck . . . I don't mean to speak ill of the dead, but she'd been a great beauty in her day, and Mrs Rutherford's older sister was lovely too. She made a very good marriage – an American businessman, very wealthy. I'm afraid that they could sometimes be quite . . . *unkind* . . . People do tend to see beauty all on the surface, you know. There was a young man during the war, but the family didn't think he was suitable so she broke it off. And she wasn't young then – nearly thirty. I suppose,' Mrs Boyce moved the milk jug fractionally to the left, aligning it with the teapot, 'that he wasn't suitable really. He was a curate. No money, of course, and he'd been turned down for military service, which didn't help matters. I always thought,' she frowned suddenly at something across the room, 'that he really did love her. It was a shame. Excuse me a moment.' Mrs Boyce rose and began adjusting various pieces of crockery on the dresser. Her back to Stratton, she continued, 'We always thought that Lady Purbeck saw her as rather an embarrassment – still a spinster long after all her friends' daughters had married, and of course they pitied her for it. I think – as the years passed, you know, and no one else came along – that they began to regret not letting her marry the clergyman.'

'But someone else did come along.'

'Eventually. She was almost forty, and it was quite a surprise to everyone.'

'Were her parents pleased?'

'Lady Purbeck was. I should think,' Mrs Boyce turned, a decorated plate in her hand, and stared at Stratton with sudden fierceness, 'that by that time she'd have been delighted if it was Jack the Ripper who wanted to marry her daughter. And of course he went out of his way to be charming to her.'

'And Lord Purbeck?'

'I don't know what he thought, but I never heard him say anything against it. I always wondered if perhaps he didn't try to stop it because he felt guilty about not letting her marry the other one.'

'Do you know how they met?'

'It was when Lord Purbeck was selling some of his property. He came to the house – the family home in Lowndes Square, that is, not here.'

'And Lord Purbeck is at Lowndes Square now, is he?'

'Yes, he lives there. But he's not . . . He no longer receives visitors. His health . . . He's become very frail in recent years, and he gets rather confused.'

'This confusion,' said Stratton carefully, 'was it notice-able at the time the property was sold?'

'Really, I couldn't say. He hasn't been well for a number of years.' Mrs Boyce looked unhappy.

'What was Rutherford's part in selling the property? Do you know?'

'I'm not entirely sure. I think he might have been work-ing for the estate agent. He came several times on business.'

Stratton remembered what Laskier had told him about Perlmann's first forays into property. He'd said that the estate agent – Rutherford, presumably – had introduced them to the solicitor who controlled the trust funds. If Rutherford had known about the trust funds, he must have known, before he set his cap at her, exactly what his wife-to-be was worth and – as Laskier had said – that she wouldn't be able to touch the capital until she was mar-ried. 'Was Mrs Rutherford present at these discussions?' he asked.

Mrs Boyce looked affronted. 'Of course not,' she said briskly. 'That was men's business. She had nothing to do with it.'

'Did Rutherford ever bring anyone with him?'

Mrs Boyce thought for a moment, weighing the plate in her hands. 'I don't recall anybody. We didn't see him for a couple of months after the houses were sold, and then one evening he arrived with Miss Virginia – this was before they were married, of course – and . . .' The housekeeper pursed her lips. 'That was it, really. They were married about six months later.'

'You don't like him, do you?'

Mrs Boyce stiffened and looked down at the plate in her hands. Carefully, as if she did not quite trust herself not to smash it, she replaced it on the dresser. 'He married her for her money, no other reason. She was certainly in love with him. She was swept away by his looks, the way he paid her attention and flattered her . . . I'm sure she must have known, in the back of her mind, that the money had a great deal to do with it – she was almost ten years older, after all – but I think she genuinely thought that he loved her. And for once her mother was pleased with her, and of course it was exciting, all the preparations and being the centre of attention, because the wedding was a very grand affair.'

'And then?'

'It was fine for a while – on the surface, at least – although he'd been seeing other women behind her back right from the word go.'

'How do you know?'

'Logan – our chauffeur – used to drive him. He never made any secret of it.'

'Mr Rutherford didn't?'

'Not to Mr Logan, no.'

'And Mr Logan told you?'

'Only this morning. He said he hadn't liked to say before.' Mrs Boyce shrugged. 'Men sticking together. In any case, I certainly wouldn't have told Mrs Rutherford. Ladies aren't meant to know about these things, and once it's been said . . .'

Once it's been said, they can't carry on pretending not to know, thought Stratton, picturing the Hon. Virginia, alone, hurt and bewildered. He could visualise her thinking that she must have done something wrong and trying desperately to remedy it, then realising that there was no remedy; could imagine her hope that she had her husband's heart dwindling, by degrees, to the hope that he would be civil to her, if only in public. What was it Fenella had said? *It's humiliating, having your husband eyeing every other woman in the room* . . . 'Well,' he said aloud, 'that certainly helps to put me in the picture. Now, what can you tell me about yesterday evening?'

'Not a great deal, I'm afraid. I left the house at half past six – before Mr and Mrs Rutherford had gone out – and when I returned just after eleven there was no one here.'

'Did you know where they were going?'

'Mrs Rutherford told me. I must say, I was a bit surprised. I'd think twice about going there during the day, never mind after dark. It's one thing going in for good works, but . . .' Mrs Boyce's eyes filled with tears and she yanked the handkerchief out of her sleeve once more. 'Look what happened. And *he* just went and left her with a pack of savages! You've only got to look at the papers to know . . . Excuse me, Inspector.' She blew her nose.

'And where did you go?'

'I went to the cinema with Miss Preston. She's the housekeeper at number 20. We went to the new Angus Steak

House in Kensington High Street and then to the Odeon to see *The Man Inside*.'

'And what did you do when you got home?'

'Miss Preston came in for a cup of tea, and then I went up to bed – I have two rooms at the top of the house. I read for something like ten minutes, and then I went to sleep.'

'Were you aware of Mr Rutherford returning?'

'I'm afraid not. I suffer from insomnia, so I take sleeping pills, and they tend to make one dead to the world.'

'What about this morning?'

'I made breakfast as usual. I take the tray up at ten o'clock on Sundays. Usually they're still in bed, but Mr Rutherford was already dressed. In fact, thinking about it, I'm not sure that he'd been to bed at all, at least not properly. The ashtray was overflowing, and so were the ones in the sitting room, and all the brandy in the decanter was gone, so I think he'd been up for most of the night.'

'Did Mrs Rutherford sleep in the same room?'

'Yes. I asked Mr Rutherford where she was, because she'd not said anything about going out early, or I'd have fetched her breakfast for her. I didn't know there was anything wrong, and then he said that you'd come, that you'd told him . . . I couldn't believe it.'

'And he explained about leaving her at the party, did he?'

'Yes. I was appalled that he'd left her in such a dangerous place, and I didn't really bother to hide it.'

'Did he give a reason for leaving her there?'

'No. Just said he was bored and she seemed to be enjoying herself, so he'd decided to come home.'

'Did he say he'd gone on anywhere else before he came home?'

'If he did I don't remember.'

'And what about later?'

'Well, he told me that he had to go and . . . identify the body . . . and that someone would come and fetch him. That was in the morning – I suppose he got back at about midday. He was in the sitting room for a while after that, and then he went out again.'

'Did he say where?'

'No. The first I heard of it was when the door slammed.'

'Did Logan take him? You said you'd spoken to him this morning.'

'He drove himself. Mr Logan came at about eleven because Mrs Rutherford was supposed to be opening a fete somewhere out in Barnet and he was meant to be driving her. We had to telephone the organisers and tell them.'

'And the woman who comes in to help – was she here?'

'Mrs Doran only comes on weekdays.'

'Do you know what Mr Rutherford was doing in the sitting room when he got back?' asked Stratton, making a note. 'There isn't a telephone in there, is there?'

'No. There's one in the passage down here, and one in the study. But,' Mrs Boyce straightened her back, a look of sudden triumph on her face, 'I can tell you what he was doing in the sitting room. He was burning papers – lots of them. The grate was chock-full of ash.'

CHAPTER FORTY-THREE

'In the light of what you've just told me . . .' Matheson leant back in his chair and tapped his fingers on the arms for a moment before continuing, 'I think we can justify a request for emergency warrants.'

'I'm guessing that Rutherford's already destroyed any papers he had at home,' said Stratton, 'but – assuming we're on the right track – there'll be more at Perlmann's office, and possibly at the club, Maxine's. And of course he might have more documents at Lower Belgrave Street.'

'I'm inclined to agree,' said Matheson. 'It sounds as if Lord Purbeck is pretty well ga-ga, so I can't imagine we're going to get any clarification from that quarter.' He sighed. 'And of course we still don't know if there's any real connection with the murder of Hampton.'

'Other than that Hampton worked for Perlmann,' said Stratton. From the moment he'd sat down in Matheson's office, tiredness had engulfed him, dulling his thought processes, and the heat – still stifling – wasn't making things any easier.

'Ye-es . . . And then there's the matter of Etheridge, who

seems to have disappeared, and the probable connection of Rutherford with Knight and Halliwell and the rest of them – incidentally, we've not yet managed to bring those two in for questioning. It's a fair old mess.'

'I'm sorry, sir,' said Stratton. 'I realise I'm not being much help.'

'For God's sake, man, you're exhausted. I'm going to get on the blower – no, don't get up. The sun's over the yardarm, and I'm sure you could do with a drink.' Matheson rose and went to the discreet cabinet in the corner of the room where, Stratton now knew, he kept the decanter and glasses. 'I know I could use one. Here.' He slid a large measure of Scotch across the desk.

'Thank you, sir.'

'Well,' Matheson raised his glass, 'cheers. It's a lot to unravel, but I can't help feeling that a couple of good tugs on some of these loose ends will do the trick. Now, you sit tight and help yourself to those,' he waved a hand at the box of cigarettes on his desk, 'while I sort out these warrants, and then,' he gave Stratton a sudden wolfish grin, 'it'll be time for some action.'

A single gulp of his drink made Stratton feel light-headed – hardly surprising, he thought, since he'd only eaten half a tomato sandwich since his meagre breakfast – and he closed his eyes and tried to unscramble his thoughts. There must be something more, something he'd forgotten to follow up . . . His gaze, unfocused, took in the top of Matheson's desk, then Matheson himself, receiver in hand, drumming his fingers as he waited for the operator to put him through, and then moved past him to the fireplace behind. He supposed that the Victorian original must have been ripped out at some stage, because instead of a mantelshelf and grate, there was a gas fire surrounded by a geometrical arrangement of shiny green tiles . . . Of course! It was that bloody green van.

Stratton took out his notebook and began thumbing through the pages. Seen by O'Driscoll outside the pub, seen by two witnesses in Golborne Road, seen by the old girl in Colville Road when the petrol bombs were thrown . . . But there was something else too. The kid with the adenoids . . . Tony Pearson. He'd said Halliwell "must have had the van off some bloke", hadn't he? And he'd said he'd meant borrowed, rather than pinched. If that was the case, it must be someone he knew well enough to borrow their vehicle. He flipped back through his notebook again. Halliwell's mother had said he'd got his driving licence a couple of months earlier, but that he didn't own a vehicle – but he hadn't thought to ask her if anyone else in the family owned one, had he? Stupid, *stupid*! He hadn't asked about a specific car or van, and of course he hadn't spoken to the father at all . . . Still, it would be easy enough to find out – and if the van wasn't Mr Halliwell's, there were plenty of other candidates. Raising a hand to Matheson by way of excusing himself, he put down his Scotch and went to find PC Dunning.

Someone was shaking his shoulder. Stratton unglued his eyes, blinked at the glare and peered at the clock on the office wall. 'It's twenty past two,' said Matheson. 'Bit of a mix-up, I'm afraid – took a bit longer than I thought.'

Stratton levered himself off the camp bed and started dragging on his trousers. After a lot of waiting about and only a few hours' fitful sleep on a narrow bit of sagging canvas with a pillow that might as well have been a piece of wood, he felt sweatily clammy all over and every bone in his body ached. 'Bit stiff?' Matheson's tone was sympathetic.

'You can say that again.' Stratton rubbed a hand over his bristly chin and wondered how his superior did it. All right, the man was over ten years younger, but he looked as spruce and alert as if he'd just stepped, newly minted, out of a bandbox.

'I'll get over to Perlmann's office—'

'I shouldn't think anyone'll be there now, sir.'

'No matter.' Matheson's eyes, Stratton realised, were actually shining with anticipation. The man was electrified. 'You take the nightclub. I thought you'd prefer it, being your old patch. I've said you'll be ready in five minutes, and the chaps from West End Central'll meet you there.'

I'm too old for this, thought Stratton, bending over to lace his shoes with thick, unwilling fingers. 'Right,' he said. 'I'm on my way.'

It being Sunday, Wardour Street at 3 a.m. was pretty well deserted. The few people still about – in various stages of inebriation, judging from the unsteady figures Stratton could see weaving their way along the pavement – seemed to be on their way home. Maxine's itself was dark, the heavy curtains drawn, as PC Brodie hammered fruitlessly on the front door.

Stratton looked at his watch again. Hadn't Laskier said that the manageress lived on the premises? He looked up as a sash window was raised somewhere above his head, but it was the house next door. The blurred, pale disc of a face emerged, looked and, seeing policemen beneath the street lamp, withdrew, pulling down the window with a bang.

'Should we try round the back, sir?' said a young constable who Stratton recognised as PC Dixon from West End Central. 'There's a passageway.'

'Good idea. Take Brodie and Dunwoody here with you, and I'll follow.'

The passageway was narrow, and the policemen's torches glinted off the filthy glass of small barred windows, the ill-fitting lids of battered dustbins and the tops of empty bottles in wooden crates. Stratton could smell the sickly ripeness of food discarded by nearby restaurants and beginning to rot. 'Door's here, sir,' said Dixon.

'Is there a bell?'

'Can't see one, sir.'

Stratton struggled past the uniforms and thumped his fist on the flaking paint. 'Open up! Police!'

There was silence, but for the breathing of Dixon and the other two and the muffled sounds of Soho at night-time. 'Right,' he said, stepping back. 'Break it down.'

'I'll take it,' Dixon muttered. There was another moment's silence and an indrawn breath as he braced himself for the kick while the other two shone their torches at the lock, and then the air was broken apart by a high, jagged scream coming from somewhere inside.

'Go!' The scream was abruptly cut off as Dixon threw himself at the door and disappeared inwards in a heap of splintering wood. Stratton, Brodie and Dunwoody followed and found themselves at the end of a tiny and very scruffy hallway. Illuminated by a single weak bulb, it was lined with crates of bottles, leaving just enough space for walking in single file. For a moment there was an absolute silence, as though the very fabric of the place were holding its breath. Spotting a door at the end, Stratton muttered 'Follow me,' and pushed past the others.

As he reached for the handle there was another scream, shriller and more frantic than before. 'Police!' yelled Stratton, turning the handle and putting his shoulder against the panels as he did so. 'I'm coming in!'

The room was an office, with two desks, a typewriter and shelves covered with messy piles of paper, more of which was stacked in two cardboard boxes on the floor. A door in the opposite wall led, presumably, to the front of the building and the whole space, which was windowless and smelt powerfully of stale sweat, was barely large enough to accommodate the four people inside.

The first one Stratton saw was Laskier, fully dressed, standing beside an open safe, a wrapped bundle of money in his hand and more in a canvas mailbag at his feet. His face was grey, the eyes sandbagged with exhaustion. Next to him stood Walker, feet bare and shirt unbuttoned as though he'd been disturbed in the act of getting dressed. With a closed expression that betrayed nothing, he was clasping the hand of Irene, who was standing beside him, shaking visibly, her face so pale that it looked translucent, like the lining of an oyster shell. She was clad in a floor-length white nightgown with a ruffled neckline, which looked as incongruous on her slight frame as though she were a little girl who'd dressed up in her mother's clothes to play at being a bride. Stratton wondered, momentarily, if she'd borrowed it from the manageress, and then, where the hell the manageress was. Not here, anyway: the only other person was Etheridge, who was standing on the other side of Irene, holding a gun to her head.

CHAPTER FORTY-FOUR

'Stay back or I'll shoot her.'

Irene shrank away as Etheridge jabbed the girl's temple with the gun. Sweating, eyes bulging with paranoia, he had the stance of a boxer up on his toes, dancing and edgy. Stratton could feel the constables' breath ragged on his neck. Making a conscious effort to slow his own breathing, he turned slightly in the doorway, murmuring, 'Stay there and keep quiet.'

'Nobody move! You told them.' Etheridge pointed the gun at Laskier, who shook his head. He looked, Stratton thought, more despairing than frightened.

'How could I?' Laskier's voice was infinitely weary. 'We've been in the same room all the time. If I'd telephoned anyone you'd have seen and heard me.'

'You tricked me, man!'

'How could I?' said Laskier again. He sounded as if, despite the gun and Etheridge's unpredictability, he couldn't find the energy to formulate a different question.

'Nobody tricked you,' said Stratton. At the sound of his voice, Etheridge whipped the gun round, pointing it at him for a few seconds before thrusting it back into the side of Irene's head. She gave a small whimper of shock and Walker, still looking straight ahead with a face devoid of expression, kept hold of her hand.

'We're here to speak to Mr Laskier,' said Stratton. With deliberate casualness, he leant against the doorframe, crossing his arms. Addressing Laskier directly, he said, 'We've got a warrant to seize your paperwork.'

'You talk to me, not him!' shouted Etheridge, the gun jumping in his hand.

'All right, Mr Etheridge,' said Stratton in his blandest tone, 'if that's what you'd prefer. As I said, we came for the paperwork, so all of this is rather a surprise. As a matter of fact, we've been wanting to speak to you ever since—'

'Don't fuck with me, man! I'll kill her.' Etheridge's eyes blazed with fury. 'I want the money and a car. I'm taking her with me.'

Stratton gave the appearance of contemplating this, and said, 'Are you indeed?'

'Yes! You get me a car or I shoot her!'

'If you shoot her,' said Stratton, 'you won't be able to take her with you, will you? I mean, she's not going to be an awful lot of use, is she?'

'Then I shoot them,' said Etheridge. 'You tell your men –' As he waved the gun past Stratton at the three constables in the hallway, Walker pulled Irene into his arms – 'to bring me a car.'

Stratton could feel the sweat trickling down his back and the insides of his legs. At least leaning on the doorframe gave him a bit of support and having his arms folded meant that he could suppress the shaking of his hands. 'I *could* do that,' he said, 'but if one of these men calls up the station and says there's a gentleman here wants a car and please can you send one round, they're bound to start asking a few questions, d'you see?'

Etheridge eyed him suspiciously. Turning momentarily back to Irene, and seeing Walker's arms around her, he tugged at her arm. 'You let her go!'

'No,' said Walker, eyeballing him over Irene's head.

Stratton straightened in an instant, arms uncrossed and ready to spring, and felt the three men behind him tense in anticipation. Laskier, to Walker's right, was motionless, apparently staring at the bundles of money at his feet. Stratton shook his head at Walker and mouthed 'Let go' but Walker ignored him as entirely as if he'd been a fly and carried on looking at Etheridge.

'Leave her alone!' Etheridge let go of Irene's arm and dug the gun hard into the back of her neck. Irene yelped and buried her face deeper in Walker's chest, sobbing.

Walker didn't budge, but stared at Etheridge implacably over Irene's head. He loves her, thought Stratton suddenly. Nothing Etheridge says will make any difference to that.

'I'll kill you,' screamed Etheridge, waving the gun at him.

'No.' Walker looked down at Irene and stroked her hair.

'I'll kill *her*!' He jabbed Irene viciously with the gun, making her cry out in pain.

Stratton cleared his throat. 'This isn't really getting us

anywhere, is it?' he asked, as though they were having a perfectly ordinary conversation.

'Shut up!' Etheridge swung the gun round to point at him. The other three were frozen in position like statues, Irene and Walker together and Laskier, who Stratton could just see out of the corner of his eye, still staring downwards. He's not afraid, thought Stratton. He's resigned.

Etheridge hesitated, looking from Stratton to Walker and back again. Keep looking at him, Stratton willed himself. Don't look at the gun. After about thirty seconds, during which Stratton felt that every nerve in his body was concentrated behind his eyes, Etheridge nodded in Laskier's direction. 'He's got a car. A Rolls-Royce. I want that.'

Laskier raised his head. 'I haven't got a Rolls-Royce.'

'You're lying! I want that car.'

'I'm not lying,' said Laskier patiently. 'I haven't got a Rolls-Royce.'

'I think,' said Stratton cautiously, 'that the car you mean belongs to Mr Perlmann. It isn't here.'

'Perlmann promised me! He said . . .' Etheridge shook his head, as if he couldn't remember what had been promised, then looked wildly around the room as if the answer might be found there. 'The deeds to the houses. He said he'd give me money, and the houses – three houses. Powis Terrace – he will make the deeds over to me. We can go into business, work together. He promised . . .' His words picked up speed, an automatic, compulsive rant, about a property empire to be run by himself and Perlmann. The talk of 'making over deeds' made Stratton think that the idea of the property empire must have sprung, in Etheridge's mind, from some small seed of truth – that perhaps there had been a conversation with Perlmann in which these terms were used. Had Hampton come into it somehow? Etheridge was certainly giving the impression that he had a right to what Perlmann had promised.

As Etheridge's voice continued to pound the walls of the small room, Irene, still in Walker's arms, had turned her head and was staring at him, her mouth slightly open, tearful and uncomprehending. Walker himself was impassive and looked, Stratton thought, almost bored, as if waiting for Etheridge to come to the end of it and leave. Laskier simply looked tired.

'I know,' Etheridge waved the gun at Stratton, 'you want to pin that woman's death on me.'

'What woman?' asked Stratton.

'At the party. That's why you're here. All your talk about how you want papers is nothing to do with it! Now,' he swung round to Laskier, 'I want the papers for my houses, and the money, and the car – you give them to me!'

Laskier looked at Stratton. 'There are no papers,' he said in a monotone. 'Not here. He can't have them, and neither can you.'

'They're mine!' shouted Etheridge. 'They belong to me. You call Perlmann. Go on – you ask him.'

Laskier dropped the bundle of money he'd been holding onto the pile in the canvas bag. 'I can't,' he said. 'Danny's dead.'

'What?' Etheridge's face was stiff with outrage. 'Bloody liar. You call him, now!'

'Danny had another heart attack.' Laskier's voice, cold and flat, cut across him. 'His wife phoned me just before you got here. You took the receiver out of my hand, remember? If you want money, you'd better take that lot,' kicking the bag at his feet so that the bundles slid across the lino towards Etheridge, 'because I can tell you now that's all there is.'

CHAPTER FORTY-FIVE

'Liar!' As Etheridge hurled himself at Laskier, Walker launched himself forward to intercept him, and then, before Stratton could intervene, the room exploded in a colossal bang.

As Etheridge scrambled for the door in the opposite wall the three policemen barged past Stratton and flung themselves at him. Through the ringing in his ears Stratton felt, rather than heard, the gun fall to the floor and saw Etheridge disappear under a mass of bodies. It took him a couple of seconds to understand what had happened, and then he dropped to his knees beside Walker, who was flat on the floor surrounded by wads of cash and clutching his chest as blood seeped from beneath his fingers. Laskier was sitting on the only chair, as if thrown there, and Irene was curled on the floor underneath the desk.

'Laskier!' shouted Stratton over the yells from the hallway. 'Call an ambulance!'

As Laskier turned away to pick up the receiver, Stratton grabbed Walker's shoulders to prop him up against the desk. Walker's hand fell away from his chest, as if its owner didn't have the strength to keep it there, and Stratton saw the hole, brilliant red above the coffee-coloured skin around his left nipple.

Etheridge was shouting something as the constables hauled him upright, but it was lost in the sound of the policemen outside smashing down the front door. As they swarmed into the office and helped to drag Etheridge into the corridor, Stratton yelled instructions over the din. 'Come on, help me. Sit him up before he chokes.' One arm round Walker, he used the other to push back the thicket of legs that surrounded them. 'One of you, for Christ's sake. The rest of you get back and give him some air.'

To his right, Laskier was hunched over the phone, giving instructions. Telling himself with wholly unfelt optimism that the angle of the shot might have meant that the bullet had gone clear of Walker's heart and that he'd survive at least until the ambulance arrived, Stratton propped the man's lolling head against the desk drawers.

'You've been shot,' he said. 'Can you talk?'

Walker's eyes flickered and his lips opened slightly, but no sound emerged. He's going, thought Stratton. 'Can you squeeze my hand, mate?'

This was rewarded by a pressure so faint he thought he might have imagined it.

'Will he be all right?' Irene, her face tearstained and her fancy nightgown greyed with dust from the floor, scrambled out from under the desk. As she knelt down beside him, Stratton's nostrils caught the sharp tang of urine.

'Yes,' he lied. 'I'm going to get one of the policemen to escort you next door, and you can—'

'I'm not leaving him.' Irene wiped her nose with a frothily sleeved wrist.

'You've had a shock, love,' said Stratton, gently. 'I really think—'

'He didn't leave me,' said Irene. 'He could have – Clinton told him to get out but he never. And I ain't leaving him, specially not now. You can't make me.' She was shaking again, but now it was with defiance, not fear.

'All right,' said Stratton. 'You stay and talk to him till the ambulance gets here.'

Irene shoved the bundles of money out of the way and, moving over so that she was beside Walker, put her hand over his. Walker's eyes flickered once more, but he didn't move his head or make any sound.

Laskier put down the receiver. 'It's on its way,' he said to Stratton. As their eyes met, Stratton saw that he didn't believe that Walker was going to make it either.

'Not long now,' Stratton told Irene. She nodded, apparently accepting reassurance, but her expression didn't change. She's realised he's dying, he thought. 'Just keep talking to him,' he said.

Irene stroked Walker's arm and began murmuring into his ear.

'You,' Stratton pointed to one of the policemen, 'go out to the front and if there's a policewoman out there, bring her in.'

'He's cold,' said Irene. Her eyes were bitter now, accusing. 'We need something to cover him.'

'You two,' Stratton looked up. 'Get upstairs. You'll find blankets in the bedrooms.' Shrugging off his jacket, he placed it over Walker's chest and tucked it behind his shoulders with care. His body was hard and unyielding, as though the life force had already gone, and when Stratton picked up his wrist he couldn't find a pulse. Perhaps it's because I'm not trained, he thought desperately, squeezing the flesh tighter. A doctor would be able to find it, a nurse . . . Come on, come *on* . . .

Suddenly Walker's chest rose in a convulsive heave as his last breath expelled itself in a long, jerky rattle; his head slumped, his eyes fixed, and he was still.

CHAPTER FORTY-SIX

Seated on a banquette with a cup of tea on the table in front of him, Laskier watched as Walker's blanket-shrouded body was carried through the club on a stretcher and Stratton, watching him, wondered what was going through his mind. In the time since Walker's death he'd said very little, remaining slumped over in his chair, head in hands until requested to move. Now he looked simply numb. Irene, speechless with shock, had allowed herself to be led upstairs by a policewoman to get washed and dressed, while bumps and bangs from the next room told Stratton that PC Brodie and the others had begun loading the contents of the office into boxes.

'Here.' Stratton pushed his Churchman's across the table.

'Thank you, Inspector.' Laskier exhaled a stream of smoke. 'What will happen to Irene now?'

'They'll take her to West End Central for the time being,' said Stratton. 'Don't worry – I'll be sending somebody to look after her and we won't question her until she's had a chance to recover a bit.' Lighting a cigarette for himself, he said, 'Were you telling the truth about Perlmann?'

'Yes.'

'Had you known there was a problem with his heart?'

Laskier sighed. 'He'd been taking pills for it and trying to reduce his weight. The doctor had told him to stop playing tennis because of the strain.'

'But when I came to your office yesterday morning, the man there told me he was playing tennis.'

'Danny didn't want anyone to know,' said Laskier. 'People wouldn't lend him the money if they thought he was ill.'

'And Etheridge did come and slam the phone down, did he, while you were speaking to Mrs Perlmann?'

'Yes. Will you explain this to her?'

'Wouldn't you prefer to tell her yourself?'

'Of course, but . . .' Laskier spread his hands in an 'anything might happen' gesture.

'I'm not going to arrest you,' said Stratton. 'Of course I can't promise that won't happen – it's not in my hands. You'll have to come to the station, but then you can go home.'

'But if you see her before I do,' said Laskier, 'I'd like her to know that I didn't hang up the phone on purpose.' He sighed and stared at the table again. 'Danny asked me to look after her if he wasn't there. This may surprise you, but he loved Maxine very much.'

'I understand,' said Stratton. 'I'll make sure she knows it wasn't intentional.'

'Thank you.'

'Can you tell me what time Etheridge arrived?'

'Maybe ten minutes before you did.'

'About a quarter to three, then.'

'If you say so. I wasn't aware of what time it was.'

'What were you doing – before Mrs Perlmann telephoned, I mean?'

'Paperwork. Danny had asked me to find certain things.'

'You saw him today, did you?'

'Yes, this afternoon. He told me about Virginia Rutherford. Some things are here, but most of the papers are kept at the office in Monmouth Road.'

'So why weren't you there instead of here?'

'I went there first.'

'What did Mr Perlmann want you to find?'

'Some contracts, details of mortgages . . . just paperwork, as I said.'

'Did you find it?'

'Most of it, yes.'

'And that was all you took?'

'Yes – two boxes. You saw them in the office.'

'At the hospital, what else did he say to you?'

'Nothing about any of this. We talked for a while about when we first came to this country, and about before. About his mother and father, when they took them away. He was studying to become a dentist, like his father, and then . . . He never talked about those things, even with me. Never. If somebody asked, "What happened to your parents?" he would just . . .' Laskier shrugged. 'Like that. Because it's too much. Too difficult.' He stared down at the table, indicating an end to the subject, passively awaiting the next question.

'So,' said Stratton, after a pause, 'after you'd been to the office, what time did you get here?'

'About eleven o'clock, I think. I didn't want to go home.'

'Mr Perlmann told me about your wife, Mr Laskier. I'm very sorry.'

'I wanted to protect her.' Laskier made a dismissive gesture, flicking ash across the table. 'I was an idiot.'

'I'm sure you did your best. It must have been a terrible shock.'

'No,' Laskier stared intently at a spot somewhere above Stratton's head for a moment, then lowered his eyes and continued, 'because already I have grieved for her. You know, the first time you met me, Inspector, you saw what's here.' Laskier tapped his arm. 'When Lola first came here, someone saw hers and asked if it was her boyfriend's telephone number.' He shook his head hopelessly. 'One can't change anything, so one adapts to it. It was a *different* life for us, but it couldn't be a new one because you can't wipe your memories away any more than you can take this mark and not leave a scar behind. I think that I had already grieved for all of us, dead and living, and so it wasn't a shock to me when Lola died. I don't know . . . Perhaps that doesn't make sense, but there it is. In there,' Laskier jerked his head towards the office, 'it should have been me, not him.'

'It shouldn't have happened,' said Stratton. 'I wasn't quick enough.'

'Etheridge didn't mean to shoot. The gun went off by accident.'

'I know. But he was trying to attack you at the time, and he had threatened all of us. I should have handled it better.'

Laskier shook his head. 'You couldn't. Etheridge acted

like a fool, but I can't blame him. When people are trapped
. . . All that about Danny – and he thought that somehow I
had managed to contact you. It was ridiculous, impossible
. . . but things weren't going as he wanted. He didn't expect
to see Irene, or Walker. He ordered Walker to leave, but he
wouldn't – and he thought everyone was lying to him. He
said that you wanted to charge him with killing Mrs Rutherford. Are you going to?'

'He might be guilty,' said Stratton.

'It's possible, I suppose. Poor man.'

'Etheridge or Walker?'

'Both.' Once more, he transferred his gaze to somewhere
above Stratton's head.

'To return to what you were saying,' said Stratton. 'What
happened when you arrived here?'

'Well, as I said, I didn't want to go home, so I stayed here.
I wasn't doing anything – just sitting and thinking – and
then Maxine called to tell me that Danny had died.'

'How did she know you were here?'

'She didn't. She had telephoned to where she thought I
might be – my house, the office, the Condor—'

'Condor? What's that?'

'Danny's club in Earl's Court. It's run by a man called
Cyril Nash.'

'I see. And who was here with you?'

'Irene and Roy. They were upstairs.'

'Roy?'

'Roy Walker.'

'He was here *with* Irene, was he?'

'I suppose so.'

'When we spoke on Saturday you mentioned a manager-ess who lives on the premises.'

'Mrs Crocetti. She always goes to see her daughter on Sunday evening and comes back on Monday morning.'

'How did Etheridge get in here?'

'The side door – I forgot to lock it.'

'And when did Irene and Walker appear?'

'They must have heard the noise. Etheridge was shouting.'

'We can go into the details later,' said Stratton. 'For now, there are several other questions I need to ask you. Have you seen Rutherford at any time today?'

'He came to the office this afternoon. I wasn't there, but he told Jan that he wanted to collect some papers.' Laskier held up a defensive hand. 'I have no idea what they were.'

'I imagine,' said Stratton, 'that they were the papers he burnt later in the grate at Lower Belgrave Street.'

He'd expected Laskier to refute this, or at least to be shocked, but his expression didn't change. 'Perhaps. I don't know. It's possible that he took some papers from here too, because he came later, with Jan. Some of the things Danny had asked for, I couldn't find them.'

'Were you here when they arrived?'

Laskier shook his head. 'Mrs Crocetti told me. He took some flowers and chocolates. I imagine those were for Miss Scott.'

'Do you know April Scott?'

'Yes. She comes here often.'

'What made you think they were for her?'

'A guess. From what I saw between them.'

'Did you ever mention your suspicions to Danny?'

'No. I wasn't sure, and it would have upset him. Especially Rutherford – that would be like a kick in the teeth—'

'Because they were doing business together?'

Laskier's eyes narrowed. 'Rutherford was important to Danny. He introduced him to the kind of people he wanted to know . . . to be friends with. I want . . . wanted . . . to protect Danny. You know, five, six years ago, I became a British citizen. I didn't tell him – he found out a few months ago – but I hadn't spoken of it because I knew it would upset him that I had this and he didn't . . . Actually, April Scott telephoned me yesterday, Inspector. Danny hadn't called her and she wanted to know where he was. I told her he'd gone away for a few days on business. I didn't want her to go running to the hospital. She'd have been over there like a shot if she'd thought he was dying.'

'Mercenary, is she?'

'Ach, she's not a bad girl. I like her. She's beautiful, she's smart, she's good company and she makes – made – Danny happy. But she's young, you know? And like a lot of people she thought he was rich, that he would keep her in luxury, maybe marry her.'

'Wasn't he?'

'Rich?' Laskier shook his head. 'Danny didn't *own* anything, Inspector. It was all mortgaged and remortgaged. What I said about the money in there is true – that's all there is.'

CHAPTER FORTY-SEVEN

'It was like conjuring,' said Laskier. 'Juggling. Keep it in the air, borrow from one to pay off another . . . But all the time he is doing these deals, he's spending the money too. This afternoon, when I was in the office, I discovered there was more debt than I had realised. I found some papers I'd never seen before. Danny must have brought them in from his house. He didn't tell me about them – perhaps he didn't want Maxine to know, or . . . I don't know, but he took a second mortgage on his house, and one on the flat in Bryanston Mews. And then the Rolls-Royce: four payments behind on the hire purchase.'

'So even the car didn't belong to him?' Stratton was incredulous.

'The never-never. And he was still spending. Two months ago he had a Cadillac delivered from the States. You know what they call that in America?' he asked, deadpan. 'A Jew buggy. And last week he was telling me about a Sheraton cabinet he bought from Sotheby's. He was having it converted for the television, to put it inside.'

'When I saw Mr Perlmann in hospital, he said to me that

you "didn't know". Was he talking about that, or something else?'

Laskier frowned. 'There are things I don't know – maybe in the sense of having no knowledge, or maybe because I chose not to ask questions.'

'So what you told Etheridge was true, was it?'

'Yes. There'll be a lot of people wanting money, and nothing to give them. They won't believe it, of course, but there it is. There's no point trying to pretend.'

'What about what Etheridge said about Perlmann promising him those houses? Do you know anything about that?'

'No, but I can believe he offered him a house – to set him up, you know?'

'Why would he help Etheridge? After all, he isn't Polish, and there's no reason. Unless you know of one, of course.'

'You mean for doing his dirty work?'

'I mean for getting rid of Herbert Hampton.'

'No,' said Laskier, flatly. 'Danny hated violence.'

'Mr Laskier,' said Stratton. 'I know you want to protect Mr Perlmann, but people don't just give away houses out of the kindness of their heart.'

'But he wasn't giving him a house.'

'But you just told me that you believed—'

'What I meant was, it wasn't as simple as saying, "Here's a house, it's yours, now you can make money." It's as I told you: Danny didn't own anything. Those houses in Powis Terrace are like all the others – mortgaged far beyond their value. After you'd paid for that, you'd make . . . oh, maybe £200 a year from one of those if you were lucky.'

'You're going to have to explain,' said Stratton, lighting another cigarette and pushing the packet towards Laskier. 'Why would Perlmann go to all the bother of setting this up for only £200 per year per house? And why would you go to the bother of helping him?'

Laskier took a cigarette. 'How much do you know about building societies, Inspector?'

'As much as the next man, I should think. But I thought you told me that you and Perlmann found some solicitor who lent you money from trust funds.'

'It wasn't as simple as that. You know that – in theory, anyway – anyone can set up a building society? Get some fancy names for the notepaper and then people decide they trust you and they start lending you their money, so you have plenty of cheap money to buy property yourself and to lend to other people at higher rates – and everybody's happy, yes? Except maybe the Association of British Building Societies – but that's too bad because it's not illegal, and people like the small places because they offer a one hundred per cent mortgage, which they can't get anywhere else.'

'So?' said Stratton. 'It's a racket, but as you said, it's not illegal, and I still don't see—'

Laskier held up his hand for quiet. 'What you probably *don't* know is that mortgages of over £5,000 have to be shown in the building society's annual return. So, what happens is this: Danny buys a property for . . . oh, £4,000 with a loan from the bank. Say it's a house with five storeys. He divides it up – in a manner of speaking – into five separate flats and then he gets five separate mortgages for £2,000 each from one of these small building societies. Say he gets £1,000 per annum in rent – that looks after the mortgage payments, with a little bit left over, as I said – and Danny takes the difference.'

'You mean he'd pocket £6,000?'

Laskier nodded. 'Dozens of times. Sets up different companies to stop the same name recurring too many times . . .'

'And he gets – *got* – £6,000 for each house?'

'At least.'

'Whose idea was this?'

'Danny's.'

'It sounds to me,' said Stratton, 'as if there was one particular society which was lending all this money. Rutherford was involved in it, wasn't he?'

Laskier sighed. 'Yes, he was.'

'How?'

'Initially as an estate agent, and then with the Porchester Building Society.'

'What was his involvement in that?'

'It was not . . . official. A man called Stephen Hamilton started it. He also started the Hythe and Hamilton Property Group. Mr Hythe is a solicitor.'

'And this is where the trust funds come in?'

'Yes, Inspector. I think you saw Mr Hamilton here, when you came. Big man, loud voice.' Stratton had a mental flash of a florid, jowly face and a plummy, booming accent – one of the men who'd been talking to Perlmann that night, he thought. 'Rutherford helped him to set it up – he found the names.'

'When was that?'

'About five years ago, I think. It's written on the paper – the letterhead. I can fetch it for you.'

The office was now almost empty. PC Brodie put down the cardboard box he was humping into the corridor. 'Done everything but the desk, sir.'

'Would there be something in there?' Stratton asked Laskier.

'It's possible.' Laskier began opening drawers and pulling out handfuls of paper. He started to sort through them, tossing aside receipts, bank statements and scraps covered in hastily scribbled columns of figures. 'Here's one.'

Smoothing out the crumpled sheet of paper, Stratton saw the words Porchester Building Society written across the top in elaborate cursive script and beneath them a fanciful drawing of a portcullis flanked by two heraldic beasts wearing crowns and surrounded by swirling chains. *Est. 1953*, he read. At the bottom of the blank page was an address in Piccadilly and underneath that, a list of directors: *Wing Commander Victor Glendinning DSO, Stephen Hamilton, Gerald Hythe LL.B., The Viscount Purbeck.*

CHAPTER FORTY-EIGHT

'There was nobody at Perlmann's office,' said Matheson, when Stratton had finished his account of what happened at Maxine's. 'And precious few papers either. Somebody'd had a clear-out.'

'I don't think it was Laskier.' Stratton was perched on the corner of a desk in the CID office at West End Central, surrounded by overflowing boxes of stuff they'd removed from the nightclub. 'He said he'd taken two boxes, and from what I saw in the Westbourne Grove office, there was a great deal more than that. He told me that Rutherford had been there before him, and he'd taken some stuff too – which I'm assuming he burnt at Lower Belgrave Street – but he didn't say anything about the place being cleared out. Perhaps Rutherford went back to the office for the rest of the papers after Laskier left, sir.'

'If he did, he didn't take them back home. DI Hanford reported that there was no one there except the house-keeper, and she said she hadn't seen Rutherford since you left this afternoon.'

'I'm just wondering,' said Stratton, 'if he might have

gone to Perlmann's house. I didn't get the impression that Rutherford and Laskier were in cahoots, but I've instructed the duty sergeant here to keep him hanging around incommunicado for as long as possible before a formal statement is taken, just to be on the safe side. I think there might be further documents at Perlmann's house, and if Rutherford's trying to cover up the misuse of his wife's money . . . It's possible that he's aware of Perlmann's death by now, but even if he isn't, he'd expect to find him at home if he'd drawn a blank everywhere else. Incidentally, sir, it might be worth having a word with Cyril Nash, who manages Perlmann's other club. That's the Condor, in Earl's Court. Rumours of unlicensed gambling, according to PC Jellicoe. Laskier says Perlmann's got a lot of creditors, and if Mrs Perlmann told Nash about his death, it's possible that he's been pretty busy on the blower already.'

'We'll do that right away, and we'd better get on to the other chaps whose names are on that letterhead too. Where does Perlmann live?'

Stratton peered at his notebook again. 'Winnington Road in Hampstead.'

'Very nice. Why don't you get over there now and see what's happening? Take Brodie and the others with you.'

'Yes, sir. Just before I do – about the girl. There's no reason to keep her here once her statement's been taken, but she's very young and very upset and there won't be anyone to look out for her at home.'

'Fair enough. A social worker?'

'There's someone I can ring, sir.'

'Do that, then – but you'd better make it quick.'

It was just about light as they drove in convoy – West End Central had provided another car for backup – down the length of Winnington Road. It was, as Matheson had said, very nice, with large detached houses, each with a sizeable front garden. Most had semicircular driveways with two sets of double gates. He'd been pleased that Matheson had been prepared to trust him about Irene without asking questions. Lamb, he reflected, would probably have insisted on contacting the girl's parents whether she liked it or not. Fenella's voice had been thick and sleepy when she'd answered the phone, but once he'd apologised for the early hour and explained things a bit, she'd seemed quite happy to have been asked to help. He'd given her a brief résumé of events, and she'd agreed to come and collect Irene from West End Central and take her home for what remained of the night. He wondered if the girl might talk to Fenella about who or what had frightened her so much on the night that Johnson had been killed. He'd not discussed it with her, but sometimes shock had the effect of making people open up . . .

'It's this one, sir,' said the driver, pulling up outside a tall hedge with a pair of elaborate wrought iron gates on either side. The far ones were open and the nearest ones slightly ajar. Through them, Stratton had a reasonably clear view of the front of the house, which was a grand affair with a portico, built in a mock-Georgian style. It was silent, all the blinds and curtains closed, but everything about it shouted wealth. There was a double garage beside the house. The door was open, and Stratton could see a wide powder-blue bonnet with a grinning radiator grille and huge, pointed chrome decorations that he supposed must be the Cadillac Laskier had mentioned. He could also see the boot of the navy blue Roller, which was parked outside the front door, but everything else was hidden by the hedge. A few hundred yards further down the road a white Jaguar sports car, its top down, had been clumsily parked, one front wheel up on the grass verge. It was the only car he'd seen parked in the entire road.

'Right. I don't know what's going to happen, if anything – but you'd best park in front of these gates and be prepared to stop anyone who tries to leave. Tell the others to do the same on the other side. Brodie and Coxon, you follow me.'

Going through the gates and into the garden, the first thing Stratton noticed was that there was no sign of the Bentley. The second thing he noticed was a small blonde figure, head down and hunched over the steering wheel of the Rolls-Royce.

CHAPTER FORTY-NINE

Telling Brodie and Coxon to position themselves at the front and side of the house to keep an eye in case Rutherford was inside, Stratton marched round to the driver's side of the Roller and knocked sharply on the window. April Scott raised her head and looked at him blankly through eyes slicked with smears of powder and mascara. Stratton pointed downwards to indicate that she should open the window. April complied, apparently in a trance.

'What are you doing here?' asked Stratton.

'Danny . . .' Her face broke up in sobs. 'He's dead.'

Looking into the car, Stratton saw that she had a pair of leather driving gloves and the butt of a cigar clutched in her lap. She'd been holding the cigar so tightly that flakes of tobacco were scattered across the tight skirt of her pale blue silk dress and the leather upholstery. 'Who told you?' he asked.

'Giles Rutherford.'

'Did he bring you here too?'

April shook her head. 'I drove myself.'

'That's your car outside, is it? The Jag?'

'Yes.' Stratton saw, behind her mascara-streaked face, a glimpse of her former hauteur. 'Danny bought it for me.' On hire purchase, presumably, thought Stratton, thinking of the missed instalments on the Rolls.

'Do you know if Rutherford is planning to come here?'

'Is he here?'

'I was hoping you could tell me.'

'If he is, I didn't see him. I was in there before, talking to Danny's wife, and he wasn't there then.'

'Did Rutherford tell you *when* he'd found out about Perlmann's death?'

'Just before he called me, I think.'

'Which was when?'

'I'm not sure. He woke me up, and I came here . . . I don't know.'

'How long have you been here?'

'I don't know that, either. Gerald didn't want to let me in, but—'

'Who's Gerald?'

'Gerald Hythe. He's a friend of Danny's. I think he's a creep.' The solicitor whose name was on the letterhead of the Porchester Building Society. That was quick. 'He tried to shut the door in my face, but she wouldn't let him, and then he pretended he didn't know who I was. She kept asking me about property deals and things like that.'

So she knows something's up, thought Stratton. 'Were you able to help her?'

'No, and I don't understand. How could Danny have all this, and be . . .' April shook her head. 'She said he didn't leave a will. I didn't believe it, but then I could see . . . she only let me in because she wanted to know if I knew anything. She said people were already telephoning her, saying Danny owed them money.'

'How did Rutherford find out that Mr Perlmann was dead, Miss Scott?'

'He'd been trying to get in touch with Danny yesterday, so he phoned Cyril.'

'Cyril Nash of the Condor Club?'

'Yes. He didn't know then, of course, but Danny's wife phoned him later.' When she was trying to find Laskier, thought Stratton. 'She told him and he phoned Giles.'

Stratton opened the car door. 'Listen, April. You can't stay here, and I'm not at all sure you should be driving at the moment, so I'm going to ask one of my men to take you home.'

April nodded, her eyes fixed glumly on the house. 'Danny wasn't ever going to leave her, was he? He used to tell me he was, but it wasn't true, was it?'

'I don't know,' said Stratton, 'but I doubt it.'

'It was only when I was in there talking to her that I realised, really. I mean, I knew he was married, but he always said that they didn't have any . . . you know . . . and that she spent most of her time in America. He said she'd helped him in business and he stayed with her from gratitude.'

'They all say things like that,' said Stratton, helping her out of the car. 'Still, you're young and you'll know better next time, won't you?'

Telling Coxon to escort April outside the gates and send

a car to take her back to Bryanston Mews, Stratton was about to knock on the front door when a figure came crashing through the shrubbery on the far side of the house: Rutherford, carrying a suitcase. Brodie, blowing his whistle frantically, made a lunge for him at the same time as five constables raced across the lawn from two different directions. A second later, hearing the front door open, Stratton turned to prevent Maxine Perlmann from coming into the garden, but instead of Mrs Perlmann, Jan the Polish giant appeared and launched himself at Rutherford. PC Dixon and one of the others immediately rugby-tackled him, one round his waist and the other grabbing one of his legs, but he barely seemed to notice and, as he threw punches at Rutherford, both men were flung about as if weightless.

'Get her out of here, and for Christ's sake get some backup,' Stratton yelled at Coxon.

'My God! Oh, my God!' Stratton saw a white-faced, swollen-eyed Maxine Perlmann dressed in slacks with a bandanna round her head, standing at the front door of the house. 'What's happening?'

'You,' called Stratton, picking out the shadowy figure of a man behind her, who he assumed must be Gerald Hythe, 'get her back inside, now, and shut the door!'

He turned round in time to see one of the giant's flying fists hit a constable, who tottered backwards and sat down hard in a flower bed. Then, elbowing Brodie out of the way, Jan got Rutherford in a headlock. As he did so, the suitcase slid out of Rutherford's hand, hit the gravel and exploded open, and a slew of typed documents cascaded out, getting trampled underfoot or wrapping themselves about the legs of the combatants. Stratton could see, in the ensuing mêlée, that Rutherford had made a grab for Jan's groin. 'Bastard! Bloody bastard! Thief!' As Jan pulled at his hand, Rutherford's head, aided by the policeman tugging on the rest of him, began to slip out from under Jan's arm. Suddenly Jan bent his own head and a second later Rutherford began screaming like a stuck pig.

'He's got his ear!' yelled Brodie. 'He's biting off his ear!'

Apparently unaware of the truncheon blows raining down on his bowed head and shoulders, Jan held on for what must have been about thirty seconds but seemed a lot longer, as two constables tried to pull him away and Rutherford carried on bellowing. Then Jan lifted his head so that Stratton saw the blood around his mouth and on his chin before he leant forward and spat something red and fleshy towards the edge of the lawn. As he did so, one of the men swung his truncheon, like a golf club, squarely at the backs of his knees and another three ploughed into him from behind, so that he ended up face down on the grass with four constables sitting on top of him, surrounded by pieces of paper and spitting out a stream of what Stratton assumed to be Polish obscenities.

'Well done,' shouted Stratton over the din. 'Cuff him.' He turned his attention to Rutherford who, still screaming, was now struggling in the grip of PC Brodie, blood streaming down the side of his face and onto his white shirt.

'The fucker tried to kill me,' he gasped.

'Yes,' said Stratton, 'we saw. We also saw you trying to

make a run for it with that lot.' He gestured towards the papers, some of which had now fluttered beneath the hedge and into the carefully tended flower beds.

Coxon appeared at his elbow. 'Van's on its way, sir. The girl's in the car outside.'

'Good. Knock on the door and ask for some towels to mop this one up, will you?'

Turning back to Rutherford, he said, 'Now, where were you off to in such a hurry?'

'I just' – Rutherford tried to jerk away from Brodie – 'came to collect what's mine.'

'We'll see about that,' said Stratton. 'In the meantime, you're under arrest.'

'What for?'

'Breaking and entering, being in possession of stolen property and anything else I can think of,' said Stratton grimly.

'You can't, you jumped-up little—'

'I just did,' said Stratton.

'Get your hands off me,' Rutherford snarled at Brodie, trying to elbow him in the ribs.

'Less of it,' said Stratton, 'or I'll have you for resisting arrest as well.'

'You can't—'

'Oh yes I can.'

Coxon appeared from the house bearing a stack of towels like a chambermaid.

'Good.' Stratton took the top one. 'Go out and call for an ambulance, will you? And after that you can make a start on clearing up all these bits of paper.' To Rutherford he said, 'I'm going to hold this towel to your ear and try to stop the blood, so if I were you I'd keep still.'

Rutherford tried not to wince as Stratton gently pressed the towel to the ragged remains of his right ear. 'Where's your car?' he asked.

'I'm not answering any more questions.'

'Aren't you?' said Stratton. 'That's a pity.' He pressed down hard on the towel so that Rutherford gave a yell of pain.

'I parked down there, round the corner.'

'Which road?'

'I don't know the name. Right and right again.'

'Thank you, Mr Rutherford. That's most cooperative. Now, if PC Brodie can just take your keys . . .'

Stratton and Brodie stood in silence after that, Rutherford sagging dejectedly between them, as they waited for the vehicles to arrive. On the lawn Jan, handcuffed and pinned down by policemen, continued to thrash and bellow incomprehensibly, throwing in a 'bloody bastard' now and then for good measure.

CHAPTER FIFTY

'Should we have given them this, sir,' said Dixon, 'or is it evidence?'

Rutherford, clutching a towel to his still-bleeding head with one hand and handcuffed to Brodie by the other, had been escorted to the ambulance and driven away. Jan, still shouting, had been carted off in the opposite direction by a Black Maria, and Dixon and Stratton were looking down at the cartilage and flesh that had been Rutherford's right ear and was now a thick red curl on the edge of the lawn. 'I mean,' Dixon continued, 'couldn't they reattach it?'

'No idea,' said Stratton, who was strongly tempted to kick the thing into the nearest bush and forget all about it. 'I suppose we'd better send it after him. Why don't you knock on the door again and ask Mrs Perlmann if she's got a Tupperware box?'

Imagining a litany of complaints including words like 'fiasco' and 'the Keystone Kops', he felt in his pockets for his handkerchief. Remembering that he'd given it to Gloria, he called out to Coxon who was grovelling about in the bushes after the remaining bits of paper. 'Have you got a clean handkerchief?'

'Yes, sir.'

'May I borrow it?'

'Of course, sir.'

Coxon lingered as Stratton spread out the white cotton square and, squatting down, covered Rutherford's ear with it in order to lift it up. It felt, through the handkerchief, as though it were made of hard rubber, and he kept the fabric bundled up so as not to have to look at the thing inside. Coxon stared at the smears of dried blood on the handkerchief and said, 'If it's all the same to you, sir, I definitely don't want it back.'

When Rutherford's suitcase, now piled haphazardly with pieces of paper which had variously been crumpled, trodden on or smeared with earth, was stowed in one of the police cars and Stratton had given instructions for the Bentley to be impounded, he decided it was high time he spoke to Maxine Perlmann.

A maid showed him into a large hall with a high ceiling and plenty of gilt-framed mirrors and ornate furniture, all sparkling and shining in the morning sun. Remembering what Laskier said about Perlmann buying things from Sotheby's, Stratton concluded that they must be antiques although – perhaps because of the surroundings – they did not quite have the same look of belonging as the things in the Rutherfords' house. Winnington Road was definitely, in its ostentatiousness, *nouveau riche* – and certainly a world away from the cramped and squalid quarters of Perlmann's tenants.

Somewhere in the background a telephone was ringing, shrill and insistent. He could still hear it, but more faintly, when the maid took him through to an enormous, airy sitting room. There was more fancy furniture here, and through the French windows he could see a vast and beautifully kept garden with a tennis court at the end of it.

After several minutes, Maxine Perlmann appeared. She'd done her best to camouflage her pale face and red eyes with a coating of make-up, but she moved woodenly, as if grief and shock had made her rigid. Without looking at Stratton, she seated herself on the sofa. Beside her, holding tight to her elbow, was a man – Hythe, presumably – for whom the word 'seedy' might have been invented. He looks like a creep all right, thought Stratton, remembering what April Scott had said. With scruffy clothes, lank, over-long hair and pro-truding teeth, there was something indefinably murky about him and Stratton had a feeling that, close to, he might smell of mildew.

'DI Stratton. We met yesterday, Mrs Perlmann, at—'

'Yes,' said Maxine Perlmann, her voice wobbling with accusation. 'Then he took a turn for the worse. Until you came, the doctors thought he was going to get better.'

'I'm sorry if anything I said distressed him, Mrs Perl-mann,' said Stratton, taken aback, 'but he wanted to see me. And I'm afraid I do have to ask you some questions now, but I shall try to keep it as brief as I can. So if you wouldn't mind leaving us, Mr Hythe . . .'

Hythe remained seated. 'You know my name, I see. I imagine Miss Scott must have told you. The stupid female was still sitting in the car an hour after I turfed her out. Pretending she'd gone into a trance or something.'

'People do strange things when they've had a shock, Mr Hythe. I'd like a word with you later, if I may, but for now—'

'Mrs Perlmann has asked me to remain. I shall be acting for her.'

'Is that so?' Stratton asked Maxine Perlmann, who nodded, her mouth in a firm line as if she didn't trust herself to speak. As Stratton was fishing out his notebook, she burst out, almost shouting, 'I need to talk to Stefan, but I can't get hold of him. When I rang to tell him about Danny he hung up on me and now he's not answering the phone. I'd only been back from the hospital half an hour when people started phoning up, saying Danny owed them money. After you left in the morning, he was obsessed with talking to Stefan – he's the only one who knows everything and he's supposed to be Danny's friend and he can't even—'

'Mrs Perlmann.' Stratton held up a hand. 'If you'll allow me, I can explain about Mr Laskier.'

Mrs Perlmann sat and nodded at intervals as Stratton described what had happened at Maxine's. Hythe, he noticed, looked sour, and he had a strong suspicion that when she had told the man her version of events he, sensing advantage, had proceeded to tell her that Laskier was not to be trusted.

'I very much doubt,' Hythe said now, 'that Mr Perlmann promised this negro anything. The man sounds deranged.'

'Mr Laskier thinks it's entirely possible that he might have done,' said Stratton, testing his hypothesis. Maxine Perlmann looked uncertainly from one to the other.

'Impossible,' said Hythe. 'In any case, the man's a criminal, isn't he?' Turning to Mrs Perlmann, he continued, 'I hate to say this, Maxine my dear . . .' No you don't, thought Stratton. '. . . I know how much Danny trusted Stefan, but we've all been quite worried about him. He's not been the same since Lola died – that was his wife, Inspector, she took her own life, I'm afraid. It's hardly surprising, and of course Danny was so loyal to his friends, he would never have said, but I know he was concerned about it.'

'Told you, did he?' asked Stratton.

Hythe nodded earnestly, as though he'd not heard the scepticism in Stratton's voice. 'Last week, in fact. He said he was thinking of trying to persuade Stefan to take a few weeks' holiday. You may not be aware of this, Inspector, but Danny and Stefan went through a lot together during the war and Danny was like an older brother to him.'

'I'm aware of that,' said Stratton, 'but when I spoke to Mr Laskier I saw no sign that he couldn't manage. Quite the reverse, in fact. He seemed to me to know *exactly* what's been going on.' He treated Hythe to a glare, mentally adding, And I've got your number, chum, so don't bugger me about.

Hythe dropped his gaze first, and turned back to Mrs Perlmann. 'I'm only thinking about safeguarding your interests, my dear. In spite of what the Inspector seems to think, I don't think it's fair to burden Stefan at a time like this.'

Very clever, thought Stratton, and of course it contained

more than a grain of truth. He'd had the impression, talking to Laskier, that Perlmann's death hadn't really sunk in – at least half the time he'd been talking about the man in the present tense. 'Mr Perlmann was keen to talk to him, though,' said Stratton. He turned to Maxine Perlmann.

'Did he say anything to you before he died?'

'Yes,' she said uncertainly, 'but he was frightened and in a lot of pain and most of it was in Polish so I didn't understand, apart from a few words here and there. He mentioned Stefan, and straight after that he said, "Give him the things from the house." '

'He said "Give Stefan the things" or "Give him the things"?' asked Stratton.

' "Him." '

'What things do you think he meant?'

'I don't know. They wouldn't let me stay. I asked afterwards, but they said he hadn't spoken again.'

'So he didn't say anything about Rutherford?'

'No.'

Stratton wondered whether she knew about Mrs Rutherford, but decided this wasn't the time to mention it. Instead, he said, 'Can you remember what time Mr Perlmann died, Mrs Perlmann?'

'Just after half past twelve.'

'And when did you leave the hospital?'

'About two o'clock, I think. I'm not sure.'

'Were you driving?'

'Yes. In the Rolls.'

'And you were alone, were you?'

'I would have telephoned my sister to come, but she's away on holiday.'

'Have you managed to contact her?'

'Yes. I rang the hotel – she's in France – and she said she'd get a flight back as soon as she can.'

'Any other family members?'

'My parents are both dead, and my brother lives in Australia. I haven't been able to speak to him yet.'

'Fair enough. So you drove home and you got here at what time?'

'For pity's sake,' said Hythe. 'She can't be expected to remember—'

'Approximately.' Stratton cut across him. 'Try to remember, Mrs Perlmann.'

'About twenty minutes?'

'OK. And what happened when you arrived home?'

'Well, Bonita – that's our maid, she lives here – was waiting up for me, and she made me a cup of tea and we sat in the kitchen for a bit, and then I thought I'd better ring Stefan, so I phoned around trying to find him.'

'Where did you try?'

'Home, first. There was no answer, so I called the Condor. I couldn't imagine why he'd be there, but I thought Cyril might know.'

'He answered the phone, did he?'

'Yes. It rang for a long time, so I think I woke him up. I told him about Danny, and then I rang the club. I suppose I must have talked to Stefan for a couple of minutes before the phone was slammed down.'

'And that would have been . . .' Stratton thumbed back through his notebook, 'about ten to three.'

'I should think so. I was going to call my brother, because it's daytime in Australia, but before I could pick up the phone it started ringing. I thought it might have been Stefan, but it was a man – he said he was sorry about Danny and then he said he needed me to sign something because Danny owed him a lot of money and there was nothing in writing.' Her voice rose, shrill and panicky. 'I said I didn't know what he was talking about and he'd have to talk to Stefan, and then straight after that another man phoned.' She shook her head, blinking away tears. 'I couldn't take any of it in, I was so . . .'

'It's all right, Mrs Perlmann. Do you know the names of these people?'

'No. I didn't catch them. All I know is that Danny's dead and I don't know why all this is happening. I said to them, I can't help you, you have to talk to Stefan, but they wouldn't listen. They were threatening to come here.'

'It's all right, Maxine.' Mr Hythe, next to her, glared at Stratton and made damping down motions with his hands. 'I'm sure we can sort it all out. I really don't think, Inspector, that now is the time to go into—'

'No,' said Stratton, 'it isn't. But could you tell me exactly what happened after you took the calls, Mrs Perlmann?'

She blew her nose. 'I suppose I must have sat there for a while, and then the phone started ringing again and Bonita came in. I told her not to answer it. I remember I went upstairs and sat on the bed after that . . . Then Bonita came up and said Giles Rutherford had arrived.'

'And what time was that?'

'About an hour later, I suppose, maybe more.'

'What happened after that?'

'Bonita said that Gertner was with him—'

'Gertner?'

'Jan Gertner. He works – worked – for Danny. Bonita said that they'd gone straight into the sun lounge and she couldn't stop him. Danny works in there, you see, in the summer, and sometimes he leaves papers and things. He doesn't like it if anyone goes in there and tidies up, so Bonita's very careful . . . I went downstairs to see, and there was quite a lot of stuff – more than usual – and Giles was in there shovelling it all into a case.'

'What was Jan Gertner doing?'

'Nothing. He was sitting on one of the chairs. He was upset . . . kept asking me if it was true that Danny was dead. When I asked Giles what he thought he was doing, he turned on me like a madman and told me he had to take it all, and then he said he was trying to protect me . . . I told him, you can't just come in here and take things, and I tried to make him put the papers down. He was shouting, and he kept saying how he'd helped Danny in the past and now I had to help him, and then Bonita came in because of the noise and I said to her to take the papers upstairs, but when she tried to pick them up he snatched them. I thought he'd gone mad. And then Jan . . .' Maxine Perlmann took a deep, ragged breath. 'All the time Giles and I had been arguing he'd just been sitting there, and then suddenly he was towering over us, pushing us apart, shouting in Polish. Giles was trying to calm him down. He kept saying, "I'm doing it for Danny." I don't think Jan understood what was happening any more than I did, but by that time I was really frightened. Bonita was hysterical so I told her to go upstairs, and I was going to call the police when Gerald arrived.'

'When Mr Perlmann said to you,' said Stratton carefully, 'that you should give Mr Laskier "the things from the house", do you think he meant the papers that Rutherford tried to take?'

'Yes. I couldn't think of anything else he might have meant, because there's no safe here. When Gerald arrived, I told him about Giles and Jan—'

'And I said I'd go and talk some sense into Rutherford,' finished Hythe.

'And this was when?' asked Stratton.

Hythe looked at him with irritation. 'About an hour and a half ago, I should think. That girl arrived just after I did.'

'April Scott,' said Maxine Perlmann wearily. 'You know perfectly well who she is, Gerald, and so do I. I told him,' she said to Stratton, 'to let her in. I suppose I wouldn't have – ordinarily, I mean – but I wanted to see if she had any idea of what was going on with all these wretched people.'

'And did she?'

Mrs Perlmann shook her head. 'She said she didn't, and I believe her.'

'After about half an hour, I went in and asked her to leave,' said Hythe. 'She wasn't helping, and it wasn't . . .

right for her to be here, but she wouldn't budge – just stared at me as if she was half-witted.'

'I must have forgotten to lock the car,' said Maxine Perl-mann. 'I didn't realise she'd been sitting there until Gerald told me just now.'

'I see. Right.' Stratton stood up. 'I think that's all for the time being, Mrs Perlmann, so I'll leave you in peace.' To Hythe, he said, 'I'd like to have a look at the sun lounge, please, so if you would be so kind as to accompany me . . .'

CHAPTER FIFTY-ONE

As soon as they were in the hall and out of earshot, Hythe hissed, 'I hope you're pleased with yourself, bullying a distressed woman.'

'But taking advantage of her distress and confusion in order to swindle her is all right, is it?'

'I'm doing nothing of the sort,' said Hythe. 'I'm trying to protect her.'

'I'll be the judge of that,' said Stratton firmly. 'In the meantime, I'll ask the necessary questions. Now, where's this sun lounge?'

The room was a large, conservatory-like structure, painted white, lush with greenery and full of rattan furniture of the type Stratton associated with the outposts of Empire. The double doors, one of which was open, led onto a patio, and the only incongruous note was a large wooden table in the centre, littered with stray pieces of paper, more of which were strewn across the floor. Beside it, a briefcase lay open, face down, as if it had been upended and the contents shaken out of it. Several of the chairs, Stratton saw, stood at odd angles, as if they'd been shoved or pushed aside in the course of a struggle, and one of the plant pots was tipped over, scattering a ragged semicircle of earth on the tiled floor.

'Did you have a fight?' he asked.

'I told you,' said Hythe. 'I was trying to make him see reason. Gertner did that,' he pointed to the tipped-over plant, 'blundering about.'

'So what were you trying to get Rutherford to do, exactly?'

'Stop him taking the papers, of course,' said Hythe.

'Sure about that, are you?'

'Of course I am. The man had gone mad. He'd just killed his wife.'

'How do you know that? Did he tell you?'

'He didn't have to. Everyone knows.'

'Who's everyone?'

'For God's sake, Inspector! I arrived to find Maxine being threatened by a dangerous lunatic – a murderer – and I did what anyone would have done.'

'But you didn't, did you? "Anyone", in the situation you've just described, would have called the police at once. Unless, of course, they had a good reason not to. Did you have a reason, Mr Hythe?'

'Of course not!' A mottled flush was spreading up Hythe's neck. 'You can see what's been going on here—'

'That's just it,' said Stratton. 'I can't. What I can see, however, is that Mr Perlmann has, unfortunately, died, and you lot – alerted, I imagine, by Mr Nash at the Condor – have descended on the place like a plague of locusts. Mr Rutherford is a business associate of yours, isn't he?'

The flush, which had now reached Hythe's face, blotched damson and red across his cheeks. 'Certainly not.'

'What about the Porchester Building Society?'

'That's nothing to do with Giles.'

'His former father-in-law is a director, Mr Hythe.'

'That's completely irrelevant.'

'Irrelevant that Rutherford helped you coerce a frail and possibly senile old man into lending his name to—'

'The Porchester Building Society operates within the law, Inspector,' said Hythe triumphantly, 'and I deny any wrong-doing.'

CHAPTER FIFTY-TWO

It was twenty-five to ten when Stratton arrived back at Harrow Road Station. Somewhere in the tangled mess of Perlmann and Rutherford's affairs lay the answers to who had killed Bert Hampton, the Hon. Virginia and very likely Clyde Johnson as well, but he was too tired to think about it any more. He still had to deal with Pearson, Larby and the rest of them as well as Etheridge, Gertner and – when he'd emerged from hospital – Rutherford.

Stumbling on leaden legs through the knots of people waiting in the foyer, he would have failed to register that Curtis, the desk sergeant, was calling his name if PC Dunning hadn't tugged on his sleeve. Turning, he saw that Fenella Jones was standing at the desk, looking worried.

'What's going on?' he asked Curtis. 'Where's Irene Palmer?'

'She's here, sir. This lady says she's supposed to collect her, but we've not had any instructions about it.'

'I went to West End Central to collect Irene,' said Fenella, 'but when I arrived I was told she'd been brought here. They wouldn't tell me why, so I thought there must have been a mix-up and I'd better come over here, but they won't let me take her and I didn't want to just abandon the poor girl, so . . .'

'. . . you've been here all this time,' finished Stratton, appalled. 'I'm very sorry you've been messed about like this. I'll find out what's going on.'

Sergeant Curtis, who had the mulishly virtuous look of one who finds himself in trouble for following orders, said, 'The duty sergeant says there's no authorisation, sir, and no one else knows anything about it.'

'When was she brought in?'

'Twenty-five to seven, sir.'

'I am sorry,' said Fenella. 'If I'd got there a bit quicker . . .'

'We're the ones who should be apologising,' said Stratton. 'Who's on duty?' he asked the desk sergeant.

'Sergeant Matthews, sir. He told the night Duty Sergeant to leave it to him.'

I bet he did, thought Stratton. He's getting his own back for those fucking identity parades. 'Where's Miss Palmer?'

'With Policewoman Jenner, sir.'

'Well, that's something, I suppose. What are you waiting for? Go and fetch her.'

'Yes, sir. It's just that Sergeant Matthews said unless it was the girl's family, it had to be through the proper channels, and—'

'You're looking at the proper channels, you idiot! Now get cracking. I really am sorry,' said Stratton, when he'd gone. 'I left clear instructions at West End Central, so I can only think that wires must have got crossed.'

'Honestly, it doesn't matter.' Fenella looked, given the circumstances, remarkably fresh and unflustered. In fact, she looked lovely, whereas he must look – and, in all probability, *smell* – like something dragged off a rubbish tip, added to which, she must now think him an incompetent fool. Seeing that she was gazing at him intently and presumably rapidly revising whatever good opinion she'd previously held, he was about to offer another apology when she said firmly, 'Really, it doesn't matter. I know these things happen, and it obviously wasn't your fault.'

'Miss Jenner's very nice,' said Stratton. 'I hope,' he added, 'that Matthews hasn't been bullying Irene for the names of her parents. He can be a bit of a . . . a so-and-so, and she'd got quite enough on her plate without that.'

'Is she the one you were telling me about in the cafe?'

'Yes,' said Stratton, surprised she'd remembered.

'So the man you said was killed, was he her . . . her lover?'

Stratton spent the next few minutes filling in the sketchy precis of events he'd given her earlier, and then Curtis reappeared, by himself and looking flustered.

'Where is she?'

'On her way, sir. Sergeant Matthews isn't best pleased,' he added. 'Says you should have talked to him first.'

'Well, he needn't worry,' said Stratton grimly, 'because I'll certainly be speaking to him later. Is DS Matheson about?'

'No, sir. Not for another hour, he said, but he left a message for you. If you could excuse us, madam,' he said to Fenella, who smiled at Stratton and went to sit down on one of the benches. 'It's about Knight and Halliwell, sir. They're downstairs. And they've found the van, sir.'

'That is good news. Where were they picked up?'

'Leaving the White Defence League place, sir, about two hours ago. The van was in the yard behind, under a tarpaulin. They're having a look at it now, sir. Turns out it's registered to Halliwell's father.'

'Even better. Have we managed to get hold of him for—'

Stratton broke off as Miss Jenner appeared, Irene at her side. Dressed now in a blouse and skirt, she was no longer shaking but looked paler and less substantial even than before, her legs and arms like white twigs and her drooping head too large for the slender neck beneath it. Her eyes widened in terror as Stratton took a step towards her, and she grabbed hold of Miss Jenner's arm.

'It's all right,' said Stratton gently, 'I'm not . . .' He stopped, realising that Irene wasn't looking at him but at something behind him. Turning, he caught a blurred snapshot of Mrs Halliwell, teased-up black hair and blazing eyes, charging towards him, but before he or anyone else could stop her she tore straight across to Irene and, pulling back her right hand, walloped her squarely across the face. Cowering, Irene staggered back against the wall, taking Miss Jenner with her.

'You bloody little *bitch*!'

'Stop right there!' Mrs Halliwell whirled round, arms flailing, clawing like a wild cat as Stratton leapt forward to catch hold of her. He felt a hot, piercing pain beneath his left eye as the sharp edge of her handbag hit his face and, bleeding and unbalanced from the blow, he cannoned sideways into Dunning, who had rushed across the foyer to help. There were gasps and yells of mixed excitement and fear from the waiting crowd as he and Dunning crashed to the ground and Curtis, above them, frantically pressed his buzzer and bawled for help.

As Stratton struggled upright there was a crash and a clatter as PC Jellicoe, accompanied by Illingworth, barrelled through the swing doors. After a few seconds' mêlée of arms, legs and curses, with Mrs Halliwell swinging her bag like a scythe and kicking out at their shins with her pointy-toed shoes, the two policemen managed to pinion her arms behind her back.

'What do you want us to do with her, sir?' panted Jellicoe.

'Interview room,' said Stratton. 'I'll deal with her in a minute.'

As Jellicoe and Illingworth manhandled the still struggling woman towards the swing doors, she made a sudden lunge towards Irene and, thrusting her head forward, spat directly into the girl's face.

CHAPTER FIFTY-THREE

'Right,' said Stratton. 'So far, you've obstructed an investigation, assaulted a member of the public and caused an affray in a police station. Added to which –' he tapped the Elastoplast he'd hastily stuck over the gash on his cheek – 'you bloody nearly blinded me, and if you don't want to find yourself trying to explain all that in court, you'd better start telling me what the hell is going on.'

Mrs Halliwell, seated on the other side of the table with PC Jellicoe and a policewoman standing in attendance, her spider-lashed eyes alight with fury, said, 'Never mind that, what you done with Tommy?'

'If you mean your son,' said Stratton, 'he's downstairs and we'll be speaking to him later.'

'She's the one should be down there, not him,' spat Mrs Halliwell. 'She's the one caused all this.'

'She?'

'You know bloody well who I'm talking about. Irene.'

'And what does Irene have to do with you?'

The hostility in Mrs Halliwell's eyes was replaced by a look of calculation. 'She hasn't told you, has she?'

'Told me what?'

'That she shopped her brother,' said Mrs Halliwell triumphantly. 'Not such a poor little innocent now, is she? Pure spite, telling lies about her own brother.'

'Are you saying,' said Stratton, 'that Irene Palmer is your daughter?'

'Calling herself Palmer now, is she?'

'Yes, she is. Is it her father's name, Mrs Halliwell?'

'Yes, my first husband. But Frank – Mr Halliwell – adopted them when we were married. Treated them like they were his own. You ask Tommy. He thinks the world of Frank. Not like her, the vicious little cow. She told lies about Frank right from the start, then she run away from home and took up with a nigger so I can't even hold my head up in front of the neighbours, and now she's telling lies about my Tommy. Always going on about her precious dad, she was, and when she come to me saying disgusting things about Frank, I told her I wasn't having none of it.'

'How do you know she wasn't telling the truth?'

'The truth!' Mrs Halliwell's entire face seemed to swell with indignation and the words burst from her, shrill and vehement. 'Given you the sob story an' all, has she? Well, I can tell you what the truth is, all right. Reg Palmer – oh, he was wonderful, he was. To hear Irene tell it, the sun shone out of him, but he never done a day's work in his life unless it was bent, and when he weren't doing that he was down the pub. Used to worry me sick, how I was going to put food on the table, never mind if he's going to come home, or if he's got himself nicked or gone off with some woman – oh, yes, he used to do that too, just bugger off for days, weeks, sometimes, and leave me with no money. We come this close,' she pinched together a thumb and fore-finger, 'to losing our home, and I couldn't sleep with the worry . . . And then he gets carted off to hospital because his liver's packed up, and that's it. What I'd have done if Frank hadn't come along, I don't know. How many men would take on a woman with two kids? Frank's a hard worker, he's reliable, and he's ten times the man that Reg Palmer ever was. I won't hear a word said against him by Irene or anyone else.' Closing her mouth with a snap, she sat back and folded her arms defiantly, challenging Stratton to argue. There was no doubt that she'd meant every word, but throughout the diatribe, he'd kept hearing Irene's voice in the back of his mind: *She called me a liar before I'd even said it – like she knew what I was going to say.*

'I appreciate what you're telling me, Mrs Halliwell,' he said gently, 'but it doesn't necessarily mean that what Irene told you isn't true.'

Afterwards, Stratton told himself he must have imagined it, but at that moment it seemed to him that her bullet stare softened for an instant, before she said, as passion-ately as before, 'Of course it bloody does! Frank's a good man.' Swiping her handbag off the table in a single, sudden movement, as if she thought he might snatch it away, she clutched it to her chest. 'And whatever she's said about Tommy, that's a lie as well.'

'She hasn't said anything about Tommy, Mrs Halliwell.'

'I don't believe you. If she hasn't said anything, why is he here?'

'He's here because we have several witnesses who've identified him as part of a gang who attacked a coloured man called Clyde Johnson on Wednesday evening. As I'm sure you're aware, Johnson died later in hospital.' Seeing that she was about to protest, Stratton held up his hand. 'Your son refused to come in for questioning and made himself scarce until we caught up with him last night. During the night of the attack on Johnson, he was driving a green Bedford van. This van was also seen' – here Stratton was aware of raising his voice to cover a weak point – 'during a petrol bomb attack at a party in Colville Road on Saturday ... *And*,' he continued, now safe in certainty, 'it was later discovered in the yard at the White Defence League place. We've identified it as belonging to your husband, Frank Halliwell, who we shall be bringing in for questioning shortly, and *that*, Mrs Halliwell, is why your son is here. What I'd like to know is why you should think Irene might have, as you put it, shopped her brother.'

Flustered, Mrs Halliwell said, 'Well, I didn't, I just thought ... I mean, I don't know.'

'You don't know? You were pretty sure about it a minute ago. What's made you change your mind?'

'Well,' she said, rallying, 'it was a darkie, wasn't it? I thought it might be one of her friends or something.'

'Really?' Stratton injected as much disbelief into the word as he could. 'Notting Hill and Notting Dale are big places, Mrs Halliwell, and they're full of coloured people.

What made you think she might know this particular man? Something your son told you?'

'No! He never – I don't know anything about it.'

'And yet you seemed so certain. What was it you said just now? Oh, yes: "She's the one who caused all this." '

'I didn't mean it like that.'

'You didn't mean it like that,' echoed Stratton. 'How exactly *did* you mean it, Mrs Halliwell?'

'I was worried about Tommy, that's all.'

'I see.' Stratton sat quite still for a moment and then, without warning, brought down both hands on the tabletop with a crash which caused Mrs Halliwell to jump in her chair so that her handbag bounced in her lap. Standing up and leaning towards her so that she shrank away from him, he continued, 'That's *not* what happened, and you know it. And in view of that – and in view of the fact that I'm still considering whether to charge you with obstruction and assault, I strongly suggest that you give PC Jellicoe here a true and accurate statement detailing *exactly* what you know about your son's whereabouts on both Wednesday and Saturday evenings. Do I make myself clear?'

Stratton had been as sure as he could be that she'd buckle but, to his surprise, she eyeballed him right back and said, 'You're never going to charge me for them things. My Tommy's done nothing wrong and you can't make me say he did.'

Dropping back into his chair again, with a weariness that was entirely unfeigned, he said, 'I'd credited you with a little bit more intelligence than that, Mrs Halliwell. Now, it's a shame that your daughter ran away to live with a black man and you can't hold your head up in front of the neighbours, but think how much worse it would be if your husband was in prison for raping his stepdaughter.'

Mrs Halliwell gasped. 'You can't! You'd never be able to prove it. It's her word against his, and she's nothing more than a . . . a . . .'

'A child who ran away from home because she was being assaulted in the most vile and disgusting way by a man she should have been able to trust. A child who was betrayed by a mother who was prepared to sacrifice her own daughter in return for an easy life. Prison isn't easy for anyone, but for that sort of person, well . . . Of course it's just possible that he might get off, but mud sticks, especially *that* sort of mud. Your Frank may be a good provider *now*, but who do you think would employ him after that? And you'd have a lot more to worry about than a few clicking tongues and a bit of gossip.'

Looking into her eyes, Stratton could see behind them a nightmare explosion of bricks through the windows, dog shit through the letterbox and filthy words gouged into the front door, and this time he knew, without a shadow of a doubt, that he'd got her.

'All right,' she whispered, utterly cowed. 'I'll do it. I'll make a statement.'

CHAPTER FIFTY-FOUR

'Any of that tea left?' asked Stratton. 'I could do with a cup.'

Fenella gave him an encouraging smile but Irene, seated next to her, did not look up from the untouched plate of toast and jam in front of her. Miss Jenner rose and picked up the battered aluminium pot. 'I should think it'll be stewed by now. Why don't I fetch us all some more?'

'And some breakfast. Anything, so long as it's not one of PC Jellicoe's rock buns. I've still got a few teeth left, and I'd like to hang on to them for as long as I can.' Fenella laughed on cue, but Irene's eyes remained lowered, her face half hidden by her long hair. 'Back in a moment,' he said, and followed Miss Jenner into the passage, shutting the door after them.

'How is she?' he asked, *sotto voce.*

'Very shaky. She's only just stopped crying.'

'Has she said anything?'

'It was all a bit confusing. We didn't realise Mrs Halliwell was her mother, and she thought we'd got her in so that she could take her back home. It was hard to get any sense out of her because she was absolutely terrified, she was *beg-*

ging us not to make her go with the mother . . . I was trying to explain why Mrs Halliwell was here – the business with the brother – but that seemed to make it worse. Your Mrs Jones was very good with her, really calmed her down.'

Stratton put his ear to the door for a moment before re-entering the room, and heard Fenella talking in resolutely normal tones about what she liked to eat for breakfast. 'I was just explaining to Irene,' she said when he opened the door, 'that I can always make her some bacon and eggs if that's what she prefers. I must say, it'll be jolly nice to have someone to cook for again.'

Irene, who'd ducked her head the moment he came into the room, raised it cautiously. 'Am I really going to stay with you?'

'Yes, if you'd like to,' said Fenella.

'I think,' said Stratton, taking a seat, 'that it's a good idea, don't you? Of course,' he added, 'we do have a few things to sort out first.' The trace of a smile on Irene's face disappeared immediately. 'It shouldn't take very long,' he added quickly. 'And before we have our chat, I'd just like to make it absolutely clear that no one is going to hurt you, Irene: not your mother, your brother or your stepfather. I've made quite sure of that.'

Irene frowned. 'But what about when you're not here?' she asked.

'I know it's a big thing,' said Stratton, 'asking you to trust me, but it is going to be all right.'

'But,' said Irene, 'even if Tommy does get put in prison, he'll come out again, won't he?'

'If he does,' said Stratton, 'it won't be for many years. Tommy and his friends killed Ding-Dong, Irene. If they're allowed to get away with it, there's every chance they'll decide that they're above the law and go out and kill somebody else.'

'What about my mum?' Irene's voice dropped to a whisper. 'She hates me.'

'That was the impression she gave me when I spoke to her,' said Stratton, 'and I think I know why.'

'It's because of Clinton,' said Irene. 'She wouldn't have minded so much if it hadn't been a coloured man.'

'It's partly that,' said Stratton, 'but it's mainly because of why you ran away. You told your mother what Frank Halliwell had done to you, didn't you? When you told me, you said it was as if she knew what you were going to say before you said it. That's right, isn't it?' Irene nodded. 'That's because she did know.'

'She said that to you?' Irene, her eyes as big as saucers, looked about ten years old.

'Not in so many words. She didn't have to. She knew what was going on, and she knows that I know she knew.'

'But what . . .' Irene looked panic-stricken. 'I shouldn't have told you. Mum'd be lost without Frank.'

'Mum,' said Stratton, marvelling at Irene's instant concern for her parent's welfare, 'isn't going to lose Frank. Not if they both do as they're told – and that includes leaving you alone. One of the reasons your mother has turned against you so much, Irene, is because, by choosing not to listen to you – not to believe you – she did a terrible thing to you, and she knows it . . . Do you understand what I'm saying?'

'Not sure.' The girl looked at Fenella for confirmation.

'Inspector Stratton's right, Irene. Very often, when somebody does something like that to another person, they feel guilty about it. What they've done is so bad that they can't forgive themselves so they sort of transfer the horrible feeling inside them onto the person they've wronged instead. They tell themselves lies about that person to justify their own action, because then they don't have to feel guilty any more.'

This was such an accurate summation of what Stratton had been trying to say, delivered with such heartfelt sincerity, that he suddenly remembered the husband with the roving eye and wondered if she was speaking from experience. How many times, sitting in interview rooms like this one, had he heard men justifying their adultery by laying the blame on their wives? Rapidly shelving this thought, and avoiding Fenella's eye, he said, 'The other reason why your mum was angry was that she thought Tommy'd been brought in because of something you'd told us.'

'But I didn't,' said Irene, looking frightened again. 'I was . . .' Confused, she stared wildly round the room, then imploringly at Stratton.

'You were frightened,' said Stratton gently, 'because you recognised your brother in Golborne Road. That's why you said "Tommy", wasn't it?'

'I can't . . .'

'Yes,' said Stratton, 'you can. Stop and think for a minute,

Irene. Why would your mother be so certain that you'd told us about Tommy being in Golborne Road? She could only know you were there *because Tommy told her about it afterwards*. And that makes her a witness, Irene. That means she has to stand up in court and tell everybody what your brother told her about beating up Ding-Dong. She's making a statement about it now, and your stepfather's going to make a statement too, about how Tommy borrowed his van – because you recognised that too, didn't you? And if I'm not mistaken, I think you might have recognised some of the other boys as well. Tommy's friends, the ones who live on the White City Estate. The ones you grew up with.'

'Yes.' The single word was barely audible. 'Yes, I did.'

'. . . and then we started walking back towards the railway bridge, and there were a group of men there, outside one of the shops, just sort of hanging about on the pavement. They weren't shouting or nothing. Well, perhaps a bit of pushing and shoving, but it didn't look, you know . . . And then we got close, and . . .' Irene faltered, and after a moment Miss Jenner finished writing and looked up expectantly.

'What happened next?' prompted Stratton.

'Well, it's like you said, I did recognise some of them. Gordon Baxter, and Ronnie. . .'

'That's Ronnie Mills, is it?'

'Yes. And then I saw Ding-Dong—'

'And you recognised him straight away, did you?'

'Yes, because of his clothes. He was wearing this suit. Stripey. Gloria used to say it looked like a deckchair.'

'Yes, she told me that.' Stratton flipped back through his notebook to find his record of the conversation. 'Go on.'

'Well, then I realised what was going on. They weren't just talking, they was all standing round Ding-Dong and he's been shoved right against the window of this shop, then suddenly he's right down on the ground, sort of slumped, and some of them were bending over him.'

'Were they holding weapons?'

'Yes. Ronnie had a stick or a piece of iron or something, and some of the others had things too.'

'And when did they see you?'

'I don't know exactly. We sort of stopped, and then one of them stepped back, away from Ding-Dong, and I saw Tommy was there. I didn't mean to say anything, but it just came out, and then they all looked.'

'What was Tommy doing?'

'Leaning over Ding-Dong like the others.'

'Did he have a weapon?'

'I don't know . . .' Irene shook her head. 'I was terrified. I thought they were going to kill us. We just legged it.'

'Did you hear them say anything?'

'One of them said, "That's a nigger's whore." '

'Which one?'

'I don't know. We both started running at once, so then they was all behind us.'

'And he definitely said those words – about one of you, not both of you?'

'No. That's what he said. It was horrible. I can still hear the words.'

'Was it Tommy who said it, Irene?'

'Honestly,' Irene looked uncomfortable, 'I don't know. It might have been Tommy, but I didn't see.'

'It doesn't matter if you don't know, Irene,' said Stratton. 'You're doing very well. I'm just trying to get a clear picture

of what happened. The suit you said Ding-Dong was wearing
– did he wear it often?'

Irene, relieved at the apparent insignificance of the
subject, said, 'Quite a lot. That was, you know, his best clothes, so if he went to one of the clubs, or something like
that, then he did.'

'And did you go about with him much? You told me,
didn't you, that Etheridge said to pretend you were Ding-
Dong's girl so that Gloria wouldn't be upset.'

Irene looked worried again. 'Yes, but it was only in fun,
and I didn't know about what you and Roy said about Clinton
and Gloria. I mean, I knew some of it, but—'

'But you didn't know that Etheridge was living off Gloria,'
Stratton finished. 'I know that, Irene, and I'm not suggesting
for a moment that you've done anything wrong. But I *am*
wondering, if Tommy – or one of his friends – had seen you
about with Ding-Dong once or twice, and he was wearing
this very distinctive suit, if they might have come to the
wrong conclusion about the two of you, and if that was why
they attacked him.'

Irene stared at him. 'No . . . they couldn't.'

'Couldn't they? We've spoken to a few of them and they
can't make up their minds about whose idea it was to get
out of the van at that precise moment. It's entirely possible
that they were simply driving round looking for trouble –
and of course one man on his own presents an easy target
– but it's also possible that Tommy, or one of the others in
the front with him, recognised Ding-Dong's suit, and that's
why they stopped.'

'But . . .' Irene looked bewildered. 'How would they know he was going to be there?'

'I don't suppose they did, any more than they knew that you and Gloria were going to be there. It was chance, that's all.'

'Chance . . .' repeated Irene. 'But if we hadn't . . . I mean, if he was coming to meet us . . .'

'It wasn't your fault,' said Stratton. 'Or Gloria's. Or Etheridge's, come to that. And what I've just said is only a possibility, nothing more.'

'No,' said Irene suddenly, sitting bolt upright. 'It's not.'

The silence in the room seemed to quiver in the air, and Stratton could hear the blood pounding in his ears. Mentally stabilising himself with a caution that the job wasn't finished by a long chalk, he said, 'Why's that?'

'When I told you,' said Irene, 'about us running away and them chasing us and one of them tried to grab me and I tripped over, I missed a bit because I didn't want to say nothing about Tommy, see?'

'Don't worry about that,' said Stratton. 'Just tell me what happened.'

'I was lying on the pavement, on my front, and I thought they were going to bash me or kick me or something, so I put my arms up round my head, but they didn't do nothing, just stood there. I don't know how long for – probably not even a minute, but it felt like a long time because I was so scared – so then I'm just peering round, through my hair, and I can see all these legs and shoes . . . Then I hear someone say "Leave it" and I look up a bit more and it's Tommy and

I know he wasn't there before because I never saw his shoes or trousers, and I'd have recognised them because he had those Italian type leather shoes, the nice ones – I remember when he got them. It was just before I run away and he'd saved up special. So then I put my head up just a bit so I could see his face, and that's when I saw.'

'What did you see, Irene?'

'I saw . . .' Irene swallowed. 'He was holding a knife.'

CHAPTER FIFTY-SIX

Leaving Miss Jenner, who'd eventually arrived with fresh tea, to take a statement from Irene, Stratton went into the office, where he found Jellicoe typing up a copy of Mrs Halliwell's statement with his two fingers. 'Another lovely job, sir.' Jellicoe thumped his way through the final sentence and pulled paper and carbon out of the typewriter. 'Here you go – all down in black and white. Funny thing, Mr Halliwell – the stepfather, that is – come in just after we'd finished up, and somehow – you know how these muddles can happen, sir – we ended up leaving them in the same interview room together for five minutes, completely unsupervised. I've let her go, of course, and DI Peacock and Dobbsie are in with *him* now, taking a statement. Oh, and DS Matheson's interviewing Knight – I gave him chapter and verse about where you'd got to and he says Tommy Halliwell's all yours and keep up the good work, sir.'

'In that case,' said Stratton, regretfully putting down the bacon sandwich that Miss Jenner had brought for him in order to read through Mrs Halliwell's statement, 'you'd better bring him up sharpish, because we've got a hell of a lot of catching up to do.'

'Right,' Stratton plonked himself down opposite Halliwell who, with nowhere to run, was looking paler and less sure of himself than he had two days earlier. 'You know why we're here, so if I were you, son, I'd do myself a favour and make it quick.' Halliwell looked as though he was about to protest. 'Save your breath – you'll get your chance later. So far, we've got half a dozen witnesses that a van belonging to Mr Frank Halliwell, your stepfather, was in Golborne Road at the time Clyde Johnson was attacked . . .' Stratton took Halliwell through everything that had happened in detail, enumerating the various witnesses as he went along. 'Now,' he concluded, 'as you will know if you read the papers, Johnson was killed by a knife wound. Not a stick, not an iron bar, but a knife. We haven't found the knife yet, but when we do – and believe me, we *will* find it – it will correspond exactly with the dimensions of the wound that killed Johnson. Oh, and by the way, we have a statement from your mother, Mrs Mae Halliwell, to say that you told her about the attack afterwards in considerable detail. Added to which, we have very good reason to believe that you recognised Johnson and, knowing who he was, you ordered the attack. That counts as premeditation, son, and that means you're looking at a murder charge. Or, to put it another way, you're fucked. Added to which, I've got this very tasty black eye from where you had a pop at me on Saturday afternoon, I've been on duty since yesterday morning and I haven't had any breakfast, so I'm not in the best of moods. Now,' Stratton stood up, and in a single, swift movement, leant across the table and, grabbing Halliwell's tie in his fist, yanked his head forward so that it was barely an inch from his own, 'if you don't want me to rip your head off and piss down the hole, start talking.'

seeing that Halliwell was sitting up a little straighter in his chair. 'Now,' he said, 'you're in trouble all right, but you can make things a lot easier for yourself if you cooperate with us. The fact is, son, we all lose our tempers once in a while, and that business over your sister can't have been easy. I reckon anyone who put himself in your shoes would agree with that, don't you, Jellicoe?'

'Yes, sir,' said Jellicoe solemnly. 'I'm sure I'd be just the same myself.'

'There you are, you see,' said Stratton. 'And I shouldn't be at all surprised if the jury think the same – but that, of course, depends on what's presented to them. After all, it's one thing to defend someone's honour . . .' Fearing that this might have been a step too far, even for someone like Halliwell, Stratton paused to see if the lad had swallowed it, and seeing from his expression of eager attention that he had, continued, 'and it's quite another to come over as a mindless thug. That'll be your lawyer's job, of course – but how your lawyer does his job depends on what we tell him.'

Stratton was relying on the fact that Halliwell, with no record, had no understanding of what went on in court other than what his less lucky mates had told him and, judging by the look on the lad's face, it was working. 'So, we could say that you lost your head and should be treated with leniency, or we could say that you're a nasty, vicious little toerag who deserves all he gets. Are you following me? Yes? Good.' Mentally poising himself, as if for a high dive, he continued, 'We might also say that you were led astray by Eddy Knight and Mr Gleeson. You know them, don't you?'

Stratton pretended to think for a second, then said, as if remembering something, 'Course you do – you were picked up at the White Defence League place, weren't you? You and your friend Eddy, and the famous green van that was hidden underneath a tarpaulin in the back yard. You don't half get around in that van, don't you, Tommy? All over the place, in fact – Colville Road, for example, on Saturday night.'

Stratton cocked his head on one side and contemplated Halliwell, who now had the look of a man waiting for the final blow to fall. 'I knew you were smart,' he said. 'You're ahead of me already. But it wasn't your idea, was it, throwing those petrol bombs? Someone put you up to it, didn't they?'

CHAPTER FIFTY-EIGHT

'Halliwell's adamant that the petrol bombs were Knight's idea,' said Stratton, 'and I believe him. Attacking Johnson because he happened to be on the spot and Halliwell thought he was Irene's boyfriend is one thing, but planning something like that, no.' He leant back in the chair in Matheson's office, punch-drunk with exhaustion.

'He says,' Stratton peered at the sheaf of statements he was holding, '*Eddy wanted to get the nigger who killed his uncle and he knew he'd be at the party.*' Stratton blinked and opened his eyes wide. The words seemed to be wriggling about on the page like small insects. '*I was a mug to get involved with it but I wanted to help my mate. I felt sorry for him because my sister was keeping company with a nigger and it broke my mum's heart. He told me . . .* Sorry, sir.' Stratton stopped, shaking his head to try and clear his vision.

'Quite understandable after the night you've had,' said Matheson. 'In fact, you look as if you could do with a sharpener.'

'Bit early for me, sir.'

'Bit late in your case,' said Matheson, getting up to pour him a measure of Scotch. 'Get it down you.'

'Yes, sir. Thank you.'

'Now, where were we?'

Stratton took a gulp – it was probably the last thing he needed, but the warmth it provided going down gave him the illusion of well-being, at least – and stared at the statement until the words stopped moving and reassembled themselves into something more or less coherent. '*He –* that's Eddy Knight – *told me this bloke's name which I think was Etteridge. We knew he was the one who done Mr Hampton. All my mates knew about it because a bloke Eddy knows told him and we reckoned it was true because this man worked for Perlmann and everyone knows he wants to put more coloureds in his houses so he can get more money off them.*'

'I take it,' said Matheson, 'that Halliwell is not aware of Perlmann's death.'

'I don't see how he could be, sir. But without any witnesses – unless any of the inhabitants of the house in Colville Terrace can identify Etheridge as being present at the time Hampton was killed – we're on a hiding to nothing as far as that goes.'

'You could be right,' said Matheson. 'However, I've just had a word with Eddy Knight. He maintains that he only heard about the attack on Johnson after it happened, but after we'd confronted him with what we found in the back of the van – jerrycans, rags and the rest – he confessed to throwing the petrol bombs. According to him, he was told by someone "very important" that Etheridge had killed Bert Hampton. He was quite cocky about it – kept saying we couldn't touch this chap because he'd got what he called "connections". When I mentioned Giles Rutherford's name and explained that we already had him in custody, he turned a very funny colour indeed. When I told him about *Mrs* Rutherford, he suddenly became very keen to convince me that the petrol-bombing was Rutherford's idea.'

'So Rutherford told Knight that Etheridge had killed Hampton,' said Stratton slowly. 'Knight denied working for Perlmann – the business with the dog – but that wasn't necessarily the truth, and given what we now know about Rutherford's involvement with Perlmann and the fact that he'd been siphoning off his wife's money behind her back, I'm beginning to think that it must have been Rutherford who put him up to the bombing.'

'Not only that,' said Matheson, 'I'm thinking that it must have been Rutherford who put Etheridge up to killing Hampton. Etheridge was full of how Perlmann had promised him houses and the rest of it, wasn't he? But I'm wondering if, before that, Rutherford hadn't promised him that if he got rid of Hampton and kept schtum about the tribunal business he could take over collecting the rents and – eventually – the houses themselves. Etheridge wouldn't have known that they were worth so little, would he? He must have looked at Perlmann and looked at Rutherford and thought he was going to be sitting on a goldmine. And petrol-bombing that party was scare tactics. According to Knight, there were only coloured people there. He had no idea what it all was in aid of – and nor, according to the statement they sent over from Shepherd's Bush, did Gleeson. And Rutherford left before the attack took place – that was confirmed by one of the MPs who were present. I'm willing to bet that Rutherford thought the petrol bombs would be enough to scare his wife off the whole business and start her looking around for some other good cause.'

'Or to provide a smokescreen for killing her?'

'I don't see how. Judging from what you've told me, it sounds as if she was perfectly happy to leave the money side of things up to Rutherford. There was no reason why she should have found out what was going on unless he managed to lose the lot. That might have happened eventually, of course, because it does appear that he has a bit of a gambling habit. After you telephoned me from West End Central, I decided to pay an early morning visit to Mr Nash at the Condor Club. He became quite talkative when I mentioned the matter of his non-existent gaming licence. Gave me a list of the people he'd already spoken to – I imagine we'll find they were the ones dunning poor Mrs Perlmann – and he also told me that Rutherford's lost a lot of money recently: £4,000 in August alone.'

'But – playing devil's advocate, sir – that might have been a reason for killing her, if he'd gambled away her money and she was about to find out.'

'You're not thinking like a gambler, Stratton. The more they lose, the greater the incentive to carry on playing and try to get it back, not to bash someone's head in to cover up the fact that they've lost. All they need is one good win, and everything will come right again . . . And of course Mrs Rutherford would have had expectations, wouldn't she? Her brother's dead and her father's over ninety. There's something else, too. I used the information you gave me to have a bit of a sniff around the Porchester Building Society, and believe me, the last thing that Rutherford, Perlmann or any of the others needed was the spotlight being turned on their affairs. According to both the specialists who've been treating him, Lord Purbeck was well on the way to mental incapacity in February 1953 when the company was registered. Besides which, Wing Commander Victor Glendinning, whose name also appears on the letterhead, has been dead since November 1952. And when we've handed over all of Mr Rutherford's precious paperwork to the legal and accountancy boys, I dare say we'll discover some other interesting facts.'

'If Rutherford didn't kill his wife,' said Stratton, who was starting to feel like a man running after a train he could never hope to catch, 'that leaves Etheridge, and I can't see any reason why he should have killed her either, if he was hoping to get something out of her, because she'd be bugger-all use to him dead, would she?' As he said this, his tired brain suddenly filled with several partially associated impressions: the spangled bright blue ruff of Mrs Rutherford's skirt standing proud beside the nettles and discarded tin cans; Rutherford's eyes, bloodshot and wide with surprise when told of his wife's death; Mrs Rutherford saying she'd often wondered how it would feel to be a hit with the chaps . . . 'Unless . . .' He stood up, draining his glass. 'I think it might be a good idea if I had a quick word with Mrs Jones, sir, if she's still here.'

CHAPTER FIFTY-NINE

Stratton managed to catch Fenella just as she and Irene were about to get into a taxi outside the police station. Blinking in the bright sunlight, he felt a physical jolt in his chest as she turned towards him. She looked even lovelier than she had before, with her shining cloud of hair – which was, he thought irrelevantly, the colour of prunes – and the concern in her warm brown eyes. 'I won't hold you up,' he said hastily, seeing that Irene was already seated in the back of the cab, 'but I just wanted to apologise again for what happened earlier—'

'You mustn't,' she said, putting her hand on his arm. 'It wasn't your fault.' Realising that she could probably smell the alcohol on him, he stepped back sharply. 'You had quite a night of it, didn't you?' she went on. 'Irene's been telling me what happened.'

Stratton glanced over Fenella's shoulder and through the window of the cab at Irene, whose profile was hidden behind a curtain of hair. 'How is she?'

'Pretty upset, as I'm sure you can imagine. Especially about Roy Walker. She was in love with him.'

Stratton raised his eyebrows. 'Bit quick, wasn't it? When I spoke to her on Friday she was in love with Clinton Etheridge.'

'I know. I met Etheridge at the party, remember, and I was just as taken in by him as Irene was . . . And she's known Walker longer than you think – she told me he's been looking out for her ever since she moved into Powis Terrace. Besides,' she added in a sharper tone, 'Irene is something of a lost soul who will latch onto anyone who's kind to her, which is exactly how Etheridge got his hooks into her in the first place. Of course we've no way of knowing what would have happened with Roy Walker, but *you* trusted him, didn't you?'

'Yes, I did. I'm not at all sure that he trusted me, though – maybe that's why he went to check on Irene on Saturday evening.'

'And one thing led to another,' said Fenella. 'That's not so terrible, is it, to seek comfort? Irene's a very attractive girl, and perhaps Walker was lonely too.'

'Yes,' said Stratton, picturing Walker's small, spotless room and remembering the things he'd said, 'perhaps he was. Sometimes, in this job, one tends to forget that not everyone has an ulterior motive.'

Fenella smiled at him in agreement, and Stratton felt as though he never wanted to stop looking at her. 'We should probably go,' she said gently. 'Irene needs to rest, and if you don't mind my saying so, you look as though you do too.'

'Yes, of course. I'm sorry. There was just one thing I wanted to check with you, about the party. You told me that after the bombs were thrown, you were on the floor and Gloria bumped into you. You said she trod on your hand.'

Fenella looked puzzled. 'She did.'

'Which way was she facing?'

'The front of the house. We both were. I remember that because I was in the front room when it happened, and when I looked up the first thing I saw was the curtains on fire.'

'So Gloria must have come from the back of the house.'

'I suppose so. I'm pretty sure she hadn't been there just before the explosion. I don't remember seeing her then, only afterwards.' Anxious now, she added, 'Is that all right? I mean, does it help with . . . whatever it is?'

'Yes,' said Stratton. 'I think it probably does.'

'Good. Well, in that case, I think we'd better—'

'Can I ask one more question? It really will be the last one this time. Would you like to have dinner with me next Saturday?'

Standing on the dusty pavement and watching the taxi drive off, Stratton had an elated, vertiginous feeling, as though he was floating on air. Almost dizzy with exhaustion and Matheson's double Scotch, Fenella's words – *There's nothing I'd like more* – echoed in his head. Seeing another taxi approaching like a mirage in the heat haze, its light miraculously on, he stepped into the road and stuck out his arm.

'Where to, guv?'

'Number 45, Powis Square, via Westbourne Park Road.'

CHAPTER SIXTY

'Have you found him?' Gloria, still in the same clothes, looked as though she hadn't slept.

The sling on her arm, already fraying at the edges, now had the colour and consistency of a dishrag, and she smelt of fags and stale sweat, but she was staring at Stratton, red-rimmed eyes full of hope.

'Yes,' said Stratton. 'We've found him.'

'Can I see him? Is he all right?'

'Perhaps,' said Stratton, 'I could come in for a minute?'

'He's not hurt, is he?' She stood back from the door.

'No, he's not.' Stratton removed a brimming ashtray and a pile of magazines from one of the armchairs and indicated that Gloria should sit down, taking a hard chair for himself. 'He's been arrested. Before you say anything, it wasn't for the murder of Virginia Rutherford. At least, not yet.'

'You mean you're going to charge him? Fit him up? Is that what you've come here to tell me?'

'No, it's not.'

'Then what did you want to arrest him for?'

'If you'll just listen to me, Gloria, and keep quiet, I'll explain.'

Five minutes later, after Stratton had given a potted version of the events at Maxine's, Gloria, now huddled on the edge of her seat, stared at him in bewilderment. 'I don't understand.'

'Don't you, Gloria?'

'No. It doesn't make any sense.'

'I have to confess,' said Stratton, 'that it didn't make all that much sense to me at the time. It's hard to think straight when someone's pointing a gun at your head. As I told you, we – the police, that is – had gone to the nightclub for reasons that had nothing whatsoever to do with him, so we were as surprised to find him there as he was to see us. He was desperate all right, no doubt about that. You'd have to be desperate to wave a gun and demand money and a getaway car, wouldn't you?'

Gloria nodded, her mouth slightly open. She looked as though she'd been struck dumb.

'But when I thought about it afterwards, and remembered what Etheridge had actually said to me, I suddenly realised what must have happened. You see, Gloria, he said that he thought we were going to fit him up for the murder of the woman at the party. Now, if he's innocent – which is something you seem very sure about – then how did he know about the murder in the first place?'

Gloria's eyes flicked around the room, as if she might

find an answer there, and then, having glanced down at the magazines by her feet, said, 'It was in the papers.'

'No it wasn't. My guv'nor made sure of that.'

'Well, I found out, didn't I? Someone must have told him, same as they told me.'

'I don't think so, Gloria. You gave me a story about how some friend of yours told you that another friend of yours had seen the body out of the window, which I took at face value because at the time there was no reason for me not to believe it.'

'It's true!'

'Does your friend happen to have X-ray vision?'

'What you talking about?'

'The gardens in Colville Road may not be up to much,' said Stratton, 'but they do have quite a few trees. When – or rather, if – we manage to find your friend, we'll test the view from her window, but something tells me we're not going to see very much apart from leaves. What's her name, this friend?'

'I don't know. She's just this girl I see around sometimes. I can't remember everything.'

'But you do remember quite a lot about what happened at the party. At least, you did yesterday. If I remember rightly, you were very keen to give me a full account of the proceedings – except, of course, for the bit about how you knew about the death of the Honourable Virginia Rutherford. And I'm as certain as I can be that the person you described arguing with her in the garden was her husband.'

'Well, why don't you have a go at him, then?'

'Don't worry, we've been talking to him. But right now, I'm talking to you, and I want to know how you knew about Mrs Rutherford, because I think that you were the person who told Etheridge.'

'How could I? I told you, I never saw him. I went to the hospital, then I come back here.'

'You told me that you went looking for him and you met your friend in an all-night caff on Westbourne Park Road called Dot's.'

Gloria blinked at him. 'Oh,' she said, in a rush, 'I'm getting confused now. Of course I did.'

'I came here by taxi,' said Stratton. 'The driver told me he knew Dot's Cafe – a lot of cabbies use it, apparently. They've got to know Dot quite well over the years, which is why they all know that she always goes down to Brighton over the August Bank Holiday, to visit her sister – and that's why the place closed on Thursday and won't reopen until the day after tomorrow. I'm surprised you didn't know that yourself – or perhaps, in all the excitement, you just forgot.' Gloria didn't say anything, but her face told him he was spot on with the last bit. 'You lied to me,' Stratton said. 'And I think you're lying about telling Etheridge too.'

'I'm not. All right, I did lie about the first bit, but not about Etheridge. You saw me, I was worried sick.'

'Yes, you were. Worried sick. And you should be now, because if you didn't tell Etheridge about Mrs Rutherford, then he must have known because *he* was the one who killed her. After all, you told me he disappeared, didn't you? When you were telling me about all this on Sunday, you made it sound as if the two people standing outside the back door – Mr and Mrs Rutherford – walked further into the garden after you and Etheridge had finished arguing. You said . . .' Stratton checked his notebook, 'that two people came past you and you thought it was them. But that wasn't right, was it?'

'I don't know. It was dark . . . I couldn't see.'

'You see, we know that Mr Rutherford wasn't in the garden when the explosion took place, because we have a witness – who also happens to be a Member of Parliament – who says that he was inside the house, talking to Rutherford, a few minutes before it happened. Which leaves us with Etheridge. And I think, when Mrs Rutherford went past you, that he followed her. I imagine he realised that she must have heard you screaming about how the money you'd earned on your back had bought his clothes and rings. He wanted to reassure her and she wasn't having it, and he lost his head.'

'No . . .' Gloria shook her head frantically. 'That's not what happened . . . It wasn't like that.'

'Oh, I think it was. Whatever else Etheridge may be, he isn't stupid. He'd know damn well that a woman like Mrs Rutherford would be shocked to realise that the man she was trying to help wasn't just some poor unfortunate with the cards stacked against him, but a criminal living off your immoral earnings. She wouldn't have minded about any of the others. In fact, she probably got rather a thrill out of being in the same room . . . But not Etheridge, and he knew it. That's why he didn't want you anywhere near the place.

You see, Etheridge was Virginia Rutherford's special project. She saw him as a "Community leader" – she told me that herself. But after she'd heard you saying all that, well . . . And all those other people Etheridge wanted to impress, the councillors, the MPs, the rich friends – she'd tell them, wouldn't she? That's why he went after her. I don't suppose that he *meant* to kill her, but he's impulsive, isn't he? I saw that with my own eyes at the nightclub. Perhaps he tries to put his arms around her and she pushes him away. Perhaps—'

'No! It didn't happen like that!'

'Then how *did* it happen, Gloria?'

CHAPTER SIXTY-ONE

'It was me who told Clinton about Mrs Rutherford. When I came back from the hospital, he was sitting here waiting for me. I said the same as I told you, about going to the cafe and all that. He said he'd be blamed for it – talked about how you'd come to the club and seen the two of them together, and how you were bound to think it was him. He begged me to help him – that's why I telephoned the police station yesterday and pretended I hadn't seen him. I wanted him to stay, but he wouldn't. I don't think he had any idea of where he was going to go or what he was going to do. He just said he'd find a place and then he'd write to me. That's the truth.'

'And the party?'

'It was like I said, I did hear Mrs Rutherford arguing with that man – the one you said was her husband – and me and Clinton had a row too, in the garden. Clinton went back in the house afterwards, but I stayed put. I didn't believe a word he'd said. I'd had a few drinks, like I told you, and I was so angry I wanted to kill him, but at the same time I'm telling myself, come on, girl, not here . . . you've got to have

a bit of pride, haven't you? And I could see *her* – Mrs Rutherford – standing in the doorway – and I thought, well, I'm
not giving you the satisfaction, you cow.'

'In the doorway? Was she by herself?'

'Yes.'

'What about before? Did Eth— did Clinton say anything
to her?'

'I don't know. My ankle was killing me where I twisted
it and my shoe's come off, so I'm trying to find that . . . Next
time I looked, there she was – the bloke with her must have
gone inside by then. Like I said, I didn't want nothing to do
with her so I look round and I can just see there's a hole in
the fence, so I thought I'll nip through there and come back
when she's gone, because I had this idea she was looking
for me.'

'Why did you think that?'

'Well, she must have heard us, mustn't she? I could see
her in the doorway, and she'd got her face pushed forward,
like that,' Gloria hunched her shoulders and peered at him.
'Anyway, I was right because I've gone towards the hole in
the fence, and I hear her come after me.'

'So what did you do?'

'Wasn't much I could do, was there? I get through the
hole, and I can't see a bloody thing, so the next I know I've
tripped over and I'm being stung by these nettles, and I can
hear her right behind me . . . And then she says, "Gloria, I'd
like to talk to you." I told her to piss off but she wouldn't.
I'm trying to pick myself up and now I've lost my bag and
she's standing there, going on about how she can help

Clinton and how she knows it's not my fault but surely I realise that if he stays with me he won't make anything of himself and perhaps she can help me too, find me a job or something. I said, "What job's that, then? Scrubbing the floor like my mum? Don't tell me about work – you never worked a day in your life." Then she starts on about she knows how hard it must be for me and all of this . . . I said, "You don't know nothing about me, and I don't want your shitty job. I want you to leave me alone." And she says,' here, Gloria broke into a plummy squeal, ' "But I'm trying to help you, Gloria." I said, "Well, I don't want your help, but I know what *you* want, all right, so why don't you just come out and say so? I'm sure Clinton'll give you one if you pay him enough." Well, I'm on my feet by this time, and she catches me by the arm and says, "Oh my dear, it isn't like that at all," and I'm telling her to get off but she won't so I give her a shove and there's all these bricks lying there so she falls back and she's still got hold of me and we both end up on the ground.'

'And then?'

'She wouldn't let me go . . . Just kept going on about Clinton and how she wanted to help him. She's trying to hold onto my wrists and we're sort of wrestling, pushing against each other, but it's like I'm fighting with a giant or something. Then she says to me, "What you're offering him isn't love." I said, "What do you know about it? You're like a bitch on heat for him," and I give a big heave to try and make her let go. She sort of goes sideways and I think she must of hit her head or something because suddenly she's pushing me right over and I'm on my back and she's on top of me. She's squashing my chest so I can't breathe and now I'm really panicking and I don't know what to do, so I just grab one of the bricks and I . . . I just wanted her to get off me, that's all. I mean, I was angry, and her talking to me like that, all those lies about helping me when she just wanted Clinton for herself, but it wasn't deliberate . . .'

'Did you realise she was dead?'

'I suppose I must have done or I wouldn't have told Clinton, but I don't remember thinking that, not at the time. Then there's this bang behind me and it feels like the whole world's exploded and I'm thrown back down on the ground. I look round and I can see all the smoke and hear people screaming. All I could think about then was Clinton, if he was in there, and the next thing I know I'm in the house and that lady's there and she's trying to get me to come out and I'm trying to find Clinton and I don't know what's happening or what I'm doing . . .' Gloria bowed her head and shook it slowly in silent misery.

'It's all right, Gloria,' said Stratton gently. 'I understand.'

She jerked her head up and stared at him for a moment as if trying to get him into focus. 'No you don't.' Her voice was flat, her eyes narrowed. 'You've no bloody idea. None of you.'

No, I don't understand, thought Stratton. Not her, nor Etheridge, nor Laskier, nor anybody, really, who isn't like me. That's the whole problem: nobody does. Not even when we try.

THREE MONTHS LATER

CHAPTER SIXTY-TWO

'Rutherford'll appeal, of course. Conspiracy's always a tricky one, and it's Knight's word against his. Have you seen this lot?' Matheson waved a hand at a stack of newspapers on his desk. The *News of the World* was on top, with the headline: *A New Era in Motoring.*

'The Preston Bypass?' asked Stratton.

'Inside page. They've really gone to town on Perlmann after what Rutherford said in court.'

'Well, Perlmann's not here to defend himself, is he? Unlike Rutherford, and he made it sound as if Perlmann had hypnotised him into ordering the petrol-bombing.' Stratton opened the paper and found himself looking at a large photograph of Perlmann wearing dark glasses and looking like a gangster and captioned 'Millionaire slum landlord'. Skimming the paragraphs underneath, his eye picked out '*fleet of Rolls-Royces . . . fond of cigars . . . grotesque appearance . . . brutal methods . . . lead piping . . . drugs . . . began his rise to notoriety working for the Messina Brothers, who operated a vice ring in Soho during and after the war . . .*'

'*Perlmann employed bands of thugs,*' Stratton read aloud,

'*many of them fellow refugees from the German concentration camps, whose minds were so warped as to exclude emotions like mercy, decency and honour.* Bloody hell. Even Rutherford didn't say that in court, and he didn't say anything about drugs or the Messina Brothers either.'

'I don't suppose they bothered to substantiate any of it,' said Matheson. 'After all, tenants' rights – that's not a story, is it? But now they can plaster April Scott all over the pages in her bathing suit, they're raking up all the muck they can think of and claiming it's a moral crusade. You know Etheridge has been offered money for his story by the *Sunday Pictorial*? They're going to send a journalist to Pentonville to interview him.'

Stratton put the paper back on Matheson's desk and sat down. ' "How I Stood Up to Evil Slum Landlord'," he said. 'Wouldn't surprise me if he claims that Perlmann was behind him holding up Laskier at the nightclub and shooting Walker. He'd probably claim that Perlmann, not Rutherford, put him up to killing Bert Hampton too – if he was ever going to admit to it, that is.'

'Which he won't,' said Matheson. 'After all, why should he? With no witnesses prepared to identify him – and God knows, it's not as if you haven't tried – I'm afraid we're on a hiding to nothing. But whatever Etheridge does decide to tell the paper, there's bugger-all we can do about it. You know, it was only by sheer good luck that we managed to keep Mrs Rutherford's death out of the press for as long as we did. If it hadn't been for the fact that all the journalists were chasing around for stories about the riot, we'd have been scuppered.'

'Yes, I know. But all the same . . .'

Matheson gave him a hawkish look. 'No use crying over spilt milk. The Lockwood girl had a choice. She didn't have to go on the streets, or take up with Etheridge – and she certainly didn't have to bash Virginia Rutherford's head in.'

Stratton sighed. 'I know. I suppose it's just how it happened – fighting over a man who didn't give two hoots for either of them.'

'Women really *are* a race apart, Stratton. We'll never begin to understand them.'

'I'd never presume, sir.' Recalling the slew of headlines about Gloria and Mrs Rutherford and all the coverage in the weeks before the trials of Halliwell, Knight and the others, he said, 'The other thing you can say about this whole business – Johnson's death and the riot and all the rest of it – is that at least it's made the powers-that-be sit up and take a bit of notice. And the heavy sentences, of course. We've not had much trouble of that sort for a while now.'

Matheson eyed him gloomily. 'I shouldn't bank on a lasting peace if I were you. Let's face it: with most people, they get a shock – mental, moral, whatever you choose to call it – when they catch a glimpse of something very unpleasant below the surface; that makes them feel shame, or guilt, or both, and that, in turn, makes them try to forget it as quickly as they can . . . But the unpleasant thing won't go away just because people fight shy of addressing it. Quite the opposite, in fact. Mark my words, we're going to see a hell of a lot more in the future.'

'What I can't understand,' said Stratton, 'is why Laskier hasn't tried to put the record straight about Perlmann.'

Fenella looked up from the menu she was studying, 'I'm sorry, Ted, I'm not not listening on purpose, I just can't make head nor tail of this.'

'The English things are on the next page, if you'd prefer.' Fenella looked round at the red paper lanterns and the Chinese scenes painted on the wall in swooping calligraphic strokes. After quite a few meals with her in conventional restaurants, Stratton had chosen the place because, despite his initial caution about food poisoning and strange ingredients, he'd often enjoyed eating there when he'd been stationed at West End Central. 'I thought it might be a bit of an adventure for you,' he said, 'but if you'd rather go somewhere else . . .'

'No, Ted. I want to stay here. It's lovely, and I'm sure the food's lovely too.' Fenella lowered her voice. 'Just as long as I don't have to eat it with those things.' She pointed discreetly at the chopsticks on the table. 'I really don't think I could manage.'

'It's OK,' said Stratton, 'they always bring knives and forks for gwailo.'

'For what?'

'Gwailo. It's what they call foreigners. It means "ghost man". At least, that's what the owner of this place told me, but perhaps he was just being polite. It might mean something much worse.'

'Well, I suppose they find us quite as strange as we find them. Why don't you choose for me?' she added, as the waiter approached.

'I'm sorry,' said Fenella, when Stratton had ordered, 'what were you saying before, about Stefan Laskier?'

'Just that I don't understand why he doesn't put his side of the story to the newspapers, about Perlmann. I know he wasn't a saint, but they're making him out to be some kind of monster and no one's defending him. I can see why Maxine Perlmann doesn't want to have anything to do with them – as well as all those wretched creditors, she's had journalists hounding her night and day ever since the Rutherford business came out, and they'd probably make *her* into a monster as well – but Laskier's different.'

'He's tried,' said Fenella.

'How do you know?'

'He told me. He said he'd had lots of offers from the papers. Some of them were prepared to pay as much as £500 for a story about Mr Perlmann, but he turned them all down because he wanted a guarantee that they'd print what he said – the whole story, not just bits and pieces. Anyway, he thought there was one journalist who would, so he agreed to talk to him, but the paper hardly printed any of it because it wasn't sensational – and he told me that the man refused to believe that Perlmann didn't have millions of pounds hidden away, even though he'd seen a copy of the will. I suppose the papers don't want the facts to get in the way of a good story.'

'When did he tell you all that?'

'Yesterday, when he came to see Irene.'

'Has she decided what she's going to do? After all, she can't stay with you forever.'

'That's something I want to talk to you about. This is nice, isn't it?' Fenella took another sip of her tea. 'I didn't think I'd like it without milk, but I can see it would spoil the taste.'

'Fire away, then. Don't keep me in suspense.'

'If you promise not to say anything until I've finished.'

'I'll keep quiet.'

'Well, Irene told me a few weeks ago that she thought she might be pregnant. At first, I thought that the ... you know, the *symptom*, was probably due to shock, because that can happen, but we went to the doctor and he confirmed it. She thinks the baby is Roy Walker's.'

'I'd have thought it was more likely to be—'

'You promised.'

'Sorry.'

'Judging from what she's told me, I agree that it probably *is* more likely that the father is Clinton Etheridge, but Irene has decided it's Walker's child and if that's what she needs to believe, then so be it. After all, it's not impossible.' Seeing that Stratton was about to speak again, Fenella held up a warning finger. 'But regardless of who the father is, the child will be a halfcaste, and whatever you or I may think, we both know that that's not going to make things very easy for either of them. She and I have had a long talk about it – several long talks, in fact – and she's adamant that she doesn't want to give it up for adoption.'

'But how's she going to—'

'Wait, there's more.' Fenella grinned. 'She's going to marry Stefan Laskier.'

Stratton stared at her. 'But . . . I mean, when . . .? What happened?'

'What normally happens: he asked her and she accepted.'

'Does he know about the baby?'

'Of course. I think he'd have asked her anyway, although perhaps not just yet – Irene's news has moved things along a bit, that's all.'

'And he doesn't mind?'

'Apparently not. I've got to know Stefan a bit in the last few months, Ted. I confess I was quite suspicious the first time he turned up, what with him being connected to Perlmann and everything, but I started thinking about all the things you'd told me, and . . . Well, you know.'

'You've got very fond of Irene, haven't you?'

'Yes, I have. And Stefan desperately needs somebody to look after, and now he's got her and the baby. I suppose it's not what you'd call a *conventional* marriage, but I don't think that matters. It's funny,' she added, 'but one has all these prejudices, and one never really questions them until something like this happens. Then you start to think about it, and you realise it's all a lot of nonsense. When I think about my life, I've been so fortunate, really . . . Oh, dear.'

Fenella reached for her handbag and extracted a handker-chief. 'I'm sorry. I didn't mean to get silly.'

Stratton gazed at her as she dabbed her eyes. He didn't know if it was thinking about Fenella's kindness to Irene, or Irene herself, or Laskier, or everything that had happened, but there was a definite lump in his throat. 'You're not silly,' he said gruffly. 'You're lovely.' And, finding it entirely beyond him to say anything else, he reached across the table and took her hand.

Acknowledgements

I am very grateful to Tim Donnelly, Katie Gordon, Stephanie Glencross, Jane Gregory, Maya Jacobs, Simon McVicker, Lucy Ramsey, June Wilson, Jane Wood, Aga Wiechowicz and the staff at the National Archives and Colindale Newspaper Library for their enthusiasm, advice and support during the writing of this book.

A WILLING VICTIM

Laura Wilson

On a dank November day in the late 50s, DI Ted Stratton is called
to a murder scene in Soho. The victim is Jeremy Lloyd, a loner with
some strange tastes. Before his death he gave a photograph of a woman
to a fellow lodger for safe-keeping.

Stratton's enquiries lead him to Suffolk, to a sinister foundation, where
Stratton meets a boy, Michael, who has been proclaimed as the next
incarnation in a long line of spiritual leaders. The woman in the photograph
is the boy's mother, but she has disappeared . . .

When a woman's body is found in woods nearby, Stratton initially
assumes he has found Michael's mother – but the reality turns out
to be far more terrifying.

'Laura Wilson's DI Stratton series is one of the bright spots of British
crime fiction . . . an intelligent, thought provoking crime novel
with a particularly poignant ending' *Spectator*

www.laura-wilson.co.uk

Quercus

www.quercusbooks.co.uk